Perfect Love

Elizabeth Buchan

CORVUS

First published in hardback in Great Britain in 1995 by Macmillan,
an imprint of Macmillan Publishers Ltd.

First published in paperback in Great Britain in 1996 by Macmillan,
an imprint of Macmillan Publishers Ltd.

This paperback edition published in 2023 by Corvus,
an imprint of Atlantic Books Ltd.

10 9 8 7 6 5 4 3 2 1

A CIP catalogue record for this book is available from the British Library.

Paperback ISBN: 978 1 83895 541 0
E-book ISBN: 978 1 83895 542 7

Printed and bound in Great Britain by Clays Ltd, Elcograf S.p.A.

Corvus
An imprint of Atlantic Books Ltd
Ormond House
26–27 Boswell Street
London
WC1N 3JZ

www.atlantic-books.co.uk

MIX
Paper from
responsible sources
FSC® C018072

Perfect Love

Elizabeth Buchan was a fiction editor at Random House before leaving to write full time. Her novels include the prize-winning *Consider the Lily*, international bestseller *Revenge of the Middle-Aged Woman*, *The New Mrs Clifton*, *The Museum of Broken Promises* and *Two Women in Rome*. Buchan's short stories are broadcast on BBC Radio 4 and published in magazines. She has reviewed for the *Sunday Times*, *The Times* and the *Daily Mail*, and has chaired the Betty Trask and Desmond Elliot literary prizes. She was a judge for the Whitbread First Novel Award and for the 2014 Costa Novel Award. She is a patron of the Guildford Book Festival and co-founder of the Clapham Book Festival.

Also by Elizabeth Buchan

In memory of my much loved and much missed parents

'Love seems the swiftest but it is the slowest of all growths. No man or woman really knows what perfect love is until they have been married for a quarter of a century.'

Mark Twain

PROLOGUE

OUTSIDE, A WINTER WIND BLEW DOWN FROM THE ridge but, to all appearances, the frost of the financial recession had only touched the fringes of the village of Dainton – the parish being a Nazareth to Winchester's Jerusalem – for the money expended on the Christmas flowers had been generous. Euphorbia, lilies, and imported narcissi do not come cheaply. Making a rough computation of the cost, Prue Valour was puzzled. Perhaps a newcomer, buying their way into the village, had donated them. Perhaps the church flowers had been put above other claims on the Christmas purse (the insulated mats for the homeless, for example) but Prue thought it unlikely.

Kate Eliot, Prue's friend and confidante, and a woman fond of a challenge, providing there was every chance she could master it, had taken the trouble to decorate the Christmas tree with real candles – not, of course, to be lit because of the insurance veto. This was a shame because the candles looked beautiful elsewhere in the church. Nevertheless, swaying on the tree, forced through the green like white asparagus, they cocked a snook at regulations, their colour suggesting the purity and hope so lacking elsewhere.

Content, certainly better-looking and more serene at

1

forty-one than she had ever been at twenty-one, and just about organized (turkey stuffed, extra fruit salad made, emergency presents wrapped and stacked in the cupboard) Prue joined in the singing of the last carol. If God had withdrawn from England in disgust, there was still a chance he might drop in, briefly, to Dainton's parish church to cast an eye over his faithful: struggling, well-meaning, frayed and nibbled at the edges by existence, imperfect and, in Prue's case, a little cushioned, a little unwilling to listen to new voices . . .

Unlike Joan of Arc, who had listened to them all too well. As Prue had discovered during her researches into the life of the saint, apparently Joan had been in her father's garden in Domrémy when she first heard the voices towards noon on a summer's day. After that, they visited her at various times, often when bells were ringing – the bell for vespers, compline, or the lovely clear tone of the evening angelus.

The bells were important. They introduced order into lives that had none. They told the time, they spread news, issued warnings and because France lay split open – so many segments of a peach over which fought French, Burgundians and English – many warnings were needed.

Whatever time it was does not matter. For into the broken silence, the backwash of displaced air that shuddered over the fields and village torn and ravaged by war, came the voices of St Michael and St Catherine and changed Joan's life for ever.

Oh, yes, thought Prue into whose consciousness was creeping the knowledge that her own life had remained much the same during the past twenty years, it was right that the voices spoke when they did – and for Joan to listen to their message.

SPRING

CHAPTER ONE

'I T'S IN THE STORIES,' JANE HAD ONCE INSISTED ON A Friday car journey home from school. 'Everyone hates the wicked stepmother, and the wicked stepmother schemes to get rid of the beautiful stepdaughter. Think of Snow White.'

'*I* don't go "Mirror, mirror on the wall",' Prue protested, only half amused.

'You don't have to, Mum.'

'Thank you,' said Prue with dignity. Beauty had never been her problem – and now that she was older and understood that more elements lay below the surface than on it, she realized that beauty *was* a problem for those who had it. Not that she considered the problem to apply to herself for, in Prue's view but not necessarily in the opinion of those who came to love her, she did not possess it. Whereas Violet did, in bucketfuls.

Happily, Violet was safely in New York with her new husband and baby and well out of Prue's way. Or she had been until that morning in January.

'*When* did you say they're coming?' asked Prue, pouring milk into her saucer for the cat. Bella placed an elegant, bangled paw on Prue's knee, leapt into her lap and was surprised when Prue clutched her hard against her midriff.

'I wish you wouldn't do that. It's so unhygienic,' replied Max, her husband, watching the milk spray the tablecloth. It was not the first time he had protested. Nor would it be the last. 'February. Because of the recession the bank is cutting staffing levels on its overseas operations. Anyway, apparently they want Jamie back home to head up the London bit of the European arm.' He pushed the airmail letter over to Prue.

Prue picked it up with reluctance and Max, aware of what was going through her mind, said, 'It's only till they can buy a house in London. Jamie can commute and Violet will be looking for a job.'

'Lucky Jamie.' Prue gave the letter a brief glance and then ignored it. Meanwhile, Max creased *The Times* into a raging sea.

'You don't object too much, do you, Prue?'

She leant over the table, nipped the paper out of his grasp and folded it into order. 'I object to you doing *that*.'

'Do you mind?'

She considered his question, the familiar sleepy look in place that meant she was thinking hard. Was sharing a kitchen with her stepdaughter a good thing because it would shake Prue's moral fibre into a bracing workout, or a bad thing because the inevitable clash would cancel any Brownie points thus gained?

I hate you, Prue . . .

'It's Violet's home and you're her father.' Fairness, she reflected bitterly, was the curse of so-called civilized, the fatal weakness. 'They can look after themselves.'

Bella's purr broke the uneasy silence which fell between them. Oh, Max, thought Prue, you look so pleased at the prospect of your daughter coming home. How can I possibly deny you?

Max looked at his watch and got to his feet, wincing at the

twinge that occasionally attacked his right hip. 'Time to go.' He retrieved *The Times*, which he had no intention of yielding up. Prue swallowed half a cup of coffee so strong it made her tongue go dry, but that was how she liked it. One day she intended to renounce caffeine, being reminded daily by the inside of her cafetière what her stomach lining must resemble – but not yet. She squinted at Max. He looked irritable and impatient, two things which until recently had been alien to his nature, brought on, she suspected, by panic. For Max was sixty and he did not like the idea of retirement.

Tick, tock.

These days he maintained, a little too frequently, that he was still in his prime. Still capable of good things. Oh, yes, his listeners agreed, but then they were not likely to disagree. To be fair, Max's large, fit-looking body gave the impression of strength and a well-oiled mind, both of which were true.

Prue did not relish the idea of his retirement either, but there was nothing to be done. Sometimes, she caught Max looking at her as if to say: It's unfair that you're twenty years younger. Other times, she sensed that he almost disliked her for it. I can't help it, she wanted to cry out. I would take on your years if I could. It did not occur to her that it was not her business to shoulder Max's advance into old age, it was his. But, then, it is almost impossible for the lives of people who are bound together by deep feeling and habit, not to seep into each other's.

Meanwhile, it *was* Prue's business to help negotiate this tricky period. She pushed a reluctant cat on to the floor.

'You've got the big meeting today, haven't you? I won't expect you home until late.' She paused to insert the first plank in the bolstering-Max programme. 'I don't know what the firm would do without you.'

Max tapped his right hand on the table and the little white

scar on his index finger – Helen's wound – attracted Prue's gaze as it had done a hundred thousand times during their marriage. 'I've made noises that I would like to take over the working party into setting up the European structure.' Max's large and profitable law firm in the City was in the process of setting up a working relationship with like-minded firms in France, Germany and Spain, the idea being that clients would get the best advice on all fronts. 'I would like to get it,' said Max, whose fluency in French, German and Spanish certainly put him in the running, 'so spare a thought.'

'I will, darling. I will.' She fingered her coffee-cup. 'They would be foolish to ignore you, I think.'

'Thanks,' he said, a touch drily. He adjusted the silk handkerchief in his lapel pocket, his only sartorial indulgence, and flashed her one of his disconcerting smiles, which told her that he was not going to let his feelings get the better of him. 'Good try, darling. Butter the old boy up. I might just bring a decent bottle back for supper on the strength of it.'

Palm up, he stretched out a hand across the table and curled his fingers in invitation. Prue tapped the edge of the table with hers and her mouth twitched.

'Darling Prue . . .' said Max. 'Don't be mean. Give me a kiss.'

She laughed, leant forward and traced a circle on the exposed palm. He caught her hand and kissed it.

'My lovely Prue,' he said.

'I love you really,' she said.

'That's fortunate,' said her husband. 'You've got me for life.'

Prue removed her hand, looked down at her lap and endeavoured to brush the cat hairs from her skirt.

*

The car nosed into Winchester station only just in time. Max wrenched open the passenger door to show his annoyance at Prue for insisting on changing her skirt at the last minute. It had made them late and the road from Stockbridge had been full of feeble drivers unwilling to go above 40 m.p.h.

'Nobody looks at your bottom half if you're behind the counter,' Max had pointed out, not unreasonably, which exasperated Prue – unfairly she knew. All the same, the goodwill of breakfast had vanished.

She swerved to avoid a squashed hedgehog, which had made the mistake of imagining the station was a safe place. There was no need to add insult to grievous injury and, besides, the idea of going over the bloody little body was too much at this time of the morning.

'I'm sorry I made you late,' she said.

'So I should think.' Max dropped his large, squarish hand on to her thigh for a second and she covered it with hers.

Although Prue's life was oriented around her husband's, the minute he was out of her sight she forgot him. She often puzzled over the conundrum. Was it a normal stage in a twenty-year-old marriage? She supposed it was. After all, she did not notice her wedding ring from one week to the next, despite its tendency to make her finger swell. It was there, much as her nose was (which she disliked), or her legs (marginally better) or the rather startling mole, positioned above her right eyebrow.

Once upon a time, as all good stories go, there would not have been a day *not* dedicated to the idea of Max. Every breath she took, every meal she ate, every stamp she licked (Prue had been a secretary when they met) had revolved around a Max-shaped space. And why not? He was older, wiser and infinitely sadder, and, thus, irresistible to a nineteen-year-old, a *young* nineteen-year-old whose favourite childhood game had been to re-enact Florence Nightingale's lamp-lit passage through suffering men at Scutari. Perhaps a too-young nineteen-year-old?

What she got with Max was love that showed no sign of running out, fishing rods, a pair of guns to which he was devoted, gentleness in all their dealings, a village life and a degree of comfort.

Prue drove through the city and concluded that too much reflection on what constituted normal was not a good idea.

With a lot of extra exhaust and gear changes, she manoeuvred the car into her secret parking place behind the market square. The morning was still sharp and exuded depression, and wherever Prue looked as she made her way to the bookshop she was accosted by 'For Sale' signs.

Whatever else she had expected, she had learnt quickly that bookshops are not peaceful places. Certainly not Forsight's. It was busy, which was good, but it was also haphazardly organized, which was bad. Any ideas Prue had entertained for browsing, paid, through Fict., Class. and Fict., Pop., or even Hist., Med., vanished by the end of the first week. Since then, she had tried for two years to impose order, but never managed it.

Books were delivered daily, others were piled up waiting to be returned, publicity material buckled in corners and gangways, and Gerald, the owner, had a knack of sabotaging Prue's ideas for display with his own. Still, most days the shop was full, and not only with browsers who had no intention of buying. You might be experiencing trauma, she reasoned, you might be a witness to the repossession of your house, be forced to sell your assets, weep at the destruction of your life, but buying a book remained an achievable goal.

'What do you think?' Gerald held up a paperback with an explicit cover.

She directed a look at it. 'It will sell.'

'Winchester doesn't like sex. Hadn't you noticed? But stack it on the table, will you, Prue, after you've served the customer by the till who wants a book on hats.'

Sometimes, Gerald sounded remarkably like Max. Prue threw her scarf into her basket, twitched at her blouse and refrained from asking if he had had a bad night.

By half past one, three people had placed orders for a book on coping with bankruptcy.

'You should stock some,' Prue informed Gerald, much struck by this neglected window in the market, as she put on her coat.

'Can they *pay* for it, dear?'

Next door to Forsight's was a bakery, the kind that sells 'Olde Worlde Bread' and pipes a smell of cooking yeast into the retail area. Prue bought a sausage roll and an almond croissant to which she allotted four out of ten and ate them as she walked to the public library. It gave her satisfaction – still – to flout one of her mother's rules: never eat in the street. In fact, the transgression gave her so much pleasure that she tried to remember the others.

The enduringness of habit . . . and Prue, now accustomed to the library and its best seats, made for 'her' niche and was forced to restrain a frown when she saw it was occupied. She retreated to a position by the door, arranged her books and began to write.

'It was in my thirteenth year when God sent a voice to guide me . . .'

This was Jeanne la Pucelle, *fille de Dieu*, as those mysterious voices addressed her, describing the moment when her life, the hardworking, simple life of a daughter of a well-to-do peasant, was stopped in its tracks. 'Say what you will', Prue wrote in her notes, then came to a halt. Say that Joan was born with the compulsive exhibitionism of many of our public figures, which drove her to invent something, anything, which would stamp her life in bas-relief on the often dark and frightening medieval chronicle of life and death. That she was schizophrenic, that she was driven to extremes by the limits of the age in which she lived. Say anything you like, but as Joan stood in the garden, carpeted with lilies-of-the-valley and wild strawberries, a heroic poetry, a meaning, a clash of arms and a terrible beauty flowed into her life.

Prue did not regard herself as a woman given to a hot rush of feeling, or a candidate for the steel grip of the *idée fixe*, and her ambition to write a biography of this woman and saint, Joan of Arc, took her, and anyone to whom she confided it, by surprise.

Do it, Max urged, when Prue faltered out the idea to him. Do it. Do it.

Do it, echoed the obstinate part of Prue which she kept hidden, folded into the dark areas of her mind (of which she was secretly afraid). She obeyed, and that was why she was to be found in the public library on every spare afternoon.

Prue's biography was intended to be the unacademic, ordinary woman's view of the medieval equivalent. Where the idea had arrived from was mysterious, but arrive it had as a sunburst over a bleak landscape. Even now, Prue maintained a level of extreme surprise at her daring, for nothing in her life had trained her for a project like this. That obstinacy, a quivering response to the colour, the boldness, the surrender, the excess of St Joan, and perhaps an unconscious need to change an element in her own life, fuelled Prue's researches. Not that she would explain it as such.

The results so far were headings, 'Life', 'Death', 'Battles', in a red-and-black notebook imported from China, and notes made on A4 paper which she kept meaning to transcribe under the headings, once she had got through the stack of reading she had set herself. This was composed of biography, to guide her as to what she should be doing, history, for its background information on labyrinthine politics, gold-encrusted artefacts, and the collection of John the Bolds, the Fearless, the Bads, and degenerate Valois that had littered medieval France.

The library smelt of polish and, less fortunately, of sweat, which was not surprising for the central heating had been turned up to furnace level, and the faces at the tables were varnished with an unnatural sheen, Prue's included. She sensed the stain that crept up her neck when she was hot and bothered, spreading like red ink above her blouse. Somebody should tell the council. *She* should tell the council.

Shopping. St Joan. Ironing. Jane. Bank managers. Max. Councils. This was a life indeed.

She looked at her watch. It was time to pick up Jane from the school where she was a weekly boarder. She stacked her books together and got up.

Outside, the cold wind blew, cooling Prue's flush and she put up a hand to her neck in a gesture that was becoming habitual. Still smooth, she thought, a little guilty that she minded.

In front of her flowed the life of the city – an arterial stream of traffic, punctuated by the ganglia of shops, precincts and the market. Looming over this commercial activity was the cathedral, whose massive symbolic and physical presence used to exert an osmotic force on the life of the city. *Mutandus mutandi* . . . (Prue was learning some Latin.) Today, having been modified by the rush towards science and commercialism, its supremacy was composed mostly of memory and the reverence the British accorded to the past. But Prue took delight in the building, and often made a detour as she did today to wander in its precincts or look inside. The January light failed to penetrate the dim interior, lit here and there by the bright, isolated stars of candles. The aisle was shrouded and echoed to the half-whispers of tourists and church officials going about their business.

Her basket weighing on her arm, Prue hovered in the transept, thinking about people and their separate circles of isolation, sometimes overlapping others, sometimes moving forward without contact. It was perfectly possible to live a life thoroughly boxed in by Christian habits but lacking the essential core of belief. She knew because she was making a good job of it herself.

A group of Japanese tourists fluttered and fussed in the aisle, and some nuns were praying in the pews. Presumably God loved this stone tribute to him. She trusted that he did, for it had been built on sweat, lives and ambition.

Prue left the smell of wax and ripe flowers and returned to the daylight.

'Wicked, Mum, you're on time.'

Jane was preceded by a collection of bags slung into the back seat, then a great deal of green uniform and green tights, and plaited fair hair.

'How's the week been?'

'Fine.' Jane always made the question sound irrelevant.

'The French test?'

'Oh, Mum. Don't ask me those questions the minute you see me.'

It was windy and rather bleak on the hill where the school was situated. To the east the motorway, always crowded, cut away to London, and to the west a new section was being hacked out of the chalk downland, much to the bitterness of local protesters. That view was not pretty.

Jane sighed.

'What, my sweetie?'

'Nothing. Just glad you're here.'

Prue drove out of the school yard. 'Violet and her family are coming to stay for a bit.'

Jane sat up. 'Oh, Mum,' she repeated, this time with a dying inflection indicating her disapproval. 'That's a real pain. Where will they all sleep?'

'In the spare room, of course. Luckily it's big enough for the baby as well. If not, they can put him in the guest bathroom.'

Jane bit her lip.

'Aren't you curious to see your new cousin?'

'Not really,' said Jane, who preferred computers to ballet and software to clothes. 'Babies are boring.'

Prue smiled. 'You weren't. You were marvellous.' She observed her daughter from the corner of her eye. The approach always worked, mainly because she meant every word. 'I used to wonder what I'd done to deserve such a good baby. Sometimes, I imagined a big foot in the sky waiting to squash me because I was too lucky.'

'Truly?'

'Truly.'

Actually, there *had* been the equivalent of the foot in the sky and that had been Violet. But Prue would not permit herself to say so to Jane.

Jane went quiet for several minutes. They drove on between hedges lightly tipped with new life – nature always got on with things much earlier than you imagined – over mud islands from last night's rain and past telegraph wires on which rooks and moisture were equally strung. The landscape was suspended, but also secretly in flux, waiting for the moment it tipped over into spring proper. Every so often, a cascade of water hit the windscreen and, as they descended the hill to Stockbridge, the road became slippery.

15

What had I done to deserve such a good baby – and such an awful stepdaughter?

The car skidded slightly and a vision of Jane lying crushed and bleeding by a roadside, calling for her mother, flashed by Prue, so vivid it almost made her choke. It was the old nightmare, come back to visit, the old anxiety. It meant many things.

Prue tried to explain her fears for Jane to Max, and how they were connected to the idea of perfection. They'll vanish quickly enough when she's a teenager with a safety-pin through her nose, he said.

Jane broke the silence. 'It's a pity you don't like Violet. You don't, do you, Mum?'

'Why do you ask?'

'My intuition,' said her eleven-year-old daughter. 'Don't worry, it's quite normal in the circumstances.'

It was then that Jane explained the Snow White theory.

CHAPTER TWO

'CAN YOU MEET US AT HEATHROW?' VIOLET NEVER bothered to ingratiate herself with her stepmother – that point had long ago been passed if it had ever existed – but since the last thing she wished was to struggle to Dainton by public transport or incur the expense of hiring a car, she managed, 'If you would, Prue.'

Prue made an effort and said she would, adding, 'It will be lovely to see you and to meet Jamie and the baby.'

'Five a.m., terminal four.'

'*Five a.m.!*'

'Afraid so.'

'Violet, that's hideously early.'

'Well, if you feel you can't, Prue, could you organize hiring a car for us?' Violet calculated two things. One, the request might shame Prue into agreement. Two, if it did not then the likelihood was that her father would pay. It was a measure of her current state of mind that she forgot that Jamie's bank was paying most expenses. Or perhaps she wished to put Prue to considerable trouble.

Same old tricks, thought Prue, powerless before Violet's determination. 'Don't worry, I think we can make it.'

'See you, then.'

17

In Dainton, Prue was accounted something of a saint – older husband with two tragedies, or at least incidents, in his past, and a stepdaughter who thought rather too well of herself and made it her business not to cooperate. Violet was well aware of Prue's putative sainthood and had lived with it for those difficult, uneasy years before she had left home; it had sharpened her quick, but essentially unsubtle, mind. Character is shaped by those we hate, as much as by those we profess to love, and Violet was very much Prue's creation, a fact that would have astonished both women.

'I hope we're not *too* much trouble.' Violet pondered the *coup de grâce*, which proved too tempting not to use. 'After all,' she modulated her voice sweetly, 'you don't have that much else to do.'

The conversation left Prue to stare at the calendar on the wall, unsettled and disturbed. Only Violet managed to prick the skin, so soft and gracious, in which Prue clothed herself without having to try. Only Violet could make her feel so angry and unwilling. Picking up a pen, she scrawled: 'Heathrow, 5 a.m.', in such a way that the whole of the day's space for 7 February 1992 was obscured.

Violet's recollection of her childhood was a fractured, uneasy jumble of dreams and memory. On one hand, she took comfort from a cosy, firelit nursery, a cross between Enid Blyton and Charles Dickens where she knew she was safe (*OED* 'safe': uninjured, entire, healthy). But, perhaps, this was wishful thinking. On the other hand, and the sensation was indisputable, her memories or dreams, whichever, precipitated Violet into a terrain across which she fled, running from a terror she found impossible to describe.

Oh, that white dust churning in her face and choking her

mouth and nostrils as she panted across her inner landscape. The torn nails she used to batten on to blank rock faces blocking her way. The sweat that ran like lava down her body. The terror that clawed at her back.

She supposed that those who lose their mothers young can be subjected to mirages like a warm nursery, and the terror swimming in the darkness outside. Violet's dream figurations could have been less obvious, but that did not diminish either their import or their impact. They were cruel fantasies, both for the fear they stirred and, worse, for the false suggestion of safety enshrined in a leaping nursery fire, the rag-rug, the rocking-chair and the cupboard in which lived Ned the Teddy and Muffin the Mule. Oddest of all, Violet bore no recollection of her mother and she had been almost six when Helen had gone away for the last time – all of six when she died.

Jamie understood. 'By dying, your mother let you down,' he said, 'and you're angry with her and you've blocked her out.'

Violet regretted her impulse to confide in Jamie – but the marriage was still young. 'I wonder,' she commented acidly, 'what the world would have been like before Freud reinvented it. Fresh and innocent, perhaps?'

'I don't mind my concern being rejected or abused,' said Jamie. 'My humour remains intact.'

His reproof did not go unnoticed. 'Sorry,' said Violet, who was still delighted by the acquisition of a new, handsome husband and, furthermore, loved him.

They were in the bedroom of the New York apartment packing the last bits of luggage. Jamie inserted a pastel wedge of Brooks Brothers shirts into his suitcase and closed it. Violet watched. Because she could not fathom them, she distrusted Jamie's occasional silences.

'I *am* sorry, Jamie.'

He placed the suitcase alongside the others by the door. 'I'll think about accepting the apology.' He had his back to her and she was unable to see his smile.

Uncertain how to take the last remark, she sat down on the bed. 'I never know where I am with you, Jamie.' When baffled, Violet had a habit of clicking a nail against another. The sound filled the pause. Then she continued, 'I don't want to be left out, if you see what I mean . . . Because I am your wife and I want to share everything.'

'It's simple.' Jamie came over and pushed her back on to the pillows. 'I love you and I can take your nastiness.'

Violet should have replied, 'I love you, too, and thank you for being nice.' Instead she said, 'Mind my breasts. They're sore.'

'I won't.' Jamie edged closer. 'Beautiful, clever wives must put up with interest in their breasts.'

This was familiar ground. Violet gave a laugh and ran her hand down Jamie's back. 'Friends?' she asked softly, meaning lovers.

His arm reached over her body. 'Friends.'

After a moment, she wriggled free. 'I must pack.'

Jamie rolled over and folded his hands behind his head. 'Are you going to have a minor panic or a major one?'

'Neither – and do you have to joke *all* the time?' Violet pulled open the top drawer of the chest and surveyed the contents. Muddle, she hated muddle, and muddle stared back at her. 'Jamie?'

'Yes.'

'You don't think having a baby addles your brain permanently, do you?' She bit her lip as the words left it. A bundle of crawling, post-partum neuroses was not the best aphrodisiac.

'It's not your brain I'm interested in.'

She raised her eyebrows. 'Ignoring the base metal of yours,

do you think I'll ever be normal again?' She sifted her fingers through a Liz Claiborne scarf and a Ralph Lauren belt and let them drop. 'My memory is haywire, so's my ability to organize. I've always been so good at remembering.' She wanted to say, 'I've always shone at whatever I've turned my hand to', which would have been true.

She poked furiously at the scarves and belts and slammed the drawer shut, trapping a belt. There was another silence. 'Jamie. I seem to have lost my will to do things,' she said helplessly.

It was so uncharacteristic of Violet. In a flash, Jamie was on his feet and cradling her in his arms. 'Listen,' he said, 'having a baby, running a department and the home takes a toll. Your body is telling you to slow down, that's all, just until you recoup your energies.'

'You think?'

Jamie stared over Violet's dark, glossy head to the New York landscape framed by the apartment window. 'I know so.'

Violet stiffened. Before meeting her, Jamie had lived with Lara and her daughter, Jenny, for ten years. That meant he had ten years' extra experience and nothing would ever alter this advantage. Violet's competitive instinct was nettled. It was not so much that she had missed out on ten years at Jamie's side, rather that she had launched herself into a relay race where she was forever condemned to the outside track. Whatever Violet did, however fast she ran, Jamie was pounding away on the inside track.

She leant against Jamie's cashmere-clad shoulder. Then she pulled back and stared into his face. I want to read you, she thought to herself. I want to gather up what is *you*. But I can't.

Under her scrutiny, Jamie's eyebrows lifted a fraction and Violet was swept by desolation for she was failing to grasp something important, and she did not know what. She reached up and pulled his head down and gave him one of her soft, dry kisses on the lips which he always found incredibly erotic. 'Thanks, Jamie.'

A howl from the second bedroom made her jump. The howl increased and Violet folded her arms across her stomach and tightened her mouth. (If she had known how the gesture changed her face for the worse, she would not have done it.) 'I can't, Jamie. He was only fed a couple of hours ago. I just can't.'

Jamie pushed his wife gently away. 'You stay there and I'll bring him in.'

As it was fashionably situated – they had agreed on fashion over comfort – the apartment was tiny and, thus, Jamie was back thirty seconds later. He held a squalling Edward out to Violet. Reluctantly, she accepted him. The baby was red and furious, and the rash sprayed over his face appeared embossed into his skin.

'Oh, baby,' said Violet, angry at his thoughtlessness. 'How could you?'

'I'll get you a cup of tea,' said Jamie.

Edward smelt and it was a toss-up between enduring the crying or the smell. The second option was easier. Violet forced herself to hold the baby and, hating herself for hating him, dragged up the front of her designer jersey and allowed him to latch on. Silence broke over the room, the kind when the breath hisses out in release.

Jamie came back with a tray and gave her a mug. With her free hand, Violet engineered it to her lips but, worried about dropping hot tea on the baby, only managed an unsatisfactory sip. Even having a cup of tea was an effort, these days. The biscuits remained on the saucer. Officially, she ignored them but unofficially their sweet and infinitely desirable image burnt a hole in her stomach.

Edward made satisfied sounds. Bully for him, she thought. She was sucked dry, an arid, slackened arrangement of tubes and organs, no longer pumping sweet juices but bile. The baby's mouth at her breast tugged and worried her flesh with the arrogance of complete possession. Violet looked down at the incubus that had recast her life, and tried not to hate him for his being hideous with spots, because he had made her hideous and her clothes did not fit, and because she was stretched to screaming point by sleeplessness and the scars from her stitches still hurt.

Nobody had warned Violet.

What shall I do? she thought with real panic. A baby and leaving New York. Can't we turn the clock back, Jamie? she asked him silently. Why are you making us go back home?

It had been four hugely exciting years. Of all the great, glorious metropolitan cities to choose from in the world, New York was Violet's. She had made herself there, and the pulse-beat of urban life thudding day and night thudded in time to hers.

New York suited her brand of good looks, her sharp, smart shrewdness, and applauded the terrier quality that made Violet excel in the rights department of a publishing conglomerate.

'I know, I know,' Jamie had said four months ago when he told Violet that the American arm of the bank was being scaled down because of the recession. He knelt in front of the white sofa where she had been sitting. 'But I'm going back to a good job.'

Violet had not moved. 'What about *my* job?' she had asked him. 'Can't you get another one over here?' In reply, Jamie had gently splayed his fingers over her pregnant stomach. 'There are other things,' he said.

'Evidently not for you,' she spat at him. 'Your job comes first.'

Edward continued to feed at her breast as though his life depended on it which, of course, it did. She placed a thumb on his chin and, with a sound of released vacuum, Edward was forced to relinquish the nipple. Face averted, Violet held him up against her shoulder and waited. After he had belched into her ear, she transferred him to the other breast.

A future of eternal broken nights, feeds, milk dripping down her shoulder and an enlarged stomach – almost worse than anything – was visited on Violet. It seemed so awful, and she felt so desperate that she bent her head over the baby and cried. Afterwards, she took Edward into his room to change his nappy.

She had taken infinite pains with the room – more pains, Jamie had commented wickedly, than she had with the baby. It had *had* to be blue and white, ordered, stacked with white towels, clean-smelling and resolutely non-adult. As with most things, Violet achieved her aim and by the time the nursery was finished it was a strong candidate for *Interiors* magazine.

That was before Edward was born and cotton-wool balls had migrated like starlings across the floor and the snowy towels had acquired indelible marks.

Violet pushed back a lock of hair which fell stylishly on to her cheek – the haircut by Kelvin requiring a bank loan. The cut was terrific with the power-suit but irritating at home. Skewering Edward to the changing mat with one hand, she felt in her pocket for a kirby-grip and jammed it into her hair. Edward whinged.

'Be quiet,' she told him.

The Filippino maid who came in once a day had left everything as per Violet's instructions, except for the Beatrix Potter cot bumper which, for some reason, she always tied on upside down. A protest? Perhaps Peter Rabbit made more sense that way. Violet untied and retied it correctly.

The baby settled into the cot without too much fuss. Violet checked his position, stuffed a nappy under his back, rewound the tape of *Womb Concerto* and clicked it on.

Unspeakable noises filled the room and she backed out.

How long? An hour? An hour and a half? Two hours? How long before it all started again?

Goodbye, New York. Goodbye, joggers, muggers, impeccably dressed women walking to work in trainers, designer salads, designer sex, designer divorce. Goodbye, Canal Street, SoHo and the best pasta bar in the world on 5th.

Goodbye, where I made myself.

Violet craned out of the plane window to suck in the last traces of land. Below, the gigantic spawn of the city heaved with life and death. Once again, New York girded itself for another night.

Goodbye, sweet, sweet New York.

Jamie smiled at his wife across the BA flying cradle into which Edward had been lowered. I understand, said the smile. No, you don't, thought Violet, because you have got your own way. Then she repented and returned the smile before settling back in her seat. Night flights were hell.

They flew on into the dawn, and it was so cold in the stratosphere that the rising sun failed to melt the ice crystals on the aircraft's wings. The light turned from bruise purple to mauve, to lilac and then rose pink. After that, came opal and turquoise and tender pink-grey. Violet caught her breath, for up here the world was beautiful and unstained.

'We'll look for a house with a reasonable garden,' murmured Jamie, who was not sleeping either. 'Near a common or something.'

'Not too far out.' Violet's instinct for the city did not desert her. A new thought imposed itself. 'And near a good school.'

'Near a good school,' confirmed Jamie.

'With an extra room downstairs so we don't have baby things cluttering up our room.'

'Anything you wish, Violet.'

Jamie was happy. After eighteen months of marriage, Violet knew him well enough to gauge a mood. She sneaked a look at him as he peered into the cradle and talked to a wakeful Edward. There were such huge areas in Jamie's life of which Violet knew nothing, and Lara was one of them. Not that Violet wished to explore the past – she was not a *Titanic* survivor who went back to look at the iceberg. No, it was better to sail on.

At that point, Edward decided to be thoroughly traumatized by the unfamilar surroundings, the strange cot and the popping in his ears. An hour later, Violet thrust a still-crying baby into Jamie's arms.

'*You* take him,' she whispered, spitting vitriol, and scrambled out of the seat.

She reached the lavatory and slammed shut the folding door. Inside, she examined her reflection in the mirror: The Woman Who Could Not Keep Her Baby Quiet, the object of every eye on board. She dabbed with a tissue at a stain on her blouse. That was mistake number two, dressing up to fly home with a manic baby. For a second, the humour of the situation struck Violet, which was not usual, and she flashed a grin at herself. Then it disappeared and did not return.

When she got back to the seat, she found Jamie holding a peacefully sleeping Edward in his arms. The baby's features were slack with sleep and his skin had acquired its usual translucence.

'Nothing to it,' said Jamie, and it was all Violet could do not to whack her handbag down on the complacent head of her husband.

*

Her father never changed much. Huge, grey-haired, a little shambling, given to corduroy trousers and green sweaters and to taking off and putting on his bifocal spectacles, Max was a reserved man except when it came to his daughters. When he saw Violet, he stepped forward and swept her into one of his bear-hugs, which came close to inflicting injury.

'Darling,' he said, with the brand of awkward tenderness that always made Violet's throat tighten, 'I had to come.'

It was a minute or two before Violet worked out what Max was talking about, until her jet-lagged mind took in that it was Friday. Max had taken a day off work because, he told Prue, he could not miss the homecoming, and added as an afterthought that she might need help with the driving.

Although neither of them had made it to the wedding – so quickly decided on, so romantic – Max had been over to the States to meet Jamie and pronounced that he was a good choice. But he had not met Edward, and as soon as he released Violet, he turned to examine his grandson, who was almost obscured by his wrappings. Virtually ignoring the other two, father and daughter bent over the pushchair, which also did duty as a pram.

'He's a fine little chap,' said Max. 'Handsome, too.'

'No, he's not,' said Violet. 'But I'm glad you like him.'

'Hallo,' said Jamie, standing by the heap of hand luggage. 'You can only be Prue.'

Prue transferred her attention from the family vignette to Jamie. For a second her eyebrows were pulled together in a frown, as if she was trying to sort out a problem, then her eyes widened a fraction. Violet's husband reminded her of someone. Who?

He turned to see to the luggage, and then she realized that Jamie was a younger version of Max. He was very tall and brown-haired, with a similarly shaped face and large but elegant hands. He wore better clothes than Max, and an expensive aftershave, which would never darken the bathroom shelves at Hallet's Gate. But, like Max, there were humour and curiosity in Violet's husband's face and the suggestion of deep feelings that the photographs had ignored. The photographs had, she concluded in that second's assessment, conveyed only two dimensions and missed the third.

'Hallo, Jamie.' Prue held out her hand.

The Basingstoke stretch of the M3 was even uglier than she remembered, Violet announced in the car after surveying, admittedly, some of the worst excesses that had mushroomed during the last four years. *If* that was possible. Violet tended to have A Subject tucked up her sleeve which she aired at parties and dinners. It was a useful defence. Having reasoned that motorway architecture was a conversation in which she could adopt the politically correct stance, she embarked on a trial run on the way back to Dainton. Max joined in and while they batted the topic back and forth, Violet searched assiduously, and unobtrusively, for signs of age in her stepmother.

It had taken her years to realize it, but Prue's were the sort of looks that responded to scrutiny. At first sight, the verdict on her was good-looking, attractive, pleasing. On second and third sight, a curve of her eyebrow, the set of her eyelids, the suggestive mouth and thin wrists prodded the onlooker into thinking: There is more.

Search as she might, Violet could not isolate much. An extra pound on the hips and stomach, perhaps. A line under the eye, which Violet hoped she had not seen before, but nothing else. Otherwise Prue's dark brown hair, swept behind her ears, and clear skin were as she remembered. Nor did her breasts show any sign of sag. Somehow, Violet reflected bitterly, her stepmother always managed not to look her age.

Violet had reached the stage where she no longer endeavoured to censor her reflections; from early in their acquaintance, Prue had been fair game. Occasionally she wondered if Prue knew how much she disliked her, and, if so, did it hurt? Prue never gave anything much away – that was what made her so infuriating, and such a difficult enemy. To the angry, grieving child, her soft implacableness had been . . . terrible.

Motorway architecture having had its airing, Violet moved on to discuss the job that was possibly on offer in the publishing house she most favoured. Underneath the Armani trouser suit, the child that she had been wept at yet another change and beat out her grief.

'Can I help?' Prue stood in the doorway of the spare bedroom at Hallet's Gate. 'You must be dead tired.'

The men had gone off for a walk to work off the bottle of wine that both, unwisely, had tackled over lunch. Edward was asleep and Violet was unpacking.

'I can't believe it was yesterday I put this lot in.'

Prue knew that Violet had not wished to leave New York and felt some sympathy. She picked up a pin-striped skirt and shook it out. 'Liz Claiborne,' she read on the label. 'How chic.'

'Yes, isn't it?' Violet handed Prue a tartan-padded coat-hanger from a stack. 'Hang it up for me,' She paused. 'Please.'

Prue shoved the wire coat-hangers she had saved from the dry-cleaners to one end of the cupboard and did as she was asked. The exiled hangers rattled as she arranged dresses, suits and skirts on their padded rivals, and inserted them in special wardrobe bags. 'I never do this,' she said.

Violet threw her a look, and Prue declined to interpret it. 'Do you have any rough clothes?' she asked. 'You'll need them here.'

'Jesus H. Christ, Prue, I've only lived here for twenty years.' Longer than you, Prue, she wanted to add, although that wasn't true any longer. But I was in the house long, long before you. All those years ago, when Helen, beautiful, drunken Helen, had abandoned her little daughter and sent shock waves through the village equivalent to the death of Grace Archer. Prue had not arrived until three years later, an interloper from London. 'I know the mud-flats as well as my face. And yes, I have plenty of sweaters and leggings.' Violet pronounced 'sweaters' with an American twang.

She flung her hairbrush on to the dressing-table, and Prue winced for the glass top. 'I think I'll get some sleep now.'

Prue did her bit. She fetched and carried hot-water bottles, a cup of tea, an extra rug and Violet, who did look grey with exhaustion, settled down gratefully.

She got half an hour's rest before Edward let everyone in the house know that he, too, had taken up residence. Furthermore, he demonstrated it throughout the small hours of Saturday and Sunday night, but spent the days in exhausted slumber. Thus, it was a frayed group that convened for Monday morning breakfast.

'I thought you said, Mum, that you can sleep through other babies' cries,' said Jane, who had been kept back from school for a dental appointment. She spooned up cornflakes in a dazed fashion. 'I would like to remind you I have a Latin test this afternoon.'

Violet was washing Edward's bottle at the sink. She swirled round. 'Think yourself lucky it isn't every night – which I have to put up with.'

Jane's spoon descended to the bowl and she observed her

half-sister without affection. 'I was giving fair warning as to why I will do badly in the test,' she said. 'That's all.'

Prue broke an egg into the frying-pan for Max's breakfast. Anyone who caught the 7.33 day in day out deserved padding, even if it was pure cholesterol.

'Would you mind if I use a ring?' Violet brushed up against Prue.

Prue endeavoured to make herself as small as possible. 'Of course not.'

Violet produced a bag of organic, cold-pressed porridge oats, labelled 'DelMonico's New York, Your Organically Sound Delicatessen' and measured a cupful into a saucepan. 'Part of the strategy to keep Jamie healthy,' she said. 'All those business lunches.'

Prue assessed the porridge, which certainly had 'organic' written all over it, and transferred her attention to achieving, within the limited space available, the perfect fried egg, sunny side up.

'Good morning,' said Jamie arriving in the kitchen smelling of soap and Vetiver. 'That bacon and eggs looks good. Can I have some?'

Violet placed the organically OK, ecologically sound breakfast in front of her husband. 'No, Jamie,' she said. 'I've done this for you.'

CHAPTER THREE

EXPENSIVE, LACY, WISPY; VIOLET'S KNICKERS STARED UP at Prue from the pile of clean laundry in the basket. Prue entertained a vision of the slender torso and entirely cellulite-free thighs to which they belonged, and sighed. Once Violet had been a skinny, burning-eyed little girl, all bones and angles, who proceeded, in the course of only one year, to surprise onlookers by developing beauty.

Beside the fantasies in the basket lay Prue's own knickers, safe and sensible ones. She bent down and picked up one of Violet's daring black numbers. Comfort versus style. The terrible old sofa versus the love seat. Knickers were a clever way of deploying and maintaining an ingrained male fantasy, and Violet would know just how it was done. If pressed, most women would admit that keeping their kidneys covered was a great deal more comfortable than wearing minuscule bits of lace but, like Violet, endured the chill and unsightly lines. As it happened, Prue was misjudging her stepdaughter – something to which well-intentioned Prue was prone. Violet wore her underwear entirely to please herself.

Prue did not doubt that Jamie loved his wife and, because she herself was loved and therefore understood its language, read the signs, but she wondered if he was at all smug at his trophy? She let the knickers drop back into the basket.

'Day-dreaming, Prue?'

Jamie entered the kitchen with the evening paper under his arm. It was seven o'clock on a Wednesday evening and he had changed into corduroys. Prue's answering smile was particularly sleepy.

'Thinking about laundry, actually.' She kicked the basket under the table because the notion of Jamie making the same knicker comparison and arriving at the same conclusion did not please her somehow.

'Can I help with the supper?'

The request stopped her mid-track. 'Is that a *serious* question?'

'Surely.'

She indicated the potato peeler and Jamie dumped the newspaper, ran cold water into the sink and set to. Taking pleasure as always in the routine, Prue chopped an onion and fried it and watched while the slices softened and turned translucent.

'Did you ever see that play when they fried an onion on the stage? The audience was in agony from hunger.'

'No, I didn't.' Jamie replenished the water in the sink, adding, 'I don't go to the theatre much.'

Prue added mince to the frying pan and the slightly rank smell of meat joined the other smells in the kitchen.

'We must be a lot of extra work,' said Jamie.

'Yes and no. Max always has a cooked meal in the evening.'

'Where is he?'

Max had phoned to say he would be late, she told him. Although he would never breathe a word of criticism against Violet, Max, Prue suspected, was finding the full house as trying as she was. Extra noise. Night activity. Stuff everywhere. A borrowed pram blocking the hall. Baby clothes overflowing in the laundry basket. A half-emptied suitcase on the landing. Every room had an occupant and the house had shrunk.

Where are the spaces in my tranquil, drowsy house? she cried silently.

'Still,' Jamie persisted, 'it's extra work for you and we're grateful.'

Prue nudged back a lock of hair with her wrist. Provisioning and providing were her business, but it was nice to have it acknowledged. 'Any luck with a house?'

'Well, yes.' Jamie launched into a description of one they had seen in Wandsworth and for which they had offered, explaining that it was expensive but he could get a cheap mortgage.

'Ah,' said Prue.

There had been a report in Max's *Economist* which demonstrated that the richest 1 per cent of the population owned 18 per cent of the marketable wealth – a member of which category was helping her to make shepherd's pie in her kitchen. This was in contrast to the poorest 50 per cent who owned only 6 per cent of the marketable wealth.

Of course Jamie Beckett would be able to secure a cheap mortgage, he was that sort of person. The sort who knew people and who had a network thrumming discreetly to his wishes.

The knowledge did not enrage Prue for, she reasoned, it did not mean that Jamie was not lacking in either morality or feeling and, although she worried about the disadvantaged and was happy to make cakes and sell raffle tickets for the homeless, the Bosnians, etc., etc., she had never burned with passionate involvement in their fate. How, then, could she cast a stone?

'How are you doing with the potatoes?'

Jamie pushed a full saucepan towards her. 'Anything else?'

'Could you lay the table? But are you sure?'

'It's my duty day,' he said. 'Or rather night. I share the nights with Violet.'

Gosh, thought Prue, silenced.

Jamie's night duty did not run smoothly. Violet had decided to get Edward completely off the breast within a week and he hated the bottle he was offered at one-thirty a.m., and the bottle he was offered at two-thirty. He cried and cried, emitting the angry, despairing wails of an air-raid siren. The members of the household not involved in the drama cowered beneath their bedclothes, including the baby's mother who informed his father that Edward had *got* to learn.

At three o'clock, Jamie took Edward downstairs and, in desperation, walked him through the hall, around the dining room, up and down the drawing room and round and round the kitchen table. In the dark, he whispered to his son to shut up and, in the dark, he remembered his own childhood nightmares and terrors.

'Please be quiet,' he begged Edward.

The baby's down-dusted skull pulsed angrily under Jamie's chin, and the little body was rigid. Back Jamie paced through the hall, and a shape emerged on the stairs.

'Is he ill?' asked Prue in a normal voice. Under the circumstances, it seemed pointless to whisper.

'I don't know,' said Jamie. 'He won't take the bottle and I'm not sure if it's obstinacy or stomach-ache.' Jamie was beginning to feel exhausted and, not unreasonably, panicked.

Prue led the way into the kitchen and turned out the light. 'Shall I have a try?'

Jamie handed over the baby thankfully. Prue took him and, in an automatic gesture, drew him into her breast. Conscious then of his gaze, she said without looking up, 'I wanted more after Jane, but it didn't happen.'

She was wearing a blue dressing-gown, minus its belt, revealing a soft, white-cotton nightdress underneath. She looked warm and rather sensual, with the blurry languor of mussed hair and drowsiness, and he was suddenly conscious that he was looking at a private side of her. Perhaps fatigue acted as a filter on Jamie, for the colours that made up Prue, blue, brown hair, and the white skin, veined and intimate at the junction of her neck and collarbone, dry and slightly stretched on her hands, painted themselves on to his vision.

'Where's the bottle?' she asked, after a slight pause, aware of his scrutiny.

Jamie handed it over. She settled Edward in her arms and tested the milk. 'It's cold,' she said. 'I bet he doesn't like that.'

'We never heat it up at night.'

Prue raised her eyebrows and then lowered them again. It was not her business. She got up and switched on the kettle, talking to the baby as she did so. Jamie could not make out what she was saying, but her voice was steadying. Evidently the baby agreed for he quietened and when Prue offered him the warmed milk he nuzzled at the teat. After a hiccup or two, he began to feed.

'This might take a while, Jamie, because he's been so upset. Do you want to go back to bed?'

Yes, he did very much. And no, he did not. 'I'll wait with you.'

The cuffs of Prue's nightdress had slipped up her arms and Jamie found himself fascinated by the movement of her surprisingly delicate wrist-bones under the skin and the long fingers that were working magic on the baby. The kitchen was quiet and very cold. Neither of them said anything, but every so often Prue shifted the baby or adjusted the angle of the bottle and Jamie was reminded of paintings of the Madonna and Child – the calm and potent icon from which we demand comfort.

'Like the Virgin,' he said aloud.

'St Joan called herself the Virgin.'

'What?'

'An interest of mine.'

'Tell me.'

Prue told him. During her life, Joan had been given several names, even more after her death which, she said again adjusting the angle of the bottle, was an indication of how puzzling and incomprehensible she had been to her contemporaries. Joan herself preferred the term *la pucelle* which means virgin, but a virgin who anticipates a change in her state.

'Oh,' said Jamie.

It was a condition, continued Prue, that suggested flux, a condition that Prue had at first found difficult to understand. 'But now . . .' she looked up at Jamie '. . . I think I do.' It pinpointed the maiden, both innocent and nubile, on the cusp.

There was a pause.

'Ambiguous, but not,' Jamie supplied.

'But how acute,' said Prue. 'How psychologically sound for a so-called unlettered peasant. And it fascinates me how she knew.'

The chill deepened. Prue addressed the now peacefully sucking baby. 'I suppose I'd better wind you.' She draped Edward across her shoulder. 'Did you have trouble at night in New York?'

'Sometimes. But it's far worse when you're responsible for someone else's household stuffing its fingers into its ears.' Jamie began fiddling with an orange from the fruit bowl and looked up at Prue with a smile rendered devastating by its rueful irony. 'I'm learning.'

She smiled back. 'If you mean that parenthood is a state of extended exhaustion . . .'

'I do. I do.'

'Actually, it's extended terror as well.'

'Meaning?'

'You're constantly frightened for your children.'

Jamie was silent.

'Do you think . . .' Prue sounded tentative. 'Do you think Violet should be going back to work quite so early?'

He frowned and tossed the orange from one hand to the other. 'That's up to Violet.'

She thought for a moment, digesting the rebuke.

The light was not good in the kitchen, but good enough for Jamie to witness the flush flooding Prue's cheeks. The desire to leap up and comfort her cut into him with the speed, thoroughness and surprise of a knife, and he dropped the orange. 'I didn't mean to be rude, Prue.'

'But justified,' she said, got up and handed Jamie his son. 'I think he'll be fine now.'

She left him holding a damp, but silenced, baby.

As a result of that last episode, Emmy Horton came into their lives for Violet insisted that she just *had* to have help. Period.

All right, Prue conceded wearily and wrote out the postcard for the village shop.

KIND, CARING, TEMPORARY MOTHER'S HELP WANTED TO LOOK AFTER FOUR-MONTH BABY AND DO LIGHT CLEANING. GOOD CONDITIONS AND PAY. REFS. APPLY MRS VALOUR, HALLET'S GATE.

The notice attracted a good deal of interest, not least because it was placed beside the one announcing the sale of bankrupt Jack Woodham's personal effects on 26 February. Jack had been the head of the local fern-growers' association and his greenhouse collection – now in jeopardy because he could not heat it – was being fought over.

'Has Mrs Valour had a baby, then?' asked Anna Vigas, reading the postcard.

'No,' said Emmy Horton.

Anna's attention span was never great and she lost interest in the subject. She scuffed a bit of mud with the toe of her Doc Martens and flipped her blonde hair over her shoulder. 'Are you coming tonight, then?'

Emmy was searching her bag, a huge, floppy leather affair with a fringe, for a Biro. 'Hang on.'

'You're not going to apply, Em? A baby *and* cleaning?'

'Unemployment plus extra cash equals nice idea,' said Emmy. 'I like babies and I want something to do.'

'You could do lots of things,' said Anna unfairly, for her own horizons were not vast.

'But I don't, do I?'

It was a bitter day but neither girl was wearing much. Thin T-shirts, leggings and jackets from the discount store. Both of them were skinny and, clearly, cold but neither appeared to mind. Emmy sniffed the air.

'It's going to get colder,' she said. 'I think I'll go and try my luck now with Mrs Valour.'

Flip went Anna's hair.

'The baby is still very young,' said Prue later, in the kitchen of Hallet's Gate, worrying about the thin T-shirt and goosefleshed arms, 'but it's reasonably simple to look after him. My step-daughter wishes to have some help because she needs a bit of a rest and she has to go up to London quite a bit.' Prue outlined the situation.

Emmy shifted on the kitchen chair and her eye lit on a

framed photograph on the dresser of a beautiful girl with black hair and rather remarkable eyes. She looked smart, in control and well off. I see, thought Emmy, who was no fool. Madam needs her beauty sleep.

Prue apologized for Violet not being there and asked when Emmy could start. Emmy replied she could then, that moment.

Aren't you going to ask me about my experience? she projected silently, feeling almost embarrassed for Prue. As if on cue, Prue produced a red-and-black notebook and scanned the last page where headings such as 'martyrdom' and 'treachery, Burgundians', were interlarded with 'check hourly rate', 'no smokers' and 'notice period' which Violet, who reckoned she knew about management, had dictated to Prue.

'Do you have experience with babies?'

'No.'

Prue stared at Emmy and then smiled. 'Nor did I when I had my daughter.'

Her smile was infectious. OK, thought Emmy, not bad. She was aware that she did not look her best. She and Anna had been out drinking the previous evening and it had been an effort to get up. She felt the outline of dark circles under her eyes, the lank feel of her awful hair at its worst, and she was thirsty.

'First aid?' Prue was searching her notes. 'Do you know what to do when a baby chokes?'

'Turn it upside down?'

It did not rank with one of the great answers, but it would do.

'Could I get you a cup of coffee?'

Emmy hesitated. 'Could I have tea, please?'

She watched Prue organize the cups, familiar with the type. Mrs Valour was the sort of person who bent over backwards not to offend but, in so doing, sometimes did. I wonder if she knows she's beautiful? Emmy considered herself ugly and measured her sex from this relative position, and Prue's well-tended hair, clear skin and unforced, untampered feel struck her. Is her husband as nice as he looks? Both Valours were well known in Dainton, but Max's large, hunched figure, his courtesy and his willingness to sit on committees and councils made him especially popular.

The warmth in the kitchen was making Emmy's cheeks glow. Evidently she had caught Prue just as she had returned from a shop. Ordeal-by-trolley at the local Sainsbury's and, judging by the amount, ordeal-by-chequebook as well. She bent down to retrieve a rogue tin from the floor.

'Thank you,' said Prue. 'Do you mind if I unpack while we talk? Some of the stuff needs to go into the freezer.'

'I'll help.' Emmy got to her feet.

'That's kind of you.' Prue shoved a polystyrene tray containing twenty-four chicken thighs towards Emmy before she could change her mind. 'Special Price', it said on the red sticker. 'Family bargain'. 'Could you bag those up in fours, please, in the freezer bags?'

Emmy touched the sticker. 'Favouritism. Do you ever get a bargain if you're an old bat on your own?'

Prue handed the roll of plastic bags across the table, and the light caught a couple of strands of hair at her temples, which were lighter than the rest, 'No, I don't think you do.'

Emmy took a gulp of tea with an unfamiliar taste, ate Prue's biscuits and began work. A stack of polystyrene, plastic and clingfilm mounted on the table. Prue stuffed it into the rubbish bin.

'I know, I know,' she grimaced guiltily, 'it's not good. I keep meaning to protest about the amount of packaging.'

'Gives someone a job, though,' said Emmy.

It crossed Prue's mind that she and Emmy might not get on, and it crossed Emmy's that this was a very different world from the one she knew.

She stood bottles of sherry and wine on the table, piled butter and low-fat spread into a heap, and marshalled tins of *petit pois*, flageolet beans and green lentils for the larder. There were bags of different pastas and pasta sauces, but no gravy browning or salad cream.

'"Farfalle",' Emmy read out from a packet. 'I don't know why they bother. It's all the same at night.'

'There's a theory that sauces bind better to the pasta the more surface there is.'

Prue gathered up the bags and Emmy repressed her reply.

The larder impressed her, however. It was one of those cold, shelved, walk-in rooms, ventilated by mesh and dubbed game-larders by pretentious estate agents. Tins – lentils, artichoke hearts, plum tomatoes – were ranged one side, jars of chutney, expensive jams, bottled fruits and emerald-coloured olive oil on the other. There was a ham, the remains of a truckle cheese and a half-empty jar of Quality Street. Someone had a sweet tooth.

Emmy closed her eyes for a moment.

'You must help yourself to anything you want,' said Prue in a rush, anxious to make up for her slightly superior attitude over the pasta. 'I'm out at work three mornings a week and Mrs Beckett will see to her own meals.'

By that, Prue meant that Violet had categorically refused to do any cooking for the mother's help. 'And, anyway, Prue, I have just gone on a *vicious* diet in order to get into trim for London.' Do you not have to be in trim for Hampshire? Prue wanted to ask her.

'Do you have a microwave, Mrs Valour?'

Prue handed Emmy the final tin to be stowed and took so

long to answer the question that Emmy was not quite sure if her question had been offensive.

'No, we don't.'

Prue had been thinking about Jamie's rebuke over Violet.

Anna was suspicious. The idea of the cash was OK, but babies spelt work. 'They want something for nothing,' she repeated, endlessly in Emmy's opinion.

'Shut up,' she told Anna, finally.

Anna adjusted a migrating shoulder-pad under her jumper and scrutinized her friend. Emmy wore her miserable-and-alone look, which she did from time to time. 'Sorry, Em.'

Emmy grinned suddenly. 'I'll watch out,' she said. 'If they overwork me, I can always clean the baby's bum with Jif.'

Scanning the gardens and fields that lapped the village boundaries for the things that interested her – earth thrown up by a mole, a stream swollen and flowing with energy, the bright green of grass sated with winter rain – Emmy walked home. Almost too dazzling for the gloomy day, a burst of winter jasmine was draped over the wall of Horton's farm. Further up the road, rooks were nest-renovating in the beeches that edged the copse up the rise. Good. That indicated spring. Not spring because the calendar said so, but spring because things were happening in the earth.

Emmy considered the subject of spring. She knew quite a lot about wildlife and bits of this and that picked up from GCSE biology and the snippets of medical detail with which her mother, a clerk at the hospital in Winchester, occasionally regaled her. Knowledge that surprised her sometimes, for Emmy, though sharp and shrewd, did not consider herself in any way bright and school had been an experience to get over and done with as soon as possible.

The wind shifted, and she responded by hunching her shoulders. Where in the damp, frozen woods were the fritillary butterfly caterpillars overwintering? Hidden in the violet leaves? She hoped so because it sounded so nice, and they must be there because last summer had seen fritillaries. Emmy had spotted a rare pair of Monarchs, too, blown 3500 miles across the Atlantic by the winds.

Imagine being blown all that way.

She bent to pick up the discarded husk of a beech nut which cracked between her fingers. Gently, she prised it open and was rewarded by a glimpse of secret, intimate green at the centre. Its unexpectedness, and the contrast – death and life, sweet and bitter – pleased her greatly.

These days, Father was on a reduced shift, Mother was on night duty, because it brought in more, and her two elder brothers had joined the army and she never saw them. In the empty space that remained was Emmy, a solitary girl, in an empty house on the edge of Dainton. Either that or it was full of people trying to sleep at awkward hours.

A green Range-Rover followed by a Volvo drove down the road and sent up a spray of water. Emmy stepped back smartly.

'Sods,' she said half-heartedly.

The Volvo had a FOR SALE notice pasted on to its back window. GOOD PRICE FOR QUICK CASH SALE.

Emmy's lack of obvious prettiness was not helped by the pinched look characteristic of someone who did not eat quite enough, in contrast with the glossy hair and skin of someone who did. Like Mrs Valour, for example.

In one respect, unremarkable bone structure and lank hair made life simpler: the race was so unequal there was no need to enter it. Observing Anna's unrelenting attention to her body – haircuts, face packs, depilations – Emmy appreciated her freedom and was grateful for the anonymity granted by ugliness. People looked straight through Emmy to the blonde, full-lipped Anna, who then had to cope with the attention.

'I don't know,' said her mother, often enough. 'You won't even *try* to look nice.'

She reiterated the complaint on Emmy's return to the house and stepped up the pressure when she heard Emmy had got herself a job. She suggested that Emmy got herself a perm, at least, and emptied the contents of her straw basket on to the table. Having located her wallet, one of those fat-bellied affairs into which you can stuff a life, and extracted a twenty-pound note, she held it out to her daughter. 'Here, have it on me.'

'You really think it'll help?' asked Emmy.

Mrs Horton's own face was framed by a construct of ice-blonde curls. 'Of course,' she said impatiently, and picked at a flaking cuticle. 'You see, Emmy,' she confided, and clicked her frosted nails on the Formica table, 'you're so much on your own and I don't do enough for you.'

'And a perm will alter that?' Emmy flashed back.

Mrs Horton was tired from having raised three children, harassed by the family's reduced income and the demands of running a home and a job. ('Thank the Lord,' she often said, 'I won't have to empty a Hoover bag in my coffin.') She did not feel equal to pulling Emmy's life into shape. A perm was the best she could offer. Emmy knew that, and knew her mum tried, and was grateful. 'Stand by for the mob, then,' she said, 'and for the suicides under my window.'

The perm, as she could have predicted, was not a success. In the seconds before her scalp disappeared under the baking foil and chemicals, Emmy allowed herself to fantasize: from under them a woman of power and beauty would emerge. Then she pulled herself together and studied her reflection in the mirror while Neil worked her over. Surrounded by lights and bottles of shampoo and conditioners promising Nirvana, it was not a kind mirror. Its object was to strip its prey to the bone, and it did. There sat Emmy, a plucked chicken with nodular wrists, peaky features and collar-bones that made lines under her T-shirt. She lit a cigarette.

'Shouldn't do that,' advised Neil, 'it destroys your Vit C levels. Have a cup of herb tea instead. Else,' he shouted across the salon floor, 'bring us a cup of Blackcurrant Bracer.'

Neil was a great deal prettier than Emmy and she could see from his clear eyes and fresh skin that his Vit C level was kept topped up. A wholesome, tutti-frutti, blow-dried walking advert for citric acid.

Else placed a mug in front of Emmy and a sweetish smell rose from a curl of steam.

Two hours later, Emmy alighted from the bus at the Dainton stop. Patches of frost glimmered in the light thrown from the houses edging the road, and the landscape was how she liked it best: stark, with gaunt, skeletal plants. She liked the smooth bark, bleached branches and cleanness of stripped winter trees. It was growing even colder and her hair fizzed and burned around her face. She pushed it back and contemplated doing a Sinead O'Connor and shaving her head.

At eighteen she had not got far with her life, but exactly what she was to do with it was as yet a mystery. Three moderate passes at GCSE, as Mrs Horton also pointed out, were not a passport to a briefcase and a company car. Silence lay over the other subjects with which Emmy had wrestled and lost. Since leaving school, she had made do with odd jobs here and there, but they never lasted more than a month or two, and never engaged her interest.

She halted by the big oak at the bottom of the lane which was flanked by hawthorn scrub. Earlier that morning, a fieldfare had been sitting there, fluffing out its grey and russet plumage. Emmy had enjoyed that.

Her shoes cracked on the frozen puddles and the sound was magnified in the cold air. In the field ahead, the livery horses were clumped together. A big bay had a New Zealand rug strapped around his girth, thicker than Emmy's jacket. Round here, livery horses got treated like hotel guests – linen sheets and hot-and-cold running.

Emmy rounded the corner and Hallet's Gate came into view. She recognized the Valours' voices in the drive as she drew nearer and saw them standing, talking.

'Don't get cold,' he said, and there was a degree of tenderness in his tone that made Emmy halt temporarily in her tracks. Sometimes the unfairness with which love was dished out, some people getting so much, made her jealous. She hovered for a few seconds more, a dark, rather anguished shadow with a perm that imperfectly disguised a spirit that longed to expand but did not know how.

Then, Mr Valour put his arm around Mrs Valour and she leant briefly against him before they moved towards the front door from which light was streaming.

Suddenly, Emmy knew. She did want something from life. She wanted her own home. Not a big one, just a couple of rooms, with a kitchen, and a bathroom with a decent bath. A back garden. She wanted white walls, fringed lampshades, coir matting and plants. She wanted order and quiet, not the deadly quiet of Number 5, but her own peace. The yearning solidified in the pit of her stomach, surprising Emmy by its physicality.

As Emmy let herself into her own home, which smelt chilly and unoccupied, the boiler leapt into life. She switched on the light, which sent down harsh rays through its frosted glass shade on to the patterned carpet.

In the kitchen, Mrs Horton had left a message on the back of an envelope. 'Get your own supper. Dad and me out.'

Emmy sighed.

CHAPTER FOUR

Emmy proved a godsend and, for someone with no experience of babies, a natural. Edward took to her and so, after the initial week, did Prue. Quick to pick up the basics, she was not too talkative, apparently reliable and, above all, willing. Prue relaxed, and Violet exploited all these advantages.

'I'll be away a lot more in the future,' she explained to Emmy, and sipped mint tea while Emmy struggled to change a nappy. 'I need to be in London to supervise the new house. After all, I've done my whack with breast-feeding, whatever Sheila Kitzinger says.'

Emmy did not hold any opinions on breast-feeding, neither did she know who Sheila Kitzinger was, but what did strike her was that Violet was on the defensive. Guilt at offloading the baby? No, Mrs Beckett did not look the guilty type. Intuitively, Emmy felt it was more complicated. People looked and sounded like Violet when they were not sure how to behave: she had seen it with her mates at school, and particularly with the bullies. Violet, Emmy eventually put her finger on it, to her satisfaction, was only pretending to be a mother.

Emmy liked the baby, without feeling any passionate attachment to him, but when he was presented with a bottle instead of the warm breast and occasionally cried, his desolation rendered Emmy sweaty and uneasy. She was not, therefore, surprised that Violet made herself scarce.

'She's a madam,' she told Anna.

Anna inspected the expensive pushchair. 'With loot.'

'With loot.'

'Are you going to stick it, Em?'

'Of course. The more spoilt Madam is, the more's in it for me.'

'You've lost your deck.'

Emmy considered Prue's kitchen and larder, the scent bottles on Violet's dressing-table, the stack of sweaters and shirts with classy labels, and shot a look at Anna. At the back of her mind, she harboured an idea that if she stuck out the job some of the luxury and exclusiveness would rub off on her – like glitter flaking from a Christmas card. Whether that was sensible or not, and what she would get out of it in the end, Emmy was unsure. Neither Violet nor Prue wore T-shirts and there was not a leather jacket to be cast off between either woman. Packets of pasta? An insider's knowledge of Sainsbury's layout? Instant recall of Radio 4's timetable, Monday to Friday?

It was not the *savoir faire* that would get Emmy by in the disco or the factory, or the supermarket packing division – if it came to the latter, the thought of which made Emmy screw up her face.

'Bear up, Em,' said Anna, flicking her hair. 'We'll go drinking tonight.'

From the first – and always – Violet had inhabited an uneasy terrain in Max and Prue's life together. 'I can't cope with her, I *can't* cope,' Prue had been driven to shouting at Max from her mess of hormones and leaking body just after Jane was born. She hates me. She hates the baby.

Max's large, heavy hand on her shoulder and his silence, which she interpreted as condemnatory, hurt badly, and drove Prue to say something she regretted: 'She's like a bad fairy in our marriage.'

Instantly, Max had removed his hand and left the room. Later, Prue discovered him in the study polishing (forever polishing) the two guns from the gun cabinet. Max always used his uncle's Purdey for shooting but the other, which had belonged to William, his father, received equal attention. She had endeavoured an apology and ended up weeping hysterically in the armchair. Max dealt with Prue's tears and moved into action. He had put her to bed, summoned her mother, who was still going strong at that point, and Mrs Blake from the village was recruited to take charge of Violet until the worst was over. All wonderfully practical solutions that he effected without drama, fuss or recrimination, and Prue was grateful.

'We all need breathing space,' he said when she tried to thank him. 'Otherwise we crowd the spirit too much.'

And Prue was left in peace with her new baby, and her mind was allowed to drift in and out of dreams, to go over and over the birth until it was settled in her memory, to struggle with the sense that she should be giving thanks to a God, but that she could not find him. At least, she had been given the silence in which to try.

Max had never commented on Prue's outburst. Yet she felt that its memory, and its import, remained, submerged but there.

'Violet looks exhausted,' said Max, sitting down and peeling off a sock. It had been a full week and everyone had opted for early bed. Violet had arrived back in Dainton after a two-day trip to London full of talk of the new house and the job she had been offered.

'I'm worried it's going to be too much for her.' Max took

off the second sock. He held up a hand to forestall Prue. 'I know, I know, it's what women want.'

The echo from the conversation in which she had been the one to query Violet's decision pricked and bothered Prue. Instead of confessing that she had been thinking along the same lines, she said, 'You sound like something out of the ark.'

'Maybe. But I watch these working mothers struggling to keep the show going and I wonder. Delphine Watson, for instance. I told you about her before. She used to be pretty but these days looks dreadful. I took her out to lunch to find out why. Apparently her two-year-old hasn't slept through the night yet and her husband's no help.'

'Being at home makes no difference if you have no sleep.' Prue got into bed beside Max and leant over and dropped a kiss on his hair. 'It was nice of you to bother.'

'I know women must work but how can she do her job properly in her state?'

Prue withdrew to her side of the bed.

'What I'm saying is this. I don't want Violet ending up half dead with fatigue and heading for a nervous breakdown.' Max punched his pillow and settled down.

He interpreted Prue's silence correctly and flung a sop. 'Actually, the working mother is nothing new, only the dames who ran the manors and demesnes in history had family back-up. Nowadays, you use girls like Emmy.'

'Emmy is very reliable.'

'Maybe.' Max swivelled on the pillow to look at Prue. Underneath the blankets his hand felt for his wife's.

Prue turned off the bedside light and composed her body into the position she preferred for sleep. After they had first married, Max had forbidden Prue to work. Well, not forbidden exactly, he had just kept up a powerful lobby. 'Look,' he said, 'I've lost one wife, and Violet and I need you at home.'

She remembered he had stood over her as she sat on the sofa, his large features creased and urgent. Then he took hold of Prue's hand and held it against his cheek. 'Please, Prue. I want a family and a home.'

There had been no glittering career for Prue to fight for – the role of secretary then research assistant did not warrant a lot of drum banging, and insisting on her right to work promised to be a Pyrrhic victory.

Practicalities were a consideration, too. The prospect of daily outwitting British Rail made Prue wilt – the cattle truck of the rush-hours, the furtive Mars Bars at the end of a long day and falling asleep over the *Evening Standard* did not seem to be positive affirmations of life. Who would look after the children, the many she envisaged sitting around the kitchen table?

Prue turned over, aware that her distaste for the commuting life would cut no ice with those who had no option but to do it. Her hand sought and found the corner of the pillowcase and she rubbed it between her fingers. She liked the feel of the texture on her skin, and to run an edge under her fingernail.

Max was asleep. This was Prue's time, and her mind flowed up and over the rocks and hills of her life, trying to make sense of problems or the restlessness that occasionally tormented her. Sometimes, in the moment suspended between waking and sleeping, she sloughed off the sense of herself and floated free. Just for a few moments. Then she would feel extraordinarily peaceful and receptive but, paradoxically, charged with energy. I have been lucky.

Yes, so far, Prue had been lucky: in her marriage, in her circumstances, in her daughter.

Men are good icon-makers, and Max had shaped Prue into a familiar and infinitely comforting one, and she had not objected. A French peasant girl wearing a man's armour and a man's haircut had also been turned into an icon through the medium of the masculine eye and pen. (Although women's tongues must have had quite a bit to do in shaping Joan's story and sending news of it far and wide.) As far as Prue knew, there was only one documented instance of a woman describing Joan, which affirmed only that from what she could observe Joan was a virgin. Stranger still, as often in the business of forging icons, men like to ascribe weird purities to the female version. Extreme, tortured virginity. Suffering. Untouchableness. Immaculate conception.

A virgin then, the *pucelle*. A woman on the brink of change.

Before she fell asleep, Prue relived the moment in the kitchen with Jamie and Edward: the sensation of the baby against her breast, and Jamie's tired, tenderly composed face. He was a stranger, and different, one whose possibilities were foreign. Of one thing only she was sure: the sum of Jamie was hidden below the surface. Her mind drifted on . . . Jamie holding his baby and telling her to mind her own business. His touch on her arm, as violent in the sensation it provoked in her as the swords of Joan's men running through English flesh.

After Prue had fallen asleep, Max turned and looked at the dark shape, tipped by a luminous lick of white linen. He stared at his wife for some time. Then, very carefully, he turned back to his side of the bed.

Jamie leant over to kiss Violet goodnight. Burrowed into the bedclothes, she was already half asleep and the waterfall of hair on the pillow was motionless. He turned off the light.

Blue was the Virgin's colour, the Madonna's colour, and it suited Prue as it did not suit the un-Madonna like Violet who favoured reds and greens. He stared at the ceiling while his eyes adjusted to night vision. Blue was a colour into which to sink, rested and calmed by its serenity.

Prue was secret, or rather private, and Jamie suddenly perceived that walls and thorn hedges offered temptation as, let it be said, they did in matters of work. How high could you, would you, climb? Did you dare to cut and slash your way through to the princess wrapped in blue who lay sleeping within?

To reassure himself, Jamie slid a hand across the sheets and placed it on Violet's slender haunch. It was cool and firm to the touch.

Goodnight, wife.

'My mum's always worked,' Emmy informed Prue over the sterilizer, which took up too much space on the sideboard and made the kitchen stink of Milton.

'Who looked after you when you came home from school?'

Emmy looked at Prue as if she was sizing up a visitor from Mars. 'No one. Mum left a meal out for me to warm up. Sometimes my brothers were home. Sometimes my nan came over. The neighbours were there if I wanted something.'

'Yes,' said Prue. 'Of course.'

Emmy flicked through her file of mental images. One of its documents was the picture of a warm house, a bright fire and a mother in the kitchen, baking. It was a picture to which she only referred after careful consideration, or after one too many at the pub, because it hurt her to think about it.

'How do you find dealing with a baby?' Prue sat down at the table to count out the housekeeping money.

'I was dead frightened.'

Prue looked amused. 'And now?'

'I like it. He's a nice baby and it's sort of planning, really. Working out a routine. Understanding his language. I should be quite good at it.'

'Oh?' Prue slid a heap of coins back into the tin, which had 'Fortnum and Mason. English Breakfast Tea' written on it.

'Yes,' said Emmy. 'I'm good at crosswords.'

Prue was not and the conversation lapsed. Anyway, she was not quite sure of the logic of Emmy's argument.

She was quite clear on one point, however: her longing to have the house back to herself. A baby provoked such big upheavals and such big emotions – panic, inadequacy, crippling tenderness. When it was yours myopia was added to the list, for it was hard to see anything beyond its milk-blistered mouth and your own exhaustion. With Jane, Prue had looked up from time to time to the world outside and found it alarmingly narrowed but, battle-happy and at that time more or less on an even keel with Violet, thanks to Mrs Drake, had longed for a bigger family. When a second one did not arrive, distance set in and, after a few years, so did relief at no longer being on the front line.

Unlike Joan, who had placed herself fairly and squarely on the front line.

Joan had possessed an advantage. God. From the beginning, Joan had been in touch with him. She had been an exceptionally pious child, even in an age of piety, if you believe the depositions of Jean Waterin and Mengette Yoyart as they appear in the *Procès de condamnation et de réhabilitation de Jeanne d'Arc*. In his deposition, her godfather Jean Morel also states that often when Jeanne (*sic*) was supposed to be watching the cattle, she played truant to worship at the shrine of Our Lady of Bermont. God must have made life easier even in war-ravaged France, particularly if he sent instructions down via St Michael and St Catherine, and less frequently St Margaret.

Instead of battling on to the 7.33 to Waterloo, or with the school run, Joan had abandoned her patched red frieze dress, the traditional costume for women in the area, borrowed a tunic and hose and taken herself off to a bigwig in Vaucouleurs, Robert de Baudricourt, and badgered him into listening to her crazy idea of rescuing and crowning their moribund Valois dauphin. This being the age that allowed, encouraged, a dialogue with God and miracles, she succeeded, and set off for Chinon with six companions wearing a new set of clothes and a horse bought by the good people of Vaucouleurs. Note: The saddle was of a design that supported the small of the back and the thighs. Otherwise, how else would a peasant girl unused to riding have mastered such a mount?

The wool stuff of her newly acquired leggings would have rubbed unfamiliarly between thighs that had known only a skirt. She would have been aware of the different freedoms permitted by a shirt and doublet, the constriction of leather boots, the smell of harnesses and male sweat. Noise, too, would have afflicted Joan, accustomed as she was to the rural peace of the village. She complained later that her voices sometimes had trouble coming through because of it. Prue empathized with this as she read of Joan searching for a little peace among the clamour of conflict and communal medieval life. Today, she would have stood no chance at all against aircraft, breakfast television and the new, improved A303.

'Did you get the organic oats?' Violet enquired, as Prue was packing away yet another gigantic Saturday shop. It was the first week in March, and everyone was waiting for spring.

'Sorry, I forgot.'

'Camomile tea?'

'Oh, Lord.'

Violet pushed the sterilizer under the window and stacked tins of infant soya milk powder in the place where Prue usually kept the bread crock. Prue bided her time until Violet was occupied with the kettle, pushed the milk tins to one side and replaced the bread crock. She felt thoroughly childish.

Violet looked up. 'Were they in the way?'

'No,' said Prue coolly. 'But I keep the bread there.' Violet's expression prompted her to add, 'Oh, for goodness sake, it doesn't matter where the bread goes.'

'Quite,' said Violet, 'that's what I thought.'

Emmy, Violet and Prue sat and drank coffee at the kitchen table. Once upon a time, Violet would have been drinking orange juice and demanding a story, a diversion she used to demand constantly.

If Prue had loved her – and she tried, she *did* try – Violet would have been fascinating. She had been a funny little girl, a great collector, comics, *Girl* annuals, cheap jewellery, shells, abnormally tidy and over-fond of fluffy toys. Each toy had a house in her bedroom, a shelf, a corner, an area of the bed and a second establishment downstairs, and it went ill with Prue if they were moved. Every so often, Violet gathered up her menagerie of bears, cats, dogs and dolls, shut herself in the bathroom and washed them. The hairdryer then whined continuously. Eventually, damp, groomed and fluffy, the objects of Violet's passionate care returned to their homes. The tidiness had created an extra barrier between stepmother and stepdaughter.

'By the way,' said Violet holding out her cup for refill, 'I've got the official letter today. Group Rights Director.'

The magnitude of this achievement was lost on Emmy, but Prue said, with unfeigned delight, 'Congratulations.'

'It's the one I really wanted.' Violet's red-tipped nails tightened on her cup. 'It's the most exciting publishing group in the business.'

'Will the house be ready in time?'

'Sorry, Prue, I forgot to tell you. Jamie told me last night.

We exchange contracts on Monday and complete in two weeks. Jamie's making them work double quick.'

'Lovely,' said Prue. 'We should celebrate.'

At her end of the table, Emmy shivered. 'I'm freezing,' she said.

Prue met Violet's gaze and, for once, there was complete accord between the two women.

'You're not wearing enough,' said Violet.

That was the weekend when Prue first became concerned about Jane who had arrived back from school subdued and pale. Prue had overdone her concern, insisting on a double dose of tonic and supper in bed. This had pitchforked mother and daughter into a battle. Jane wished to stay up to watch *Home and Away*, *Neighbours* and *Eldorado* and Prue had said no. Jane had insisted on three good reasons as to why the ban was in force, and Prue had made the mistake of saying she did not want Jane's head stuffed with that rubbish. 'You don't want me to be left out,' Jane wailed as she went upstairs, 'everybody watches them. Anyway,' she added, 'we see them at school.'

This left Prue to reflect bitterly on the relationship between school fees and soaps. She came to the conclusion that the subject was so enraging that it was best not to dwell on it.

She was tackling the ironing after lunch on Saturday when Jane surprised her by sneaking up behind her and sliding her arms around her waist.

'Hallo, poppet,' Prue said.

Jane pressed her cheek into her mother's back. 'I've done my prep, Mum.'

This was Jane's apology. Touched by its elliptical approach, which was so typical of Jane, Prue inserted the tip of the iron under a shirt collar and the material wrinkled into creases. 'Bugger,' she said under her breath.

'I did an extra bit as well because it was easy.'

'Well done.'

Jane's arms tightened around Prue. 'Victoria's mum and dad are getting divorced, you know.'

Prue did not know. She plonked the iron down on its stand and swivelled round to face her daughter. 'That's awful. Poor Victoria.'

'She's quite happy. She says she can play them off against one another. Me and Sally have a bet that Victoria will have a pony by Christmas.'

This report did not accord with Prue's image of Victoria who was a shy, rather withdrawn child, and she ached to think of the bravado that had gone into her statement.

'And what would *you* aim for, Janey . . . if you were playing Dad and me off against one another?'

Jane's eyes gleamed. 'You know what I want, Mum. A computer with all the trimmings . . .'

Prue searched her daughter's face, so little and so unfinished, and smoothed back some hair from the unmarked forehead. It was a source of amazement that she had produced a creature of science and mathematics, of computers and suchlike when she herself cared for and knew nothing of these subjects. 'I should have known,' she said tenderly.

'Can we light a fire, Mum, and watch telly together?'

When Max came in from his walk, mother and daughter were settled in front of the drawing-room fire enjoying themselves. They made a good picture and he watched them fondly for a moment.

'Hallo, darling.' Max leant over the sofa and gave Jane a kiss.

Jane reached up a hand and Max tugged at her fingers. He pointed at the newspaper lying on the table in front of the sofa. 'Did you read that the pound's in a mess?'

Prue sat up. 'They won't put up interest rates, I hope.'

'It's possible,' said Max.

It was only then Prue registered that another figure stood behind her husband.

Quite by accident, Prue's and Jamie's eyes met, explored, and exchanged a message which neither quite understood.

CHAPTER FIVE

AT LAST THE BECKETTS HAD MOVED INTO THEIR HOUSE in Austen Road. Prue had longed for their departure but, in the contrary manner of the human psyche, found the space left behind in Hallet's Gate empty and unsettling.

'It's odd,' she told Max as they wheeled the borrowed pram back to its owner, 'how ungrateful you are for getting the things you want.'

Max's expression was inscrutable. Then, looking straight ahead, he said, 'I'm grateful for getting what I wanted, even if it is obsessed by a saint.'

For a second Prue was blank, then she realized he was joking. She prodded him in the ribs. 'Unlike wine, Max, your wit does not improve with age.'

He laughed, and they walked on together and, because they were enjoying the walk, took the long way home.

But the peace was not to remain unbroken.

A couple of weeks later the telephone rang.

'Can you help, Prue, do you think?' Violet managed to make her request sound remarkably similar to a command, explaining that it was imperative that she attend the spring sales conference as a run-in to the new job. Apparently, the nanny hired for the week had phoned to say that, after all, she did not fancy the job.

Not fancy it? Violet was not often floored. Not *fancy* it? was all she could manage at her end of the phone, the grail of the sales conference whisking out of sight. You *can't* do that to me, I have a job to do. Tough, said the defaulting nanny.

In Dainton, Prue toyed with the idea of saying no.

Violet, knowing she was at bay, changed her tactics. 'I'm desperate, Prue.'

It was true. She was desperate to get out and away and shake off her appendage. In her more anguished moments when she fell back on cliché, Violet thought of herself as a bird unable to take flight, caged and encumbered – which, of course, she was.

Prue checked out the *Prunus autumnalis*. Planted strategically so that washers-up at the sink – her – could benefit from its winter blossom, it was now past its best, but tanking up nicely underneath were the narcissi and chinodoxia she had planted at the last minute. London was another world. Not hers and, she suspected, dangerous.

'It's only from Tuesday to Thursday afternoon,' said Violet, who did, indeed, sound desperate.

Prue relented. 'I suppose I could do some work on Joan when Edward's sleeping.'

Violet refrained from replying that she thought it most unlikely. 'Of course,' she said in the tone she had found useful in New York when lying, business lies being part of business. 'I would be so grateful.' Gratitude was not an emotion she usually felt for Prue, but Violet was a strategist.

*

There was no one at Waterloo to meet Prue, not that she expected it, and the taxi queue was enormous. Nudging her case along with her foot, she took stock of the city, a station being as good a place as any to begin. As a child, Waterloo, to which she had journeyed frequently on school trains, had seemed immutable and unchanging, like the areas in her atlas stained pink which, her teacher insisted, represented decency and order.

Now the station was under wraps. Bits were falling off it and a skin of litter, leaves and dust overlaid the pavements. A couple of homeless men had set up base by the entrance. One of them had a puppy stuffed into the front of his coat, which was tied with string. The other breathed in greedy slugs from a paper bag and turned a drugged, drowning face towards passers-by who did their best to ignore him. Prue supposed he was in his twenties.

According to the taxi driver, Albert Bridge was out of commission, and life was a bloody nightmare. Prue sat in the taxi, swamped by a sea of cars. She sniffed at the benzine and exhaust, overcome by the miasma of houses and humans competing for existence in a confined area.

Colours in the city are cast in a different foundry, she thought. Leaves are heavy with yellows and ochres dripping acid tints into the greens. Dun-coloured cement pointing in brickworks is slicked by a powdering of carbon. Curved grey roof-tiles gleam in the rain; a flat counterpoint of greys sit alongside the harsh, unbeautiful red of London brick.

Prue pressed her gloved hand against the taxi window and rebellion at being there streamed through her fingertips and on to the glass. Was her protest at Violet? Or was she protesting about the fin breaking through the surface of the now calm, unstormy waters of her marriage?

A cyclist paddled alongside the taxi and flipped the wing mirror.

'Idiot,' said the driver, mildly, out of the window.

The Becketts' house was situated in a road wider than the others, in the area between Wandsworth and Clapham Common. Prue was deposited outside a late-Victorian house with good proportions and a brown front door.

Violet had been hovering and opened the door before Prue had rung. 'Hideous colour, isn't it?' she said, referring to the front door.

Prue followed her into an open, light-filled hall, littered with painting equipment. Almost at once, she sneezed. From upstairs came a clatter of boots on bare floorboards and a volley of interesting language. Violet apologized.

'I thought you said nothing needed to be done to the house.'

'Well, you know how it is,' said Violet. 'In the end, Jamie needed a dressing room and the nanny must have her own bathroom. Some of the rooms needed decorating, and the kitchen wasn't quite as I wanted it, so it's being redesigned. Don't worry, they're working on the nanny bit at the moment and won't bother you.'

It is possible to know how you feel about a house when you step over the threshold, and Prue was interested in this one's incompleteness.

'There's a good feel to the house,' said Prue.

'That's lucky.' Violet led the way into the kitchen. 'I'm not moving again for a long, long time.'

The kitchen was large, sunny and the floor had just been relaid with planks of sanded wood and varnished to mirror brightness. Prue negotiated a pile of builder's overalls and huge tins of varnish and sat down.

Violet loomed over her, a creature, Prue fancied, out of a Fuselli engraving, brooding darkly, wings straining for flight.

'Edward's in the next room, asleep. I've made up his bottles for the day and they're in the fridge. He should sleep for an hour or so. Give him a drink when he wakes. After his lunch he likes a walk, then pray for six o'clock when you can put him to bed.'

'Bath?'

'If you like.' Violet seemed indifferent. 'Have some coffee.'

She disappeared and returned ten minutes later, groomed and made-up, wearing an olive wool suit, her eyes sparkling with a different light.

'Do you think you can cope, Prue?' Violet was straining to be gone.

Prue transferred her gaze from the garden (20 ft x 50 ft) which currently resembled a municipal tip. 'Good luck.'

Suddenly, momentarily unsure, Violet hugged her briefcase. 'I'll need it. I've got to make a good impression. Show them that the baby makes no difference at all.'

'I think that's impossible,' said Prue gently. 'You can't have a baby and pretend that nothing's happened.'

'I can,' said Violet, and the old, assured expression was back in place. 'By the way,' she added from the doorway, 'you'll have to buy something for supper. Northcote Road. The *A–Z* is in the hall. Alfalfa sprouts are in the fridge.'

Edward did not bother to wait for an hour and was yelling for his bottle within twenty minutes of his mother's departure. Prue gave it to him – there was no point in not and she had been blooded in the Baby-Knows-Best school. The afternoon walk was advanced by three-quarters of an hour but Prue enjoyed snooping. Anyway, the prospect of a supper composed entirely of alfalfa drove her shopwards.

Colonized by late-Victorian housing developers, the area had mouldered during the fifties and sixties but, clearly, was now enjoying a renaissance. Many of the houses had been painted in pastel colours, a backwash from the British love affair with the Mediterranean, and wreathed in fashionable plants, clematis and old roses definitely favoured over utilitarian mahonia and laurel. The effect reminded Prue of medieval gardens she had seen in Books of Hours, indisputably pretty but lacking robustness.

Pelmets were in fashion. Tart's-knickers blinds had been ousted in favour of swags, poles and ornate curtain rods. Velux windows sat fish-eyed in roofs so that neighbour, it seemed, was looking into neighbour.

Edward stirred in the pushchair and opened his eyes, which were now bright blue, blinked and, soothed by the motion of the chair, dozed.

'You little blighter,' Prue told him.

By the time she reached the butcher, she had decided that her taste in curtains was boring, and she should do something about it. On an impulse, she bought a copy of *Interiors*, which featured pages devoted to old Swedish furniture, swathed in muslin and photographed in light as white and sunny as a dream. They were delicious and beautiful, and utterly removed from her life.

Prue took the magazine back and exchanged it for *Good Housekeeping* and a part-work on computers for Jane.

The shop local to Austen Road turned out to sell French cheeses, Italian salami and extremely expensive vegetables. Next door was a florist whose window display was composed of lilies and mimosa, and the off-licence further down the street had Australian wines stacked in bins.

How like Violet. How clever she was at situating herself. No run-of-the-mill corner shop for her. No wedges of cheese wrapped in industrial strength cling-film, or one-size pop socks. All the same, Violet was right. These commodities exuded attraction. Vignottes and Chaumes cheese sitting on a bed of, admittedly, fake straw, pesto, up-market ice cream and Bach Flower Remedies exuded the allure of fantasy made real.

Back at the house, which seemed cold and dark, Prue sat in the kitchen and fed Edward, conscious of the uncurtained window. Because he was tired, Edward fussed. Suddenly, two days seemed a long time.

She phoned Kate, at home in Dainton, and did not feel at all guilty at talking for half an hour at the Becketts' expense.

'You are kind,' said Jamie when Prue served him sausages with baked potatoes. 'We batten on you, I'm afraid. Do you mind if I start? I'm so hungry.'

They sat opposite one another at the table, with a candle stuck into a bottle. Prue was wearing a jersey in her favourite blue which allowed Jamie to see the outline of her breasts.

Jamie made himself concentrate on his plate.

'Ketchup?' she asked.

They passed mustard, chased sausages around their plates and drank wine out of tumblers, because nothing was unpacked, and shared the kind of intimacy that is usually shared by people who know each other well.

Jamie talked about his work in the bank, and used his knife and fork to emphasize points. He talked about the Australian economy and European politics. Prue described the protest against the motorway extension at Twyford, which was gathering momentum, and explained that she was concerned it might turn violent.

'I'm not sure how to act,' she confessed. 'I disapprove of violence but I feel driven to wield a stave.' She drank her wine. 'I know I'm talking liberal middle class . . . but it's the best I can do.'

The thinness of her aspirations struck Prue with depressing force, and if she expected to be reassured about the purity of her intentions, she was not. The motorway reference had reminded Jamie of a file he should have checked before leaving work and his attention wandered. Frightened that she was boring him, Prue came to a halt and then sneezed a couple of times.

'It's the dust, sorry.'

'Like Lara.' Jamie poured out more wine.

'Lara?'

'I lived with Lara before I met Violet. She always sneezed.'

Prue was unprepared for this knowledge. 'I didn't know about Lara. What happened?'

'She met someone else, upped with her daughter and left.'

'I'm sorry.'

He looked down at his empty plate. 'I was too. But I went to America soon afterwards and met Violet, so I gained in the end.'

After a second or two, he looked up, his expression suggesting that he appreciated the sympathy. In fact, he had just noticed that the electric light gave Prue's hair fascinating highlights.

'Do you keep in touch with them?'

'I write to Jenny now and again.' Jamie sounded sad. 'I watched her growing up, you see.'

Prue drank several mouthfuls of wine. 'Do we regret mistakes as much as we regret the things we don't do?'

An ancient but renascent message was sent over the table. A second elapsed. Then another.

Jamie took his time to reply, rolling the possibilities around his mind, well aware that if you took even one tiny step across a boundary line it is impossible to return.

'You don't look as though you make mistakes, Prue. You're too careful a person.'

*

Was she? Prue asked the curtainless bedroom, and went to look at the London-scape spread beneath the window. Roofs touched by tungsten-light. Black tree shapes. Patches of gloom where the back garden met others. Who knew what was sliding through them? Foxes? Cats? Burglars?

At home, she thought with a catch in the throat, the earth would be wet from the rain and sodden mulch would be masking the spring growth. In the moonlight, her *Prunus* acquired the witchy grace of a Rackham painting, and silence spread under the night sky, with only the occasional fox bark to break it.

Prue let the sheet which covered the window drop. She had discovered that Jamie was thirty-nine. She had not imagined he was virtually her own age.

Nanny agencies kept Prue busy on the phone for a good part of the day, time she had wished to spend on Joan but which was filled instead with taking details of Alisons, Sarahs and Annes for Violet to consider. Were they NNEBs? Could they drive? None of them seemed ideal.

She rang Max and told him that it was the job to be in, car, flatlet, good pay, and you could demand the world. One had asked to bring her own baby, the other was into riding and wished to stable her horse at the nearest livery. Even the last failed to raise Max's interest. 'Tell me the news,' she begged.

'Met the new occupant of the Dower House, a Lady Truscott.'

'And . . . ?'

'Silly woman. Huge pearls, nicotine-stained fingers and when I asked her what her husband had been she said, "A gentleman."'

Prue laughed with real enjoyment. 'Wonderful,' she said.

'When are you coming home?'

His need for her was palpable down the phone and Prue, once again, was conscious of the seethe and prick of rebellion.

'Friday morning,' she said. 'How's the cat?'

Max was not to be deflected. 'I hate meals from the freezer.'

'Darling. Half our meals are from the freezer.' She visualized him, hunched over the phone, performing his ritual dance with his glasses. 'Have a fry-up or something.'

'It's lonely without you.'

'Max, it's only two nights. What has got into you?'

His voice cleared. 'Nothing.'

'The baby's crying, I'll have to go.'

'Bugger the baby,' said Max, but Prue knew it was a good-natured cut-off.

Unable to settle to research, she spent the time while Edward slept rifling through Violet's glossy collection of cookery books. Her finger stopped on a recipe: to cold-press a tongue first scrub it, soak for half a day in cold water and cook. The tongue is ready when the skin along the surface has blistered, and the T-shaped bone at its root comes away easily. After this destruction, it is arranged in a suitable dish, port-flavoured jelly is poured over it and it is pressed down by a heavy weight until it is ready. It is completely unrecognizable when it is served.

Prue's finger released the page, and she moved on.

On Thursday morning, Edward woke late and refused his milk, screwing up his mouth and pushing aside the bottle. Tramlines dribbled down his cheeks and on to Prue's sleeve. She put the bottle down to examine him more closely – and a fist squeezed in her chest. There was a blue shade to the baby's mouth, and a red flush on cheeks normally like pale shells. He did not look well and when Prue took the minute hand in her own and gently felt the matchstick fingers, her flesh made

70

contact with burning heat. Without thinking twice, she phoned the doctor.

After an interminable wait in a hot, noisy, overflowing surgery, a young and indifferent-seeming doctor took a look at Edward. Just a passing temperature, she informed Prue. Babies do that. It always seems worse than it is. Give him plenty of fluid and don't bundle him up in too much clothing.

Her coolness only intensified Prue's anxiety, otherwise she might have laughed at the patronage. Instead, she drove back to Austen Road and spent an uneasy morning hovering over the cot. From time to time, Edward wailed and his body twitched in between fractured dozing. Each time Prue forced Dioralyte down him, he vomited.

At half past three, Prue was once again on the phone to the doctor. The receptionist, who could detect genuine panic from 'panic', promised to talk to the doctor when she had a moment.

An hour passed. Prue sponged the little body with warm water and, in her fright, she imagined that flesh had already slipped from the bird-like bones, and the frog stomach was hollowing – like the poppyhead which ejects its seeds and dies.

Not to worry, that wretched doctor had said. Babies do this. Yes, they do. Babies do this and have died. Think, think of the millions of babies' bodies which have piled up during the centuries.

Edward seemed to appreciate his blanket bath, for he sighed after she had finished, tucked his hand up by his neck and fell asleep.

Prue got herself some tea.

Edward's piercing wails interrupted her and she rushed into the nursery. The baby was bright red and had been violently sick. Prue phoned Jamie.

'I think he needs to get to hospital.'

Jamie did not hesitate. 'Get a taxi. I'll meet you there.'

He was waiting by the time Prue arrived, white and anxious-looking. 'I've cleared it with the receptionist,' he said, taking the baby from her. 'We go straight in.'

Prue discovered she was trembling.

Jamie held Edward while the doctor examined him. He looked up once to thank Prue, otherwise he concentrated on his son. Prue held her shaking hands tight, and went outside to wait.

Casualty was awash with people, sitting on benches in the corridor in various states of dejection. Each time a nurse or a doctor went by, they looked up. Along with their bodies, perhaps they were hoping that their spirits would be patched up as well.

Prue closed her eyes and opened them when Jamie emerged, walked over to her and took her hand in his. 'Don't fret. They think it's only a twenty-four-hour bug.'

He was followed by the doctor, and a nurse hovering at his heels carrying Edward.

'Mr Beckett, you can take him home now. We've given him a thorough examination and paracetamol to bring down his temperature. He is a little dehydrated so you must try to get some liquid into him. If you're worried, bring him back.'

They made the journey home in the taxi in virtual silence. Prue leant back against the seat and closed her eyes, luxuriating in relief. Her eyes opened a crack and she found herself observing Jamie, narrowed to a squarish shape which smelt of expensive aftershave and a whiff of cigar. Emptied of everything, she absorbed the contrast of his brown hair against his navy coat, the skin tones and the way in which his big, elegant hands emerged from his cuffs.

'Why are you looking at me, Prue?'

Prue's treacherous hands trembled in her lap. 'Am I?'

Light-headed and consequently reckless in the aftermath of

adrenalin, Jamie leant over, pulled Prue towards him and kissed her.

'Oh, Prue, oh, Prue,' he muttered into the white skin of her neck, relief for his son translating itself into physical need.

She felt her own body burn with desire and knew that if she gave it only the slightest leeway, pandered to it in the minutest form, it would make her forget that she was someone else's wife, and that Jamie was her stepdaughter's husband.

Back at the house, Prue fed Edward boiled water and Dioralyte, and Jamie hunted for a bottle of sherry.

'It's only five o'clock but . . .' Prue drained her glass.

Jamie said he would ring Violet because she would want to come home. A conversation took place on the drawing-room phone with a great many pauses. Prue concentrated on Edward who was taking his time, the sherry warming her gullet, sweet and wonderfully welcome.

Jamie returned and poured himself a glass. 'Violet isn't coming back till tomorrow. It would be difficult to leave as there's a big dinner tonight, especially if Edward is over the worst.'

Prue found it impossible to gauge his expression. Instead she held out her glass for a refill.

'I can't,' Prue said gently when Jamie appeared in her bedroom in the small hours as she lay thinking about him.

He looked down at the coils of hair and rounded shoulder illuminated by the light from the corridor, and his gaze travelled down the shape under the bedclothes.

'No,' he agreed, but in his imagination he was imprisoning the full, tempting breasts under the white cotton and the un-known territory of her body with his own. He bent over, and brushed her cheek with a finger.

'Goodnight, Jamie.'

'Goodnight.'

Chrysalis-like, the sheets enclosed her body. She felt their weave against her skin, smelt the detergent and wool in the blanket. In the dark, the sheet across the window became a mask, hiding the slippery feelings and heated imaginations that raged behind it.

Prue had imagined that her desire centred solely on Max. It was a shock to discover that this was not true.

Violet arrived home on Friday morning. She stepped out of the taxi wearing a defiant expression and hugging her leather briefcase. Prue knew that look. It meant: I am not going to show that I feel guilty.

Brushing past Prue, Violet ran upstairs into the nursery. A couple of minutes later, she emerged holding Edward. 'He looks fine,' she called down. 'You gave me such a fright. I couldn't concentrate.'

You couldn't concentrate. Reminding herself of the scenes with Jamie, Prue fought with herself to give Violet the benefit of the doubt. After those, how could she climb on to the rock of moral superiority? It was hard work turning into a mother, a process that did not come automatically. Violet, as she had, needed the time to learn.

Was Prue overreacting? Lusting after your stepdaughter's husband, though bad enough, is not quite the same sin as neglecting a baby.

Talking to Edward in a breathy way, Violet came downstairs and went into the kitchen and put him in his chair. 'It wasn't very kind of you, baby, to get ill. I almost think you did it on purpose.'

She was aware that Prue would judge her, and knew she

should have come home. But she had been frightened to leave, and equally frightened to return. She put Edward into his chair and surveyed the kitchen. 'Goodness, how untidy.' She began stacking the china on the draining board.

'Sorry,' said Prue, 'it's been a bit hectic.'

'Of course,' said Violet.

Prue made an effort to remove the constellation of saucepans that had migrated to the stove, and then thought: Dammit. 'Was the conference successful?'

Violet put out a foot and prodded Edward's chair. The baby juddered like an apple at apple bobbing. 'You know,' she said vaguely, 'lots of talks, too much to drink and far, far too much food. I'm sure I've put on masses.'

She was busy opening and shutting drawers, rearranging contents and stacking plates, with the result that Prue felt deeply inadequate.

'Did you impress the bosses?'

A smile spread across Violet's beautiful face. 'Yes, I think so. They were very nice about me. And there is some good business coming up.'

Prue produced the bit of paper with the doctor's name written on it, and the dosage for the Dioralyte. 'You should have this.'

Violet glanced carelessly at Edward who, mercifully, had stopped bobbing. 'I hope I won't need it.'

With obvious reluctance, she peeled off her olive jacket and draped it over a chair. 'Thank you, Prue, for all that you have done.' She spoke like a child at the end of the party. 'Do you want me to call a taxi?'

CHAPTER SIX

EMMY DID NOT REQUIRE MUCH TIME TO THINK OVER Violet's phone call, inviting her to accept the post of nanny to Edward.

'*Pro tem*,' Violet added hastily (none of the Alisons and Sarahs having measured up to her standards), leaving herself leeway to say goodbye to Emmy if she found someone better. 'You might not like London. Or us.' She gave a laugh which suggested that the latter would be unlikely.

At Number 5 Hallet's Lane, Emmy stared into the mirror positioned above the Phone 'N' Sit table and grimaced. She moved her foot, sending a wave of static across the nylon carpet. 'I'll come,' she said.

Violet rattled out some details about pay, conditions and use of a car. Emmy kept on repeating yes, it all sounded fine but could she ask if Violet would deal with the PAYE?

'PAYE?' Violet's tone sharpened. 'I don't think that will be necessary.'

Emmy realized she had made a mistake. On the other hand, her rights were important – they were all she had. 'And National Insurance,' she added.

'Oh.' Violet became thoughtful. '*That* makes it a lot more expensive.'

Emmy thought it wiser not to comment.

Violet recouped. 'If you decide to stay on permanently, Emmy, then, of course, we will be putting you on PAYE.'

She was cursing silently, having relied on the grapevine that alleged that nannies preferred to be paid in cash.

'Thank you, Mrs Beckett.'

'Er . . . Emmy, that being so, if you *do* stay on, I might reduce your pay a touch because of tax and insurance, which makes it a little expensive for us at the moment. I'm sure you understand, with the recession and everything.'

Lying b—, thought Emmy, and made conciliatory noises. How come Madam was so mean? She had plenty of money. Enough, as Anna pointed out with irritating frequency, to have a boob, hip and face job when the time came.

Question: Did having money make you meaner or were you mean in the first place? Never having had any, Emmy could not hazard an answer. As she moved through Number 5, dusting her mum's horse brasses from Devon, the blue Maltese glass and bulbous china cherub from Portugal, the problem occupied her.

No enlightenment, however, emanated from the silent lounge and hall. In the kitchen, early spring sunlight filtered on to foil rectangles which sat thawing under a tea-towel for tonight's microwave banquet. A solitary tea-leaf decorated the shining sink. Emmy removed it between her finger and thumb and the kitchen was perfect once again, scrubbed sterile and as ordered as a sergeant-major's kitbag. Suddenly, she felt desperate to get away, from the silence and the unyielding concordance of crimplene and nylon.

As the days lengthen with the approach of spring, it sometimes happens that the cold increases, and the last week in March had been icy. A hard chill hugged the bottom of the valley and, in defence, birds had gathered close to the houses.

They were hungry and probably frozen. Emmy hauled a pair of secateurs out of her jacket pocket and headed for the holly tree at the end of the garden, which formed part of the hedge bordering the road. For some reason, the birds never touched it. Emmy cut off the largest branch she could without doing damage and backed on to the lawn where she stuck the branch into the grass. Then she retreated.

After a minute, the first berry-eating birds arrived hot-foot and tucked in. Hand on hip, Emmy watched. Eat up, she advised them silently. It's on the house.

Emmy headed up the road towards the airstrip which sloped up from the depression in which Dainton was sited. Up in the open, the frost which had closed in a week or so ago had rampaged unchecked and had burnt sections of hedgerow which gaped like lost teeth. A partridge ran across the field on Emmy's right and she came to a halt. Partridges would be paired off by now and if she was lucky she might spot some.

Most people had paired off by now.

Wasn't it better, though, to hold your life in your hands, cupped and shaped as you wished?

Emmy swung to her right and plunged into the tiny strip of wood that led up to Danebury Rings. Her feet sank into the softened earth and gathered mud as she passed. As she reached the foot of the steep rise, the first primroses greeted her.

She tucked her frozen, ungloved hands into her jacket, pulled it tight across her thin stomach and felt better.

The builders were creating a bathroom out of a cupboard and Mickey was regaling his team with a story to make a sex therapist blush when Emmy pushed open the spare bedroom door at Number 6 Austen Road with her foot. A flush stormed into her cheeks and, not at all sure what to do, she stood awkwardly with the heavy tray.

'Hang on, love.' The tall, glossy-skinned one with a ponytail took pity. He detached himself from the Black and Decker and removed the tea-tray from Emmy. 'Don't listen to Mickey, he's a throwback.'

Was her face scarlet or bright scarlet? 'Thanks,' she said. 'I've heard it all before.'

'Have you, now?'

She liked ponytails on men: they stirred a residual memory of childhood fairy tales, complete with illustrations of men in boots with flowing hair, where the maiden is saved, or is merely the helpless female swept away by a superior masculine force. Whatever. Emmy reckoned that being passive had its advantages.

Ponytail winked at her. Why, he's beautiful, she thought. The counterpoint that never failed her echoed: And I am not.

Later Emmy – having sorted the kitchen, emptied the tumble-dryer, washed the floor and changed Edward – was watching the birds feeding on the fat she had hung from a branch of the sycamore tree. After a minute or two she became conscious that she was being watched and whipped round.

It was Ponytail bringing the tray back. 'Thanks.' His physical presence filled the room – all hair, skin and bones covered with lean flesh. Beside him, Emmy was transformed into a delicate and tiny nymph, the maiden trapped on the rock waiting for rescue.

'Do you want seconds?'

He nodded and Emmy moved towards the kettle.

'What's your name?'

She told him and he replied that his was Angus and she suppressed a giggle for Angus always went with kilts.

'Are you interested in birds?' He pointed at the tableau outside.

'Love them,' she said, handing him back the tray.

Angus appeared to consider her reply. 'No accounting,' he said finally but his expression was kind. Emmy flinched, for she imagined it was the sort of kindness reserved for losers.

'No accounting,' she agreed.

London was a shock to the system that kept Emmy reeling for the first weeks. How did people breathe in this air? How did they sleep with the noise, traffic, alarms, late-night talks in the streets, crashing milk bottles – and the constant light?

For much of that time, Number 6 Austen Road was in uproar. In places, the house resembled a building site, the baby was teething and fretful and Violet was too snappy and nervous to help her son.

Emmy found herself at the beck and call of an employer whose rage for order was as bad as her mother's – a difficult situation since the builders made it their business to import an impressive percentage of London clay into the house.

'I'm growing shoulder pads on my knees,' Emmy confided to Anna on a long and surreptitious phone call.

'Very sexy,' said Anna.

'How does she suppose I'm going to look after the baby if I spend my time on my hands and knees scrubbing?'

'Don't do it, Em.' Emmy could hear Anna inhaling cigarette smoke. She longed for a fag herself but Violet had laid down battle-lines and informed Emmy that if she ever caught her smoking that would be *it*.

London notwithstanding, Emmy did not want it to be *it*.

'What's her clothes like?' Anna performed another noisy exhalation in Emmy's ear.

'Must have cost a packet. Mind you . . .' Emmy paused. 'They don't look comfortable.'

'Yeah,' said Anna. 'Don't expect they stay on her very long.'

'Don't think she's that type.'

'Where do you shop?'

'Sainsbury's.'

'And . . . ?'

'What?'

'The bill, stupid.'

'About two hundred quid. She's very fussy. The cleaning stuff is all ecological. Trouble is, it doesn't clean very well.'

Anna pressed for more details and Emmy obliged. Thus did the tom-tom beat out all sorts of private facts. If, thought Emmy, the employers of nannies and mother's helps ever considered the extent to which the detail of their lives, down to their chosen brands of soap powder, were in the public domain, they might have had second thoughts about working. Was it worth it? A salary in return for an itemized list of your habits, your knickers, the colour of your toothbrush and what precise terms you flung at your spouse when he came home drunk from a 'quick one after work'.

'Met anyone, Em?'

Emmy reflected on the lonely evenings spent upstairs with the television tucked up with Bovril and a smelly gas fire because the heating did not *quite* reach that far up the house. 'No,' she said.

Apart from registering that she was pleasant and capable, Jamie did not pay much attention to Emmy. He was thankful that the problem of childcare had been dealt with and, once satisfied that his son was in good hands, switched off. But Emmy watched Jamie and compared him with the men with whom she was familiar.

For a start, Jamie took a lot of stick from Madam. On the

81

other hand, he was capable of dealing with it and telling her to get lost. From time to time, he helped out with Edward and got up in the night and changed nappies. He even did his bit at breaking eggs into a bowl and whisking them up. Accustomed to bad-tempered men, Emmy found his good humour puzzling, then suspicious, then seductive. Nevertheless, just in case she was tempted to elevate Jamie to sainthood, he succumbed at intervals to patches of irritation. They tended to occur when Jamie and Violet both arrived back late from work, played out and hungry. Edward, of course, was always at his worst.

'You deal with him,' Jamie ordered Violet one Friday evening. 'I'm going to have a bath.'

'I'm too tired,' said Violet flatly. 'Anyway, why does it have to be me?'

'Because you're his bloody mother, that's why. Although no one would guess it.' Jamie ripped off his tie.

'That's outrageous and unfair,' said Violet.

'Is it?' said Jamie in a dangerously quiet voice.

Edward's screams interrupted further discussion and Emmy, who was hanging about in the corridor feeling useless and a gooseberry, retreated to her room. Later, percolating through the *Coronation Street* theme, she heard sounds of impassioned argument over who should do what, which intensified until she heard Violet clattering down the uncarpeted stairs.

She wished she was not living on top of the Becketts and she wished she did not have to be a fly on the wall.

At seven o'clock on Monday morning, Emmy tramped blearily downstairs to join Jamie and Violet in the kitchen.

'She has a long enough day as it is, Violet,' she caught Jamie saying as she arrived in the hall. 'You can't ask her to do any more.'

'Try me. She sits here and eats us out of house and home.' (Emmy started at that one. Whatever else she may have been, her appetite was modest.) 'She is warm, housed, uses our phone, makes free with the car, it won't hurt her.'

Emmy grasped the banister. It was bad enough breaking into someone else's intimacy – and at breakfast time at that – worse if you were the subject of discussion. It made her feel raw and jumpy. Emmy had no intimacy to safeguard and no pacts to make over the toast. But although she did not mind her solitude, indeed sought it, she did mind being discussed as if she was a fitting for the bathroom or kitchen.

Violet was scraping vegetable spread on to her wholewheat toast as Emmy entered. Jamie looked up.

'Hallo, Emmy. We were just talking about you.'

Still at war with her perm, Emmy had scraped her hair on to the top of her head and anchored it with an elastic band. Bits of it fell down her neck, which Emmy was aware resembled a plucked chicken's. It was, however, a remarkably slender neck.

Violet rubbed at hers as she spoke. 'Emmy, would you be prepared to put the baby to bed? I *know* I said I would do it, part of the bonding process and all that. But, frankly, Edward leaves me very unbonded and I feel exhausted. If you could do the evenings, then I can cope with the mornings.' Violet's manicured nails were like scarlet petals on white silk.

Emmy shot Jamie a look. Whatever he was thinking, he was keeping quiet. He returned her look and, suddenly, Emmy felt her mouth twitch. Jamie did not appear to have the situation under control. Despite this, Jamie's mouth also curved at the corners and she felt that she and Jamie understood one another.

'If it'll help, OK.' Emmy sat down, remembered that the Becketts drank coffee and she liked tea, and got up again. Jamie took refuge behind the *Financial Times* and Violet quivered almost visibly with impatience to be gone – out and away. She cast a look at her husband.

'Men have it easy,' she said, clicking her nails on her coffee-cup, and her bitterness was both shocking and ageing.

'For God's sake,' said Jamie, and retired into the paper.

Emmy ate a piece of toast and drank lapsang souchong, which she did not like, preferring plain old teabag.

It was odd, she confided to Anna later, being a sodding Peeping Tom. She wasn't quite sure what she felt about the Becketts. 'I mean,' she said, 'they get quite lovey-dovey and all that,' but she wondered if they got on as well as it first looked. When ordered to explain, Emmy said she didn't know what she meant.

She returned from taking Edward on his afternoon constitutional, as long as the cold would permit, and was unloading baby and shopping in the hall when Angus peered over the banister.

'Thought you'd done a runner,' he said. Emmy gave an uncertain laugh, conscious that the tip of her nose was raw. Worse, it might have a drip.

'I've got something for you.'

Emmy heaved the enormous bundle that Edward made in his outdoor things into her arms and followed Angus into the kitchen. He pointed through the window and Emmy's gaze followed obediently until it rested on the sycamore. Her eyes widened. Nailed on to a lower branch was a small wooden platform. She turned to Angus and he nodded. Clasping Edward under one arm, Emmy fumbled to open the back door and flew down the lawn.

If rudimentary, the bird table had been made with care and sited out of reach of the cats.

'I thought the birds should eat in comfort.' Angus stood behind her as Emmy inspected his work.

Emmy felt a smile begin at the corners of her mouth, pulling them gently but inexorably wider and wider, until she was smiling all over her face. In her head, the sound of a nightingale in full throttle trilled clear and joyous.

'Thanks,' she said, shifting the baby. 'That was dead nice of you.'

In the days that followed, however, Emmy began to wish that Angus had not singled her out. Not that the bird table did not give her pleasure. It did – a lot. She spent a great deal of time gazing out of the window at the tits and yellowhammers and shouting at the starlings to get lost and to pick on someone their own size.

No, it was because Angus had opened a floodgate to a different type of self-consciousness, whose newness acted as an abrasion on soft skin, rendering her uneasy, expectant and vulnerable all at the same time. Why had he made the bird table? It can't have been friendship. It could have been impulse. Or . . . surely to God he didn't fancy her?

How could he?

This was one problem on which Emmy did not consult Anna and remained silent.

One morning, having disposed of the breakfast things and made a stab at the ironing, Emmy sneaked upstairs, washed her hair and larded on conditioner and spent an uncharacteristic amount of time drying it.

The results were not much different. Emmy fingered a lock and assessed the image in the mirror. At least, it *felt* soft – she had been afraid that the perm would leave her with a permanent Brillo pad on her head. Then she searched for a sweater which had some pretensions to style.

Her efforts were wasted for Angus did not turn up with the team that morning. Emmy spent the day in an uncomfortable state when every nerve was on red alert. Was he going to come? If not, why not? Perhaps he had moved on to another job?

She made tea for the team as often as she dared without overdoing it and padded upstairs with the trays in the hope of discovering some information. It was not forthcoming.

As she gave Edward his evening bottle, Emmy debated fiercely with herself. Was she *so* deprived, *so* insecure that a small gesture (which he would have forgotten by now) started her thinking she was a cross between Meryl Streep and Madonna? OK, nice gestures were thin on the ground, but that was no reason to prance around wiggling her bottom.

Where was her famed liking for independence? Solitude? For the rewards of organizing her life just as she pleased?

Emmy's highly developed instinct for self-preservation told her that blokes spelt trouble.

Edward choked and she ripped the bottle out of his mouth and held him up while she dealt with the paroxysm. After he had regurgitated enough to float the London docks, Edward resumed a normal expression. His eyes travelled up to Emmy's face. He studied it, blinking now and then and breathing noisily in through his mouth. Who are you? he appeared to be asking and Emmy found herself grinning. Edward blinked again, awarded Emmy a ravishing smile and pulled himself into a sitting position, using Emmy as an anchor.

'My God,' said Emmy. 'You little devil. You've never done that before. Wait till I tell your mum.'

On the face of it, Mum did not seem interested. 'At least he's developing normally,' she said. 'We need a reward for all the hard work.'

Having just got in from work, Violet was burdened by a long camel coat and a bulging briefcase. She fiddled with her gloves (Italian, black leather), squatted down, stuck her face towards her son's and parted her lips. Edward did not care for this – perhaps his mother had startled him – and wailed.

'Oh, no,' said Violet in a resigned fashion. 'We're in for it.'

On Sundays Emmy was free. Technically, Saturdays were too, but Violet had pleaded with her to help out, just for the first few weeks while she settled into the job, and promised that if Emmy stayed on permanently the contract proper would be drawn up.

'It's either that, or I'll have to get Prue up to help,' she said when Emmy showed distinct signs of non-cooperation.

'Mrs Valour?' Emmy said stupidly.

'Yes, my stepmother. I said that, didn't I? I really don't want her around unless I have to.'

'Oh?'

'She's . . . she's not very good with children. As well I know. I use her only when I have to.' Violet sounded strained.

As far as Emmy was aware, Mrs Valour appeared to be a warm, comforting and more than adequate mother. She raised her eyebrows and started to fold a stack of Babygros. Better not to enquire closely about how many pots were calling kettles black.

That Sunday, she got up late and, armed with the *A–Z*, let herself out of the house. In her bag were two weeks' worth of wages which she had not had an opportunity to broach. The *A–Z* informed her that Clapham and Wandsworth Commons were close and because she was hungry for a sight of some green she decided to explore.

Emmy spent a reasonable half-hour circuiting Wandsworth Common, watching parents masterminding toddlers and children on tricycles and skateboards. Dog-owners were exercising every kind of breed and the keep-fit brigade was out in force.

Emmy was curious. Londoners seemed to be so much more aware of themselves. In Dainton, the village people lived, worked, pottered and walked without thinking about their image. She avoided the puddles dug by bicycle tyres and the quagmire that spread from the toddlers' play area and, hungry for breakfast, made for the terrace of shops. Once there her heart sank for it was very smart with a wine bar, and a restaurant that looked expensive. Not a McDonalds in sight. Emmy's skin goosefleshed with fright. She could not go into any of those places. Not with those glossy joggers, mothers and dog owners.

The only place remotely approachable was the newsagent and Emmy went in to buy a paper. When she emerged, she had persuaded herself not to be intimidated and made her way to the brasserie and ordered coffee and a sandwich. The coffee arrived all fluffed up and sprinkled with chocolate and the sandwich was made from French bread.

Emmy stared at these with a new and acute insight into how an alien might feel when he arrived on earth. She took a bite and the sandwich filling spilled over and dropped yellow egg dollops on to her jeans.

She walked back past big Victorian houses and past a pub whose windows glittered. A group of people stood outside by the railings, bikers in leather with serious leather boots and lots of fastenings. One of them had his back to the road and Emmy's stomach contorted for she imagined she recognized the big back and the ponytail.

Head down, she hurried on past. Whoever it was did not look round.

CHAPTER SEVEN

Prue had left a jumper behind in Austen Road.
'Typical,' said Max folding his arms across his chest
when she told him. Since he felt fondly tender about Prue's
occasional lapses, and enjoyed the manifestation of what he
considered a mild dottiness, and Prue was aware of this, she
had not, in the past, minded Max's superior attitude. Indeed,
she had not considered it as such.

Apparently, the relativities of the position were changing
and, in this instance, she did mind. Yes, there was an unfinished
tapestry in her work basket, *circa* five years ago. Yes, she did
mean to go back to the art classes, *one* day. And, yes, Joan of
Arc *was* waiting to be written. But, she protested hotly, ram-
ming her weekend case back into the cupboard, anyone who
runs a house, produces a meal each night, has a job (granted
part time) and does more than her bit with flower rotas, village
fêtes, and masterminds the 'Teddies for Tragedy' sew-in could
reasonably expect to be considered organized.

'I think you're most unfair,' she finished.

Max blinked at his wife's unaccustomed tartness, looked
blank for a second or two, and then a wariness crept into his
face which Helen would have recognized. Prue did not.

'Sorry, darling. That was a bit tactless.' Max unfolded his

arms and held out his hand and the white slash of Helen's wound caught her eye. 'I expect coming back after the dazzle of London is a letdown.'

'Dazzle of London? Max, I spent the whole time changing nappies and coping with a sick baby. Don't be witless.'

Max went quiet. He turned on his heel and left the room. Prue heard him later, moving around the study. She heard, too, the soft clink of cold metals and smelt Rangoon oil, so she knew what he was doing.

Jamie left it a week. The telephone rang at Hallet's Gate and he suggested that Prue and he meet for lunch when he could hand over the jumper.

Prue struggled to say, 'Please put it in the post,' and failed. 'I'm coming up to do some research next Wednesday.'

'We owe you a big thank-you, Prue, especially for your suggestion about hiring Emmy as the nanny. How about the Ivy?'

Prue would have needed to have possessed the detachment of a St Augustine, sated to the point of asceticism, to say no.

'Yes,' she heard herself say, resolving to sort out a few points with him. '*Yes*, please.'

When she arrived at the Ivy her jumper was waiting, exquisitely packed in tissue, in a smart carrier bag. In it, Violet had also put several give-away samples of face creams from one of the most exclusive and expensive make-up houses as a thank-you present. 'I thought you should try these', she had written. 'Thank you again.'

Prue replaced them carefully at the bottom of the bag. 'How thoughtful,' she said.

Flushed from a struggle with the *A–Z* and the briskish walk from the London Library, she sat down at the table, spread her napkin over her knees and realized she had made a mistake.

This lunch – knives, forks, some meat, a salad, a bit of bread – would be a profoundly disrupting experience, and the needle carefully balanced between the poles of contentment and tormenting yearnings would be set quivering.

Why did she do it? Why did she sit there, innocent of her understated beauty and its effect, dressed in a grey crêpe wool suit and white blouse, and eat the lunch?

Who knows? Perhaps it was something to do with the search for St Joan. For a second, Prue was back scrutinizing Decari's mezzotint of Joan's burning. Already, the toes were disintegrating, the bony, slender fingers (this was a highly idealized representation) cramping in agony, and Joan herself was translucent and insubstantial, like a photographic negative.

She directed her attention at Jamie and, once again, his likeness to the younger Max nagged at her. 'I gather this is the place to be.'

'It is,' he replied. 'And I intend to be smug about the ease with which I procured a table.'

Prue decided she was impressed by the close proximity of two actors and a television mogul. 'Wait till the WI and Kate hear about this.'

Jamie gave her a look usually reserved for clients who wished to play the coy game. Prue, do I look taken in by the hick-comes-to-town bit?'

Prue's eyes were hidden suddenly by her eyelids. Behind them coalesced a picture of Joan riding away from Vaucouleurs, an ignorant, unlettered peasant girl with ideas above her station, struggling to master a warhorse and the unfamiliarity of her longed-for breeches.

'You should be,' she said coolly. 'I am from the country. And the WI has a healthy interest in most things.' She sipped her wine. 'You're being rude about them.'

Jamie sent his knife spinning in a circle and watched the flash of silver. 'Yes, I was,' he said.

She enquired after Violet and the new job, and then how Jamie's new job was going. 'What *qualities* do you need for it?' Prue was anxious to understand what an asset manager did. She cut a piece of *carpaccio* and ate it slowly.

Jamie was amused, then intrigued, by her interest. 'Energy. The nerve to know when to act when the consensus is right, and that's difficult. You have to play devil's advocate, and keep your ear finely tuned to what's going on.' In contrast to Prue's slow progress, Jamie's Caesar salad disappeared rapidly. The energy that he cited flowed over the table and sucked her in, pulling her, unresisting, along. Jamie was over twenty years younger than Max and it made a difference. Jamie was expanding: his knowledge, his job, his life. Max less so. As he had once remarked when they had talked about his retirement, he had finished climbing the mountains and was now on the plateau. At the time, Prue had not understood.

It is a matter of luck when you meet someone. Prue smiled across the littered table at Jamie who smiled back. It was luck whether or not that person had reached the same point as you, and bad luck if you were too far ahead.

Jamie made a joke. Prue laughed. Then she became quiet, and so did Jamie. Holding her gaze, Jamie offered her a second piece of bread from the basket which she accepted.

'Sleepy Prue,' he said.

Her eyes widened at his tenderness, and the bread turned to stone between her fingers. Dressed in that deceptive grey, Prue Valour gazed, with an abundance of . . . what was it? . . . illicit interest and delight, at her stepdaughter's husband and, for once, felt remarkable.

She knew suddenly that she needed to have everything quite open and honest between her and this man. It was important that the dark things, the past and its accretions, its mistakes, should be laid on the table between them. 'I don't know what Violet has told you, but she was cruel to me sometimes,' she said with a rush, breaching a dam she had resolved would never be breached, but impelled by an honesty that determined he should see her worst side. Now. Before it went any further. 'And I wish I could say that I don't blame her, but I did mind. Still do. That is not to suggest that Violet did not suffer. I know she did, and badly.'

It was not a pretty piece of self-justification, but Jamie had a Lara in his past, and understood what prompted Prue's confession. Vulnerability always stirred him, and Prue looked so woundable, and so embattled by a complicated family situation, not unlike a child herself. 'You tend to see things the way you're told them,' he said, 'and I had no reason not to accept Violet's version.' He wiped his mouth with his napkin and threw it down on the table. 'Violet never said *that* much, you know.'

'I'm sorry about the disloyalty,' she said quickly. 'It's unforgivable. Yours, I mean, in listening to me. It's not your fault, and you didn't start the conversation.'

He lifted and let drop the crushed linen. 'If we accept truths about those we love, does it make us disloyal?'

'"I hate you, Prue. He didn't want you. He wanted Mummy but she's dead."' Prue repeated the words that had reverberated in her mind for so long, and which she had kept hidden from Max because she knew she should not pay attention to them. But she had.

Equally, her loyalty at this lunch, or lack of it, was past retrieving, and the intimacy of the confession had . . . well . . . she drank more wine very quickly, an erotic compulsion to it.

Daddy doesn't really like you. He loves me and he wants Mummy only she's dead. Granny says she thinks Daddy married you because you were convenient.

'I was cruel, too, Jamie. First from ignorance then, perhaps, because she hurt me so often. It made me understand that being innocent doesn't prevent you being wicked.'

Jamie listened in silence. Then he refilled her glass.

'Sorry,' she said. 'That's enough of that. I won't mention it again.'

No fool, Jamie understood when it was time to back off. Besides, it was a long time ago, before he was on the scene. He steered the subject away from Violet and, because his work was never far from his thoughts, asked her if she thought the City had changed.

A little surprised, and disarmed, Prue considered. People tended to solicit Max if they wanted an opinion, and Prue if they wanted help with the school-run or harvest-supper. It was habit, and Prue forgave male chauvinists and related species, like maiden aunts, for she herself was as habit-bound as they were. Still, she had felt some resentment in the early days and then grew used to it.

'What do I think?' Prue prodded into action a brain that felt as murky as Loch Ness. 'I think recent events show that politics doesn't influence the City anymore. Money markets influence politics.'

'Politicians are past their sell-by date?'

'Sort of.'

'Is that a good thing? At least, we elect politicians.'

Prue's attention was caught by a blonde in a short black suit settling herself at an adjacent table. Pulled back by a tortoiseshell clip, her streaked hair framed a face cherished by artifice into plate-glass flawlessness. She was as unlike Prue as it was possible to be.

She returned to unemployment and the City's underbelly. '"The centre isn't holding,"' she remarked.

'That's a quotation, isn't it? I can't remember where from.'

'Nor can I.'

Joan might have said the same thing, except she was not given to philosophy and mysticism. France was in a mess, Domrémy was in a mess, its church partially destroyed. How did she feel about her tranquil, fertile Meuse valley as she watched dawn slide over the dew-laden meadows and tear apart the mist draped over the famous *bois chenu*? What did she think after the Anglo-Burgundian band had swooped down on the cattle and plundered the church? That the centre was not holding?

Jamie talked on about the Russian aid programme, a junk-bond trader's deal with the courts to reduce his sentence, and the rise of the new right in Germany which had grabbed a share of the vote. Prue listened to the world being dealt with across the lunch table – economics, high finance, bomb explosions, the politics of greed, aid and consensus. Such a big place, the world, in which small acts repeated themselves until they became huge – greed, power-seeking and polluting habits.

Jamie was in his stride. Prue listened and interjected now and again, and it seemed to her that a transparent bell-jar lowered itself over the table, trapping them inside its shiny, revealing dome. Prue knew she should beat at the sides to be let out, even smash through them, but did nothing.

Afterwards, they walked down St Martin's Lane and Jamie asked Prue why she was so interested in Joan.

'Because she practised the art of the impossible, I suppose,' she said.

When she looked back through the window of the taxi into which Jamie had handed her, he was standing quite still, looking at the pavement. Nothing had been said about the shaming incident in the other taxi, or what had taken place afterwards.

The interlude is over, it is closed. Prue sat back. Cradled and protected as she had chosen to be, she now understood that passion could arrive out of the blue, like a bunch of flowers with a tag on it saying: Your turn.

Jane's rats were giving problems. When had they ever not? thought Prue, disloyally reflecting on their brief, but incident-strewn, careers. Not only did they act as a magnet to Bella the cat – and the danger of a rat holocaust was ever present – but they had acquired a taste for liberty. Thanks to Jane, in whose scale of priorities animal comfort ranked highest, the rats took morning and evening constitutionals around her bedroom, driving Prue to shampoo the carpet at regular intervals and to reassure herself constantly that domestic rat droppings could not possibly be harmful.

Worse: a rat's life runs out fast and, for the past fortnight, Toffee had been ailing. When Prue picked up Jane that Friday, Jane insisted they took him to the vet.

'He's ill. I *know* he's ill.' Jane pressed her nose against the wire cage where Toffee's tail stuck out cold and limp from a pile of shredded newspaper.

Prue bent down and studied Toffee. Her heart sank. 'OK. Let's take him.'

Jane's expression was a compound of distress, fear – and complete reliance on her mother. 'Do you think he'll be all right?'

Do you lie to reduce a child's terror? Should you erase that look, which strikes straight to an adult's heart, for the sake of few minutes' grace? If Jane suffered, Prue suffered, and she was never sure if she lied to ease Jane's pain or her own.

In the event, the journey to the vet proved to be Toffee's last. By the time they had manhandled the cage into the surgery, he was dead. Prue would long remember Jane's cry of anguish, and the sight of her daughter sitting on a plastic chair surrounded by a clutter of *Country Life* and give-away magazines clutching a dead rat to her chest.

'I'm trained in bereavement management, Mrs Valour,' whispered the vet, gently disengaging Toffee, 'I'll deal with her.' In his experience, humans grieved more bitterly for their animals than for other humans. He produced a cardboard box from a pile under the counter for Toffee's coffin and laid him gently in it.

'Come and choose the label to put on it,' he invited Jane, closing it up. 'You must write his name and his dates.'

'If you want any help, Mrs Valour, in the grief management – it takes a little time you know – come and see me,' he said as he examined Buttons, the survivor, whom he pronounced fit and well. Just a little top-up of vitamins to make sure, he said, producing an enormous syringe and an equally enormous bill.

'What will Buttons do without Toffee?' Tears washed in a sea down Jane's cheeks. 'He'll be so lonely.'

Prue's own throat jammed up at this point, and she cursed the day the rats had entered the house. 'Perhaps he won't notice too much, darling. It's not like a human being.'

Jane interrupted her crying to stare at her mother, and Prue felt as if she had been chastised with a whip.

'How do you know, Mum?'

She drew her daughter close. 'I don't, darling, but I think there is a good chance he doesn't feel like us.'

Jane clung to Prue. 'It's so awful that everything has to die. Why do they?' and added, 'Toffee wasn't doing anything. Just living in his cage.'

Prue stroked the wet face. 'People have been asking those questions since time began and I don't know the answers.' She thought for a second or two. 'You might think this odd, but death improves life, Janey.'

Perhaps, she reflected, piloting a still weeping daughter into the car, a rat mortality in the home is a useful aid in the teaching of metaphysics to one's offspring.

Jane got up on Saturday having slept badly. Pale and heavy-eyed, she spent the morning hanging over Buttons in his cage. At lunchtime, Prue went upstairs to investigate.

The bedroom resembled a bombsite, but Prue bit her lip and merely drew back the curtains. She bent down to pick up a pair of rollerboots apparently left in the middle of the room with express intent to kill.

'Lunch,' she said. 'Didn't you hear me calling?'

Jane looked up from the cage and Prue's irritation vanished. Her daughter's eyes were underlined with what a previous au pair had termed 'suitcases'. From long habit, projections of the direst kind – anaemia, leukaemia – surged into Prue's mind.

'Are you feeling all right?'

'Fine.'

Jane was lying. Prue sat down on the bed and studied her. 'Everything OK at school?' This time the hesitation was obvious and enlightenment (with relief) dawned on Prue. She patted the space beside her. 'Tell me what's going on.'

Jane tensed, and Prue divined that a battle was being waged between keeping up the pretence and the comfort of casting her troubles on to her mother.

'Everyone hates me.' Jane made the confession sound shameful. 'They all tease me.'

'Ah.'

'Nobody wants to be my partner. I was left by myself at CDT lesson and Miss Cook had to do it with me. I thought I'd die.' Jane slumped against Prue's shoulder. 'If I died at least I'd see Toffee.' Jane tried hard to stop her lip trembling, and she said, 'I don't care really, Mum.'

Any suggestion of attack on their daughter drew elemental

feelings from both Max and Prue, chief among them desire for vengeance, mixed with hurt for the child. It did not matter how often Prue lectured herself, and Max, on being too emotional, or that Jane needed to learn some lessons for her survival or that they, the parents, could not, should not protect her. Not trusting herself to speak, she took Jane's hand in her own and rubbed her thumb up and down the palm.

'Alicia hates me, and she makes everybody else say I'm stupid and ugly. Even Lydia.'

Technically, Lydia was Jane's best friend, with whom she had swapped wrist snappers and, in a major demonstration of best friendship, Julip Horses. Prue concentrated on achieving a perspective while suppressing the wish to shake Alicia until her teeth rattled.

'What shall I do, Mum?'

The virus of hate in the fourth form was as disfiguring and contagious as smallpox, and here it was disfiguring her eleven-year-old daughter's face as surely as the evil blotches. Prue cradled Jane's head between her hands, feeling the bony plates of the skull as if it was her own, and kissed it.

'Listen to me. It won't last. Nothing ever remains the same. I know, it happened to me.'

Jane went rigid and still against her mother. 'Did it, Mum? Did it really? You're not just saying that?'

'I begged Granny and Gramps to take me away from my school. They didn't, and I discovered that being unpopular is like a switchback. Sometimes you are, sometimes you aren't. I bet you next term Alicia hates someone else.'

'A whole term, Mum.'

'Listen. If you show you mind, Alicia will make it worse. She wants you to look miserable, so don't. And tell her to shut up if she attacks you. Bullies don't like to be told to shut up.'

Jane appeared to be absorbing the advice. Prue breathed in

the smell of her daughter – a combination of Prue's best jasmine soap and cheap shampoo – acutely conscious of the growing body against hers. Love flowed out of her in a hot, aching tide and lapped the suitcase-eyed little face, unformed hands and too-thin shoulders.

Please (God?), please, see to it that I carry on protecting her until she's big enough to cope.

'Just one thing, Janey. If they start on someone else, don't forget what you've felt. Don't forget what it feels like to be miserable.'

Jane grabbed Prue's proffered handkerchief. 'Thanks, Mum,' she said in a small voice. 'I don't know what I'd do without you.'

Never, ever will I take risks with Jane, resolved Prue. She is my absolute responsibility.

Never, ever.

Jamie telephoned.

Prue gripped the receiver until her knuckles turned white.

'Next time you're up, perhaps we can have lunch again?'

She shut her eyes and thought of Jane. 'I don't think it's a good idea,' she addressed her corpse-like knuckle, and thought, If I bang you hard against the table perhaps it'll kill the devil that has got into me. She was taking the call in Max's study, facing the photographs on his desk. One was of a family group – she and Max with Jane between them. Max was looking towards Prue, fondly and she now perceived, a little possessively. Her knees felt weak, and her heart was pounding. She inhaled deeply and continued. 'I think you know why.'

The pause at the other end of the line became ominous with unsaid words. She pictured it as a summer sky grown plum with incipient storm.

'You don't have to worry, Prue.'

With breathtaking fickleness, Prue's emotions did a volte-face. She had been wrong, after all – the kiss in the taxi had been one of pure relief from tension, only that. The nocturnal visit a politeness in a circle that took making love as one did meeting for a drink, or for a meal. Not wishing to insult her after the taxi episode, Jamie had made it a point of honour to invade the bedroom – from which he undoubtedly retired in relief. That was it. Jamie had not wished to hurt her feelings. All that had been required of Prue to extricate herself from a solecism was to hide them. Instead she had blundered. In the blessed privacy of the study, she balled her fingers into a fist and knocked it against her stomach hard.

'I'm sorry. I made a mistake.'

'No, you didn't.'

She found herself smiling like an idiot with relief. You've gone mad, Prue Valour. Mad and dangerous.

'But you're right, Prue. Lunch is probably a bad idea.'

The study seemed very cold and dusty and the silence that followed the replacing of the receiver an ungrateful one. Prue studied one of the photographs. She had been thinner in those days and it had suited her. She studied her younger image critically, comparing it to the photo of Helen that also sat on the desk.

'I don't like you at all,' she told the beautiful countenance for the umpteenth time, 'and, dead, you have been nothing but a menace.' Helen's glistening eyes and scarlet lips did not move. Neither did a tremor disarrange the shining hair.

Prue picked up Helen's photograph and placed it at the back of the desk so that it was partially obscured by one of Max at a company dinner.

*

At his end of the phone, Jamie sat in his office twirling the Biro stamped with the bank's logo around and around between his finger and thumb.

'Daydreaming?' asked Dyson, one of his fellow asset managers, putting his head round the door. 'Of the millions you're going to make?'

'I was thinking about clichés.'

'Good God.' Dyson parked himself on the chair in front of Jamie's desk. 'Have you got the answer to the great cliché of the economy?'

Jamie was suffering from a sense of shock at his own behaviour. 'Just because a cliché is a cliché it doesn't mean you should underestimate it.'

'Good God,' repeated Dyson, unimpressed.

CHAPTER EIGHT

THE ALARM SHRIEKED INTO THE DARKNESS AND TORE Violet from sleep. For a few seconds she lay motionless, flattened and exhausted, before the adrenalin shuddered through her limbs.

The Scandinavians devote a whole vocabulary to snow. Mothers have evolved one entirely for sleep. Oh, that leaden, deliciously unenabling warmth. That languor licking softly over a body quivering with need. Come, come fast. Stay.

Sleep.

Get up. Dress. Make breakfast. Feed Edward. Brush teeth. Go to work . . . Come back. Make supper. Brush teeth. Go to bed . . . Struggle up to Edward.

A cry sounded from the baby's room and uncapped the borehole that fed Violet's rage. Anger streamed through her and she jerked the sheet up over her shoulders. How much more could a baby demand of its mother? And how old would he have to be before he slept properly? She had been up twice during the night to service the ravening monster that apparently inhabited her son's body and refused to respond to her nurturing. There was no *reason* for Edward to cry; and her anger was fed by the unreason. He received every possible attention. He was fed. He was clean. He was talked to. He was cuddled. But no amount of feeding, changing or rocking pro-pitiated the ever-open mouth whose *raison d'être*, it seemed, was to scream.

Under the bedclothes, Violet strove to remember what it was like, not so long ago, for God's sake, when she had no baby, and failed.

Jamie was making groggy-sounding noises and she turned over towards him. 'See to Edward, Jamie, please. I'm finished. There's juice in the fridge.'

'Must I?'

'Yes,' said Violet sharply.

Jamie struggled out of bed and padded out of the room. Violet sank into the goose-down pillow. She craved peace, stillness, the utter bliss of not being wanted – and the certainties back by which she had lived her life before Edward.

She listened to Jamie talking to the baby, and to Edward responding with little grunts and giggles. Father and son went off downstairs. Violet let out her breath, rolled out of bed and stripped off her nightdress. Low-cut and lace-edged, it was part of the pre-baby existence, inadequate for night sorties, and she reminded herself wearily to buy some sensible ones. The idea of her, Violet, in a sensible nightdress intensified her rage. Gritting her teeth, she forced herself into the bathroom and to the mirror to start the armour-plating process with which she began the day.

The nakedness of her face never failed to set Violet's fingers metaphorically itching, for here was the best, and most docile, material of all to shape, refurbish, alter and mould into the image she wished.

Cleanse, tone, nourish. Violet rarely deviated from the regime self-imposed after reading articles on skin care at an impressionable age in the sixth form. The articles had been high on scientific data, and a slightly sceptical but determined

Violet had taken note and looked to the products they recommended much as the fully paid-up atheist might secretly cleave to the idea of the saviour – you have nothing to lose by assuming the benefit of the doubt.

If you wanted to believe, then liposomes offered one possible route to eternal youth. Violet was canny, choosing the most exclusive and thereby enhancing its mystique.

She glanced at the clock and picked up a moisturizer which had come in an icily elegant package and apparently incorporated these desirable liposomes in spoonfuls. A gremlin dancing at the back of her mind informed her that she had been conned: advertisers lie, it said, it's their business. From long practice, Violet ignored it.

She applied the cream over her face and neck. Then she brushed her hair vigorously, this way and that, and studied the effect, checked her eyebrows, combed out her eyelashes and nipped at her cuticles with a special pair of pliers.

Jamie padded back into the bedroom and deposited Edward on the bed. Reluctantly, Violet yielded the bathroom to her husband. The baby's gaze locked on to his mother and a smile revealed four white teeth.

'He seems all right this morning.' Jamie retrieved a towel from the floor. 'Thirsty, though.'

Violet proffered a finger to her son. She did not pick him up, however, because she was now in her office clothes and there was dribble on his face and a patch of something dubious on his Baby-gro. Edward seized her finger and transferred it to his mouth where he bit.

'Ouch. Little beast.' Violet removed her finger and Edward whimpered with disappointment. In the bathroom, Jamie frowned at his shaving-soap-wreathed reflection.

'Careful,' he said through the door. 'I've just got him into a good mood.'

Violet interpreted the remark as criticism and yet another wave of fury crashed over her.

'I'll sort out the breakfast,' she said bad-temperedly, and meant: Lay off me, Jamie.

'Do you have to be so cross, Violet?'

She wanted to run at him and bang her head hard against his chest until the breath was driven from his infuriating, superior, smug body.

'Oh, do shut up,' she said.

A flare of meanness and dislike leapt between husband and wife. Sensing the atmosphere, the baby began to cry but Violet made no move to pick him up.

Jamie looked at Violet and turned his back.

At weekends, Violet anticipated the relief of walking out of the front door on Monday mornings, much as the patient antici-pates relief from the dentist. The click of the lock, two paces down the red-tiled path, out of the gate, into the street – and there it was. Freedom. Air.

All weekend she toyed with the vision. A whole day, a whole week without my baby.

'Morning, Vi,' said Lavinia, her secretary, as Violet came in at nine fifteen sharp on Monday morning, 25 May, the day after a Palestinian assassinated a young Jew and the day before a tribunal opened in Nantes enquiring into the alleged child murders of Gilles de Rais, executed in 1440 for the crime. Gilles, of course, fought alongside Joan of Arc.

Not that Violet would pay attention to matters so re-moved from her world, but her good mood was punctured. 'Good morning,' she replied, took off her jacket and hung it carefully over one of her padded tartan hangers. 'Any messages?'

Lavinia scrutinized her pad covered in hieroglyphics. 'Don't think so.'

Violet squeezed behind her desk. 'Lavinia, would you mind not calling me Vi.' Lavinia looked blank and then turned pink. 'It's not my name.' Violet's tone was kindly – and deadly. 'It's a bit like me calling you Lav or Lavvy.'

'Sorry,' said Lavinia.

Violet requested a cup of camomile tea and began preparing for the marketing meeting, which promised to be difficult if not stormy. She arranged facts in her mind, honed what she knew to be a tricky argument over overseas discounts and read a report on a 'big' book that had come in for auction which, in the attempts to secure it, was reducing everyone into mania.

Gradually her irritation lessened and a warm, happy feeling began to grow inside Violet.

Unfortunately, the meeting *was* stormy and the wash hit Violet. Having neglected to produce some figures (which on reflection she should have anticipated), it was then pointed out that she had permitted a contract to go through that specified overseas royalties on the old basis of the published price, instead of the new practice of price received.

The criticism was listened to in silence. Nevertheless, it was a fair bet that behind the studiously blank faces – including Sebastian Westland's – ranged around the table, busy minds were constructing defences to cover their backs, or engaging in *Schadenfreude.*

The room grew stuffy and a scent of animals on the prowl hung suggestively over alert bodies and faces, blanched like mushrooms by city light.

Violet fixed a slightly widened gaze (it usually worked) on the publishing director, an attractive man but given to bouts of temper.

Even if you'd had one baby, two babies, three babies, and were hollow-eyed and boneless from lack of sleep, it made no difference. You couldn't fall back on the excuse of exhaustion. That was no quarter. She had to be up there with the rest of them: just as tough, fighting and hungry as they were.

'It would have been helpful to have had those figures,' the publishing director reiterated and his tone was biting. 'Can we have them next week? If not, someone else can do it for you, Violet.'

Never. Violet would have flung herself to the wolves first.

'Leave it to me,' she said, and arranged her mouth in what she hoped was a convincing smile.

There was a pause after this interchange before the next topic was introduced. Violet scribbled something, anything, on her notepad. They're all looking at me, she thought, forgetting that most people concentrate on themselves (a school in which Violet was a premium scholar). They think I can't cope. Or else they're pleased I got it in the neck.

'Violet?' probed the publishing director. 'What's your view?'

The obstinacy and pride that lurked in Violet came to her aid and she raised her head and told them.

When she got back into her office, Lavinia had decorated Violet's phone with a yellow Post-it sticker. 'Emmy phoned: what do you want for dinner?' For one moment, Violet thought she might scream aloud. For heaven's sake, couldn't Emmy work that one out? She seized the phone.

'Is there something in the freezer, Emmy?'

'Stewing steak, I think.'

'Could you make a stew?' Violet did not approve of them but she was beginning to see the benefits of their elastic properties.

'I don't know how.'

'Didn't your mother teach you anything?'

'No. We bought them ready-made.'

Violet could hear Capital Radio playing in the background. 'If you bought some mince round the corner, what about a shepherd's pie?'

'Sorry. I'm not sure how to do that either. Could you tell me down the phone?'

For God's sake!

'Right.' Violet spoke very carefully. 'Get down to Marks and Spencer's and buy one of their fish pies or something. Do you have any housekeeping money left?'

'I used it up when I bought Edward's juice.'

In a very even, careful tone, Violet told Emmy where to find an additional supply. Meanwhile a buzz cutting through their conversation every thirty seconds informed her that calls were backing up. Lavinia was also waving at her from her desk and mouthing, 'New York.'

Violet's sense of well-being had well and truly dissipated. Irritation (I pay this bloody girl, why can't she use her wits?), fury (why is everything left to women?), and a niggle that she had not made up the morning's spat with Jamie threatened to swell into neap-tide proportions.

'Look, Emmy. Just do what you think fit. Get anything just as long as there's something to eat tonight. Got it?'

Violet flung down the receiver and then, to Lavinia's extreme surprise, dropped her head into her hands. Pressure from the ball of her thumb made sparks float across her vision – great, flaring, yellow sparks that danced with a freedom that Violet no longer possessed.

Jamie thought about a report he had read on the Israel–Palestine situation as he struggled through St Mary Axe, which was still being cleared of millions of pounds' worth of damage from the IRA bomb.

He tried to put himself into the terrorist's mental shoes. How could anyone be so driven by hate or doctrine – the one usually involved the other – that he or she was prepared to set foot over a line dividing those that did not act violently and those that did? It took only one step, but once taken the irreducible logic of the foot over the line made it impossible not to go forward. Jamie did not enquire of himself whether kissing his stepmother-in-law in a taxi constituted stepping over the line.

'Jamie. Do you think your life has changed much having Edward?' Violet asked later, over the Authentic Fisherman's Pie and (not often seen on Violet's table) tinned peas.

'Of course.'

Violet took a tiny forkful of mashed potato while her desire grew to wallop down greedy mouthfuls until her stomach ran with juices and food. She put the fork down on the plate. '*You* are not rung up at work and asked what's for supper.'

'True.' It was a fair point and Jamie always tried to be fair. In times past, it had made Violet love him. Tonight it appeared to madden her.

'I think you should share running the house. I have an important job, too.'

She knew perfectly well that her sharpness stemmed partly from the drubbing she had received at the meeting, but she was not going to tell Jamie that.

It was quite clear that Jamie considered her suggestion a bloody awful one. Violet sharpened the whirling blades and went into battle. 'Don't interrupt my important job with questions about baked beans and nappies, is that it?'

'In a word, yes.'

'I see,' she said. 'Come home and expect to find supper on the table but ask me not how it gets there.'

Jamie had the grace to look sheepish but he also knew that, with Violet, attack was the best form of defence. 'Don't be so nasty. I promise to help when I can.'

His half-apology lanced the atmosphere which had threatened to grow poisoned, but did nothing to solve the problem – which was probably insoluble anyway.

Nevertheless, Violet returned to the subject of their changed life during the nine o'clock news. A Royal had, apparently, jetted off somewhere exotic and pictures of her arrival flashed on the screen.

'We can't do that anymore,' said Violet. 'I thought we would be able to, but we can't.'

'Why ever not?' Jamie picked up a strand of his wife's hair and smoothed it between his fingers.

Violet considered the logistics of going on holiday. Pushchair. Sterilizing equipment. Nappies. Baby food. Travelling cot. Bottom ointments . . . An anchor chain had wrapped itself around her neck and was tightening.

'Think of transporting all the stuff we need.'

'It's been done before. Successfully, too.' Jamie stroked her cheek. 'Cheer up.'

'How do you know?' she flashed at him before she could stop herself and added, 'Of course. Jenny and Lara. You've done it all before with them.'

She wished then that she had remained silent: Lara and Jenny were the big, burning areas which she knew, *she knew*, were wise to avoid. Jamie's hand dropped away from the back of the sofa and he turned on her with a mixture of pain and anger that conveyed more clearly than words that Lara's defection had inflicted a massive hurt.

'Shut up, Violet. Leave the subject alone.'

It was so unusual for Jamie to show anger, or to reproach her, that Violet was silenced.

On the television screen, figures focused and faded, and the images danced.

'Sorry,' said Violet. 'Kiss me.'

He bent over her, considering the beautiful but stormy face, and she breathed in his smell which she found so attractive. 'Sorry,' she repeated.

Jamie kissed her gently and without passion, then got up and left the room. The anchor chain jerked tighter around Violet's creamed and liposomed neck.

'We'll do the assessment first, Mrs Beckett.'

The supervisor assigned to Violet in the gleaming gym to which she had rendered up a staggering fee for membership was dressed in pedal-pusher leggings and a T-shirt which said: 'Workouts are healthier than sex.'

Violet did not feel qualified to comment and allowed herself to be ushered into a cubby-hole, grandiosely labelled 'Assessment Room'. It contained a treatment couch, a machine which disgorged coloured wires, an exercise bike, a computer and various charts in different typefaces and colours, which specified respiration rates, calorie values and fitness categories.

The supervisor shut the door, thereby trapping air so laden with sweat that the effect was of an old-fashioned wet woollen blanket. Violet swallowed.

'I'll measure your body fat first, Mrs Beckett, on the machine here and the computer will work out your needs and then we'll construct your personal fitness programme.'

She spoke with the driven energy of the fanatic and Violet began to relax.

'Thank you,' she said. 'I need attention because I've had a baby and I've not had the time or energy to get myself back on form but I need to look my best for my job.'

The girl nodded sympathetically. 'It's hell on the thighs and hips,' she said.

Violet did not ask her if she meant the job or the baby.

'My name is Carole,' said Carole, scrawling it across a virgin chart which she had clipped on to her board. 'Let's go . . .' She produced a tape measure. 'Bust first.'

Violet gazed at the bobbing head busying itself around her hips and thighs and, for the first time in months, felt curiously liberated and soothed.

'Thirty-six and three-quarters hips.' Carole flicked the tape measure. 'Waist twenty-seven.'

'Thighs?' Violet hardly dared to ask.

Carole told her and threw in the circumference of her upper arms for good measure. The two women shook their heads at each other.

'Not good,' said Violet between clenched teeth.

'Well, we'll soon see to it.' Carole spoke as the zealot faced with the task for which she had been searching. 'Let's measure the composition of your body. Please lie down.' She indicated the narrow treatment couch. 'I'm going to attach these electrodes to your feet and wrists. Don't let your thighs touch each other.'

Violet gazed at the ceiling and recollected that the last time she had been strapped to machinery her legs were raised and something dreadful was happening to her exposed body. She closed her eyes.

Carole applied the pads, read the machine and fed data into the computer which, after a couple of seconds, flicked up a breakdown of the constituent parts of Violet's body.

'Not too bad,' said Carole. 'Actually quite good. You need to lose three pounds of fat. That's pure fat, remember, so you'll have to lose about seven pounds altogether to do that.'

Three pounds of fat! Violet stared at the screen. On top of everything else – fatigue, work, food, baby, house, husband – how was she going to peel away those glistening yellow collops?

'Blow, please.' Carole held out a lung-capacity monitor. Trusting it was germ-free, Violet blew into it as directed. The result was not startling, but not bad either.

Carole wriggled herself up on to the couch and swung her purple lycraed legs in a relaxed fashion while she wrote busily on the chart.

'Now, getting thin is your primary objective. I shall put you on the thigh abductor. Then the abdominal stretch and the treadmill.' She wrote on. 'Your next assessment will be in six weeks and we'll keep a close eye on progress. But first, the Stair-Master. I promise you, it will make your buttocks beg for mercy.'

'Good,' said Violet.

Thereafter, as the days grew longer and warmer, Violet went to the gym whenever she could, plunging out of the spring sunshine into the dark, electrically lit intimacies of an exclusive female mystery. She invested in a plunge leotard, leggings and designer trainers, and with her dark hair and magnolia skin, she resembled an exotic hummingbird.

At first, she was wary of exposing her body in front of so many potentially critical gazes, but soon discovered that she had been judging others by her own standards. Granted, the gym was a temple to narcissism, lined from floor to ceiling with mirrors designed to catch every muscle twitch, and, granted, it was filled by women driven to desperation by a culture that demanded they should be thin. But the neophytes at the temple were too absorbed in the drama of thigh abduction and abdominal stretching to take much notice of others.

Violet was effortlessly absorbed into the ranks, snatching every minute to come and worship, to tread out the litany of hope on the StairMaster and watch Jane Fonda on the video screen, whose changes of outfits were as numerous as stars. (Even Violet wondered if a black lace body cinched in at the waist by a designer belt was quite suitable.)

By the middle of June, Violet had lost an inch all round and Carole, who regarded it as a personal triumph, was delighted.

'Your thighs are looking *really* good. We'll beef up the programme.'

Oh, yes, thought Violet, bending her will to master her protesting, hungry body. More, please.

Jamie did not approve. 'You spend all weekend at that place,' he said as Violet handed Edward to him on Sunday morning. 'Don't you think you're overdoing it?'

'No.'

They were in the hall in Austen Road and Violet was packing her holdall. Jamie hefted Edward from one arm to the other. He was in playful mood and bumped around on his father's shoulder and reared back in what to him was a wildly funny game.

'Don't go again, Violet. After all, we only have the weekends to be together.'

Violet stuffed a pink towel into the holdall. 'It's only an hour or so. I'm not disappearing for the weekend.'

Just in time, Jamie prevented Edward from dive-bombing to the floor. An inner, and honest, voice insisted that it was not only the prospect of being deprived of his wife that was driving him to protest, but the knowledge that even an hour with a demanding child is a long time – especially when you want to read the Sunday papers.

'Why don't we go for a walk instead and then have a drink somewhere?'

Violet's face set into obstinate lines. Jamie was acquainted with the look but had never quite appreciated how etched in stone it was. She bent over and her hair fell in a waterfall over her shoulders. She looked smooth, sweet-smelling and very desirable and Jamie ached to have her back as they once were.

'Don't nag,' she said. 'I'll be back to cook lunch if that's what you're on about.'

(Which she would not eat.)

Jamie hunched his shoulders, a habit when he was offended, and put Edward down on the floor where he made for the doormat and the curls of mud lying on it. 'It wasn't what I was getting at,' he said untruthfully. 'Don't worry, I shall demand my pound of flesh and go for a jog when you get back.'

He was left looking at the freshly painted front door which closed with a snap, aware that Violet would be hurrying out of the gate and into the street as if her life depended on it.

Perhaps it did. But Violet left behind a vacuum and into vacuums creep replacements. Or sometimes they arrive with a roar. Jamie bent down to retrieve Edward and an image of Prue flashed across his mind. What was she to him? A pair of grey eyes above a grey crêpe jacket and a pair of delicate wrists. She had raised one towards him when she had told him to leave the bedroom that night. Yet she had been willing, flattering to him, interested, her stillness infinitely seductive. *Her* foreignness begging to be explored.

I must have been mad, he thought.

Scented, yielding, mysterious. His image of Prue. Always softness, and the idea of fire burning quietly inside her.

Jamie held Edward's compact, wriggling body and stroked the now curly head and, once again and against his better judgement, fell in love with his wife's stepmother.

'Who's the hottest kid on the block, Violet?'

Violet concentrated on keeping her eyes open. She was

lunching in a fashionable restaurant in Covent Garden, the kind she loved, with a visiting American rights director with whom she had been friendly in New York.

Nicole was a highly successful, blonde-streaked, long-nailed career woman without children. Her colleague, however, with whom they were also lunching (who was Nicole's lover), was married. His name was Chuck and the trip to London provided an admirable opportunity for a real get-together with Nicole.

The bout of drowsiness routed, Violet studied Chuck over the undressed radicchio and artichoke hearts for a trace of guilt that might indicate he had mixed feelings about what he was doing. She found none.

'Come on.' Nicole was impatient. 'You look half asleep.'

Violet bit back the urge to say, Oh, God, I'm going to die if I don't get a night's sleep, but knew it would expose her flank. Instead, she said, 'There's a rumour that Dinsen and Fraser are going to be taken over.'

Her companions digested this admittedly not very exciting gossip.

'Honey,' said Nicole. 'I've got a hundred times more dirt than that.'

She drank tiny sips of her wine as she told Violet who was sleeping with whom, which famous novelist's book had virtually been rewritten by the editor (who had then been sacked), and the cock-up on Helen Hines's publicity campaign which had cost Nicole's firm close on a hundred grand.

A little scene re-enacted itself behind Violet's dark eyes. Of her stumbling up at night, of cold creeping up her legs, of a wide-open baby's mouth and the horrifying but quite clear urge to smack him. Hard.

'What did you think of the Hines novel?' asked Chuck.

'Very good,' she answered, automatically. 'I liked the way she handled the love story.'

'But, Violet, it's an anti-love story. It's a hate story. Love is a piece of cultural crap according to Hines.' Chuck looked smug in his Armani shirt and well-cut suit. Pleased to have caught her out, she thought.

The world, it seemed, was full of vindictive, uncooperative men.

'Yes, that's what I meant,' she said.

Nicole laughed and poured out more wine. Her bracelets clinked against the bottle and Violet forced herself not to wince.

'Do you have children?' she asked Chuck.

For a few seconds, she imagined that colour stained the tips of his ears, then concluded she had been mistaken.

'A three-month baby and a two-year-old.'

A baby and a two-year-old and you are sitting here in the pink of health and energy . . . with your lover. She was surprised by the strength of her outrage.

'Your wife holds the baby, then?'

'Sure, she enjoys all that,' said Chuck. 'We agreed that was her role.'

Violet drank her wine and said nothing.

Across the table, Nicole raised one shoulder in a little shrug which said: What did you expect, darling?'

CHAPTER NINE

'JAMIE,' WENT THE MESSAGE, WRITTEN ON THE BANK'S distinctive yellow memo paper, 'I think you have been ignoring me and I find your attitude difficult. I would appreciate a good morning when you come in. It would make a great difference to our working relations.'

Jamie read it twice to make sure he was not hallucinating. Dyson was a good chap, friendly, co-operative, clever, and not given (overtly) to indulging in scenes.

Written communications such as this one between colleagues were not uncommon. Jamie was also well aware that flare-ups of irritation, hurt and worry were not the sole property of either sex and, in the pressurized world of high finance, flare-ups raged like bush fires in unexpected places.

The points where humans make contact with each other require insulation grease of the thick electrician's kind, a viscous, stabilizing blanket which protects against the pinpricks and uncertainties of this world. Stroking it on was part of the business of life, Jamie knew that well. He grabbed a cup of coffee from the machine, made his way to Dyson's office along the corridor and said, 'Good morning,' pointedly. Flushing, Dyson looked up from a spreadsheet.

'Look, I'm sorry if I've offended you, I certainly didn't mean to.'

Cup in one hand, Jamie lounged against the door jamb. 'I don't know what I've done but whatever it was, I'm sorry.'

The casual pose irritated Dyson and he said stiffly and with an effort, 'Perhaps I've overreacted, but I felt I had to say something after that meeting.'

Jamie searched his memory until he remembered that he had confronted Dyson over the issue of privately funded motorways. That in itself was not a problem; locked antlers frequently resulted in spilt blood. It was rather that both the chairman and the chief executive had been present at that particular meeting – and Dyson had lost the argument.

'Sure.' Jamie heaved himself upright a little, shocked at how little he cared about Dyson's pique. That and the knowledge that the London job he had so keenly anticipated was, for the moment, of less importance than he had imagined – a state of mind that was new to him. 'Why don't we meet for a drink after work and sort it out?'

Back at his desk he chucked Dyson's memo into the bin and stood looking down at it.

The world's great sins – murder, torture, rape, the taking of a good name – claimed the headlines' attention. Yet was it not true to say that laziness and evasion did as much damage in a quieter way, and were practised on an even larger scale.

Oh, yes, continued his inner dialogue, given that human beings were endemically lazy and evasive, it was astonishing that goodness infected the world at all.

'Personal' in familiar writing. It was from Jenny who, young as she was, had quickly grown old in the ways of jealousy and taken to sending letters to Jamie at his work address in order to avoid Violet.

Dear Jamie [she wrote],

I'm off to the Brazilian rainforest to work for a couple of years. If you would like to contribute some dosh to a good cause, I need a pair of boots.

Love Jenny.

Jamie smiled and pulled out his cheque-book. Jenny was very dear to him and he did not like the idea that Lara's new man saw more of her than he did. 'Good luck, Jen,' he wrote. 'Make sure you have the right jabs.'

Jamie had not meant to loop his life into an extra twist and, a conventional person at heart, had intended it to run along a straight line. It had not been sensible, therefore, to hitch up with the fascinating but unstable Lara. But she had been ripe and golden – and on the search for a new man. He had been romantic, passionate, and in a hurry. That was that.

Jamie looked out of the window. The dusk outside possessed the white, peeled quality of late spring that he loved. It made him think of Prue walking down the lane at Dainton, and an unfamiliar tension gathered in his throat.

How he wanted her, as he had once wanted his wife. His hand moved towards the telephone and stopped.

Jamie folded up Jenny's letter. As the years lay down hard accretions round the body and soul, it is harder to fight through habits of selfishness to find those initial impulses towards niceness that, once, he had been so ready to deal out. Indeed, he wondered if there was anything left of that in him at all.

Eve Watts knocked and came into the office. She was the corporate PR officer. Tall, slim and given to linen suits with short jackets that showed off her waistline, she had long red hair which she wore in a French plait. She wanted to talk to him about the company's results and how they should pitch them to the public. Eve was clever and fluent and, after they had sorted out the strategy she stayed on to gossip. Eve made it her business to know down to the last sneeze what was going on. They discussed office antics and the row brewing between a couple of banks in the city.

'Could be quite a fight ahead.' Eve's linen skirt hitched up to reveal a very nice thigh. 'Stand by for heads on Tower Bridge.'

Jamie recollected a conversation with Prue. She had been describing Joan of Arc's famous relief of Orléans in 1429, and how Joan had woken one morning to sounds of the citizens of Orléans attacking an English garrison outside the walls at St Loup. Joan had leapt to her feet and dashed into battle. Apparently, she had wept at the sight of spilt French blood before planting her standard on the edge of the ditch and storming the *bastille* built around an abandoned church. All manner of English blood had then been shed, but it was not recorded if Joan wept for it.

Eve, sensing his distraction, twitched her skirt down. 'Do you have any views on the situation?' he asked her.

She did, of course, and confidently planted her standard on the edge of what Jamie suspected could be a financial disaster.

After a while, she got to her feet. The red plait danced back over her shoulder and the linen skirt was pulled straight.

'See you, then.' She paused. 'Perhaps we could have lunch?'

Jamie's 'Let's' sounded unconvincing.

She got the message and shrugged elegantly and disappeared.

It occurred to him later that the word 'evil' was 'live' spelt backwards. Once again, he stared out of the hermetically sealed window. What did 'love' spell backwards? What did 'love for someone else's wife' spell backwards? What did 'fool' spell backwards?

Should he phone Prue?

In Dainton, Prue knelt on the kitchen floor, like a bloody penitent, she thought, and scrubbed at the tiles decorated with the stew she had just dropped all over them.

I won't phone him.

The pain of being married and forty-one, of saying goodbye to expectations that youth enjoys without thinking about them, knowing you are passing over a bridge and you will not return, was sharp. People Prue knew were beginning to die. Her parents had gone, and one or two friends, in particular Mary, who had died protesting that she still had so much to do. Their ghosts sometimes haunted her. Elements of Prue were also dying. Relinquishing the right to nourish intense feeling – or, worse, the ability to provoke it because cellulite, slackening skin and gravity interpose themselves between your desires and their object – was harder than she had ever supposed.

As she listened to the wind blowing rain and cool wet air through the garden, Prue grieved for her youth and listened to the voices from the past. Once, she had imagined that she could touch the furthest planet if she had wished.

So Prue scrubbed, her hands stinging from the hot water and detergent.

Max and Jane, she thought. Max and Jane.

The phone rang.

Jamie's mother came from Scotland, he told Prue on that phone call, the last in a long line of a family that had gradually lost its faith in itself and, more important, its capital. Beautiful in her way, she had Celtic black hair and white skin and not a spare ounce of flesh. She always dressed in tailored tweed suits, linen blouses, and wore diamond earrings and a double-stranded rope of pearls, the remains of the MacIndrews' assets. She did possess one thing, however, in abundance: a strong sense of family. One of her chief amusements was to cart Jamie and Amelia, his elder sister, around the relations.

'You should *know* who the family are, darlings,' she would say when her children protested. 'You must know where you belong.'

We should know each other, darlings, because we are responsible for each other.

Imagine, he told Prue. Picture the scene. And Prue, who wanted to suck in every detail, listened with a hunger bordering on the ravenous. Imagine.

One of his abiding memories was of being made to recite Kipling's 'If', dressed in too-big grey flannel shorts and a tie, in front of a panel of great-aunts who lived in a vast and gloomy flat in Edinburgh. They had been a grey, fluttering group, smelling of camphor and Indian tea. After he had finished, several pairs of hands, worn down to the bone by age and making-do, patted him and offered cups of tea and sandwiches of the kind that would have fainted at the word 'filling'.

'Great-aunt Dorothy,' said his mother, who was not without a certain sadistic humour, 'would like you two to come and stay by yourselves.' Her eyes widened with the tease, knowing they would rather die. 'I've said you would love to explore Edinburgh properly . . .' She took pity on her offspring, 'but I think we are rather busy these holidays.'

Jamie had no time to feel relief. A bony hand in the composite mass of great-aunts across the table raised a cup of tea. 'But, Isobel,' said a voice, 'we won't be around much longer, will we?'

One by one, Great-aunts Jean, Ellen and Margery nodded

like flowers in a herbaceous border on which the gardener had left the dead heads.

Yes, he remembered it so well, he said to Prue, who was at this point in the long conversation struck by the thought that it was a good thing Jamie was ringing her, else how would she explain the phone bill? The great-aunts, the lace curtains shrouding huge windows, and the silver teapot on the table. Gloom and hush. Annie the maid in black and white, oatcakes and hot scones wrapped in linen napkins. Prints of the Highlands on the wall, soft linen sheets, the old Jacobite wine glass with a spiral trapped in the stem, the agony of repeating 'If' every day after tea and *utter* agony of trying not to laugh when Melly (who had taken up ballet and should not have done) was ordered to do a swan dance to Tchaikovsky on the wind-up gramophone.

Great-aunt Hilda had spotted his giggles and demanded that Jamie apologize to his sister 'Because, little boy, manners maketh man.'

Those were pieces Jamie picked out from the jigsaw of childhood which had gone.

Edward was wailing as Jamie let himself in at the front door. Violet appeared at the top of the stairs, clutching him.

'Thank God,' she said. 'Where have you been?'

Further up, on the second landing, a clearly worried Emmy was hanging over the banisters.

'He hasn't stopped crying for an hour.' Violet sounded frantic. 'I don't think I can take any more.'

'Give him to me.' Jamie flung down his briefcase. 'Have you rung the doctor?' He examined the agonized little face of his son. There was a tinge of blue around the open mouth and flared nostrils.

'He's on his way,' said Emmy.

The doctor took another hour to arrive by which time Violet and Jamie were on the whisky and the baby was limp with exhaustion and pain. The doctor was clearly exhausted, too, but examined Edward carefully.

'I think it's colic, but it's just possible that the gut has twisted.' He fingered the tight little belly. 'I'll give you a letter and if he continues to cry after I've given him some Calpol, drive him to St Thomas's. They'll have his notes from last time.'

After she had shown the doctor out Violet sank on to the sofa. 'Oh, my God.'

Jamie held Edward close to him. It was warm and comfortable in the drawing room. Violet's carefully chosen paintings were on the walls, her chair covers were tasteful, the grey carpet immaculate. It seemed too insulated a place for this kind of drama.

Love for his son tightening his throat, Jamie breathed into Edward's tiny neck, 'Get better.'

Emmy hovered in the doorway with a tray of tea. She was white and anxious and there were dark circles under her eyes. Jamie warmed to her.

'What about a hot-water bottle on his tummy?' she suggested. 'I think it would help.'

Jamie flashed her a smile of gratitude.

In conjunction with the Calpol, the hot-water bottle wrapped in a couple of tea-towels did appear to help. Jamie sat with Edward on his knee and Emmy held the bottle carefully against the baby's stomach. Gradually, Edward quietened and the stiff little limbs began to relax. Violet sat on the opposite side of the room watching the tableau, and remained silent.

Edward's eyelids fluttered and drooped, then fell over his wet eyes with the suddenness of a steel gate banging shut.

Sweating with relief, Jamie looked up at Violet who had turned as white as the lampshade on her expensive marble lamp.

After Emmy had borne the sleeping baby upstairs and retired to a hot bath, Jamie dropped on to his knees by Violet's chair and put his head in her lap. He could feel damp patching his shirt.

'All right?'

'Yes.' Violet spoke through dry lips. As an afterthought she asked, 'And you?'

'Yes.' In the darkness of Violet's lap, he closed his eyes. 'Thank God, there was nothing very wrong.'

He felt a hand tugging at his hair and raised his head. 'I never want another one,' said Violet, her mouth twisted with emotion. 'Never.'

Jamie sat back on his heels. 'You don't mean it?'

'Yes, I do,' said Violet, avoiding Jamie's eye. 'It's too . . . too distracting. I mean wearing.'

'Don't be silly.' Jamie climbed to his feet and eased his shirt away from his back. 'Of course you do.'

Violet gulped whisky. She looked up and Jamie realized that she was furious.

'Stop patronizing me, Jamie. You have no idea what I think and I'm telling you I don't want another one.'

She put down her glass and got to her feet. Despite her anger, her pallor made her look vulnerable . . . and, he saw with a shock, lonely. Jamie responded by pulling her to him, and kissing the silky hair and the cool, pampered skin of her cheek.

'Don't feel like that, Violet. Every parent must have this sort of experience. Edward's fine now.'

'Yes, you know all about that,' said Violet, harshly. '*And* you keep reminding me.'

He released Violet and took a step back. 'Jenny was five when I moved in with Lara so I don't know everything.'

She gazed down at the carpet with a secret expression. 'Even so, I know you think you've done it all before and this gives you a licence to lecture me. Poor old Violet, she doesn't know nought from ten but I'll teach her a thing or two.'

For a second, Jamie was completely taken aback and then his anger flared. With a little tsk, Violet gathered up the glasses, arranged them tidily on the tray and walked out of the room.

Jamie could hear the clink as she stacked them in the dishwasher.

Along with Scottish great-aunts, Jamie's mother had often indulged in proverbs. He could hear her saying one of them now, in the light, amused, ironic manner she had: 'You've made your bed, darling, and you have to lie on it.'

In her bleached- and limed-wood kitchen, Violet stared down at dirty china in the rack. She was profoundly exhausted and slightly nauseous from fatigue and whisky. Throughout the drama, various thoughts had sifted through a mind that had refused to work with its normal celerity, chief among them that if Edward was ill she would not be able to attend the programme meeting for which she had planned so thoroughly.

The paucity of her reaction to her son's distress appalled even Violet.

CHAPTER TEN

'DO YOU HAVE A BIOGRAPHY OF CHARLES DICKENS?' A girl dressed in black leggings and Doc Martens with bright green hair cut into a cockatoo crest, asked Prue the question.

Prue considered the figure. Crested cockatoos and Dickens did not figure in her list of obvious combinations. 'We have the Ackroyd in stock.'

'I'll take it,' said the girl. 'And anything you've got on Elizabeth Barrett Browning.'

The bookshop was crowded and Prue was forced to dodge browsers and tables piled with new publications. She stretched up to 'A' on the biography shelf. Where you lined up in the alphabet influenced your success as a writer. Authors whose names began with 'A' or 'B' were read by tall people. 'LMN' got both tall and short.

The girl paid for the books, counting out the money from a leather purse which had almost fallen apart. Prue hoped the books proved to be a fair exchange and did what they were meant to do. Entertain? Teach? Act as a doorstop?

She pressed the till button: the drawer sprang out and hit her in the stomach, as it always did, and the coins clinked into the compartments. Prue recollected that the last time she had seen a pile of coins was at the Ivy when Jamie had emptied his pockets in search of his credit cards. Then, she had remarked on how much loose change he carried.

'Hurry up,' said Gerald who was waiting to ring up a bill.

You see, Prue admonished herself, you're slipping.

She drove home with the delicate scent of flowers for the church filling the car, and the week's shopping rattling and bouncing in plastic bags. At the Dainton turn-off, she remembered that she had forgotten Jane's favourite pizzas and cursed. As part of the strategy worked out between Max and her to help Jane, Prue had arranged that Jane bring a friend back for Friday supper, promising a special meal.

Just because you're busy doesn't mean you let go, she told herself fiercely, meaning, I have a conscience, and spent the remainder of the drive mentally reshifting her timetable in order to propitiate it.

She parked the car in the lane leading up to the church, threw the rug over the bags containing the dairy foods, and extracted the flowers from the back seat. The weather had altered and a warmish wind was blowing, fresh and sweet, along the valley and up towards the airstrip, and the air smelt fresh and soft. The trees' silhouettes were blurring with new growth and the gardens had been given a fresh topcoat of green.

The wind tugged at Prue's clothes, sweeping the moraines of dust and leaves into new patterns and covering a footstep imprinted in mud, a rut – and the evidence of a long winter.

Dazzled and goaded by the onset of summer, Prue trudged up the lane and stopped by a patch of briar which had grown so thick that it impeded progress. No one had got round to cutting it back, which was nothing new. She pulled out the secateurs she always carried and hacked at the worst bits, then decided to send Max up to deal with it properly. She disentangled a blackberry branch from her sleeve. Someone, Emmy perhaps, had told her there were only ten basic structures in nature which were repeated *ad infinitum*. That prompted her to think: I must call on Emmy's mother and tell her Emmy is doing fine.

Her gaze shifted to the stump of the grand and glorious beech that had been sent crashing to the ground in the Great Storm. The tree lovers in Dainton had mourned it, and Prue was cheered to see that suckers were struggling out of the grass. What did that tell her? Rising from its base, like a glove, were black projections with their characteristic twist. Prue smiled: Dead Men's Fingers made Jane giggle for Carey Scholfield's elder sister had informed the girls they were phallic ('What's "phallic", Mum?').

That was to ignore their strange, almost sinister quality suggesting deformity and . . . weirdness. Prue's expression became troubled. The deformity of living a lie when she had been used to truth – or, at least, straightforwardness? Of living on two levels where once one had been sufficient? The fungi's 'third' finger had been broken off near the top, to reveal secret, creamy flesh and rows of spore sacs. What did *those* tell her about herself and the dark fingers that were pushing through her consciousness? Searching for the pattern, Prue touched the fungus with the toe of her shoe.

'Prue, dear, just the person.'

Molly Greer came up behind Prue, and she whirled round. 'Hallo, Molly.'

Molly was carrying a mass of daffodils and catkins from her garden wrapped in the local newspaper. Prue eyed them and knew immediately that her tastefully chosen, expensive offerings from a Winchester florist were destined for relegation behind the pulpit.

'Do you mind?' Molly shoved her hand under Prue's arm. 'The slope is bad on my hip.'

Prue tried not to feel rebellious, to give this gesture of support graciously, and failed. Molly was wearing her sale bargain, a tweed coat designed expressly to keep a dreadnought warm and which exuded a damp smell. Beneath it, she wore socks over thick green tights and sheepskin boots. Molly did not bother with her appearance. Waste of time, she often reiterated, an expert in making a virtue of necessity. My face is my face – which, said Max, who could be moved on occasion to rudeness but not originality, needed to be said otherwise it might be mistaken for a bus.

They deposited the flowers in the church porch, and Molly ordered Prue to fill the vases from the outside tap. Prue bit her lip. Molly Greer might be the keystone of Dainton, fifteen years older and a tireless defender of the village against the threat of motorways, supermarkets and boundary realignments, but unchecked power (particularly if unelected) provokes rebellion. Grimly, Prue filled the vases and hefted them one by one into the church, fully aware that any objections to Molly's dictates achieved little.

Her resolve hardened. 'I'll do the altar,' she said firmly, ashamed of her past pusillanimity and, a little ashamed of her present victory, surged into the church before she weakened.

When Prue finished she went back down the aisle to judge the effect which, she congratulated herself, was good. Purple freesias and green euphorbia were an interesting combination. To her credit Molly said approvingly, 'Very nice, Prue.'

'Thank you. I thought it was worth splashing out.'

'Oh, really?' Molly gave Prue the benefit of one of her searching looks. 'Prue dear. You're not getting yourself into any kind of trouble, are you?'

'Why do you ask that?' Prue did not turn round to look at her.

'I'm no fool, dear.'

'No, Molly, I never thought you were.'

Molly finished a huge arrangement for a window in the east wall below one of the two wall paintings, or 'Moralities', for which the church was famous. This one depicted St George doing away with the dragon who was about to consume a large-eyed Princess Cleodolinda. Understandably, her parents, on the battlements of the nearby castle, were watching the proceedings with anguish etched into their faces. Parents were bound to their children by a pulsing, tensile rope of feeling and obligation, whether men wore tights and women wimples, or not. Of course. And wept and broke their hearts when their children died, tiny replicas from the mould. Ever since the first caveman dragged a bison back to the cave, the affectionate family had been alive and thriving and parents had torn out their own breasts to feed their young. As Prue would do for Jane. As Max would do for his daughters. Oh, yes. She pictured him, the slumbering giant, provoked to whirling rage, aiming his Purdey at anyone who threatened them.

'Can you give me a hand, Prue?' commanded Molly.

Prue resigned herself to several journeys to the compost heap and to washing out spare vases in the vestry.

'How's that stepdaughter of yours?' Molly asked as they returned to their cars.

'Busy. Working. Baby. New house. You can imagine.'

'Flown the coop, that one.' Molly's grip tightened on Prue's arm as she lurched round treacherous mud patches. 'You'd never think she once lived here.'

Violet's gilded, expensive qualities did not belong in Dainton – as perceived by Dainton. This was a little unfair as the village was as worldly as any other.

Prue steered Molly into the village square which had broken out in a rash of 'For Sale' signs and caught sight of Clive Carter standing motionless in his front garden, which he had taken to doing since he lost his job from his engineering firm. Prue waved at him. Clive did not wave back.

'Time I made the old man's lunch,' Molly said, and added that he was damn well going to have cabbage because she had heard on the radio it was good for heart conditions. Since Keith Greer had made a career out of his bad heart, it did not bode well for Keith. Prue suggested that it was unwise to believe everything you heard. Molly looked her straight in the eyes and said that was true, and one did hear an awful lot of things, didn't one?

While Prue was washing up her lunch, she listened to the radio and Schubert's violin concerto filled the kitchen. Its beauty made her catch her breath and dealt a blow to her heart. She dropped the washing-up brush back into the suds. Then she gave up and finished the dishes with tears running down her cheeks into her neck.

Jamie [she wrote]

When Thackeray finally met Charlotte Brontë he expected to meet in the notorious author of *Jane Eyre* an Amazon. Instead he encountered 'an austere little Joan of Arc marching in upon us, and rebuking our easy lives and our easy morals'.

How infuriating the Joans and the Charlottes of this world are. Except, I think Thackeray's assessment is wrong. Joan was not so much concerned with the world as with what she made of herself. She tilted at the commonly held idea of what a woman should be, should think, should do, succeeded in doing so and suffered atrociously.

But she had her moments. I like to think of her dressed up in breeches, tight boots and the golden *huque* that she enjoyed so much (Joan liked clothes), riding off to battle. That and her communication with

God. Joan was lucky, she lived in an age that allowed a dialogue with God, you were allowed to speak to Him and Him to you. Much more than our own, it was an age that, if it knew it or not, made allowances for the richness and variety of the human psyche.

Yes?

Nevertheless, I shall take Joan/Charlotte's rebuke to the easy life to heart, and ask you not to phone me again. You *do* see, don't you?

Prue knew perfectly well that she was not going to send this letter, but got as far as addressing the envelope before she tore it up and threw it in the dustbin.

When Prue opened her eyes the next morning, a fully dressed Max was standing by the bed looking down at her.

'I thought you were crying,' he said.

He seemed even more impassive than usual – a sign that he was in the grip of strong feelings.

'No,' she said and forced a smile. 'I've a bit of a snuffle, that's all.'

'You won't forget to pay the gas bill.'

'No,' she said, trying to hide her misery and failing.

Max assessed her expression, then turned and went over to the window and stood gazing out. Outside the wind blew in great racing gulps and exuberant whorls of air. Prue watched his back, so large, so contained, so easy, she knew, to wound. Max always hid his wounds well.

'Good luck for today, Max.'

He swung round from the window. 'You remembered?'

She felt ashamed at the pleasure in his voice and the panic that underlay it. 'Of course, darling. You've got the big brainstorming session on the European set-up. Have you got your notes?'

'Yes.'

Max sat down on the bed and took her hand. 'Are you sure you're all right? I've been a bit worried about you.'

Treachery sat in her heart like soggy mixture in an unsuccessful sponge cake. Prue rubbed his fingers with her own and said, 'Everything's absolutely fine. Don't worry about me.'

Again he watched her and then bent down and gathered Prue in his arms and held her close. 'Is it, my Prue?' he said into her neck, and kissed the hair spilling over her shoulders. 'You must always tell me.'

How lucky, he had said, when Prue had eventually prodded him into proposing. How lucky I am to be given a second chance.

That was twenty-one years ago when Prue had been working as a legal secretary in Stephenson Blackwell's in the City. A bored, underdeveloped, unrealized Prue.

How many people do what Prue did? Mark time. And how many look up from an uncongenial desk, light on a figure and listen to the click in their head (*not* their heart) which tells them it is time to take action?

Max was tall – a definite plus for tall Prue – well dressed, kind, with the additional advantage of suffering. Two years previously, Helen, his wife, had left him and, in doing so, had rammed her car into an oncoming lorry and taken a further six weeks to die. Max was now struggling to bring up his small daughter by himself, a situation made more difficult by his refusal to move out of Dainton to London.

'It was whisky,' Max said later when Prue had finally willed him into inviting her out to dinner, a process that had taken a great deal of trouble and a fortune in scent and stockings.

136

'Helen had been drinking for some time and I was drinking it like water too.'

Prue considered. 'It was not your fault that Helen chose to leave. Or your fault that she chose to have half a bottle of the best malt before she did so.'

Max sat back in the chair. The restaurant was noisy and full, but he was quite still and removed. 'She was so beautiful,' he said at last. 'And my dreams were full of her.'

And Prue had turned away from such feeling and such grief and fled to the cloakroom'.

Later, she made it her business to find a photograph of Helen and was disappointed for she looked artificial and Prue was forced to conclude that her beauty had been the sort that had to be seen live. Either that, or the idea of beauty was like Bostik: once it had been applied it stuck.

Still, since competing on that front was out, it left her the task of scoring over Helen on character. Tell me about Helen, she coaxed a reluctant, reticent Max. Tell me.

Clever Prue. For, in the end, Max talked as much as he was capable of, and got Helen out of his system and into better proportion. It was not comfortable listening, for Max had inflicted wounds as well as suffering them, but none so deep as the one that Helen made when she told him she was leaving.

'I remember,' said Max, struggling for the precise words, 'the moment she told me. I felt as if a knife had been driven under my ribs. I remember thinking it had reached my backbone and was scraping along it.' He held out the hand marked by Helen's Wound. 'I even drove a knife into my hand to test which hurt most.'

Oh, God, thought Prue, and shut her eyes.

Jack was younger than Helen which, Max said, surprised him. Helen preferred the strong, older types. She had accused Max of growing old before his time, and said it was making her feel old, while Jack was both young and vigorous. Then people grew older younger than they do now, if Prue saw what he meant.

'The irony is,' said Max, putting down his knife and fork at one of their weekly dinners, 'Helen won't be growing old. Unlike me. She will never wrinkle or droop and when I meet her again she will be in her time, and I will be in mine. So, you see, it was a final parting.'

Prue did not think she could bear any more and dropped her head over her wine-glass while she decided on a course of action. When she looked up, it was to corner Max's dark eyes with her own and to ask, 'Will you marry again?'

Max caught on at once. For the first time, he smiled properly. Then he ordered a second bottle of wine. 'It will have to be someone who does not mind growing old.'

'Good God,' said Prue – who by now had fallen thoroughly in love – with all the emphasis of the nineteen-year-old. 'You're only thirty-nine now.'

Their future was set from that conversation. Max would marry Prue, they would grow old together and Prue was determined that the age-gap would make no difference.

For their honeymoon, Max, having been prised from a screaming Violet, bore Prue off to a country hotel tucked away on a Devon estuary. Throughout the short summer night, he told Prue how lucky he was and how he loved and needed her, and this was the beginning of the rest of his life. Then he fell asleep.

Rasping-eyed from fatigue and nerves, Prue lay until pink light slid under the chintz curtains, held her sleeping husband in her arms and wondered why it had not been just a little more, well . . . cataclysmic.

Within a month, she felt as if she had been married all her life – falling into a comfortable sofa where she had been expecting a Louis Quinze *fauteuil*. Except for Violet, of course, who set her face against her stepmother with the determination of a seven-year-old.

She had been lucky. But when friends, such as Kate, asked her if she minded about Helen and Violet, she replied, 'No,' and crossed her fingers.

Knowing the past, it's terrible mistakes and the penalties incurred, knowing she had a great obligation to guard Max and Jane, knowing that she endorsed the behaviour that she had perfected over twenty years, knowing she was content in a marriage and in a community, why was it that Prue's flesh felt so firm and expectant this early summer, this growing season, and her eyes hid secrets?

Why not?

Why not?

HIGH SUMMER

CHAPTER ELEVEN

JOAN TOOK CHARGE OF HER OWN DESTINY, PRUE WAS fond of telling Max. She made things happen.

What sort of man was Joan's Dauphin, the king-in-embryo, for whom she risked so much? What fusion of lasciviousness, political nous, religious gift and insanity had he inherited from the stockpile of Valois genes?

'The Dauphin's father,' Prue noted, 'had been subject to fits of madness which effectively caused breakdown in the French government.'

The first attack took place in 1392 when the King went berserk and killed four of his attendants. Subsequently, he suffered at least forty-four attacks, 'crying and trembling as if pricked with a thousand points of iron'. The verdict today would, in all probability, point to schizophrenia.

Isabeau of Bavaria, his mother, was not much better. Despite being embarrassingly short in the leg (a characteristic she passed on to her son), Isabeau had been attractive in her youth but also subject to wobbles in her mental equilibrium. Phobic and agoraphobic, she was terrified by thunder, by the slightest suggestion of disease (not unnaturally given the mortality rate of the period) and could not be persuaded to cross a bridge unless it had railings – a quirk which, again, her son shared.

At first, the quality of Isabeau's mothering was not questioned, but, after 1425, statements wriggled into the records accusing her of neglect. Her extravagance was notorious and so was her intimacy with Louis d'Orléans, her husband's brother. By 1417, a bejewelled Isabeau was the centre of a dissolute court at Vincennes, and scandal reached fever pitch. Rumour was saying that the Dauphin was not the King's son, but his uncle's bastard.

You see, a small but insistent voice spoke to Prue, once a family begins to break down, the effects never end. Think of the stone thrown into the pond. Think of dominoes. Think . . . of what?

The telephone rang in the study where Prue was making these notes.

'Mrs Valour?'

'Yes.'

'It's Emmy speaking.'

'Oh, hallo.' Prue went over various disasters in her mind. 'There's nothing wrong, is there?'

'Everything's fine, but Mr Beckett asked me to call you as he had to leave for the early train. He's coming down to Winchester today for a meeting and wondered if you would like to meet him for lunch at the Coaching House Hotel? He says just turn up any time after 12.45.'

Prue supposed that Jamie supposed that by making the assignation above board, it became acceptable.

Sophistry.

'Thanks, Emmy,' she said. 'I might just do that. I'd like to catch up on the news.'

I bet, thought a sharp, less peaky Emmy, as she put down the phone. It sounds all too matey to me.

Prue scanned the reference books on the shelf above her desk where she had been writing up her notes. Vita Sackville-

West's *Joan of Arc*, a monograph on jealousy, a critical appreciation of nineteenth-century women writers and *Footsteps: Adventures of a Romantic Biographer*, by Richard Holmes. The wrestlings of biographers, and psychologists, to pin their subject to the page were not as fierce as the battle raging in Prue.

How dare Jamie do this? Put her on the spot. *Force her to make a choice.*

Would you rather, then, that choice was taken away?

What would Emmy make of her role as the pander? Lucky it had been Emmy and not Molly Greer, whose curiosity was as sharp as a predatory bird's beak inserted into his prey. Jab. Jab. Plucking bloody bits of information to wave at the world.

Jamie had counted on her saying yes.

Prue picked up her Biro and wrote 'Rouen'. The Biro had been part of a job lot bought in Andover market and showed its dicey provenance by its uneven flow of ink. She shook it and a glob landed on the clean page. She stared at her fingers whose secret identification was now whorled and circled into stained relief.

How dare Jamie send messages via a third person? Most of all, how dare he expose her flimsy defences?

She made herself continue.

It can only be imagined how the quicksand of doubt, sown with phobias and madness, hampered the thin, weak, pendulous-nosed Dauphin. Couple that with high intelligence, bouts of drunkenness and physical unattractiveness, and the ground becomes almost impassable. He was capable of attracting great loyalty but, more often than not, only – in the manner of his parents – to betray it.

This was the man Joan sought to ratify as king.

Footnote, wrote Prue: Isabeau became obese, so much so

that she was prevented from being regent because it was considered that her size would impede her.

Second footnote. Although she was ostentatiously pious it was doubtful if religion nourished her life. Nevertheless, in one of those curious biographical and historical collusions, Isabeau commissioned an illuminated life of St Margaret of Antioch for her library, a great, jewelled tome. Unlike St Catherine who was associated with virginity, St Margaret was associated with motherhood. Perhaps that was why Isabeau (in hasty retrenchment? fit of conscience?) chose her.

St Margaret was, of course, with St Catherine and St Michael, one of Joan's voices.

Prue looked at her watch and stopped writing but declined to read through her work for, she knew of old, it was at this point that she plunged into a crisis of doubt about her ability to handle the project. Perhaps Rembrandt experienced this blankness half-way through the *Night Watch*? Certainly, Tolstoy did not spare Sonya his artistic doubts throughout forty years of writing masterpieces. How could she possibly be different?

Max was good at urging Prue not to give up when the doubts became an impediment to progress. He was punctilious in encouraging her efforts, talking things over, even doing a spot of research – and it drove her frantic. Joan was hers; her private property. Sometimes Prue dreamed that Max was taking over the project himself.

Quite often he rang in his lunchtime on the days she was at home. 'How's Joan?' he would ask.

Don't, she wanted to say. Don't.

The Platonic deal decrees that everything has its appropriate nature. Joan came up against that one when she declared her voices had bodies, wore clothes and talked in French. In the medieval Church's view, abstract things should remain so

146

and the Church condemned her for suggesting otherwise.

Upstairs in her bedroom, Prue contemplated the appropriate nature of herself in the mirror. The outer woman, arranged in the scoop-necked Viyella blouse that suited her so well, complete with the unfurled fan of lines at the corners of her grey eyes and the long fingers which were reddened from too much washing up.

The inner, hidden woman? Hesitating over a course that, until recently, had been unthinkable. Unthinkable because it had not existed, said a voice in her head. Prue turned away from the mirror. She began to undress. On went jeans and a white T-shirt. Over those went a navy blazer, which used to belong to Max but, if she rolled up the sleeves, looked stylishly baggy. Prue's role model was the scene from *Pretty Woman* where, thus attired, Julia Roberts signalled that she was now a serious, decent woman united with Prince Charming.

Unfortunately, she did not possess the Roberts haunch but the T-shirt, made of Sea Island cotton, looked expensive and flattering against her skin. Deciding on the jewellery took several minutes. Wedding ring, of course. Pearl studs? Far too small but fake ones did not seem right. Gold chain?

The silver-topped pots on her dressing-table needed cleaning and she rearranged them, thinking what a bother they were. When she opened the drawer containing her scarves, she was as usual confronted by a swirl of materials. Prue fingered the silks and wool, old, of second-rate quality and bought when Max was not earning as much as he did now, drew out an expensive new red one and shut the drawer with a little bang.

The eyes in Max's photograph on her dressing-table followed Prue around the room. She had not noticed them do that before.

Hanging on the handle of the wardrobe Max's ties, mostly striped, established his territory in the bedroom as surely as if he had been there. To Prue, they now seemed thin and worn – like the skin that stretched over his elbows and knees and folded, just a little, over his stomach.

She avoided the photograph and sat down to brush her hair which she tied back. As she lifted her arm, Prue noted its fullness and the slack which should have been taut. Fear of her age gnawed at her briefly and was routed by a shiver of excited apprehension.

'Don't look at me,' she said to Max's photograph. What she meant was: don't judge me.

She got up, wriggled into a pair of shoes and picked up her shoulder-bag.

Don't go.

Don't.

But she did.

The hotel – which Prue knew well – prided itself on chintz, judging by the generosity with which it had been lavished around windows and ruffled on to chairs and stools.

Prue paused in the lounge entrance and Jamie rose from a flower-encrusted armchair.

'Have I kept you waiting?' she asked, brushing back strands of escaped hair.

'Do you like chintz, Prue?'

'Depends.'

'I loathe it and the three minutes forty-five seconds I have been waiting for you surrounded by it have been deeply uncomfortable.'

She laughed and then was serious. 'Why did you ask me to come?'

'Why *did* you come?'

She shifted her handbag strap. 'Because . . .'

'Exactly,' he said gently. 'Because . . .'

He took her hand as he spoke and with the other smoothed back Prue's rogue strands of hair. Registering her quickened heartbeat, she allowed him to do so, and forgave him everything.

He smiled in reassurance. 'I am here on a genuine work project and there's nothing wrong with lunch.'

'That's what Caligula told his victims before eating them.'

Over coffee, Jamie told her about Lara and Jenny, and Prue, listening hungrily, realized with a sense of *déjà vu* that she had heard the story before. It was Max's story, too, and the pain that had been inflicted was as deep as his, although Jamie was not as honest or perhaps as wise in himself to acknowledge it as Max had been. Prue dropped her napkin on to the table. Perhaps there was something about her – face? expression? lack of glamour? – that attracted men who carried these secret histories?

If taxed, Jamie could have explained. Prue was peaceful-looking: so warm and still and intent that she would invite anyone to break their habit of silence.

Later, he suggested Prue show him around the cathedral and they walked down Jewry Street and into the cathedral grounds. The tourist season was well under way and the city was crowded but the precinct escaped the worst excesses. Summer had arrived and the sun had come with it. Hot and vigorous, it shone down on air that pulsed with heat, on flesh slicked with damp, on the rounded curves of women, fattening buds in the gardens, and grass that was still plump and juicy from the spring rain. People sat in groups, or meandered down the paths, and children wheeled like noisy starlings.

Prue and Jamie sauntered towards the entrance to the cathedral.

'Like pilgrims,' said Jamie, who was not usually given to poetry or history.

'Your name *is* Beckett,' Prue pointed out.

Jamie rarely considered the implication of his name. 'A wastrel and a saint.'

'If you're true to it, you'll have a wonderful excessive time and then repent at leisure.'

Prue's hand brushed Jamie's, and flesh whispered together, tasted the impulse to cling and a fleeting of warmth, and fell apart.

Inside the cathedral, Jamie admired the thirteenth-century floor tiles in the retro-choir and the Great Screen behind the high altar.

'The original statuary was broken up during the Reform-ation and replaced during the nineteenth century.' Prue pointed at an example. 'That's why Queen Victoria's up there with the Saxons.'

That amused Jamie. Secretly Prue watched him, her gaze a moth pulled to the flame. He was standing with one hand in his pocket, the other holding a pamphlet they had picked up at the entrance about the cathedral. Absorbed, slightly tense, eyes narrowed, an assembly of flesh tones, of blue veins, of light indrawn breaths, of pulses beating in his neck and at his wrist, of grey suit against the blue-green stripe of his shirt, Jamie, contrasted with the gloom and sanctity of the cathedral, became a voluptuous object.

Assaulted by colour, smell and yet conscious of darkness clutching at the circles of light, Prue inhaled candlewax and incense. Jamie turned to say something to her, something about Queen Victoria not being a Good Thing, something she never could remember and, with a little sigh, Prue yielded and leapt.

Shaken and shaking by the feelings that had been unleashed, Prue, a forty-one-year-old – with lines, for goodness sake, at the corners of her eyes – who had not meant this ever to happen, said 'Jamie?' Her tone conveyed that for which, unconsciously, he had been listening and waiting. Very gently, lightly and with care, he touched her fingers with his own.

After a second or two, she moved on down the aisle.

'Why don't you light a candle?' he called after her, producing a coin. Prue looked at it. A simple twenty-pence piece held between lean fingers. He had made a similar gesture at the Ivy, and he was doing it again, only now he was offering it to her as a symbol of whatever lay between them. She hesitated only a second or two, and took it.

'If you pray you can pray here.' She led him towards St Swithun's memorial where racks of candles were burning.

'Not for me, Prue.'

A flare from the candles caught Prue's face in profile as she touched the tapers to the wick, and traced her generous features with soft light. Jamie drew in his breath.

The candle joined the others. Flames shifted in the draught, and, mesmerized, Prue gazed at them until the light fused into a dazzling expanse that hurt her eyes.

Outside, the colours were equally dazzling. Prue retied her scarf, which had worked loose. 'Jane Austen died in Winchester,' she said. 'Do you want to see the house?'

She led Jamie through the Close into College Street and he gazed dutifully at the bow-windowed front. 'This is a private house', proclaimed a notice on the door.

'They must be driven crazy.' Jamie ignored the house and looked down at Prue.

'She died from Addison's disease, you know.'

'What's that?' Jamie continued to look into her face, and search her eyes with his own, and she shook her head. It was like having the components of her body taken apart and put together in a different arrangement.

He was due to catch the 4.05 back to London and they turned north and set off for the station. Half-way down one street they passed a shop selling electrical goods and videos. *Dances with Wolves . . . Thunderbirds . . . Jean de Florette . . . Brief Encounter . . .* With its distilled forties agony, the expression on Celia Johnson's face accosted passers-by. A camcorder had been placed in the window, trapping pedestrians on the screen. Prue caught sight of them both as they passed, grainy, unreal and turned into fiction, ratified by being imprinted on celluloid – as so much was.

'Look, Jamie.' She stopped. On the screen the space between them was filled in by a shop front. Jamie moved closer and the image on the screen responded obediently. She felt him draw her closer and his fingers press into her back, exploratory and possessive and she thought that she had waited all her life for that touch. Then she thought: I'm going mad.

'You'll be late,' she said.

At the station, Jamie told her not to wait and Prue obeyed. As she walked down the platform, the down train from London drew into the station. Because she made a point of not looking back, Prue did not see Max alight from the carriage where he always sat.

Max saw Prue. Or rather, he caught sight of the distinctive scarf over the blazer. At first, it did not register in his brain. Then it occurred to him that Prue sometimes wore a red scarf and his navy blazer. Later, as he stood in the taxi queue, having rung home twice for a lift, it dawned on him that it had been Prue.

In the train, Jamie occupied himself by staring out of the window, his neglected briefcase lying beside him on the seat, thinking about Prue.

Little things. Strands of hair that required tying back. A red scarf caught in a knot over her chest. Sharing fried sausages in a kitchen filled with rubble. Her trick of looking at him. Sleepy-eyed but very much there.

How could unimportant things awake such yearning? Such frantic hunger? And was it not true that the clichés – a pitching stomach, unreliable knees, a wildly beating heart – were part and parcel of falling in love?

Jamie shifted in his seat. Violet would never eat two sausages and ask for more. Violet, Jamie now realized with a major shift in loyalties, never listened.

As the train sped through southern England, past back gardens filled with apple trees and a litter of plastic toys, washing and lawns pocked by weather and pollution, past ugly office buildings, strips of wasteland encrusted with abandoned cars, through complicated railway junctions, the life that Jamie had constructed, and which had seemed so solid, began to assume dream-like qualities.

Fear pricked at his neck. Fear that the centre of his existence was not going to hold and that he had been instrumental in its dissolution.

'Were you at the station today?' Max asked his wife over tea. 'I thought I saw you.'

They were sitting on the patio outside the kitchen. The air was warm and filled with summer scent. Prue poured out her cup of tea and during those seconds made a decision.

'No. Why should I be there? I didn't know you were coming home early.'

'I should have let you know before I left the office and saved the taxi fare.'

'Never mind, darling.'

Prue's teacup rattled in the saucer.

His memories were still sharp.

153

. . . No, no, Max, where *have* you got that idea from? Of course, Jack and me are nothing more than friends.

Jack and *I*, Helen.

Stop being so pedantic, Max. It's so typical.

Eyes narrowed in anger, hair scraped back over a face that seemed peeled back to its bone. Scarlet lips mouthing untruths.

Helen later amended her statements to something more approximate to the truth. Yes, Max, actually Jack and I did have a *little* something. Not serious, you must see that. But I get so bored, darling, stuck in Dainton. It wasn't my fault he came sniffing round.

It wasn't your fault that you didn't send him packing?

Helen had got used to a glass of whisky, or four, by this point and had almost stopped eating. Drink and semi-starvation gave her a transparent, insubstantial look, like a leaf skeleton tracked with veins to which flesh had once clung.

And Violet? Max persisted.

Along with the whisky, Helen had taken to shrugging.

And Violet?

Violet's all right, Max. Don't worry about her. Everything's fine if we all calm down. I'll get rid of Jack if that's what you want.

Yes, Max had wanted that but, like everything Helen promised, it did not turn out quite that way. By the finish of the bloody battle of their marriage, it did not matter any longer what Max wanted. It mattered what Jack wanted. And why Jack did not have the grace to get himself killed in the car crash that eventually killed Helen, Max had never worked out, or accepted.

Finding yourself, an ordinary person, at the mercy of a

beating, onrushing tide of pain, impotence and ugliness were, at best, bewildering. Max had not anticipated such swirling depths in his ordinary life . . .

Over the teacup, a tempered Max, wise in the art of lying, regarded his second wife. He had known for some time that the twenty-year difference in their ages might surface eventually. No matter, he was prepared. He felt differently now about fidelity than he had at forty. No, the struggle now surely was to yield to the possibility of his wife looking elsewhere with the grace and common sense that he had, in theory, perfected.

Allow her an episode, he had sermonized to himself, falling into the error of imagining that bowing to the inevitable was the only course to take. The past can dictate the blueprint for the future – and there was, after all, much to lay at Helen's door. Or, when the thought was too painful, Max amended it: allow that it is probable, that it may happen.

He did not regard his conclusions as presumptuous, which they were. Or that he was traducing Prue by prescribing her infidelity. It seemed right to be sensible, to understand, to take a step back. After all, he had a lot for which to give thanks. He had his home and his daughters, and his feelings for them were so satisfying that they were sufficient.

Then again, he was not getting younger and the pricks (he excused the wordplay) and promptings of his flesh were not what they had once been. To make love these days required a different combination of engorged flesh and triggered hormones. It took the thought and preparation of the voyager embarking on a taxing journey.

Prue refilled their cups, and had an extraordinary feeling that Max was looking at her along the barrel of a gun. She drank the cooling tea and listened to the evening birdsong. Guilt . . . She tried to concentrate on guilt. Guilt creates lies and monsters.

Instead she felt the most complete and utter joy, as wild and beautiful as the swallow's cry from the hot sky.

'When?' said Jamie on the telephone the next day. 'When, Prue?'

'I don't know,' she said hopelessly, and tried to be correct and right. 'Never.'

'You don't really mean that.'

'Yes. I do.'

'I'll find a way,' said Jamie. 'Tell me when you can get away.'

She opened her mouth to speak, stopped and tried again.

'Prue. Don't renege. Prue?'

She told him when.

CHAPTER TWELVE

Emmy upended the baby and laid him on the changing mat. The nursery at Austen Road was not as pristine as it had once been. A pile of soiled baby clothes lay on the floor, cotton wool littered the top of the chest of drawers, and baby lotion dripped from a plastic bottle lying on its side.

Edward did not want his nappy changed and squirmed. Clamping one hand on his stomach, Emmy reached for a clean one. After a struggle, she managed to attach it to the baby.

'You horror.'

She bent over him until their noses met. Edward's eyes did a wild dance and he giggled and pulled at her hair.

'No, you don't.' Emmy unlocked his fingers and levered him upright. 'Pull your own.'

The telephone rang as she was negotiating the stairs with a wriggling Edward in her arms. Emmy made herself take the last few treads very carefully before plonking the baby on the floor and launching herself at speed towards it.

'Everything all right, Emmy? I thought I'd give you a quick ring before the meeting.'

She may not have shone at school, but Emmy had quickly learnt that the phrase 'a quick ring' hid many meanings. Because she was charitable and innocent (for it never occurred

157

to Emmy that people might misconstrue her motives) she had, at first, concluded that 'a quick ring' equalled guilt – until she realized she was being checked up on. Violet never deployed subtlety unless she thought it was worth her while. It drove Emmy mad.

Today disappointment made her snippy as well. She pictured Violet at her desk, coffee (real) steaming beside her in the French cup and saucer on which she insisted, perfectly cut and conditioned hair swinging, nails varnished a (perfect) bright red. Perfect because Violet never did the washing-up.

'Fine, Mrs Beckett. I've just changed him.'

At her feet Edward was discharging a pool of dribble into the brand-new carpet. Emmy rolled her eyes at him.

'Make sure he eats his lunch, won't you?'

Safely out of sight, Emmy raised her eyes heavenward and twirled the flex around her finger. 'Steak and chips,' she muttered. 'Rare.'

'What did you say, Emmy?' At her end Violet frowned, suspicious suddenly.

'Nothing, Mrs Beckett.'

'Look, I must go. There's a meeting. Tell him I rang, won't you?'

Emmy replaced the receiver. Either Violet had lost her tea trolley or she was thinking of something else – which would not surprise her. She squatted down beside Edward, grasped each hand and pulled him up until he was half off the floor. The baby's head fell back like a plum on a spindly branch and he made pleasurable noises.

'Your mum rang,' Emmy informed him, blowing softly on his hands. 'Had to dash to a meeting and rule the world so couldn't talk to you. Sent her love.'

Edward had no intelligible comment to make on the subject. Emmy carried him into the kitchen, managing to avoid looking at the telephone gleaming so whitely on the wall.

'Lunch, Teddy-bear.'

Lunch – any meal – required preparations as for battle. Emmy spread a sheet of newspaper on the floor and dragged the high chair on to it. Then she locked Edward into the harness and poked the fastening of a plastic bib that reminded her of a landing-stage on the moon around Edward's neck.

'Steak,' she said, spooning repellent-looking yuck – apparently braised beef and carrots – from a jar (Violet had approved the brand) into his mouth. 'Without the chips. Tough titty.'

Edward sucked at the spoon with the strength of a sumo-octopus and ate the lot. Emmy gave him puréed apple and Edward hurled the spoon on to the floor and bent over to stare, owl-like, at the results. Emmy swore.

The phone rang. Emmy let it ring for precisely five rings and then grabbed it.

'Hi,' said Angus.

Emmy sat down hard. 'Hallo.'

'What are you doing?'

Emmy eyed the horrors on the floor. 'Ducking flying baby food.'

'Fancy a beer?'

She found it hard to articulate and swallowed. 'Now?' she managed.

'Why not? I'm in the area and I've got the van.'

Emmy sighed and proceeded to explain why not. Bring the baby, said Angus. A warm little picture took shape in Emmy's mind of being tucked up with Angus and Edward in a pub with a fire and horse brasses and a beer. A real couple, saying nice, warm things to each other like: 'You make me happy' or, better than that, 'We are so happy together.' (Emmy's experience of real couples was limited mostly to what she had read.)

'Nonsense,' Angus insisted, 'you can bring the baby and his mother won't know if you don't tell her.'

That was how Emmy found herself crouched over a beer-stained wooden bench in a wind made colder because it was supposed to be summer with Edward grizzling beside her in his pushchair. The pub overlooked Wandsworth Common, which was pleasant, but was on a main road and traffic thundered past. Emmy's nose was running and the beer was not marvellous either. A full ashtray lay between her and Angus.

'Aren't you glad you listened to me?' Angus ignored the grizzles.

Emmy had made a discovery. Love – or lust, she was not sure which – did not keep you warm. June had chucked in one of those days designed to keep you on your toes, which conveyed in no uncertain terms that if you had hoped for summer, forget it. Emmy felt guilty about Edward whose little hands had gone almost blue. For the fifth time, she leant over to pull on his mittens.

Edward pulled them off.

'Bugger you,' said Emmy.

Angus was telling her about his latest job, a conversion in Wandsworth.

'Pity the Becketts have just done the bathroom,' he said. 'We've just ripped one out. Practically brand-new. Avocado.'

Pale green, stroked with cream . . . Emmy's fantasies took off. Shimmering, slippery, iridescent temples to cleanliness. Water sliding off skin, flushed pink and white, oozing into folds, between toes, along flat planes. Heat meshed with steam and tuberose scent from the bottles on the shelves.

'Pity,' she agreed, amazed at how quickly imagination could slip the leash.

Angus shoved the ashtray aside. 'What are you doing at the weekend?' he asked.

Emmy shrugged. 'Not much.'

'Fancy coming out with me?'

Emmy wanted to say no. She wanted to get up, seize Edward and run – away from the golden youth who was issuing tantalizing invitations which, she knew, *she knew*, would end in disaster.

Why did she know? Because, it did not make sense that he, beautiful, beautiful Angus, wanted to invite her, plain Emmy from Dainton, out on the best night of the week. Independence, an unscalded heart, caution, were better things by far than the release of saying yes and an aftermath of regret.

'Come on, then,' Angus urged.

A trio struggled down the street: an old lady in a motorized wheelchair, accompanied by two equally ancient companions in headscarves tied so that they resembled nuns' wimples. The three limped and bumped along, a dance of hovering death.

'Yeah. I'll come,' said Emmy.

Violet dumped her briefcase on the kitchen table. It was an aggressive gesture. Alerted, Emmy looked round from the sink. In his chair, Edward grizzled at the sight of his mother.

'I want a word with you, Emmy.'

Emmy dried her hands. Violet stood with hers on her hips.

'Did you or did you not go to a pub at lunchtime?'

Emmy swallowed. 'Yes, I did.'

'With Edward.' It was a statement not a question.

'Yes.'

'How *dare* you?'

Taken by surprise by the explosion of rage, Emmy backed up against the draining-board.

'How *dare* you, Emmy? I could not believe it when Mary Louder rang to tell me she had seen you with a man outside a pub, drinking. What do you think you were doing?'

'Having a drink, Mrs Beckett.'

'I do not pay you to conduct a social life, Emmy. You are paid to look after my son. It was a thoroughly irresponsible thing to do. Edward might have caught cold. Anyway, I don't allow him near pubs.'

It was only half an hour.

Emmy thought of the countless evenings she had worked late, and the weekends she had babysat ('as a favour to us, Emmy'). Unfamiliar rage – partly at Violet's unreasonableness and partly because she had never truly appreciated until this moment how unfair people could be when their own interests were at stake – which she only just succeeded in controlling pricked underneath her skin.

'I can't trust you.' Violet was speaking in a low, dramatic voice which concealed both a real panic that Emmy was not reliable and the fear that she, the super-manager, had made a crucial misjudgement. 'Looking after a baby is a very serious thing. I *must* be able to trust you.'

How much did trust cost? Eighty pounds, a hundred pounds a week (plus tax and NI, of course)? Cheap at the price, Mrs Beckett. Violet's expression wavered under Emmy's enraged stare and, then, it dawned on Emmy that the boot was probably on the other foot: Mrs Glossy Beckett did not trust herself either.

'Who was this man? Was he a complete stranger?'

'He's . . .' well, what was Angus? Emmy explained that Angus was, at least, known to the family. Thankfully, Violet seized on the let-out (for which she had been searching): at least she would not need to resort to anything drastic and inconvenient like giving Emmy the sack.

'Listen, Emmy. I shall give you one more chance.' You bet, Emmy thought. Procuring nannies takes time. 'But,' Violet judged it best to moderate her tone, 'if I ever discover again that you have been doing this sort of thing you will have to leave.'

Perhaps I want to anyway? What do you think about that? Emmy prudently remained silent.

But a curious little pulse beat close to her heart. Hold on, it said. Emmy listened to its thuds. Of what else did it speak? Of stubbornness, a wish to give Violet as good as she gave. Of dawning feelings that would not be controlled.

'I'm sorry,' she said. 'I thought it would be all right to have a drink. I took good care of Edward.' She gave a little shrug which, more than anything, convinced Violet. 'Of course I did, Mrs Beckett.'

Violet opened the briefcase, extracted the latest edition of *Vanity Fair* and tossed it on the table. Her expression had turned remote – the sort of expression that suggested it was unfair she should be so bothered by these domestic matters. From experience, Emmy knew she had lost interest.

'Let's forget it, Emmy. In between drinks did you manage to do the shopping?'

Emmy sighed. Denied attention for so long, Edward opened his mouth and yelled.

On Saturday evening, Angus took Emmy bowling in Streatham with his mates. Violet eyed him when he turned up at the front door in black jeans and boots, said nothing by way of greeting, left him standing on the doorstep and returned to the drawing room. Jamie, however, was more forthcoming and invited Angus into the hall and made conversation until Emmy appeared from the top of the house.

'Have a good time,' said Jamie.

Emmy cast him a look from under her lids and nodded. He was smiling good-naturedly and without the least side.

'Stuck-up bitch,' said Angus, not quite out of earshot of the front garden. 'I wouldn't give her house room.'

Because she was nervous and wanted it to be all right with Angus, Emmy found herself agreeing, although she now realized there were some things about Violet that she quite liked and – almost – admired.

Feminine solidarity can take many forms but perhaps its strongest manifestation is of one woman for another who has been betrayed by a man. Emmy was not at all sure about Jamie and his lunches with Mrs Valour. It was possible that her own newly sensitized feelings were leading her astray, but still she wondered. It was only an instinct, the prod of a half-formed thought, but she sensed a feeling between them, the more surprising for being so unlikely. Unfurling her wings in the world as she was, Emmy had yet to trust her judgement.

She looked back to Number 6 from which sounds of Mozart's *Così Fan Tutte* were issuing. It looked so solid and painted, a cradle for clean shelves, beeswaxed furniture and ironed sheets. The empty home in Dainton hovered in her mind, a boiled, sterilized repository of her childhood, until Angus dropped a gloved hand on to her knee and Emmy forgot everything. Rankled by Violet's attitude, Angus did a lot of accelerator revving, the van rattled noisily and he drew out of the parking space with as much noise as he could muster.

Angus's mates, Ted, Bill and a six-footer introduced as Nails, were distinguished by their earrings, ranks of them, mounting in glittering concordances to the outer reaches of their earlobes. Emmy was fascinated. Serious male plumage had not reached Andover. *One* earring, perhaps . . .

Cherry and Sal, the girls, did not wear jewellery at all, apart from plaited-wool friendship bracelets. Their uniform, however, matched the boys'. Black jeans or leggings, T-shirts, a thicker shirt worn on top, very often tartan, and cropped hair. One of them, Sal, was luscious.

Emmy trembled inside her Doc Martens and cursed the day she had ever heard the word 'perm'. These girls were so sharp, so icily streetwise. So London – and she was so not.

They eyed her up and down, these Juliets and Portias fo the streets, decided she was a negligible threat and proceeded, in the main, to ignore her. Not surprised, Emmy was gratified, nevertheless, to discover that her bowling skills more than matched theirs.

'Not bad,' said Sal critically at the end of the third round. Underneath her grey T-shirt, her pointed breasts swayed like palms in a tropical breeze and her lips, like plump sofas, glistened.

Emmy permitted herself a mental tick, and then intercepted a look between Angus and Sal, a sultry exchange into which was mixed anticipation. Her satisfaction vanished and a cocktail of terror, jealousy and sick apprehension slipped into her bloodstream. What on earth was she doing here? Here they were, the Sals, Cherrys and Emmys, displayed like buds on the apple tree for the hovering bullfinch, and she reminded herself what happens when the bullfinch has been and gone: no apples.

At the end of the game, Angus came over and slipped his arm round Emmy's shoulders. 'Fancy Indian or Chinese?' His eyes slid from one girl to the other, charm and sex and, yet, a kind of easy tenderness, mixed into his face. He could so easily have been repellent, but he wasn't – he wasn't at all.

Emmy did not like curry, which she tried to hide over the baskets of naan bread and Chicken Vindaloo. The restaurant into which they had piled was cheap, crowded, hot and smoky. The air was like damp cling-film and moisture glistened on the green flock wallpaper. Emmy swallowed a mouthful of chicken and regretted it.

Sal eyed her. 'Not up to your standards?'

Emmy endeavoured to answer, a tricky procedure if the

roof of your mouth has been blasted off. Meanwhile, Angus focused on Sal's bosom.

'You eat enough to sink a tanker,' he said.

Sal preened. 'I can take it.'

Yes, well. Emmy shot a covert look at Sal's Titian hair which owed more to Body Shop than to nature.

'If you like it,' said Angus, and leant over towards Emmy. 'Had enough?'

Sal lit up a cigarette and blew smoke in Angus's direction. 'Where to next?'

Next? Emmy had been cherishing fond thoughts of her hot-water bottle and her silent, unshared bed.

'I think it's time I got back,' she said, and reached for her fringed bag. She forced herself to look into Angus's face. 'That was great. See you all around.'

'Don't be stupid,' he said. 'You don't know your way back. Stick with us. I'll see you right.'

They piled into the van and hit the South Circular with a screech of brakes and made for Brixton. The disco there had a couple of fridges mounted above the entrance and the queue to get in was mainly black, funky and noisy. Getting down from the van, Emmy shivered.

Her mental horizons were shifting bewilderingly.

Inside the disco, the noise drilled holes in eardrums. Sal hijacked the opportunity to collar Angus and a dazzling show of body language went into operation. Angus was all male and no male could possibly resist the delights being flaunted – practically unveiled – in front of him.

Keeping a tight clutch on her bag, Emmy watched them dancing amid the shrieks and screams, the coloured lights and smoke-wreathed figures. A dream coalesced, tantalized and splintered, and she was left jolted by shocks of jealousy accompanied by an equally coruscating current of desire.

When Angus disengaged himself from Sal to claim Emmy, he was met by a blank, wooden face.

'I want to go,' Emmy reiterated, her face paled by the light into a ghost's. 'Point me in the right direction. I'll walk.'

'Running away, Emmy?'

There was no point in not being honest. 'Yes.'

The funny thing was, Emmy was sure Angus understood.

'I'll drive you,' said Angus, and flicked her under her chin. 'You are stupid, you know.'

'What about the others?'

Angus glanced briefly over his shoulder at the heaving mass and Sal sent him a smouldering look. 'I'll come back.'

For some while, Emmy had been convinced that a fox was living in the garden of Number 6. A flash of red, a bark in the night, the scatter of refuse round the dustbins, a hint of feralness in the air: these were clues she had quickly picked up. She spent several nights subsequent to the bowling outing watching out of the window in the small hours.

If she was not sure about the fox, there was no doubt about the pair of grey squirrels which had colonized the scrubby bit at the end of the garden. Manky they were, and cheeky chappies, who danced and spun along the garden fences like a chorus line.

During the day, Emmy watched them, and envied their busyness, and the manner in which they cheeked cats who juddered with aggression but who had grown too large and indolent from tinned catfood to do anything about it.

One of the pair had hidden a treasure under the lavender bush, a nut perhaps, and, tail at full mast, he returned again and again to root under the spiky grey branches. Emmy watched him. He knew better than to find what he was seeking.

Angus had bent over her that Saturday night – no, Sunday morning by then – when he delivered her back, and Emmy, suborned by her longings, had raised her face blindly to his. Then she turned abruptly away. She might not have been wise enough to keep her feelings under control, but she knew enough to hide them.

Perhaps it was as well that she was not going to find out what lay behind Angus's golden head and tawny skin for that might spoil the magic, too.

CHAPTER THIRTEEN

'WHEN, PRUE?' JAMIE ASKED.
    When?

Jane's long summer exeat usually coincided with Max's fishing week in Scotland. It was a pity, but there it was. In Max's calendar, the date shared equal rank with his shooting days in autumn, both as immutable as Christmas. Prue had long since accepted these slots in the year and, after the first few occasions when she was inclined to feel abandoned, looked forward to them as a break in the routine and a chance to rearrange her mental furniture.

The departure was generally accompanied by last-minute panics and late-night searches for fishing equipment and the fittings for the special picnic basket Max had inherited from his father. Each year, Prue meant to earmark a place in the attic for them where they could be easily located, and each year failed to do so.

She was up early making egg sandwiches and decanting coffee and tea into the old-fashioned Thermoses from the picnic set. With their echo from another age, she had grown fond of them. They were solid and did not let you down. Prue chopped mint on to the egg, admired the colours, added mayonnaise and spread the mixture on the bread.

Dressed in his favourite corduroys and the jersey that suited him so much better than the city suit, Max seemed pale and preoccupied. Prue put it down to the restless night both of them had spent, which neither had acknowledged to the other. Admitting to insomnia in a marriage was an intimacy only possible when it was going well, she thought.

What was unusual was Prue's lack of enthusiasm to sort it out.

Max kissed Jane goodbye and instead of saying, 'Look after your mother,' as he always did, held his daughter tight and said nothing.

'Bring me back some Edinburgh rock,' she muttered into his shoulder. Jane liked its colours better than its taste, and it was a request that she knew would not give her father any bother to carry out.

Max released Jane who, sensing that he was a little troubled, assumed an expression that suggested goodbyes were an awful bore. Max looked as though he had already departed mentally, and he said in a manner that warned Prue not to fuss, 'I'll phone when I reach Edinburgh.'

'Have a good time.' Prue handed Max the fishing bag and the picnic.

Much later, mulling over events, Prue remembered that Max had not kissed her goodbye.

'So what shall we do with ourselves before we go up to London, Janey?' she asked, as they sat down to lunch *à deux*.

Jane had spent the morning huddled into the sofa listening to the radio but she perked up at the question and expounded at length on several ideas. These involved an outing to the Romsey Rapids, a definitive update of her wardrobe and an excursion to buy a new pair of roller blades.

'What about taking a picnic tea on the bikes?' suggested Prue, warming to a mental vision of mother and daughter idling down flower-studded country lanes. 'We could do a day trip somewhere.'

Jane looked at Prue as if her mother had only recently alighted on Planet Earth. 'No way, Mum. It isn't warm enough.'

Prue propped her elbows on the table and cupped her chin in her hands. 'No way,' she conceded.

Jane was quiet for thirty seconds or so. 'I've got some prep to do,' she said, and chewed a tiny mouthful of pork chop. Prue had finished hers and sat waiting. Then she asked. 'Mum, what's adultery?'

Prue fought to control her expression for, quick as any reflex, guilt mastered her stiffened jaw and widened eyes. *Guilt for what she had not yet done.* Unfamiliar with it, untutored in dealing with it, unsure of its properties (did it always stretch, lie, distort?) Prue's panic made her forget that connections did not necessarily exist between things even if they appear to do so. Nevertheless, she *was* familiar with the teaching which held that the distinction between the intention to commit a sin and actually doing so was negligible.

'What *do* you mean, darling?'

'We've been discussing it in RE.' Jane seemed impatient with her mother's slowness. 'You know in the Bible, the story of the woman taken in adultery.'

Prue subsided. 'Oh, her,' she said rapidly. 'I'd forgotten.' Normally, Prue took seriously her parental duty to explain. Today she gave only the briefest of outlines.

Jane considered what Prue had told her. 'Wasn't she stupid, Mum, to get herself into trouble?'

Prue fiddled with her glass of water. 'It's not always straightforward, Jane. You will discover that as you grow older.

Think of when you get into trouble at school. You don't mean to but you do.'

As a defence it was not notable. Prue knew that. But at the final count, the matter was simple. You either did something, or you did not.

'But, you see,' said her daughter, pushing away her half-finished plate. 'In a funny way I do want to get into trouble. It's more fun.'

Framed in the window, the beech tree at the end of the garden swayed in counterpoint to the *Prunus autumnalis* which was now fledged in green.

'Bloody hell,' Prue said.

'Mum! You tell me not to swear.'

Prue leant over the table and caught her daughter's hand. Its slightly grubby arrangement of skin and bones lay trustingly in hers and, more than any theory, had the power to make Prue stop in her tracks: to reconsider what can be disgorged from the most ordered and ordinary lives once they become muddled and out of control.

Prue stroked the hand resting in hers. 'You, my girl, are becoming bossy.'

A trip to *Phantom of the Opera* and roller blades it was, the latter resulting in a crop of bruises to which Jane would not allow Prue to apply arnica because she wanted to display the war wounds back at school.

The plan was to spend two nights at Austen Road, which would allow time for the show and, as Prue explained to Jane, for research in the London Library. Jane enjoyed the show and so, in a masochistic fashion, did Prue, who found herself biting her lip at the spectacle of the Phantom's agonized, racked desire. But such was the decibel level that she emerged from their fabulously expensive seats into the cool night feeling as though she had been hit on the head with a hammer.

'Brilliant,' said Jane happily. 'I love it when it's sad.'

Later, Prue lay in the freshly painted spare room and listened (as Emmy was doing) to the bark of Emmy's urban fox. Max, fortified by several whiskies, would be asleep in his hotel lapped by mountains, shadows and the rainsoaked Highland air. Sleep peacefully, she willed him across the miles, and felt the burn of her treachery work its way down her body.

She endeavoured to concentrate on the things that mattered: the WI meeting, the manure that needed to be dug into the vegetable patch, Jane's half-term report. What had Molly been going on about? Ah, yes. How dreadful it was that the parish magazine had been requisitioned for the debate over fox-hunting, which was rapidly reaching flashpoint. These were the bricks that built a life. Prue's fingers searched for the edge of the pillowcase. They mattered and should not be carelessly overlooked. But, faced with a solid, undistinguished municipal building or the breathtaking achievement of Michelangelo's Sistine Library, or the grey-tiled fantasies of Joan's jewel-like, turreted cities, it was difficult not to turn away and seek out the beauty of the soaring line.

The unhunted fox in the London garden barked again and Prue dozed on and off. Animals were safer in cities than in the country. No one would dream of setting hounds on the scabby, bone-thin scavenger rooting in the dustbins set out like plastic tombstones along the street.

Along the beige-carpeted landing lay Jamie. She pictured him sprawled under the duvet in the pyjamas that, in a strange anticipation of intimacy, she had washed several times. Prue imagined listening to his breathing and with a curious finger traced the outline of his body.

She hovered. She watched. She breathed kisses over the silent body and tasted cool, silky flesh under her hot mouth, and tried to sleep.

The next morning, she woke early and dressed in an emerald green silk shirt and jeans. She brushed her hair, which she was allowing to grow longer, tied it back and put on a pair of new pearl earrings which were large enough to make a statement about her confidence and finances.

A Woman Taken in Adultery?

Leaving Jane to fuss happily over Edward with Emmy, she assembled her notebooks and said goodbye. Eyes shining, Jane glanced up at her mother. 'Take care, Mum.'

Prue hesitated, and then let herself out of the door.

The foliage in the gardens and on the trees was lit by an emerging sun, and pollution wrapped the road in a thick nap. The tube was hot, slow and littered with discarded morning papers. Someone had been sick and the combination of vomit and sickly sweet disinfectant made Prue gag. She picked up a free newspaper . . . Dan Quayle was criticizing a television soap for depicting a main character giving birth to an illegitimate baby, and was also of the opinion that the Los Angeles riots were due to a 'poverty of values'.

Poverty of values. Prue cast aside the paper.

At the entrance to the London Library, she bumped into Adrian League, one of Max's colleagues who had retired the previous year, a fellow fishing enthusiast. Then he had looked eighty. Now he looked a brisk sixty or so in studiedly casual clothes.

'Goodness,' she said. 'You look twenty—' and realized she was being tactless. 'You look wonderful.'

Adrian had never been one for small talk and got to the point at once. 'What are you doing here, Prue?'

'Research.' She felt she did not sound as convincing as she

should. Adrian's eyebrows lifted, the implication being that the last thing he associated with Prue was research. That annoyed her.

'Yes,' she said. 'I'm writing a biography of Joan of Arc. Practically finished, in fact.'

Adrian drew Prue to one side and his expression sharpened. 'Have you got a publisher?'

It was a question that worldly people always asked Prue, and Adrian was very worldly.

'Yes,' she lied, and smiled sweetly. 'In fact a couple of publishers are vying for the rights.' She popped the cherry on the iced bun and completed her perdition. 'I have to make up my mind very soon. Good, isn't it?'

Afterwards in the concealing recesses of the history shelves, Prue's cheeks burned. Not having a track record in lies – hers tended to rebound – she was amazed by the speed and determination with which she had resorted to them. Nevertheless, Adrian's superciliousness had won him a poke in the ribs and she had enjoyed watching him struggle to readjust his expression. How she was going to extricate herself from it she didn't know. Did it matter?

All these lies.

Yes, no, yes? She supposed they did, otherwise she was removing the base on which she had pitched the tent of her life.

Prue bent her head over the books. Every so often she looked up. The seconds walked slowly past. She smelt dust, assorted scents from the women in the room, a whiff of someone unwashed, felt her own warmth. The books on the shelves seemed so solid, so large, so formed, and their dun, rich colours deep and mysterious.

At twelve thirty, Prue packed up her books into a large, reinforced plastic bag that bit into her fingers and made her way into Oxford Street.

Oxford Street was full of women carrying similar plastic bags and similar secrets, a feminine conspiracy silting down layers to create a petrified forest of lies.

At Great Cumberland Street, she turned right, walked north to a hotel set back in a crescent, and halted by the entrance, which was spruced up with a red and white striped awning. A further step forward was required.

Or a turnaround and retreat.

Why hadn't adultery just happened? It was so much easier to be dragged out of turquoise waters on a Caribbean beach and ravished. Or to be thrown down into summer hay. Or to be woken at midnight and told by the equivalent of the man with the box of Milk Tray that you had no option but to yield.

Setting your face north up Great Cumberland Street was harder, an operation edged around with the mundane and small decisions that made it unbearable and took away the joyous, glamorous elements that had made it inviting in the first place.

Then why do it?

The bag was making Prue's arm ache and her back twinged. Strands of hair stuck to her cheek and her tights felt damp around the waistband. She did not feel *fatale*, but shaky and unconvincing. According to novels, and to Kate who listened to tales from other women, other women did this sort of thing with style. Or they should. There was no point in transgressing if you did it meagrely.

I can't do this. The traffic beat on in its uncaring fashion and Prue fled back down the street. She stopped at the first junction and looked back over her shoulder to the red and white stripe.

If you are hungry, why don't you eat? said a voice in her head.

Prue breathed in the traffic fumes, tasted sulphur and

carbon monoxide and felt them stream through her blood, alongside the slippery ache for Jamie. Oh, yes, she couldn't deny she *was* hungry.

Jamie.

Max?

Two minutes later she was standing in the hotel entrance, a depressing mixture of cream paint and fake crystal lights.

'Can I help you?'

The clerk at the reception desk was a brown person: eyes and hair of the same colour, and no doubt his thoughts were brown. Prue instantly took against his expression which she imagined combined knowingness and contempt. Because – the voice in her head had switched tack – you are not the first awkward-looking woman to hover in a strange hallway, and certainly not the last.

She declined the offer to be shown upstairs. Number 35, first floor. Prue made for the lift and then changed her mind and trod up the stairs.

Why did this have to be so obvious?

The anchor pattern in the carpet transfixed her, mainly because she kept her eyes fixed on the floor. When she raised them, it was to read the numerals 3 and 5. Her heartbeat jumbled with anchors flashing across her vision.

Jamie was waiting. Two seconds after Prue knocked, he opened the door and she slid in.

'I feel like something out of those made-for-telly American movies,' she said in a tone that did not sound like her.

The door was of a cheap composite wood and it shuddered as Jamie closed it. A DO NOT DISTURB notice swung from a peg on the back with instructions on how to use the fire escape if necessary. Prue found herself reading it.

'Prue,' said Jamie who had not touched her, 'are you here or not?'

Holding tight to the plastic bag, she turned. After a moment, she said, 'I'm here.'

Jamie took the bag from her. 'Are you frightened?'

She nodded. Jamie dropped the bag on the floor and stood quietly waiting. Then Prue knew why she was in this fake hotel. It was lust. Lust to possess the bones, skin and feel of Jamie. To have his flesh bury itself in hers.

He smiled. 'Chintz again.' He indicated the bedspread and she smiled back.

'That's easy.' Prue went over to the bed and rolled up the bedspread and tried to stuff it inside the wardrobe. The material was slippery and refused to go quietly and she found herself laughing.

'Diary of a chambermaid,' she said, and sat down on the denuded bed.

Jamie stood over her and she looked up at him.

'Why, Jamie?' she asked. 'Violet is so new to you.'

He raised his hands and spread the fingers wide in a gesture of non-comprehension. 'It wasn't a process. It just was.'

She looked down at her own clenched, shaking hands.

'You can change your mind, Prue.' Jamie pushed his hair back.

He looked pale and washed-out – as if this whole thing was too much. It seemed to Prue that Jamie was looking right through her, and she saw, too, that his hands also were shaking. She concentrated on those tiny indicators, for it meant they were equal. It meant that neither was able to do this lightly.

'But please,' he added.

At one point Prue shrank for she did not want her imperfections to be catalogued. Daylight is not prejudiced, and there was nowhere to hide the slack skin at the top of her thighs or the stretch marks on her breasts. Not that she had minded these stigmata, particularly the stretch marks because they were a result of having Jane and branded her as a mother, but she did not want to spoil things for Jamie. She wanted to save him from the corrosions of her femininity. She wanted to give him a perfect body.

After that, Prue did not think very much. And after that, as they unfamiliarly entwined, Prue gave up the pretence that it was only lust. Lust had been left behind in the cathedral at Winchester. It was worse, far worse. For what she – used and smarting – knew was love.

Jamie's arm tightened across her body and his hand swept as light as sand running through an egg-timer across her quietened body.

'Prue,' he said with wonder in his voice. 'Prue.'

Violet liked to eat dinner at eight thirty sharp. Jane, she had informed Prue, was too young to eat with them and Prue had not argued. At half past six she fed Jane pizza and packed her off to bed with *Goodnight Mr Tom*, a favourite book that went everywhere.

In the kitchen, Violet was making a mung bean salad and something unspeakable with tofu. Prue tried not to shudder and rolled a glass of Australian chardonnay between her fingers. The idea of food made her queasy.

'Tell me how you met Jamie,' she asked, needing to say his name.

Violet swivelled and directed an unfriendly look at her stepmother. 'I thought I'd told you.'

'Not properly.'

A piece of tofu quivered at the end of Violet's knife. Prue watched it, fascinated.

'It's funny how you recognize people.' Violet tossed the

salad. 'I was having lunch at the Four Seasons in New York.' She paused for Prue to register the right degree of impressedness. 'Jamie was sitting in one of the corner tables. I took one look at him and thought: He will do.' Handfuls of tossed salad rose and fell in a green landslide into the bowl. 'He says he took two looks. The rest was simple. I suppose we're the same kind of people.'

'You've dropped some lettuce,' said Prue and pointed to the floor.

Violet retrieved it. 'Of course, Jamie being in the Four Seasons helped because I knew he was the kind of person I wanted. Seeing him in a Donut Diner drinking through a straw would have been different.'

Violet's honesty was sometimes startling. And, Prue acknowledged to the chardonnay, admirable.

She drank more wine. All of us have a dark side, she thought, but it is fortunate to encounter it earlier in life. The reason? If you stumble on your rotten side in, say, your forties, you are unprepared.

Prue went upstairs to check on Jane who was reading in bed.

'Are you having a nice time?' Jane asked pointedly without looking up.

Prue sat down. The anti-Violet axis was alive and well. 'Sorry about the early bed, darling. But I wish you'd eaten all the pizza. Violet was put out.' A trace of moisture on Jane's face alerted her. 'Have you been crying?'

Jane shrugged. 'Not really.'

'Sure? You can tell me.'

'It's nothing,' said Jane angrily. Her wet eyes bored into her mother. 'You look odd.'

Prue swept a hand over her face. 'What sort of odd?'

'Odd, that's all.' Jane chucked her book on to the floor where it lay, a broken-backed reproach.

'*Don't* do that.' Prue was extra sharp. 'You know you don't treat books like that.'

Jane pulled the sheet up around her face and said, 'Sorry', in such an offhand manner that Prue wanted to spank her.

'If this is what London does to you,' she told her daughter, 'then we won't be coming back.'

Unexpectedly, Jane struggled to hold back tears. 'You're not so nice yourself.'

Stung, Prue clicked out the light and went downstairs to eat tofu and mung beans.

Violet had laid the dining-room table and lit candles. Jamie poured glasses of wine and, outside, the evening dimmed to grey and opal. A white clematis was reflected, pale and thoroughbred, in the dusk from a neighbour's garden and fixed itself in Prue's stimulated imagination – innocence retreating as the dark pulled it further and further away.

The wine played tricks on her body, stretched by nerves and flooded with adrenalin, and sent a rush to her brain. There she sat, suffused by the relief of being defenceless against emotion, and drenched in desire, opposite the woman she had just betrayed. She drank her wine, watched Jamie and her flesh pricked and burned with love.

Across the table, Jamie ate and drank and occasionally looked directly into Prue's grey eyes and she knew, without question, there was no going back.

As she and Jane waited by the ticket barrier at Waterloo for the Dainton train, Prue constructed a pattern of departure.

First the cluster around the notice-board, followed by an eddy towards the platforms. Then, a whitewater rapid of last-minute passengers who knew the form, succeeded by the desperate dash of those who did not.

Girls in short skirts, opaque tights and high heels, carrying *Bella*s, *Best*s and *Hello!*. Men wearing mackintoshs over Burton suits. City slickers in Gucci loafers or the more solid-looking solicitor types in a three-piece pin-stripe. Women in Barbours carrying Harrods' bags and overlarge brown leather handbags, relics from the seventies. Prue was surprised by how many men were eating sweets.

The carriage filled up within minutes, rustling with paper and snatches of conversation. Flashes of colour, movement and smells: scent, aftershave, sweat and bad breath.

Hands clasped in her lap, Prue looked out on to the emptying platform. A vast, surf-crested tide of feeling roared in her head and swept her away.

'Sorry about last night, Mum.' Jane tucked her hand under her mother's elbow. 'Thanks for taking me to London.'

CHAPTER FOURTEEN

RAIN SWEPT DOWN THE GLEN IN SHEETS AND WRAPPED Max in a dripping blanket. It had that special soft texture of Highland rain associated with skin creams and expensive bottled water, and Max raised his face to the sky and allowed it to stream down his face.

It was not the sort of gesture in which he usually indulged, and he hoped that Peter Broughton, fishing further down the bank, had missed it. He checked the clouds: cumuli nimbi were stacked further to the west with glimpses of blue showing between them. Meanwhile, the rainclouds overhead were thinning, which meant the rain would stop as suddenly as it had started.

Max liked to think of himself as an expert on Highland weather. Years – how many? – of observing it first-hand gave him grounds for this harmless piece of back-patting. All those holidays. All those years lodged in his memory.

As predicted the rain was easing, and the noise of water hitting grass gradually ceased. Apart from the murmur of the river sliding between its banks, silence reclaimed their spot. The silence of solitary sky, earth, rocks and the bleached bones of animals.

Max's silences could be equally terrifying, so much so that, sometimes in their grip, they frightened even him. They were a habit acquired during a childhood of watching adults behave badly and, like all habits, proved half relief, half burden.

Once he had learnt the knack of retreat, it was easy. Silence is a good weapon and, in using it, the wielder conveys all manner of power and self-knowledge. The relief of turning inward, of setting the face against the misery of the dormitory or playing-field, of being bullied and tear-stained (and, later, a man with a spoilt marriage and a successful, but not brilliant, career) and moving to a quiet, sunlit interior landscape, there to crouch and lick wounds.

No panacea remains indefinitely. Bacteria mutate to combat penicillin, ampicillin and trimethoprim. So, the retreat into silence became, as Max's life progressed, less of a life-saver and more of a monster that controlled him. Certainly, to remain silent in the office, where making a noise is essential, was not a wise tactic, and Max's comparative lack of advancement could be ascribed, in part, to this unwillingness to make enough noise.

Helen tumbled to that early on. Coward, she taunted. Why don't you say what you really think? On this, of all points, Helen was justified because she never scrupled to hold back on her own opinions.

Typically, Prue was kinder and sought out the reasons. Please tell me what you're thinking, she had begged him six months into their marriage, after a two-day period of Max barely speaking. (They had disagreed over where to take their holiday.) How can I understand otherwise?

You can't, Max had wished to say. No one can understand anyone else. The secret quarries of the mind are just that. Neither do I wish to be helped.

No?

Prue had helped him, lovingly and carefully. Although Max would not, perhaps, admit it, that was why he had married her. It was not Prue's fault, either, that Max had learnt the art of survival in much tougher hands. In those days, Max found it difficult to accept that trust and partnership could flourish between men and women. Neither, at that stage in their infant marriage, was Prue quite wise enough to point out that if you assume the worst it becomes impossible to accept the best. But they had learnt together.

Max began to pack away his fishing equipment. He was beginning to feel the effects of being older. It mattered less that his career had not taken him to the top – and for that release he was thankful. Frustration and envy were not good bedfellows. But, from time to time, it concerned him that he no longer minded so much about behaving well. In other words, he had become like his father.

And here, wooed by the air and the drama of the mountains the impress of his parentage had particular sharpness, the Scottish Highlands, fishing, the annual summer holiday at Northwater House having been one of the gorier battlegrounds of his parents' marriage. The panicked odour of dying fish and fresh blood cracked from their heads on stones, the sting of a midge bite, damp clothes, the acrid tang of peat soil were memories that dripped constantly over the line between the past and the present . . .

'What are you doing, Max?' The voice came out of that past, peremptory and demanding of an answer.

'Nothing, Father.'

'You must be doing something. And if not, why not? Idle blighter. Help pack up.'

Max's thirteen-year-old self had been watching the play of light on the pool formed by a conjunction of rocks and the bridge footings where trout – according to a notice in the guesthouse – lay with the express purpose of impaling themselves on the fisherman's hook. So far this afternoon it appeared that the deathwish had deserted the fish and his father was leaving in disgust.

His father's five-o'clock-shadowed face was darkened by irritation. 'Buggers. I've a good mind to demand my money back.'

In the tundra of post-war austerity, money was not a word to be taken lightly and its value was beaten daily into Max. He thought of the scene that might ensue and closed his eyes. *Please, no.*

This summer the weather on the Ardnamurchan peninsula had been unpredictable: blazing hot one day, sodden the next. Today it was muggy and a storm-cloud of midges rose from the river. Max felt the sweat spring across the ridge in his back and soak into the waistband of his grey flannel shorts. (Don't get them dirty, dear.) Beyond father and son rose the nursery slopes of the mountain, tender green and brown, and, above them, the curlews circled in the breathless hush.

'Get on with it,' bellowed his father.

Max hauled himself to his feet and they stowed away the equipment. A folding army stool (which Max still used), the cumbersome picnic basket, huge mackintoshes stiffened with age, a tin of peppermints, whisky and a battered tin which held the flies. He sighed. Holidays were supposed to be noisy, jolly affairs with campfires, paperchases and fry-ups in the evening.

With a great deal of noise, William Beckett tried to man-oeuvre the Rover out of a mud patch in which he had, foolishly, parked it. (He was the kind of person who said, 'Rubbish,' when warned of obstacles.) The Rover stuck and Max piled out of the passenger seat and set his weedy body to shoving. The wheels churned. Mud splattered over the car body – and his shorts.

'Can't *think* what's wrong with the car,' said his father when Max climbed silently back in.

On the way back to their dull guesthouse, they passed a young woman trudging along the road with her shopping. She had a young, Celtic-pale face and hips that swung to the rhythm of her walk.

'I could . . .' said Max's father, slowing down, an expression contorting his features that Max only recognized when he was older as that of lust. 'I'd . . .'

Max turned his head and stared out of the window.

His mother was waiting at the guesthouse in which they stayed each summer. It was a mean-windowed, stone-walled place dedicated to the suppression of high spirits. Not that Max possessed those in abundance, but he was young and, sometimes, the hunger to run and shriek, or merely laugh loudly, tore at him. But he knew better than to indulge it.

On seeing him, his mother attacked him for dirtying his shorts, her air of permanent injury sharpened by having done nothing all day. To compensate herself for marrying Max's father, Antonia took refuge in order. She possessed four pre-war tweed skirts, rotated weekly, and a dozen twin-sets, which were worn according to the season. Today, she sported lime-green – this alerted observers to the fact it was summer – and a string of grey river pearls which reminded Max of teeth.

'It's been a long day,' she said when they assembled in the dining room with the other guests for herring high tea. 'I thought you were never coming back.'

'Bloody waste of time,' said Max's father, camouflaging the first of many whiskies with the water glass. 'We've been bloody had this year. No bloody fish at all.'

Antonia winced visibly and a faint pink tinged her complexion. 'I wish you wouldn't be so coarse, William.'

William's cold eyes raked the dim figure of his wife. It was not fair, but it so happened that Antonia was sitting in a light that showed her to the worst advantage. She looked more than usually worn and lustreless, not from overwork, for she lived a privileged life, but from disappointment. Deliberately, Max's father raised his glass to his lips and Max shuddered for he knew that gesture.

'And I wish you had breasts like a white dove,' his father articulated, 'instead of the scrag end you have hanging off your chest.' He leant forward, paused and added in a a whisper, 'And the wit to fuel a man's needs.'

'Oh, my God.' Antonia looked wildly round the prim dining room. The words fell like stones into the dampish air reminding the occupants of unspeakable things they preferred to ignore. The colonel and his wife at the next table stared like wooden replicas at the window sill on which a dead fly reposed.

'Oh, my God,' whispered Antonia. 'I'll die of shame.'

. . . After that scene, Max hardly spoke for three days. Along with the silences – which got mixed up with subject of sex – his hatred of porridge and herrings were acquired at Northwater House.

If porridge and herrings were banished from Max's agenda, it was odd that fishing remained. Each year, he swore he would no longer indulge in the stupendous expense, but back he went to stand for hours in the wind and the rain, or bucket about in a boat and returned with a fresh complexion to tell fisherman's tales. I can't understand the attraction, Prue complained. The point is, Max answered, usually through a cold contracted from a Highland dousing, neither can I.

As Max drove back south with the smell of fish perfuming the car, damp clothes and muddy boots piled in the back and a selection of fishy parcels wrapped in brown paper, he wrestled with a mental picture that would not go away. It was of soft brown hair blowing in the draught of grimy air created by an incoming train, and a woman wearing a red scarf outlined against a hoarding advertising British Telecom.

He put his foot down and the car speeded past the blue motorway signs, past the rash of ugly buildings in the 'style motorway' (which favoured clock towers and red paint) through slices of wet, lonely countryside, past villages hanging on the edge of survival and the squat buildings of Britain's industries. Max crouched over the wheel – no car really catered for his height – and aimed to be home by late afternoon.

Jane would be back at school and Prue, he knew, would be working in the library.

Prue's desk was in the drawing room and forbidden to everyone. Her insistence that no one else touched it was the only truly tiresome thing about his wife that Max could think of. He teased her sometimes as to what the desk contained. Now, as he entered the empty house and abandoned his luggage in the hall, Max wished he had not.

The desk was made of rosewood and smelt of the polish that Prue favoured. On the mantelpiece beside it the tortoise-shell clock ticked noisily. An antique blue and white plate they had bought together in Hay-on-Wye hung in its accustomed place on the wall. Dust motes swirled in the afternoon sun which spread a glossy light over a pink and white china ballerina on the desk. It was minus a hand which had been Sellotaped to the tutu. A message in Jane's handwriting was also stuck across the ballerina. 'Don't touch. Very, very precious.' Max grimaced. The ballerina, acquired after seeing a performance of *Swan Lake* in London, was one of Jane's very few girlie manifestations.

Your father is unspeakable.

Your mother is a fucking desert.

My mother.

My father.

My wife.

My daughters.

Myself: a full bag of neuroses, disguised by six decades of living, worn corduroys, tartan handkerchiefs, aftershave, good shoes, a taste for biography (the Richard Ellman was *so* good) and a greed for malt whisky. That is me.

Max stretched out his hand. Like Jamie, his life had been rendered uncomfortable by the effects of the bomb in the City, and the idea of it preyed on his mind. Thus, as he made the gesture, he equated it to the terrorist's action when he or she first pulled a pin or depressed a plunger. His fingers tensed. Once the action was done the result became the only thing that could matter. From then on, normal restraints were in the past, and it was not possible to go back.

One drawer was devoted to bills . . . Sainsbury's, Fenez of Farnham, Marks and Spencer at Marble Arch – Max frowned at that one. There was an invitation to contribute to a pension fund. Max's frown remained in place. He had, he thought, discussed their financial arrangements carefully with Prue, and seen to it that she was provided for when he died. More than anything else, the idea that Prue was thinking independently of him financially suggested that she was evading his control.

No, Max did not mean control – that was just a slip of the mental tongue. Control was not the word he wished to apply to his marriage.

The second drawer contained a mish-mash. A letter from an old au pair bewailing her new lot and could she come back and work for *dear* Mrs Valour whose good heartiness (*sic*) she so admired and wanted to service (*sic*) again. The postscript to this touching appeal informed the reader that she was only being paid thirty pounds a week compared to the forty-five Prue had doled out. There was a photograph of Jane dressed as a Merrie Man for the school play. A key with no label. A broken watch. A tiny white hospital bracelet which read:

Daughter of Prudence Valour, 24.7.81 at 15.26 hours.

Max's hand shook a little.

Three is a number common to fable and fairy stories. It holds magical properties, the key to structures, the promise of spiritual reward. Three times a prince endeavours to win his lady. The third and youngest son is the one blessed with strength and success. The third daughter is the one marked out by Fate. In 'The Tinder Box' the soldier is asked to choose between copper, silver and gold.

In the third drawer Max discovered the following in Prue's handwriting on a folded sheet of paper. 'I have thought and thought about us and I regret . . .' This had been crossed out and underneath was written, 'One is ready to do anything to find peace once more. I have done everything; I have sought occupations . . . That, indeed, is humiliating – to be unable to control one's thoughts, to be a slave of regret, of a memory, of a fixed and dominant idea which lords over the mind' (Charlotte Brontë to Monsieur Héger).

Underneath that Prue had also written, 'How serious and dangerous it is curiously to examine the things that are beyond one's understanding, and to believe in new things . . . and even to invent new and unusual things, for demons have a way of introducing themselves into suchlike curiosities' (admonition addressed to Joan of Arc).

It took all of Max's self-control not to crush the sheet of paper into a ball. Here, he saw in a flash, his intuition primed by his love for Prue, was the message in the bottle. The tablet of stone. As he replaced the paper where he had found it, he noticed a smear of polish on the rosewood, a curl of dust behind the china ballerina, his big, shambling figure caught in the mirror above the fireplace.

*

Articles about jealousy had sometimes appeared in Sunday newspapers and, over the years, Max had read them. He knew then from his experiences with Helen, as he knew now, that such journalism usually failed its readers. Nothing could adequately describe the sear of feeling: the isolation, the sensation of being unable to draw breath because it hurt, the shame of being jealous. Second time round was no help either. As with childbirth or injury, the mind constructs its defences and buries the sharper memory.

Max had truly believed that he had found the formula which balanced reason with emotional and physical need. He had believed that at sixty, it was possible to accept what, at twenty-five, was unacceptable and to understand the quirks of sexuality and to place them in a context to a life. To understand that these quirks could be dealt with, and tamed.

On the Sunday following his return from Scotland, Max and Prue were alone. In a further bid to help Jane, Prue had arranged for her to spend the weekend with one of her classmates who showed signs of extending friendship.

At lunch, Max said he could not finish his roast beef. Surprised, Prue looked up from hers. 'I thought you'd like a roast.'

'It's tough,' said Max, who did not normally comment on the cooking.

'Sorry, darling. Obviously, I didn't cook it very well.'

He shrugged and got to his feet. 'I'm not hungry so I won't have any pudding.'

This succeeded in astonishing Prue. 'I've made lemon meringue. Your favourite.'

There was a silence and Prue's stomach contracted. Max looked away. Prue's expression jarred on him: eyebrows slightly raised, a questioning curve to her bottom lip, the mole so marked on her skin. Once, he had imagined that her face was transparent and open. Now, he considered it the opposite.

'I'm off for a walk,' he said, and pushed back his chair with a screech.

'*Max!*'

I sounded like my father. Max paced up the hill towards the airstrip. I talked to Prue as if I was William.

Nature was not in tune with Max's feelings. It was one of those exhilarating summer days with blue sky, warm sun and a tantalizing suggestion of greater heat to come. Washed by winter and spring, colour had spread along neutral hedgerows, through the fields and along the horizon. Mallow and dog rose scattered soft pinks among the green.

As he crested the hill and encountered the breeze which always blew off the crest, Max began to cry. As he was unused to crying, it took him by surprise. He had almost forgotten how the throat ached, or how water could force its way out of the eyes and down the cheeks. He stopped to search for a handkerchief.

'Hallo, Mr Valour.'

Emmy Horton came up behind Max so noiselessly in her rubber soled Doc Martens that he jumped. Embarrassed, he turned towards her, a big, tear-stained figure and Emmy's heart contracted with pity for she recognized suffering. Without thinking, she did the only thing possible and touched him on the arm to give comfort. For a moment, they stood frozen, Emmy's hand on the waxed sleeve, and she thought he would protest at her presumption. She removed her hand.

'I thought you were in London, Emmy, with my daughter.' Max blew his nose.

'Down for the weekend,' she replied. 'Wanted to see my mum.'

Fresh air had whipped some colour into her face and her hair – from what Max remembered – had improved.

'Are they well?'

'Yes. Edward has lots of teeth now.'

'I hope my daughter isn't doing too much.'

'Oh, no,' said Emmy and, naturally, Max missed the irony.

A group of birds circled overhead and Emmy's face jerked upwards. 'Bullfinches,' she said, her tone implying that Max would know exactly what she was talking about. 'They must be nesting. They're vegetarian, you know.'

Max did not reply and Emmy felt she should move on. She dug her hands into her jacket pockets. 'Nice to see you, Mr Valour.'

At that moment, Prue came into view over the rise. 'There you are,' she called.

To Emmy's embarrassment, Max swung round 360 degrees and turned his back on his wife. Prue came to a halt.

'Max?'

Emmy looked from husband to wife uncertainly. Aha, she thought and said, 'I must go.'

'Everything all right in London?' Prue asked.

'Yes, I was telling Mr Valour here that the baby has lots of teeth.' She decided to make a run for it. 'Bye.'

Prue waited until Emmy was out of earshot before turning on Max, white with fury. 'What on earth's the matter? Why were you so rude?'

'Don't be melodramatic, Prue.'

She calculated what to say next and modified her tone. 'You've been impossible since you've got back from Scotland. I don't know what's got into you.'

Prue's voice trailed to a close. If she felt her indignation was spurious, why should Max believe it? What if, she thought, he knows? Then she thought: He does. In all her life, she had never felt fear like that which now rose in her like oil from the bore, hot, strong and choking. No, Max can't know . . . She struggled to master the fear with common sense. He can't *possibly* know.

'I think I'm owed an apology.'

'Are you, Prue?'

He stared down at his wife and realized that he did not know the woman who stood with her arms folded across her body against the breeze, a typical pose. He had made the mistake of imagining that he did – as he had imagined he had summed up Helen all those years ago.

But what Max really did not know was himself.

Suddenly, he was ashamed. Ashamed of his prying into Prue's desk, of the shaky conclusions that, as a result, had taken up residence in the raw areas of his heart, but on no real evidence – *and ashamed that he could not live up to his own precept that infidelity was merely a spasm of flesh*. And, yes, he was ashamed of the jealousy that raged inside him.

'Max.' Prue, in turn, was beginning to feel sick and shaky. 'Are you ill?'

He wanted to shout that he had had enough of everything. He had no proof, only some words on a scrap of paper – and marriage should not falter on something so flimsy.

'No,' he replied. 'I'm fine.'

'Since we are here,' said Prue after a moment, 'why don't we have a good walk?'

Still struggling with the painful shortfall between theory and its application, Max bit out, 'Oh, do shut up, Prue.'

It was then Prue gave herself away. Normally, if talked to in that manner she stormed off. Now she stood quite still for a second or two, then moved towards her husband.

'Darling, I can't bear to see you angry.' She tucked a treacherous hand into his elbow where it rested against his sleeve. 'Please don't be so cross.'

In silence, they progressed up the road towards Danebury

Rings but, since the wind had veered and was blowing sharp and cutting, they turned back before they reached it.

'I'm going to paint the outside of the house,' Max announced the following week.

'Couldn't we get someone to do it for you?' Prue was struggling with WI accounts and not very interested.

'I can manage.'

Prue shrugged. Since the weather had turned wet it was not ideal for painting, but she said nothing. Instead, she was a witness to a great deal of bucket-rattling and virtue up a ladder and could not rid herself of the notion that Max was making a point.

It was a tough, uncomfortable job and Max sometimes felt nauseous from the paint. He also fell off the ladder and bruised his right hip. Watching him limp around with tins of paint was worrying. So were the livid bruises that spread like purple mud under his skin.

He, too, refused Prue's arnica and asked that she please leave him alone.

CHAPTER FIFTEEN

MAX PHONED VIOLET ON SUNDAY NIGHT AND ASKED if he could stay with them for the week. He was sorry to impose, but his club was booked up. The reason he had to be in London, he told her, was Maastricht. Not unreasonably Violet expressed bewilderment until her father explained that the firm's senior partners were holding a brainstorming session on the latest developments in Europe and how it affected corporate law. It was also intended to aid Max to put into place his plan to tie up with other law firms in Europe, and it was vital that he attend day and night.

'Terrific,' said Violet drily when she heard the venue was Claridges. 'You won't starve.'

Glacé nougatine, garnished with praline, cream and white chocolate. A sweet, oozing picture darted and fretted across Violet's unrested mind. Violet replaced it with the steamed fish she planned for supper. She herself had been struggling to master the latest intricacies of the European open market with relation to book publishing and said, 'You can give me some tips, Dad.' Only then did she make a rapid mental review of the fridge and gritted her teeth.

When he arrived on Monday evening, Max seemed tired and to Violet, who was not given to a great deal of observation, older. The more intense for being unfamiliar, a sudden panic made her remember her father's mortality – and, come to that, her own.

THIGH-ABDUCTOR DEATH OF TWENTY-SEVEN-YEAR-OLD. MACHINE SPLITS RISING PUBLISHING STAR VIOLET BECKETT IN TWO. HUSBAND SOBS: 'SHE ONLY WANTED TO BE THIN.'

Death bobbed into Violet's mind – a grinning little mannikin who stuck out his tongue and perched on top of a toadstool. Violet could not take him seriously.

Apart from his (unhealthy, as Violet pointed out) desire for meat and two vegetables at his evening meal, Max was an undemanding guest. He played with his grandson, entered into the spirit of bathtime and talked to his daughter while she cooked.

'It's good to be here,' he said as they sat in the freshly painted, sanded, tile-decorated kitchen. 'You've made it very classy, darling.'

'Thanks, Daddy.' Violet sat down opposite her father and poured out wine. 'How's the brainstorming?'

Max hunched over his wine. 'Fine,' he said, without enthusiasm. He roused himself to offer one or two facts but, clearly, the subject was not uppermost in his mind.

Violet's attention focused on her father's hands. Big hands, with fingers bruised and slightly swollen from the DIY, flecked with age-spots. They were gentle hands, and ones she trusted above all else. Succumbing to a rare impulse, Violet leant over and held one against her cheek.

'My darling Dad,' she said as those trusted fingers stroked her hair. Father and daughter stayed thus for a moment or two and then, as ever incurably restless, she leapt up to finish the meal. He let her go and drank his wine. Max's untidy feelings for his daughters were so huge and volatile and subject to their own laws, that he could only deal with them in short, concentrated gunbursts.

It was good to have her father in the house, Violet acknowledged, as she turned off the light that night. It made her feel safe.

She turned on to her side. 'Have you had words with Daddy?' she asked Jamie drowsily. 'I noticed you avoided him.'

She felt him edge further away. 'No, why?'

'You've seemed to get on, but you've hardly said a word to him while he's been here.'

'Max understands,' said Jamie, his voice harsh-sounding in the hush. 'He knows about relaxing at the end of a day's work.'

'You selfish toad.' Violet woke up. 'It's not too much to ask for you to be polite. I'm the one that does all the work. All *you* do is dish out the drinks.'

'You've missed my point.' Jamie bunched the pillow around his ears. He tried to woo sleep. The room was too warm and he wished he had opened a second window.

After a bit, Violet resumed the conversation. 'Emmy tells me that Mary Latham has run off with a lover and left the children behind.' Her voice cut like a pair of scissors into the silence. Snip. Snip. Shaping pieces to sew up into gossip – in this case about the family further up the street. 'I've often noticed a strange chap coming out of the door when I get back at night.'

Jamie said nothing.

'Imagine,' said Violet who, to give her credit, did not normally gossip, 'Rod has refused to give her any money or allow her to see the children.'

Jamie had been alerted to Mary's activities well before Violet's announcement. He recognized the signals – a strange car outside the house, Mary's lack of sweat when he met her on a so-called early morning jog, her reluctance to mention her husband, her obvious misery and strain. In London, it was easy to run an affair – just like a business, really.

'Poor Mary.' He turned over.

'Poor *Mary*! Poor Rod.'

Jamie did not sleep well and asked himself, over and over, why he was doing what he was doing. He had had no intention of ever risking his marriage, or of disregarding the rules, or losing integrity. But all those things were happening, had happened . . . and he had made the mistake of taking them for granted, of not understanding that they required policing. Why?

The answer was simple. Love.

Love, which involves all-consuming sex, has no regard for social rules, neither does it care about timing (much) and it is unencumbered (unlike the rest of us, whether we like it or not) with morality.

At breakfast, Jamie was horrified to discover that Max was considering remaining with them over the weekend. Fortunately, Violet reckoned that enough was enough.

'You've got the midsummer fête, Dad,' she pointed out.

Max shrugged. 'Somehow I can't work up the energy. It's nice being here and I'm enjoying a break from home.'

The word 'refuge' slid into Violet's mind.

'Don't be silly,' she said, more sharply than she intended. 'Prue would be furious. You've never not done your bit.'

'Grammar,' said Jamie.

Violet whirled round. 'Shut up, Jamie.'

A vision of Dainton bathed in summer goodwill, redolent with a smell of home-baking, decked in bunting, forever sunny, took shape in the minds of the three people around the breakfast table, hand-tinted like an advertisement – and just as reliable.

200

Before he could stop himself, Jamie asked, 'Does Prue mind being left on her own?'

'No,' said Max curtly. 'I don't think so.' He looked across the litter of jams, butter and plates at his son-in-law and acknowledged the younger version of himself. He registered Jamie's charm, his intelligence (but not brilliance), his habit of smiling with all his face and his knack of focusing his full attention on whoever was speaking to him. The country was not ruled by first-class degrees, it was ruled by charm, and the application of good second-class degrees, like Jamie's.

'Boo,' said Jamie to Edward who was sitting in the high chair. Looking furious, the baby banged his spoon on the rim of his plate. Jamie laughed, reached over and pulled his son into his lap. The baby's expression rearranged itself into contentment. Jamie stroked the top of his head and kissed it.

Then Max perceived youth and confidence and recognized in Jamie a capacity for passion and feeling – elements that, if he had ever possessed them, were slipping away from himself.

Violet made a remark about Prue's homemade cakes and Jamie smiled at her. What that smile contained, Max was not sure, but he knew then he should go home and face whatever was there.

Prue was deep into fête preparations and did not have time to do more than serve Max a scratch meal on Friday evening and leave him to it. It had been a tiring week and she never slept well when left on her own.

'You look exhausted,' Molly greeted her on Saturday morning. 'And you've lost weight.'

'Good,' said Prue.

'Losing weight,' Molly poked Prue in the soft part of her hips, 'usually indicates something.'

'Surely not,' said Prue.

'Waste of money losing weight.' When Prue looked puzzled Molly amplified the statement. 'You have to buy new clothes.'

'That's one way of looking at it.' Prue dumped a load of linen tablecloths on to the nearest bench. 'Shall we get these on?'

'Max back?' Molly shook out the sheet on top of the pile.

'Yes.'

'Been away some time,' said Molly as if it had only just struck her.

Prue turned away to steady a vase stuffed with irises which was threatening to topple. Molly said nothing more.

However well aired, the village hall always retained a lingering, slightly unpleasant smell, a combination of must, used-up air and drains. By eleven o'clock, the stalls were up and overflowing into the courtyard outside. Prue congratulated herself. There had only been one altercation, between the ladies on the cake stall and the ladies on Ideas for Presents, an argument that threatened to take on Joyce Grenfell overtones, as to whom should locate where. After sensitive negotiations, Ideas for Presents was persuaded to retreat to the courtyard where it was supposed to act as a draw. Since Dainton featured in tourist pamphlets and was situated smack on the tourist ley-line between Winchester and Salisbury, and the holiday season was in swing, there would be, Prue concluded, enough potential victims to be seduced with brooches cunningly wrought from dried leaves and paper-clips.

The hall filled up with the as yet imperfectly homogenized mixture of village inhabitants. Elderly couples from the council estate and retired couples of the sherry and Rover variety. The younger generation of tired-looking mothers in leggings ('I really shouldn't but they're so comfortable'), clutching clones of daughters and accompanied by sons wearing T-shirts which bore slogans such as 'Save the Whales'. Their husbands wore olive corduroys and bright-coloured sweaters, and made jokes over oven gloves, lavender bags and tomato plants. The tourists were generally identified by their shell-suits in pear-drop colours.

Whatever, the money spent here today meant that refugees, Guide Dogs for the Blind and the Church would be beneficiaries to the tune of a couple of hundred pounds or so. Not much, thought Prue, unaccountably depressed, buying a particularly awful example of macramé and then worrying that she had been patronizing because the macramé would hit the throw-out box by the end of the day. Pity was an uncomfortable emotion and Prue avoided it wherever possible. Instead she concentrated on the broad brushstroke of the many ills in the world and the belief the money would do some good, some-where.

Max only showed up in the last stages of the fête, just before the raffle was drawn by a journalist whose claim to fame was that he once worked for a couple of months on the *Sunday Times*.

Having made a short speech about how flattered he was to be officiating, the journalist picked a ticket out of the metal drum.

'Pink. Number fifty-seven,' he announced.

'Me, me, me.'

Prue heard her daughter shriek from a long way away while a freezing sensation stole over her limbs. The first prize was a ride in a helicopter which could be heard tuning up, untunefully, in the field below the church. The prize had been donated by its owner, a dealer in fertilizers, who had recently bought the manor house and was not, as yet, quite sure of his reception, which veered between acid remarks about the *nouveau riche* and the if-you've-got-it-why-not-flaunt-it? variety.

'It's me. It's me.'

Red-faced with excitement, Jane pushed through the phalanx of disappointed boys who emitted visible hate signals. His moment over, the ex-journalist gave a world-weary smile and turned to Prue. 'The owner insists that children are accompanied by an adult. Just in case.'

'You mean half of the family but not a quarter can be wiped out.'

'Something like that.'

Over the heads of the crowd, Prue sent desperate signals to Max. You go. You go. But Max ignored eye contact and turned away.

Damn him. Max knew that she was terrified of flying and he also knew she would be unwilling to make a scene. He was, in effect, abandoning her.

Damn him.

Someone once told her that you lose consciousness before you hit the earth. Either that or you died of terror.

The rotating blades switched up from a whine to a scream as soon as she and Jane were strapped into the seat of an alarmingly small cockpit and, wishing to disgrace neither her daughter nor herself, Prue prayed for control.

The pilot shouted something that Prue could not hear and she shook her head. He pointed at the sky, grinned and flicked the switches. Prue watched her hands fasten the seat belt.

The engines crescendoed, and a noise returned to haunt Prue. It was the sound made by the man who had fallen? thrown himself? out of the ninth-storey window in Victoria one ordinary day as she had walked to the station from the Tate Gallery and encountered the cluster of onlookers grouped around the smashed thing on the ground. Fear clawed at her stomach and she prayed that she would not faint.

Jane made an excited face at her mother. The sky loomed large and unwelcoming and, as they rose, the field and church shrank and became toys arranged tidily on a patchwork quilt. The air was as nacreous silk, the type so thin that, allegedly, it can be pulled through a wedding ring. As they rose higher and higher, the propellors tore it apart.

Still placed vertically in the sky, the sun spread blinding light across their vision. The pilot altered course. An ant colony of cars moved along the A13. Beyond that, the curves of the Danebury Rings were peeled back for intimate scrutiny. Further away lay Stockbridge and sweeps of downland country that had settled to the cultivator. An ancient landscape, hugging the past, woven by the resonance of past lives.

Poised, free of earth, lit by a wash of light, Prue was rocked into quiescence and, for a moment, she struggled free: of love, anger, fear of the past and fear of the present.

The earth tilted and the sun beat down on her daughter's head. All lives should have such a moment, she thought gratefully.

Violet phoned during the week – Prue could hear the hum of office life – and invited herself and the family down for the following weekend. The baby, she said, could do with some fresh air.

'You're not known for your love of the country weekend,' commented Prue.

'Yes, well,' said Violet. 'People change.'

They arrived on Saturday morning with a heap of baby equipment, and the house no longer belonged to the Valours. Once the chaos had subsided, Edward was changed, put into the second-hand cot Prue had bought at Oxfam, and Emmy was dispatched back to her family. Violet cornered Prue in the kitchen.

'Have a drink,' said Prue, who was behind schedule.

Violet ignored the invitation and came straight to the point. 'What's up with Dad?' she said, in the tone that Prue recognized from the days of failing to be a good stepmother.

She chopped at the onions. 'Nothing. Your father is fine.'

'No, he isn't. I know Dad. He's worried about something.'

Prue's knife reduced the onions to pulp. 'He's fine,' she repeated.

Violet regarded the mush on the chopping board and a plucked eyebrow arched upwards. Prue followed the line of her gaze and tipped the onions into the frying pan on the stove. Losing one's moral superiority was harder than Prue had imagined, particularly when dealing with Violet. She gave a final savage chop to a segment of onion and caught her finger. Red trickled over the board. Prue stared at it. 'I can never see French blood,' Joan said, 'without my hair standing on end.'

'I'm not so sure,' said Violet. 'He's not ill, is he?'

'No.' Prue's wooden spoon hovered for a second or two above the frying pan. 'No. But he might be worrying about work, of course.'

At that point, Max came into the kitchen holding a pair of secateurs. Violet swivelled around.

'I was just asking Prue if you were all right.'

And Prue, who knew Max's repertoire of expressions well, was aware that he did not look as surprised as he could have done. Max dropped his free hand on to his daughter's shoulder and let it rest there. Violet smiled up at him.

'I'm fine,' he said, looking directly at his wife.

Prue scrubbed at her wet cheeks with an elbow. 'These onions', she said, 'are very strong.'

Max snapped the secateurs open and shut. Open and shut.

'I've been asked to tackle Mrs Ryder's jasmine,' he said, and did not sound particularly pleased about it. 'It's growing across her window and blocking the light.'

'Don't be late for lunch.' Prue turned back to the stove.

Violet said she had to unpack.

Someone once wrote that to cook divinely required love. Nonsense. Guilt did just as well. Prue fried mince and the onions in virgin olive oil until they were the colour of a sun-tanned thigh. She opened a tin of plum tomatoes and mashed them into the mixture, added orange in the form of grated carrot, and green basil. Then she melted butter in a cast-iron saucepan, spooned in flour and waited until the roux solidified into yellow and back to white before pouring in the milk. A good cheese sauce should be made with Swiss cheese to give it that stringy, tangy flavour, suggesting clean air, hot sun and café life.

A layer of mince, a layer of pasta, a layer of sauce.

A layer of blameless married life. A layer of adultery. A layer of . . . then what?

We have the power to choose, Richard, the vicar, had preached in one of his better sermons. That's what distinguishes us as spiritual beings. Our sense of good and evil sets us apart from the animal kingdom. Rubbish to that. Prue had reacted strongly. We have simply specialized in intelligence, as the lion has specialized in speed and strength, and intelligence feeds on convenient fantasies. Good and evil are myths.

Nevertheless, we *do* possess the power of choice.

She was conscious of Jamie's presence in the kitchen before he said anything. The hairs rippled up her arms and tightened the muscles in her pelvis. Then came a rush of blood flooding into her chest.

'Prue.'

She waited until she had smoothed the final layer of mince and poured the white sauce before she turned round.

'Jamie.'

He was standing just inside the door, cradling a sleepy

baby in his arms. Years later, when other details had slipped away, she savoured this epiphany, for that was what it was. She remembered thinking how odd it was to see Jamie in her kitchen and how her kitchen, cluttered with so many familiar things, was the wrong place for him. She remembered thinking: I love him above all else and I *have* no choice.

Jamie looked tired, a little transparent and worn at the edges. She did not know him well enough – yet – but if Max had worn the look that sat on Jamie's face she would have known that he needed her. In return, Prue ached for him, her body suddenly limp, out of control.

She shoved the lasagne into the oven and shut the door with extra emphasis.

'Edward needs some fresh air,' said Jamie. 'Why don't you come with me if you've finished? Violet's doing some phoning.'

As they pushed the baby up the main street, Prue said, 'This feels very odd.'

For a second or two, Jamie looked grim. 'Are you going to say you regret everything?'

She considered. 'That would be another lie.'

His expression relaxed. 'Promise me you won't ever say anything remotely like it.'

'Hush,' she said quickly. 'I see Molly coming our way,' and she asked him about the atmosphere in the City.

'General gloom. Not helped by the muddle in Europe.'

'*Do* you think it should be ratified? The Danes seem pretty adamant that it's dead.'

'If we've elected to go the Europe route, we should get on with it.'

'Nice day,' said Molly, her tone drier than usual as she passed on her way to the vicarage with a bag of spinach.

Mrs Ryder's jasmine did not look pruned and neither, Prue

noted, was there evidence of Max. Normally, Prue never gave a moment's thought as to the whereabouts of her husband but now she ran through the places he might be. Now it mattered. Of all the anticipated consequences of an affair, compulsive checking up on the whereabouts of one's spouse had not figured on Prue's list.

'If there is banality in evil,' she said, as Jamie helped her to heave the pushchair up the bank, 'there is, certainly, banality in adultery.'

'Quite,' said Jamie, and held her hand a moment longer than necessary.

The pushchair creaked over bumps and outcrops of dried mud. Prue's skirt was much too thick for summer, and her beaten-up walking shoes had acquired a patina of dust. She took off her jersey and slung it over her shoulders.

Across the pushchair, Jamie looked at Prue.

Memories of what had passed between them surged back – hot, strong, trembling with astonishment and the slap-slither of flesh that had been turned by their wishes into the witchery of high emotion. A rage to possess Jamie, to dig deep under that transparent skin, down into blood and bone, and to seize the sinews of his spirit between her teeth and tear at it, filled Prue.

Embarrassed, she quickened her pace.

'Hang on,' said Jamie.

Prue led them up a track, only just negotiable with a pushchair, towards the footpath leading between Jacob's Farm and the tongue of hazel copse. She gestured towards the latter.

'I wanted you to see it. Old England. Apparently, the copse is medieval and the Heritage people are watching it like a hawk.'

At the top of the rise where the path widened, Jamie wedged the pushchair into a root bole and snapped on the brake. Lulled by the bumpy ride, Edward had fallen asleep, his heavy head pulled to one side.

Jamie reached out and pulled Prue towards him. She felt his face join hers, felt the outline of his teeth through his lips, tasted him, smelt him. A fire leapt in her and incinerated her disbelief that this should be happening to her, Prue Valour.

Hampered by their clothes, Jamie undertook an awkward passage towards her breast. Prue was still. His hand slid under her blouse and under her bra. His touch was rough – so, too, were his finger-tips on the smoother, warmer skin under her breast. She closed her eyes. Jamie stopped what he was doing.

'Silence, Prue?'

She opened her eyes. 'I don't honestly know what to say. I've not had many lovers. I have not committed adultery before, certainly not in front of a baby. Neither do I understand.'

Jamie's hand now cradled her breast and she added crossly, 'I'm not a cup-cake either.'

He laughed but kept his hand where it was. 'What don't you understand?'

'This is egocentric to the point of eccentricity. But why me, Jamie?'

Not privy to the female psyche, he seemed genuinely puzzled at the question. 'I could ask, why me?'

It was on the tip of her tongue to list his advantages in looks, intelligence, etc., etc., and that she had none of those things, but she stopped herself in time.

Jamie was persistent. 'Well, Prue, why me?'

She turned her head away and presented him with a profile softened by emotion and lust. 'I don't know. I didn't choose you. It just happened.'

Can you retrace the pathways of desire back to source? Pick your way through threads of memory? Select a precise moment when a decision was made?

Oh, yes.

She turned back to Jamie and he brushed the hair back from her eyes.

'I don't know what to do, Jamie.' Prue disengaged herself. 'I can't find it in me to resist.'

'Stop talking,' said Jamie. 'It spoils things.'

'Yes, I suppose it does.'

For the second time, he kissed her, and again, further down the path, against an oak tree.

Edward slept on, a picture of innocence.

Because there were so many of them, Prue served the (over-done) lasagne in the dining room. Max opened a couple of bottles of Bulgarian pinot noir. Due for her next assessment at the gym, Violet only sipped hers. Jamie left his almost un-touched, whereas Max was into his fourth glass before the cheese.

Outside, the sun shone down on Dainton, revealing smudged windows, curtains in need of cleaning, cracked roads and peeling paint. It shone, too, on FOR SALE notices that had been up for months on end, on the blue rusting Volkswagen, dumped by the village pond, which the owner could not afford to repair, and on the newly heaped grave in the churchyard covered by brown-edged bouquets. Unemployment had finally got to Clive Carter and he had killed himself in the company car before it was impounded by the firm.

The sun warmed, promised, and clarified.

Inside Hallet's Gate, Prue's body was irradiated with lust and what remained of her resolution disappeared as easily as the pinot noir.

I cannot not love Jamie.

CHAPTER SIXTEEN

HE WAS NOTHING IF NOT PERSISTENT.

Emmy could not understand why Angus continued to single her out when there was luscious Sal and the rest of the London tribe of hummingbirds for him to, well . . . Emmy did not dwell on the precise nature of what Angus might be doing.

What exercised her was the exhaustion of living with the five senses operating on red alert. She hated her vulnerability, and the way Angus ate up her time.

So much for the independent Emmy Horton.

How about this: when she woke, Angus was there occupying her mind; when she washed up or changed Edward's nappy, vacuumed the hall, listened to the telephone ring, he strutted, preened and made as free with it as only a usurper can. The newspaper, *Neighbours* and a novel by Virginia Andrews were no antidote. Neither were her plans to watch for the tawny owl that she hoped would be nesting at Tarrant's barn back home. She had been taken over by an image, a voice and a shape whose powers extended deep into her subconscious. In had slipped cunning Angus, demonstrating to Emmy the limits of her power – and the extent of his.

She learnt that there is no release from the suffocation

of a head occupied by the squatter who will not be evicted. As yet Emmy was unaware that time would do the job efficiently.

Come on the hike on the last weekend in June, Angus invited her. The gang's going and there's a good pub to get ratted at the other end. We go in the van.

Thus, one Saturday morning, an Emmy made boneless with nerves laced up her Doc Martens and ironed her best black T-shirt and jeans and followed Angus to a village near Midhurst on the South Downs.

The group – all right, the Londoners – were displayed incongruously against the green and chalk of the Downs . . . black-clad, flowing-haired townies splattered across the green turf that swept over the ridge and down the fields.

'It looks so green,' said Sal, shading her eyes with her hand.

Feeling superior, Emmy said nothing. Any fool knew that a landscape looked uniform but contained within it variations of colour and texture so minute and myriad that it made the word 'green' meaningless.

On this weekend, the sun chose to beat down and it was hot. Sweat sprouted on Sal's upper lip and her hair hung lank against the tartan lumberjack shirt she wore over her leggings. In desperation, Emmy had bundled her hair into a scarf where it lay on her neck like unaired washing.

Half-way to the pub, Sal and Cherry began to flag. 'Not used to this.' Sal hoicked up one breast with a hand. 'It's tough on the tits.'

Emmy strode over earth crusted into chalky lumps and pitted with flint, felt it crumble under her boots and, framed against the expanse of the world, cautiously admitted to herself that she was happy.

The grass was young, sappy and tough. She bent to pull up a stalk and it bit into her finger. Angus came up behind and poked her bottom.

'Move on.'

Emmy did not appreciate the prize heifer treatment or her mood being broken. 'Naff off.'

They reached the summit of the chalk ridge and the path turned and ran east–west towards a large patch of woodland. Under the tree canopy the sun was filtered of its heat, and the change in temperature made Emmy shiver. The air was still and the light spread in patches over the woodland floor. Violets edged the paths with occasional red and blue splashes of other flowers.

So much texture and so much nourishment on which the senses could feast. Emmy breathed it in, and knew then that her roots ran deeper than she had supposed. She belonged here and her body responded to the changeable light and unmistakable scents of leaf mould and growing things. In a dream she walked on.

'Have some cider,' Angus urged in the pub. It was one of those resolutely fake-beamed and horse-brassed places which served everything in a basket, even the crisps. In a fine example of British inability to handle the weather, a fire had been lit and the place was tropical.

Sal and Cherry were into the vodka, Vince and Nails into the draught bitter. Emmy sipped her cider. The talk was not of jobs for, Emmy and Angus excepted, the group did not have one between them. Neither was it of job prospects, because those had been discounted and the future was something to ignore. No, sensibly the talk was of films, benefits, gigs and *Sun* scandal.

By two thirty, Cherry, Sal and Vince were drunk and Nails had retired to the gents where he remained. The heat inside the pub had become oppressive: Emmy was sweating and Angus's ponytail was wet.

'Let's go,' she said.

Sal moaned. 'Why don't the health freaks go back, get the van and pick us up?'

Emmy could not get out of the pub quickly enough. Angus trod behind her and they walked in silence in single file towards the wood. Once there, the tantalizing, elusive smell of flowers and new leaves again sifted over Emmy and brought her to an abrupt halt. If she could absorb this rioting life perhaps she could steal its confidence and vigour for herself.

Angus's hands slid around her waist. Her thin, whippy, inelegant waist.

'What are you doing, Emmy?'

Drugged by scent and her feelings, Emmy turned and waited the second or two until Angus kissed her. Behind her closed eyelids light splintered across her vision.

'Nice,' said Angus, and released her. 'And you smell nice. I've fancied doing that for a long time.'

'What about Sal?'

'What about her? I fancy you both. Have you both. No point in being exclusive.'

'Get off, Angus.'

'Not yet,' he said and turned her face none too gently towards him and kissed her again.

The out-of-body dimension to Emmy's pilgrimage vanished, replaced by a tension that quivered, almost visibly, between the two. Emmy endeavoured to concentrate on the now milky sweep of sky spread between the horizon and the sun, and failed. She thought, instead, of lust, all flesh and tumbled limbs – not that her experience amounted to more than could be written on a full stop. Her good sense also warned her that at this moment her feelings were not reliable.

At the van, Angus fitted the key into the lock and prised back the door.

'Come to my place tonight, Emmy?'

215

She paused in the act of clambering in, catching a jigsaw piece of her reflection in the passenger mirror. Her lips were uncharacteristically red and her wretched hair had escaped the scarf.

'No, thanks.'

'Why not?'

Emmy shrugged. 'I don't want to.'

'I'll make it worth it.'

She did not doubt it. 'Bad times come after good. I'll pass.'

Dear Marje. What do I do? I am hopelessly, shamingly in love. But he is just after one thing. I'm after several, but I don't know what they are.

Emmy stared out of the window and Angus headed the van towards the pub. There was one advantage of not being a *femme fatale* – a hard head.

Hard head. Soft body.

Angus let his fingers trail up Emmy's leg. 'Quite sure?' His relative indifference stung her until he flicked his ponytail over his shoulder with a gesture that suggested he knew he was the coolest, hottest lover since Casanova. It was so peacockish, so akin to the male sparrow's mating behaviour . . . fluffed-out chest, preened feathers, swagger . . . that Emmy smiled.

'Quite sure,' she said.

'Like the bloody Crown Jewels, then? All locked up.'

She turned and looked at him and, after a minute, he slowed the van down and returned the scrutiny. 'I'll get you, Emmy. Don't worry.'

Saturday at the Blue Orchid in Croydon was *the* night, Cherry informed Emmy. Angus nosed the van into a parking place only a street away, and the girls immediately headed for the ladies' in the club. It was lit with neon light and smelt of hair lacquer and fags. A row of girls, faces and bodies in various stages of contortion, stood in front of the long mirror.

'Here,' said a big blonde, balancing a lit cigarette on the edge of her Marks and Spencer's travelling cosmetic box. 'Help me lace the bustier up, would you?'

Her auburn friend had a go.

Sal stripped to the skin and pranced around in briefs and long tight boots. Emmy ground her teeth, for Sal's figure was everything that had been promised, and watched as she poured herself into a Lycra mini-dress, with high heels, and Cherry did a paler imitation. Emmy ran a comb through her hair and applied a coat of mascara to her lashes, which gave her a startled look.

'Effing Cleopatra, are we?' said Cherry.

The noise on the dance floor backed up under the roof in a smothering blanket. Glitter balls hung in the ceiling; the room was cut by electric strobes and swivelling light. This was a temple indeed.

Sal raised her glossy arms, wriggled her Lycra rump and her hair flamed around her head – a sleek, confident goddess who ruled over youth, sex and gratification.

'Get on down,' screamed the DJ through the microphone. 'Get on down there.'

The egg-smooth floor was covered first by a trickle, then a stream, of bodies, oscillating like cornstalks in a stiff breeze.

'Right,' said Sal and sent Emmy a look. She seized Angus, who had emerged with Vince from the shadows that formed the perimeter of the floor. By the look of him, Vince had taken in another skinful and he grabbed at Cherry with a movement that owed more to luck than control.

'Lover boy.' Sal hung on to Angus and moved her hips suggestively.

Oh, yes, Emmy could tell that Angus was not unaffected

and she was furious with herself for minding. You told him no, she repeated to herself. No. No. No.

She watched them dance – Vince's lurch, Cherry's spaced-out bop . . . and Angus and Sal – until too many dancers had poured into the space and they were lost to view.

'Fancy one, then?' A dark youth materialized by Emmy, fingering a bottle of beer in a manner that betrayed his nervousness. He was sweating, too: drops sat on his face and blackened his T-shirt.

Emmy stared at him. Somehow, she had got into this and she had to go with it. 'Don't mind if I do.'

A damp hand descended on to her arm, and the youth sent his empty beer bottle spinning into the shadows and pulled her into the centre.

At the edge of the floor, packs of youths hunting females grew bold and ferocious. Their willing prey preened and re-formed in their groups whenever one of their members was snatched away. The music drilled into the brain.

At first, Emmy moved like a wary animal, stiff-legged and eyes flicking. The beat grew louder, the smell of sweat, feet and beer stifled the remaining senses and, suddenly, she heard a click in her head, the distinct, decisive sound of a switch moving from negative to positive, from 0 to 1, and, to the beat of soul, house, rap, whatever it was, to the flash and throb of the strobe, Emmy gave herself up.

Her sweaty youth pressed against her. 'Nice?'

'Nice,' she echoed, lost in the sea of bodies. The youth ran his hand down Emmy's back and between her buttocks.

She let him.

She had no idea how long she shook and strutted with her partner, being conscious only of the sensation of release pouring like liquid through her body. To celebrate her rebirth, she raised her face towards the strobe's fractured glitter.

Angus reappeared and shouted into her ear. 'What are you doing?'

Emmy's face was patched with silver. Angus reached out and pulled her towards him until her body was arched against his.

'Get rid of him,' he ordered.

She was tempted to reply, 'You get rid of Sal,' but the youth had gone. Angus's grip did not slacken and they stood together. Then he began to dance and made Emmy dance with him, and her heart began to beat with a wild rhythm. Angus bent over and Emmy felt his mouth move over her chin and rest briefly on her lips.

'Why not, Emmy?' he said into her ear.

For the second time, Emmy asked, 'What about Sal?'

'She's hotting it up with another guy.' Angus jerked a hand in the direction of the dark, heaving mass where the faces and bodies had been reduced to blanket homogeneity.

'Good for Sal.'

His mouth made another journey across the unmapped continent of Emmy's face and she shuddered.

Later, how much later Emmy was not sure, Angus led her through discontented prowlers who had failed to make a kill and around couples who did not care or could not wait to find privacy, towards the exit.

He pulled her into the street. They were out in the night where air was cold water and music a dull pulse. Emmy wanted it to stop right there, but Angus had got this far and he meant to go further. He opened the van door and gestured for Emmy to get inside. Felled by panic, she hesitated.

'Come on, Emmy. Get on with it.'

So Emmy climbed inside.

*

Between Emmy's pale, slippery body and her mind stretched a gap. Thus, when she dwelt on Angus's naked body and face, sometimes readable, sometimes not, it was with the curiosity of an onlooker viewing a painting. What did those closed eyelids signify? Or the way he rolled over at a certain point? When he whispered, 'That's good'?

She could not remember her own words but she did know that she had wanted to cry out with the love that bound her as tightly as the chrysalis is bound by its carapace. She had wanted to try to convey how she felt, what it all meant. But Emmy lacked the vocabulary, and years of being solitary in the real sense had taken away the habit of many words – or, conversely, nurtured a healthy disrespect for them.

Noises from the street trickled into the hot van. A conversation. A shout, the echo of a can rattling in the gutter. Inside, it was close and lit by ragged filtrations of neon. The blanket Angus had spread on the floor felt scratchy against Emmy's back. Each time she moved her foot, she encountered their clothing or the bulky packages of Angus's work tools.

He lit a cigarette, lay back but made no move to take Emmy into his arms. She coughed and desolation washed her, seeping into the crevasses of her spirit and the hairline cracks of a fantasy that had formed with ill-advised, lightning speed.

She reached for the cigarette packet.

'What's it like having a virgin in the back of a van?' she asked, and could have bitten her tongue.

Angus's hand encountered Emmy's buttock. 'Nice one,' he said.

'Are you sure you're giving Edward enough vegetables?'

'No problem, Mrs Beckett. He likes them.'

Today, Violet was having an acute Working Mother attack,

which tended to happen on Mondays, and Emmy was, as usual, the target. She shot Emmy a look which implied that Emmy was guilty of doing all sorts of unmentionable things with the puréed broccoli, including throwing it away. Emmy, who had grown wiser in the ways of her employer, did not drop her gaze. Have you, she was asking silently, ever made love in the back of a van?

Violet prodded a pile of laundry in the basket. 'You will do this today, won't you, Emmy?'

Violet was thinking, It's *so* bloody exhausting having an employee. They never do anything. You have to check, check, check, and you can't ever, *ever*, rely on them.

If Violet had allowed her reading these days to extend beyond the fashionable blockbuster, she would have been reminded that a large proportion of literature has been devoted to the battle between employer and – more powerful than supposed – employee. Neither side won.

'I'll do the laundry first thing, Mrs Beckett. I was a bit pushed last week.'

Violet's pursed lips apparently suggested that she could not conceive how, compared to the rigours of running an office, looking after one small baby at home could leave you pushed. Emmy was not to know that beneath the Yves St Laurent foundation and Chanel lipstick churned relief, spiced with guilt, that it was not she, Violet, who was having to cope with Edward. In her heart of hearts, Violet suspected she was not up to it.

While Emmy thought, This woman is unbearable.

Violet's heels clicked over the kitchen floorboards. Her shoes were black, very high-heeled and of extra supple leather. Above them, she was wearing a Chanel suit with a long jacket and a short pleated skirt which she had enhanced with an abundance of gold buttons and chains.

Emmy pulled her faded T-shirt down over her bottom and over the leggings which had developed a hole in the crotch.

'How's my boy?' Violet bent over Edward's chair.

Edward regarded his mother solemnly and Violet inserted a finger into the centre of one curled hand. Edward pulled. 'He's getting very strong, isn't he, Emmy?'

At the sound of Emmy's name, Edward loosened his fist and swivelled to look at Emmy. For a moment or two, Violet remained as she was, then she withdrew her hand.

'He's fond of you, Emmy, isn't he?'

Emmy reckoned that if Violet said her name again in that particular tone she would say something shocking. Go away, she willed silently. Go to your work or whatever keeps you so busy.

From upstairs, Jamie gave a shout. 'Are you ready, Violet?'

Violet sighed and picked up her briefcase and an unfamiliar look spread over her features. Emmy knew why: she had heard the Becketts quarrelling the previous evening. The unwilling snooper, the keyhole witness, she had sat in her top-storey sitting room and listened to their voices raise in anger and discord and wondered if they realized how much was revealed. Eventually Violet had retreated to the drawing room and Jamie had gone to bed in the spare room.

'If you could make that vegetable pie, Emmy.'

Emmy looked at Edward. 'Yes.'

Violet lowered her briefcase on to the table. 'Emmy, I think you could call me Violet. After all, we are living under the same roof and I do trust you.'

There, she thought, that will encourage Emmy.

Jamie stood in the doorway. 'Hurry up.' He spoke curtly and without his usual smile.

'Thanks, Emmy,' said Violet.

The front door banged. Immediately Emmy switched from

Radio 4 to Capital. Pop music filled the room and Edward banged his spoon as an accompaniment. Emmy picked him up and he settled in her arms with complete familiarity. She nuzzled the top of his head, and smelt his funny little smell composed of nappy cream, talc and a faint echo of regurgitated milk.

'Vegetables, huh?' she said to him.

If the result of making love in a van was a house whose rooms were occupied by separate and angry people, then Emmy knew better than to enter it. She knew she was right to be careful.

Her eye drifted across the piece of garden framed by the window. A clematis had caught blight and hung in a blackened tangle from the trellis. The lawn needed mowing. The frame also caught the bird table on the tree at the bottom of the garden.

Angus's bird table.

Emmy sighed and closed her eyes.

CHAPTER SEVENTEEN

PRUE'S LOVE AFFAIR WAS ALSO FLOURISHING. WHILE Emmy's peace of mind was encumbered by caution and anxiety over Angus's motives, Prue's was being fed on a cocktail of intense sexual experience, astonishment, wild joy and terror.

What is *happening* to me? Prue asked herself as she made arrangements, once, twice, three times to meet Jamie at the hotel, and there to sink, shaking and slippery with desire and hunger, through waters of oblivion.

And he as hungry and seeking as she was.

Why is this happening?

But Prue was too happy, too saturated with emotion to do anything other than surrender.

In the early summer of 1429 ('check 7 May correct', Prue wrote in her notes) at approximately 6 a.m. Joan, having spent the night in the besieged city, arrived at the Tourelles (a stone fort held by the English near the head of the damaged bridge across the Loire) outside Orléans and immediately called a council of war. A woman, circumstance and place had come together in one of those significant, delicately timed fusions that make history. Joan's moment had come – *la journée des Tourelles* – and for ever after her name would be associated with Orléans.

The city had survived the siege for six months so far, partly because the English, under the Duke of Bedford, showed a marked lack of enthusiasm for engaging in action. Instead, from time to time, the English Passevolant tossed its one-hundred-pound stone balls into the city and, from time to time, the French Rifflard returned the compliment. Such was the lack of action that on Christmas Day 1428 the English had borrowed a troupe of musicians from the French ('N.B.' wrote Prue, 'Does that remind you of another war?'). Although Joan was not a soldier, knew nothing of strategy and, above all, was not a man, the citizens were greatly cheered by the news that the famous *pucelle* of Domrémy was to take up their cause.

Joan and the captains discussed tactics, although the course of action was obvious: to storm the earthworks from the south bank of the river before launching an assault on the Tourelles.

It began at seven in the morning and the English fought as one chronicler phrased it, 'as though they were immortal'. From their advantage on the earthworks, they rained down fire, cannon and lead slingshot on the French in the great *fosse*, or moat, below and succeeded in repulsing them.

Towards midday, the French retired to eat their lunch. How characteristic, and how trying for Joan, who was famously abstemious in her eating habits and often, after a hard day's battle, had to be coaxed to eat (giving rise in our generation to the conjecture that she was anorexic – another pointer to her extraordinary willpower). Afterwards, they reassembled and launched themselves yet again at the earthworks. Joan helped to raise a scaling ladder. The air was once again ringing with noise and thick with flying objects, and the embattled French and English hacked at each other with axes, lances, guisarmes and bare hands.

It was at this point that Joan was hit by a crossbow bolt between her neck and breast, piercing her shoulder. Both St Catherine and St Margaret had warned her of this wound. Indeed, a letter exists, written from Lyon a fortnight before the attack, in which Joan states clearly that it would happen.

Predicting a wound is quite separate from experiencing it. Apparently, Joan wept and shuddered with shock and pain. She was pleased that her prophecy had been so exact but a solid wedge of steel-tipped bolt driven at speed into flesh hurts. As she pulled it out of her shoulder to an accompanying gush of blood and splitting of flesh, one of her soldiers offered to put a charm upon the wound.

Joan refused. 'I would rather die,' she said, 'than do what I know to be a sin.'

Such decisions were easier then, were they not? Prue said to Jamie as they lay in bed in the hotel bedroom. You were given a scheme, a set of rules, the notion of direct retribution for veering off-course, all of which left you in no doubt as to how you should behave.

'Sounds terrible,' said Jamie drowsily. 'Who wants rules?'

'People,' said Prue, and nipped his bare shoulder with her teeth.

Potential sinners, of course. The ones born with fleshly lusts and the normal quota of selfishness, greed, cunning and the ability to lie. Natural saints do not require rules for they are never tempted. Their goodness is absolute.

'I don't know about that.' Jamie rolled over and kissed Prue. 'I always thought St Simon the Stylite was a roaring exhibitionist,' he said. 'Anyway, the only way he could manage being good or a saint, or whatever, was by sitting on a pillar.'

'We're sinning,' said Prue, and sat up in bed.

Jamie pulled her down. 'And very nice it is too,' Prue grimaced. 'If it makes you happy, it could be argued there are rules that apply to us, Prue, and this situation. What's more, we're obeying them.'

'Do you really believe that?'

Jamie shifted on to an elbow so that he could gaze down on the face he had grown to love more than he could say. As a consequence, love, rather than morality or philosophy or even good sense, directed his arguments. 'Things are never as simple as you see them, my Prue,' he said and stroked her cheek.

'That's what I told Jane.' Prue relaxed back on to the sheets.

'But do you believe it?' Jamie's fingers walked light as a feather down Prue's sensitized body. 'We're just us. Nobody else. This is a bit of our lives that is particularly private.'

She had a feeling that she was missing something vital, but Jamie's finger had stopped.

Later she said, 'What shall we do this afternoon?'

It was shaded in the hotel bedroom and Jamie's eyes were dark and unreadable and, therefore, exerted particular fascination on Prue. 'I rather imagined you wished to remain on this bed. Am I wrong?'

Prue bent over him. Her lips were sore and her body felt battered, wonderfully beautifully battered. 'I want to do something with you. Cinema, gallery, anything.'

She wanted the pleasure of walking down the street holding Jamie's hand. Of being on display as a couple in public. Or sitting at a table in a café. She wanted strangers to look at Jamie and herself and to register the rope of plaited emotions that stretched between them.

The hotel staff knew them by now and the clerk behind the counter nodded neutrally as they walked out of the front entrance.

'He will be used in evidence against us,' Prue remarked.

'Your conscience is guilty today, isn't it?'

'It's always there,' she said. 'How can it not be?'

He took her hand. 'Don't, Prue.'

Wanting to handle it well, she thought carefully before saying, 'It's fine, Jamie. I'm not going to make you carry my burdens.'

She pressed her thumb into Jamie's palm and they walked down to Oxford Street and, via the underpass, into Hyde Park. Here they maintained a space between their two bodies, Prue hugging her shoulder bag which was full of books. Jamie stuffed his hands into his pockets, looking out of place in his grey city suit among the tourists and children.

'Ice-cream?' he asked. Prue shook her head and Jamie bought himself a vicious-looking thing from a vendor. He had an idea. 'Dinosaurs,' he said. 'Let's go and see them in the Natural History Museum.'

'If you knew,' Prue emphasized each word, 'how many times I've been to see the dinosaurs you would not suggest it. Anyway, you'll be taking Edward later on. Lots and lots of times.'

The thought struck home to Jamie. 'Yes, I suppose I will.'

Instead, they fetched up in the basement of the Science Museum admiring the original Crappers, blue and white china lavatory bowls, old gas fires, early stoves and other domestic developments.

'A bullseye,' concluded Jamie after examining an early Aga. 'A machine for cooking and a cosy ideal all wrapped up in one parcel. Whoever invented it was quite brilliant.'

'Not as clever as the wheel,' said Prue, who had been very taken by the steam engines upstairs.

Jamie pinched her bottom and she laughed. Together, they gazed into the glassed-in displays of electric lamps.

'When did you first know?' asked Jamie, his breath frosting the glass.

'That time in the cathedral.' Prue knew exactly what Jamie was asking. 'I knew I should be looking for, well, I don't know, but I found you.'

'*Are* you searching?'

She pointed at a lamp whose design intrigued her. 'I don't know. Are you?'

She slipped her hand into his and he drew it up against his chest and held it tight.

Jamie insisted on seeing Prue off at Waterloo. Don't feel too guilty, he said as she got into the train. I'll try not to, Prue replied, but it would be a strange thing if I didn't worry about it. You *are* in it unless you choose to get out, he said, and kissed her quickly on the cheek.

No wonder rationalists distrusted love, she thought. No wonder Church and moralists have striven to keep it under lock and key and searched for ways to diffuse its power. No wonder love is perceived as a monster that gobbles up whatever lies in its path. Children, spouses, households. Money and good sense.

Yet as the tide rushed towards Prue and caught her in the tow, she bent willingly to receive it as it crashed over her (and pounded over Jamie, too), dragging with it the shingle and débris of her life.

Which, she found herself thinking, was similar to the pounding that took place at the Tourelles on that bright May day where the French fought the English from seven o'clock in the morning until eight o'clock at night, but made no headway.

Her shoulder bandaged with cotton to staunch the blood, Joan took stock and withdrew to an orchard where she prayed. Then she galloped back, seized her standard from the Basque who was carrying it for her and shook it vigorously. 'Whereupon', the chronicler wrote, 'all the Maid's army rushed together and immediately rallied.'

Thus renewed and inspired, the English resistance collapsed and the French seized the day. A triumphant Joan shouted to the English commander to yield to the King of Heaven: 'You have called me whore, but I have great pity on your soul.'

The accusation of sexual impropriety – 'the harlot of the Armagnacs' – was always one that upset and enraged the Maid. She was right to guard her reputation: her virginity, her virtue, was beyond price for it gave her power not so much over women but over men. She knew that to engage in any sexual activity would both corrupt and taint her body, and her power would leach away into tales of lechery and defiled flesh.

It would have been finished for Joan.

Footnote: the English commander who had called her a harlot drowned in the river as the Tourelles was finally taken.

Max observed his second wife as, twenty-five years previously, he had watched his first. He was almost sure that his suspicions were correct. Almost but not absolutely.

She seemed happy, she had lost weight, she was a little abstracted. Nothing significant in itself, and there was danger in deciding, as opposed to knowing, that something was true – because it became so.

Max repeatedly asked himself what was the point of knowing. Of course he would prefer – desperately wanted – his wife to remain faithful, but since, courtesy of the age-gap and the ageing process, it was probably an unrealistic expectation, was he not muddying already dangerous waters? If he conceded the principle then, surely, it did not matter if he was aware of the chapter and verse of his wife's infidelity?

After tackling the outside paintwork of Hallet's Gate, Max organized a complete programme inside. Dining room. Drawing room. Kitchen. The double bedroom – and began with the latter. When Prue grumbled at the disruption, Max told her to stop complaining, threw a dust sheet over their bed and blotted it out.

'Same again, Prue, I take it?' Max indicated white on the colour chart.

Prue, who had often considered pale pink and grey, but was unsure of what Max was up to did not dare to suggest otherwise. 'Fine,' she said.

Max prepared the walls. Stripped of colour, the room acquired a monastic look and Max was reminded of the reconstruction of a monk's cell in Beaulieu Abbey. How long did it take a blank wall to hone your mind into obedience and equanimity? he wondered.

Grimly, he washed the walls down, wiped the skirting boards and rubbed them dry. Then he Polyfillaed as if it was an art-form, sandpapered until his arm ached, and spent the weekend applying undercoat.

'I'll finish next weekend,' he informed Prue over a dismal Sunday supper of scrambled eggs, and they retired to the single beds in the spare room.

In his dreams, Max returned to childhood. To the discomfort of being born to parents who embarrassed him to the depths of his soul and yet exacted a painful love. How could he not love them? They were all he had.

Max dear, don't put your feet on the settee.

Max, do you have to spread your stamps all over the table?

Max, do . . . Max, don't . . .

When you roger a woman, his father advised him, you must remember that you are in command. It's like driving a car. *You* shift the gears. *You* control the performance. Remember that, otherwise they get the upper hand. Doesn't matter if it's a Morris Oxford or a Rolls-Royce, the mechanism is the same.

Max discovered later that his father could lay fair claim to these statements having taken, as it were, his advanced test and driven a sizeable number of women – in fact, a disgraceful tally. Then, of course, there was the incident with the gun, which drew from Max both pity and horrified amusement. Later, he tried to feel contempt for the big, foul-mouthed philanderer, until he remembered the fishing trips, the cricket, the long companionable car journeys and the pints of beer in the pub, the sense that he was being watched over by a kind of love, and his contempt was replaced by a deep, unhealed loss.

To which Helen had contributed . . .

Sergeant Miles had been one of those textbook soldiers, all 'booger you', handlebar moustaches, a taste for bullying and a righteous mission to knock the scions of England into shape on their National Service.

National Service! National Bloody Misery.

The Sergeant set about his task in a shed, marked out by a double row of beds, smelling of sweat, unwashed blankets and semen expended in loneliness and frustration. Otherwise Sergeant Miles permitted nothing: no pictures, no books. His material was the raw, spotty recruit.

'Now, you boogers. You won't be seeing the outside of these barracks for some time.'

Max willed himself to think of other things. Fishing, pellucid water and undulating mats of underwater weed. A painting he had seen in a Mayfair house. Sex, the non-onanistic variety, a tantalizing taste of which he had been lately introduced to by Betty, his mother's obliging housemaid.

'Are we composing poetry, Corporal?'

'Yessir. I mean, nosir.'

A heavy hand descended on to Max's shoulder. 'It's a

funny thing, Corporal, but I have an idea I don't like your attitude. You have a sorta look that tells me that you don't give a tinker's about what I'm saying.'

Clearly, Sergeant Miles's light blue bully's eyes were strangers to finer points of feeling. Max gave in. He knew the type, he knew the score, he wanted to get by and he wanted to get by without being noticed – which was difficult with his height.

'I'll keep your secret, sonny, never fear.'

'What secret, sir?'

Sergeant Miles attacked one of his handlebars. 'That you are a useless, overgrown nancy, if ever I saw one, who thinks he's going to sail through this little episode of slumming with the oiks but who thinks wrong.'

The conversation marked the beginning of a programme of attrition that the Sergeant dished out at every opportunity. During the next eighteen months, Max learnt it was necessary to be tough to survive misery, physical exhaustion and, worst of all, boredom – but it had to be real, bone-deep toughness, not a pretence. Max knew, too, that salvation lay in humour but it was hard to laugh. Fling an intake of youths together, put them in the charge of the Mileses of this world, subject them to every physical coarseness you can think of and what, during those fifties years, did you end up with in the way of English manhood?

Max for one. The aching, trembling thing that was Max Valour at twenty. Somehow, out of the jelly, the fear and longing for death, Max had to shape himself up for life.

Several times he asked himself why it was that, in theory, life contained so much – music, beauty, powerful emotion – when he had been dished out a boil on the neck, sweaty underpants, bloody awful food, hatred of anything militaristic and, at night, the sounds of men snoring.

When he walked into the Boffin nightclub with Dickie

Bennett a couple of months before his release back into civilian life, Max spotted Helen immediately. She was talking to a couple of men in grey suits and her beauty struck a blow to Max's starved heart. As a Boffinette, Helen was dressed in a tweeny outfit with a plunging neckline and very high heels which gave her an unbalanced look. Rocking on those heels, she had turned and fixed her eyes on Max and Dickie and the curve of her breasts and intelligent dark eyes (he did not notice the too-thin mouth) and, as yet, an untouched quality in her face almost brought Max to a halt.

He should have deduced from his behaviour on the shooting range (dogged, dogged practice until his aim was dead-eyed and the envy of the squad) that he possessed untapped resources. He had imagined that he had no courage, no terrier qualities, not enough sense of self to endeavour to capture another.

But he did. Endless telephone calls, elaborate arrangements to get out of the barracks, flowers and letters later, Helen agreed to come out to dinner. By then, Max had been past eating and drank instead of the fathomless pools of her eyes and rejoiced that, at last, life was yielding up some riches.

The humour, so painfully acquired, stood him in good stead for Helen was not easy and never concealed boredom. Max's boil refused to heal, and his rawness and over-eagerness bored her mightily. He wanted her body: the white breasts, slightly too full thighs and the tiny pocket of fat that sat on her hips. Above all, he wanted to capture the grubby, selfish, grasping spirit that inhabited the body that so fascinated him.

'Stop it, Max,' she would say through her thin, scarlet-slicked lips. 'I want someone adult.' They were the same age, but Helen imagined she was older.

This was where Max's terrier came in and he held on, with jaws that grew stronger every day.

'All right,' she said at last, worn down by the siege, fixing him with the eyes that promised oblivion and Nirvana, 'we can go to bed. I owe you that. But only once.'

'That's enough,' said ignorant Max, fingers already fumbling at his shirt.

They were at his flat and Dickie had been bribed with beer to stay away. The gas flared in the filaments and gave off its distinctive smell. Outside its ring of warmth, the room was icy and Max's bed occupied a polar region in the corner.

In her electric blue dress (a colour in which Prue also looked good), Helen watched Max. His torso emerged from his shirt and he stopped, unsure how to proceed, failing to take Helen into his arms and to undress her. After a second or two, he continued and took off his trousers and stood, very white-skinned, in socks and underpants.

'My God,' said Helen from the safety of the clothed, 'what have I let myself in for?'

Life may have dealt Max largeness and a boil but he expected such to be his lot. Unlike his fantasies of making love to Helen. Despite Betty the housemaid, he had envisaged that sex just happened. One moment, you are dressed, the next not. He had imagined, too, that romance was a solid thing.

It was not. It fled under the assault of bony knees, Helen's unconcealed contempt, the Arctic temperature, his inability to take charge and his desperate need. Thus, instead of surging like a triumphant fish through tropical waters, Max was brought up against his ignorance.

Helen showed him. He had known she was experienced but it hurt to have it demonstrated quite so brutally. This way, she told him. That way. And Max who had so wanted to lead, followed.

Never, never again, she said afterwards. I want a rich man who wants a wife. Not you. Max argued that he would be reasonably well off as a solicitor. Articles over the next twelve months, then a partnership. Equity partnership within ten to fourteen years. 'Give me ten years,' he begged.

Helen looked at Max as if he was mad, and her dark eyes were contemptuous. 'I'm not sitting in a semi in Guildford wearing gingham while I wait for you to get rich.'

He wanted to slap the jeer from the scarlet lips and take her by the shoulders and shake until her teeth rattled. But he knew he was just as likely to press kisses into the hollows made by her collarbones and suck like a drowning man on that jeering mouth.

'Where will you find him, Helen?'

'There will always be someone,' she said.

After that exchange, Max allowed himself to get drunk and took Helen home. Her flat was in a decaying house off Sloane Avenue in the days before Chelsea became fashionable. At the front door, she said goodbye in a final-sounding voice and turned away. He caught a whiff of jasmine scent and tobacco, and a madness gripped him.

'No you bloody don't,' he said and, grabbing her by the hand, he pulled her upstairs to her room and bundled her inside. Then he pulled off Helen's mackintosh and ripped at her blouse.

'Stop it, Max.'

Helen fought him as best she could but, hardened by two years of army life, he was stronger.

Instinctively, Max knew that Helen enjoyed what followed. As he pushed his way towards what he wanted and ignored her cries, he saw the thin mouth suddenly slacken with desire and felt the white body respond as it had not before. He held her arms tightly and inserted a knee between her legs.

'You will listen to me,' he muttered through clenched teeth.

'You bastard,' she spat back, but the last syllable was teased out, silky and heavy. Triumphant finally, he smiled down at her.

'Got you,' he said.

A month later, Helen knocked at Max's front door and stood, hunched and ill-looking, on the threshold. He had not seen her since that night but his dreams were filled with images of their thrashing bodies that caused him to wake shaking with desire and frustration.

'I've got to speak to you, Max.'

He lit the gas fire and made a pot of tea. She was sullen but accepted a cup and balanced it on the inelegant wing of the armchair.

'What is it, Helen?' Max's cup clattered in the saucer.

'Don't do that,' she said. 'It's irritating.'

'Well?'

'I'm in pig.' She shot him a quick, calculating look. 'And I want you to pay to get rid of it.'

Max went back to the kitchen to replenish the pot, Helen's news knocking around his brain like a loosened atom. Carefully, he directed a stream of boiling water into the china pot. Then he replaced the lid and listened to the pop, pop of the gas fire.

He walked back into the room. 'No,' he said. 'I'm not going to pay for an abortion. You are going to marry me instead.'

With a snarl of dislike, she looked up at him but Max did not mind. He knew he had Helen where he wanted her.

'Got you,' he said to himself.

Thus it was that Max Valour married Helen Beech at Chelsea Town Hall with Dickie Bennett as best man and witness. The bridegroom looked very cheerful in his best, and only, suit. The bride's hair was scraped back into a ponytail and the waistband of her cheap cotton skirt did not quite meet.

Six months later, Violet was born.

And out of that semi-rape had come adultery and death, and Max had been forced to learn detachment over matters of the flesh.

So you see, my Prue, he told her silently as he mixed paints, rolled walls and inhaled paint stripper on his journey towards his personal Calvary, my armour is heavy and, like your Joan, I risk everything. I have to be vigilant with myself. Coercion does not do. To rout the enemy, I have to give you freedom, that is my gift of . . . love.

I can do no more. Enough. Enough.

CHAPTER EIGHTEEN

VIOLET POUNDED AWAY ON THE STAIRMASTER. THIS was the final assault before the holiday. The final push. Clenching her teeth, she switched the programme up to level nine and sweat poured down her face. One, two. Left, right. Gloria Estefan pounded in her ears and her legs followed suit. Up, down. One minute gone. Two minutes gone . . . She visualized the straining muscles, the hasty conversion of her fat into energy, the breakdown into carbon monoxide and the acid left pooling in her flesh, the blood arriving to vacuum it away.

In a gesture that was becoming habitual Violet looked over to the wall, entirely composed of mirror, for a quick check. There she was: body hunched over machine, stick legs working. If the botanist's pin had skewered Violet through the heart, she would resemble nothing so much as a gaudy pinioned insect in the collector's display cabinet.

She paused for breath and, without warning, her mind swarmed with other, forbidden, images, each one as lasciviously detailed and complete as a master pornographer's fantasy. Only this morning, Violet had caught sight of the extra-*extra* forbidden as she had driven past the shop, but the three-second glimpse was sufficient for a starving mind to lick and garnish into luminous temptation. Brushed with whipped cream, glistening with caramelized sugar, light, airy, confident, perfect, it had been a Gâteau St Honoré to outdo all Gâteaux St Honoré.

What a bully the mind was. Violet summoned other images to help purify and rid it of its succulent devils. The Pope. Gérard Depardieu. *Hello!* magazine. She felt her mind bend and strain to her will, as she bent and strained on the machine, but it was useless. Violet was helpless, as hobbled and spread-eagled as Gulliver in Lilliput, when confronted with the powerful chimera of *fois gras*, chips and steak, and chocolate-hazelnut spread smothered on thick white bread. In desperation, she called up the final defence.

Cellulite.

Thick brown circles of fat like potato peelings that snaked and draped and clung to the hips – in pitiful contrast to Violet's Platonic ideal – solarized into her mind. But even the spectre of cellulite failed to force Violet's fantasies to their knees.

Knees . . . Paul Gascoigne's knees. Jamie's knees, rather bony ones. Edward's knees, all pink and plump like sugar mice. *No!* Not sugar mice.

Violet scrubbed at her face with the end of the colour coordinated towel hanging round her neck, adjusted her position on the machine and stepped up the pressure on her pressurized thighs.

Afterwards, she rested in the changing room and waited for her heart to return to its normal rhythm. It was the lunch-hour and the room was full of women whose flushed bottoms, thighs and shoulders were slicked with sweat and glossy with heat.

The ubiquitous mirrors witnessed, refracted, distorted and told truths, many unwelcome. Violet studied her reflection: sucked-in-stomach, sucked-in cheeks, a sweat-splodged Lycra ensemble.

Gâteau St Honoré.

No, you don't. She swivelled to obtain a sideview of her flat stomach and lean thighs.

Mirror, mirror on the wall
Who is the fairest . . . ?

Certainly not Prue, and Prue would soon be old.

When Helen, still beautiful, had been dying in hospital from the car crash – and taking some weeks to do it – Violet had saved up and spent her pocket money on a doughnut to give Helen. It was a plain one, dusted with sugar, into which ersatz cream had been piped. This she had presented to her mother in a brown paper bag as she lay propped up by pillows and fed by tubes.

Helen reached out fingers that were by now skeletal, looked into the bag, retched and turned her head away.

Violet now understood why but, at the time, it had seemed that her mother had rejected her gift of love but, then, love offered in a brown paper bag is difficult to accept when you are dying painfully.

Violet had not been sure how to react to Helen's death. Should she cry? Should she be terribly, terribly brave giving onlookers the opportunity to exclaim how extraordinary a child she was? On the other hand, the idea of screaming artistically during the funeral and casting herself down by the coffin in a flurry of smocked dress and Start-Rite sandals, an image taken from a film, rather appealed.

In fact, Violet had been banned from the ceremony because her grandmother declared that children did not go to funerals. Why death was considered only for adults was not explained. Violet beat the ban by sneaking up to the churchyard where she watched Helen's coffin being lowered into the earth with an expression, had she but known it, of avid interest. It was impossible to deny that observing your mother being buried is a unique experience.

241

Later, she had escaped once again to stand alone and cry, in the pouring rain, by her mother's grave. Just standing, alone, until she was sodden.

Violet got to her feet, peeled off the Lycra and headed for the shower, which she ran until it was ice cold. She clenched her teeth and stepped under it.

I will not think of food, she mouthed the words through numbed lips. I will not think of food.

When she emerged, she felt that her mind had been washed as clean as her body and was now, for the time being, safely under control.

'Hallo, Dad.'

'Hallo, darling.' Max was surprised to be rung up in the office. 'Is everything all right?'

'Fine. How's Jane and Prue?'

Max hesitated a couple of seconds. 'Fine.'

At her end, Violet raised her eyebrows. 'Is Prue still wrapped up in Joan of Arc?'

'To tell the truth,' said Max, 'I wish I'd never heard of the bloody woman. Anyway, why are you ringing me?'

'Darling Daddy. You know you said if I ever wanted anything . . .'

Max's laugh cut across the rest of the sentence. 'What is it?'

'I've run out of money and I need some to buy clothes for the holiday in Italy. I don't have anything to wear.'

'Why don't you ask your husband?'

'I don't want to ask Jamie. It's none of his business. Please, Dad. I love you very much.'

'You are absolutely outrageous.' Max was already reaching for his cheque-book. 'How much do you want.'

'A couple of hundred. Three,' she added quickly.

Max hunched his shoulder around the telephone and wrote one thousand pounds on the cheque. 'I'm giving this to you, my darling, on the condition that you put half of it into the account set up for Edward.'

'How much, Dad?'

He told her, and immensely enjoyed the gasp at the other end of the phone.

'I was thinking about your mother when you rang.' Max stuck the phone under his chin and signed the cheque.

'How funny. I've been thinking about her too.' If Violet was strictly truthful, Helen's memory was like laddered tights in the drawer – there and requiring attention, but only taken out from time to time.

Max's next comment took Violet by surprise. 'Your mother and I did have some good times but, unfortunately, we let each other down. Every marriage makes its accommodations, but perhaps with mine I read the wrong notice-board. I hope you've read yours correctly.'

'Oh, yes,' said Violet, totally bewildered.

'And we've all survived.'

'Oh, yes.' Violet recollected her dream landscapes and her terror as she ran across them.

'And you, my darling daughter, are more important than anything.' Max's voice dropped and became soft and loving. Sometimes he feared for Violet's bright, glossy beauty and her bright, glossy life. He added, 'And Jane, of course.'

His tenderness reached Violet in a way that she seldom allowed anything to do. 'Thanks, Dad,' she said, with a catch in her voice. 'That's nice to know.'

Because of Jamie's commitments at the bank, the Becketts could not take their holiday until mid-July. Typical, said Violet.

How come we're the only family with a pre-school child mug enough to pay high-season prices?

The destination was a villa in Tuscany and, not to miss a day, they planned to drive there in one all-out marathon down the motorways.

Prue told Jamie they were quite mad. 'How will you cope with the baby?'

'Edward will sleep in the back of the car,' Jamie said, airily.

'He won't, you know.' Prue poked Jamie with a teasing finger. 'Haven't you learnt yet about babies? They *never* sleep when you want them to.'

'Yes, he will.'

Prue bit her lip. 'I wish, I wish . . .' and suddenly the mood shifted back to the one that nourished their passion so satisfyingly, and with which they were now familiar. Yearning, hunger, which was in no danger of being assuaged, spiced with an edge of the illicit, and sadness – the wine and bread of an affair.

I wish I was coming with you, she meant to say.

Jamie understood. 'I know, Prue. So do I.'

'Kiss me goodbye.'

He felt a shiver run through Prue's body, and held her tight. The goalposts were shifting and, for the first time, Jamie acknowledged that the situation was slipping out of his control.

'I can't bear it, Prue,' he said, spurred by the idea of parting, 'I can't go on like this. When I come back we must talk about it.'

'*Kiss* me, and don't be silly.'

Several times during the nightmare journey Jamie recollected Prue's warning which, of course, he could not repeat to Violet, Violet requiring no encouragement to dislike Prue, particularly as Edward was busy re-creating Dante's voyage into Hell.

The ferry crossing made Edward sick. Violet spent most of the time in the passenger lounge grimly clutching him to her lap with a wad of tissues, surrounded by Rotarians from Yorkshire and schoolchildren giving in to demented urges. Under Edward's assaults, Violet's carefully assembled new outfit of designer shorts and a tartan jacket became stained and smelly.

At Dunkerque, the driver in the car behind them in the queue was distracted by an official mouthing an instruction in French and banged into their rear bumper. Not too much damage was done to the company BMW but, from then on, tempers deteriorated.

'I've forgotten how fast the French drive,' said Jamie, once they were on the motorway.

'Careful.' Violet spoke through gritted teeth.

Jamie put his foot down. 'Just testing the speedometer.'

Violet leant back in the seat. France flashed by. It grew hotter, the tarmac shimmered and in the back, packed into his chair, Edward grizzled without ceasing. The car was not suitable for transporting a baby and the heat accentuated the smell of vomit, which Violet had tried to eradicate with duty-free Chanel No 5. Sweat poured off both of them and Violet's thighs were glued painfully to the seat.

Violet decided she hated both her husband and her son.

'Can't you shut him up?' said Jamie at last, as if it was Violet's fault that Edward was crying.

A couple of small Peugeots shot past and, without thinking, Jamie pushed the accelerator. Violet, who had turned round to see to Edward, was jolted backwards.

'For crying out loud,' she shrieked and, at the sound of his mother so cross, Edward opened his mouth and screamed.

'Stop the car, Jamie. *This minute.*'

'How can I?' Jamie lost his temper. 'We are on the bloody autoroute, remember. I *can't* stop.'

'Well, the next *aire de* whatever it is.' Violet's French had deserted her. Somehow she thrust herself between the two seats and crouched in the back beside Edward. 'Shush, you little beast,' she said, dabbing at Edward's hot, swollen little face. 'You're not making things easier.'

Why didn't I bribe Emmy? she was thinking furiously. Why did I let her go on holiday? The baby's gaze locked on to his mother's. Help me, it said. It's your fault I'm so uncomfortable. Caught between guilt and fury that Edward was not behaving reasonably, Violet hauled him out from the nest of straps and padding and, crouching at a dangerous angle, held him against her swaying shoulder until Jamie swung off the *autoroute* and stopped the car . . .

The villa, which had promised so much in the brochure, fell short. The garden was not the formal sweep interspersed with patches of mysterious, cedary cool that had been suggested, but a dry scrub-pocked patch overlooking the road with no privacy. The rooms were unkempt and the kitchen erred on the side of the primitive. Next door, at least five families appeared to be in occupation, none of whom ever went to bed or turned off the radio.

'What did I tell you?' said Violet bitterly. 'If we couldn't afford a decent villa here we should have gone to Umbria.'

Jamie badly wanted to sit down and drink a glass of wine. He wanted Violet to see the funny side. Suddenly he turned on her. 'Do you ever shut up?'

Violet went quiet.

The baby did not thrive in the heat. 'Why', Violet ground out between white lips, 'are we landed with such a sickly baby?' Edward was hot at night, then cold. Sweat and urine gave him nappy rash which, because Violet did not deal with it quickly enough, suppurated. Then he went off his food, developed a stomach upset and the rash turned from pink to flaming red and his eyes became huge in his shrunken face.

'I think it's time for the doctor. Again.' Violet held Edward's wailing form to her breast. It was their fourth uneasy day and she was shivering from fatigue and frustration. 'God knows how we'll manage the Italian.'

Jamie put down a volume of Larkin's poetry (which Prue had bought him for the holiday) and took his son from his wife. Despite an application of her scarlet lipstick, she had lost her customary gloss, and he was reminded of how dimmed she had been by exhaustion and bewilderment after Edward had been born. Guilt at what had happened since then made his stomach twist painfully.

Experienced in anxious holiday-makers clutching ailing children, the doctor took one look at Edward, issued antibiotics, rehydrating fluids and the equivalent of Calpol. His instructions in broken English were admirably clear. He advised them not to worry, how to proceed and hinted that, in future, it would be better to wait until the baby was a little older before venturing into the heat.

'Point taken, my son,' Jamie told a sleeping Edward in the pushchair, signing away a good proportion of his traveller's cheques for the medicine.

Violet's frustration with motherhood was not diminished by this episode and she weighed it alongside her other resentments. The role of women. The role of men, husbands in particular. Badly equipped villas. Nannies who required holidays. Why, she asked herself as she selected the best tomatoes for their lunch, do babies prevent you doing anything normal, like sleeping? They gobbled you up, babies, and their wailing, smelly forms went suck, suck, suck at what remained of your lifeblood that had not been shed in giving birth.

Chop, chop, went Violet's knife.

Even your head no longer belonged only to you. Everywhere

you went . . . Violet chopped on . . . babies came as well. You could not work without thinking about them, lunch without worrying if the baby was getting his, enjoy a drink with a colleague without feeling guilty. A mind split like Morton's Fork spelt muddle, mess and inefficiency, and Violet hated those things with a passion that might have surprised Jamie had it been fully applied to him.

Her friends managed, however. They hefted their snotty beasts under one arm, took them out to diners and restaurants, went on holidays and all seemed fine. Stranger still, these women appeared to enjoy it.

'Better?' Jamie touched Violet on the shoulder and proffered a glass of red wine.

'I suppose so.' She drank the wine and shrugged. 'I keep asking myself why having children is so difficult.'

Once, Jamie would have wrapped his arms around Violet and taken into his keeping whatever anguish was plaguing her. Instead he said, after a moment's reflection, 'We all have to grow up, I suppose.' He inflected the 'suppose' and Violet remained uncomforted.

Still, there was the scent of thyme and hot stone, the sweep of Tuscan hillside replicated in Renaissance paintings, punctuated by the dark green exclamation marks of the cypresses and grey-green blocks of olives. The air felt heavy and scented, and the sun, delicious in the slight chill of the early morning, was a pounding ball of metal by midday. Sometimes in the early morning a chiffon mist was thrown over the valley. Sometimes, a hint of cloud spread like thin paste over the sun moving down the sky. Always, the allure of herb and resin and hot stone filtered through the lazy air, and the seductiveness of the strange.

Now that he was better, Edward slept soundly for an hour or so after lunch, leaving Jamie and Violet free to make their way to their bedroom under the tiles to sleep if they wished, shutters closed against the glare, bars of hot light arranged across the floor, sheets dampening under their bodies. The air in the afternoon felt solid with heat and, more often than not, tension. Or, if both had been honest, disappointment.

Violet's skin had turned light gold, Jamie's an older gold. Both began to look well and rested. Nevertheless, if her hips were satisfyingly slender, Violet's expression was increasingly troubled.

During the Monday afternoon siesta of the second week of the holiday, she turned to Jamie and wrapped her arms around him. He did not repulse her – exactly – but lay on his back, unmoving. She pressed herself against his chest, placed her head on his shoulder and listened to his breath, worrying that her position made her look rather ridiculous.

'Jamie? Do you want to?' Her hand followed a familiar path.

He stirred and responded at last. 'Of course.'

'Of course' was a long way from the approach Violet was used to and had taken for granted. Jamie had always been the one to initiate and had always been gratifyingly persistent. Until recently, that is. Violet thought back over events in the bedroom and the cool nip of reason made her realize that 'recently' had turned into a comparative term. 'Recently' Jamie had not been on form – a state of affairs difficult for Violet to accept, for her mental map of sex was drawn to the specification of herself as the desired object. If the map had been redrawn without her knowledge, it left Violet lost.

'Do you think I've lost weight?' she said, stretching so that her tanned and exquisite haunch was displayed to its best advantage.

'Yes,' Jamie confirmed, but without real interest.

He made love to his wife with his eyes firmly shut – as if, she thought indignantly, the sight of her put him off. The episode was not a success. It was too hot, and both she and Jamie were more than a little drunk from lunch. Worse, Violet felt that Jamie had been indulging her.

She lay on her side and stared at the wooden lampstand with its gingham shade. Someone had allowed it to rest on the bulb and it had burnt on one side. A foot or so distant, a motionless Jamie lay with his arm across his eyes. It struck her that things were altering and that it was much easier to control a career than a marriage.

After a while, Violet found herself going over the fine detail of an auction she had set up to take place the day she returned to work. The book was the latest hottest development in diets, and publishers in the States were baying for the rights. Violet totted up figures in her mind. The probable ones first and, as she grew drowsy, fantasies that ran into telephone numbers. Before she fell asleep, she decided to search out a fax machine in the village to ginger up the leading bidder . . .

'Prue?'

'Jamie! Where are you?'

'In a café in Siena. I haven't much time or change. I just wanted to see how you were.'

Prue felt her throat constrict into an aching lump and blinked back tears. 'I miss you terribly.'

'It's bloody hot here. The baby's been ill.'

And Violet? Prue wanted to ask, but pride would not let her. 'Hope Edward's better.'

'Yes. Thank God. How are you?'

'Fine. Absolutely fine.' Prue wiped her cheeks with the back of her hand.

'Look, I've got to go. Violet might come at any minute. She's trying to send a fax to the office.'

'Thanks for ringing.'

'Prue. I love you.'

Back in England, Prue sat down with a thump in a chair and wept and wept until her eyes felt like boiled potatoes.

Jamie discovered that the evenings were the worst. Then the light lapped a landscape flushed with pink and gold; a rounded, soft, feminine light. It picked out the dark cypresses and overpainted the gold and brown of the hills over which the early merchant bankers had ridden in search of trade. (It had not escaped his notice that the twentieth-century variety were much in evidence. The biggest villa in the village, which was owned by a merchant bank, boasted security systems, stables, a pool, a personal masseuse and, even, a consecrated chapel.)

'It's so beautiful here,' he confided to Violet, 'that it's almost painful to look at it.'

Violet glanced at the volume of Larkin lying beside him. 'You feeling all right?' she said, and felt his forehead.

He missed Prue, and the light and the ravishing landscape pressed on a raw spot, which he hoped was not sentimentality. It did not feel like it, for he missed her with an ache and a yearning that he had never before experienced.

To tease and test him, Italy assembled an *enfilade* of ravishing views and buildings, and Jamie's awakened sensibilities continued to suffer for them . . . a hill swelling like a breast, the languor, the aromas, the seduction of the hot nights and good wine. Yes, Jamie suffered because of them.

Quite right?

During the velvet, slumbering nights, he compared the feelings that had once belonged to Lara, then Violet and now,

251

after a frighteningly short time, to Prue, and asked himself what this switchback of loyalty and passion made him. The answer was not that he was facile, because he was not and he knew that. Jamie always tried to do things well, and he tried to think them through. That he had taken an unpredicted deviation forced him to the conclusion that, far from being absolute, love and desire were extremely adaptable.

It did not, however, make them less intense.

He hoped he was not smug, but Jamie prided himself that his life and work were conducted within the limits. He had never cheated on Lara and, in the office, he tried always to take decisions within a context. What did an investment, or the lack of it, mean to local people, the landscape, future generations?

Nevertheless, context had not crossed Jamie's mind when he fell in love with Prue and took her to a London hotel for the afternoon. He had not considered the context of home, wife and child when he ran his hands through her hair and moulded her body this way and that. Or when he had stroked the flare of passion into those grey, beautiful, sleepy eyes.

And what would be the context if he left his wife and son and took another man's?

Took his father-in-law's wife . . . and his own wife's step-mother?

Two days before they were due to return home, they were eating dinner, tomato salad, pork chops fried in olive oil with sage, on the balcony when Violet asked abruptly, '*Do* you want another baby, Jamie?' Her manner indicated she had been brooding.

The piece of meat balanced on the end of Jamie's fork dropped to his plate. He must have looked astonished for she leant forward and said, 'It's not *such* a strange question.'

'What's made you decide to consider it?'

Violet leant back in her chair and raised her hands above her head to admire how dark her tan seemed in the candlelight. 'Maybe I was being foolish. And perhaps it is better to get it over and done with.'

'What about the job?'

'That's a bit of a problem as I won't have done my two-year stint before taking maternity leave. But I think I can wangle it.'

Jamie had the sensation of a fish-hook being inserted into the tenderest part of his flesh and yanked. 'But I think you were right when you said no. It would be silly to get pregnant when you've just got your feet under the table at work.'

Violet thought for a moment and then proceeded to astound him. 'I'm willing to take the risk.'

Over the candles, she sent him one of her least aggressive looks. 'What's wrong, Jamie? You were always the keen one.'

'Work, tiredness. Money. The recession is bad. What else do you think?'

'I think . . .' Violet got up and walked to the edge of the balcony. Below the house stretched the darkened valley and above the Italian night, laced with stars and a plump, luminous moon. When she spoke again, she sounded unhappy. 'I wish we were back in New York. It seemed easier there. I'm not sure London suits us. If only the recession hadn't meant that you had to come back.'

'We're OK.'

She rounded on him. 'Don't patronise me.' The heat and darkness emphasized her frustration.

Jamie pushed the bottle of wine over the table. 'Calm down and have some more wine.'

He heard her click her tongue impatiently against her cheek. After a silence, he dug in his shirt pocket, produced a packet of cigarettes and lit one.

Her turn to be astonished, Violet looked up in the act of pouring. 'Good God, Jamie. Smoking. What has got into you?'

No decisions were taken. Nothing further discussed. On the penultimate day they made an effort to visit a couple of galleries they had missed. Here, the paintings assembled a colourful, tender theme of maternity: da Siena's *Maesta*, Botticelli's *Madonna and Child Between Two Angels* and Martini's canopied Madonna and standing child.

Jamie had forgotten that strong emotion rubs sandpaper over responses that have become dulled by time and habit, and the, radiant Madonnas and Child threatened to overwhelm him. Violet did not say anything much except to roar at Edward when he dropped his teddy for the umpteenth time.

Faced with packing up and driving north, they discovered better teamwork. They had learnt a few things on the journey down and Violet acquitted herself at managing Edward, who was persuaded to sleep at the right times. Keeping to practical topics, she and Jamie talked companionably over the long haul and enjoyed a picnic in the mountains.

While Violet disappeared in search of a convenient bush, Jamie unpeeled a wrapper from a sponge finger and gave it to Edward.

'*Che cosa fare?*' he asked his son.

CHAPTER NINETEEN

PRUE WAITED. IN HER TRADITIONAL ENGLISH VILLAGE for her lover to return.

Two weeks. Less than a menstrual cycle, less than a lunar cycle, less than the flowering period of the Fantin-Latour rose. Measured by chronology it was less than any of these things, but measured in *chieros*, the long chilly time of the mind, it seemed to Prue infinity.

Molly Greer caught her as she was backing out of the drive and held up her hand for Prue to stop. Prue applied the brakes and the gravel crunched. Molly motioned that she should wind down the window. Amused by Molly's assumption of command, Prue obeyed. 'Prue. I don't see your name on the flower rota.' Molly's head was framed in the window.

Prue dropped her hands into her lap and smiled. 'I felt like a change and I'm a bit busy at the moment.'

'How can you be too busy for the Church?' Molly was sharp.

'I've been on the rota for a long time. I think a year off would not be unjust.'

Molly's expression hardened, but she could not quite bring herself to say what she thought. She did not have to: Prue knew what Molly was thinking.

'I see,' said the latter, in a freezing tone. 'I do hope this book business isn't going to take you from us.'

Prue was too happy and too absorbed by her happiness to take offence. 'No, I don't think so but I need a little break,' she said and restarted the engine.

'You can't give up on us, Prue, you know.'

Prue shook her head. 'I'll see you soon, Molly.'

She left Molly to stare after the car.

My darling Jamie, I am in the process of retreat, she told him as she drove to Winchester. You won't appreciate what pains I took to dovetail into the rituals of village life because I believed it should be given a chance to survive. Not quite, I know, the bold and dashing action of Joan who, after watching the pillage of Domrémy, goes off to save France, but flower rotas and summer fêtes have their place. Don't you think?

Here I am, Jamie, after twenty years of being good at it, and the wadding has been unexpectedly unwrapped from around my heart. I expect it is a commonplace, but to me it seems like a miracle.

What, Prue asked herself again and again, was she going to do with an exposed heart?

'Darling,' said Max after she had collected him from the station and they were driving back to Dainton, 'I know it's a bit late but what about a holiday for us? If I could get the time, how about ten days in Scotland?'

'No,' said Prue, before she could stop herself. 'No. Don't let's this year.'

'What's happened to the I'm-stuck-all-year-in-Dainton argument?'

'I'm just at a vital bit with Joan,' she said, meaning she could not bear to go away just as Jamie returned.

Max hauled the irretrievably crumpled newspaper out of

his briefcase and Prue frowned with annoyance. 'Pity,' he said.

Prue concentrated on the traffic and drove back to Hallet's Gate as fast as she could.

What about their marriage, which had nourished and sustained both for so long? Surely with so much change taking place in Prue, Max must sense something. But, apart from his obstinate insistence on redecorating the house, Max appeared to be behaving normally.

True, he was a shade more bad-tempered, more prone to irritation, endlessly pottering with the compost heap, sorting his fishing flies and polishing the guns – the habits accrued from a lifetime.

'How could he *not* know, Bella?' Prue asked the cat who was sitting on the boiler in the kitchen. 'I know I would.'

Bella's green-eyed stare suggested that Prue was fooling herself.

'Yes, perhaps you're right.' Prue stroked Bella's paw.

Blindness to the centre of the other was how a marriage survived. If you knew too much about your spouse, the marriage stood less of a chance when changes occurred.

Prue derived comfort from her conclusions but took to observing Max secretly – from the kitchen window, from under her eyelashes – and to listening for hidden messages in their conversations. At the same time, she was making comparisons and hating herself for doing so: between one pair of eyes and another, between one mouth and another. Not surprisingly, Jamie's face took on the dazzle of the younger and fitter – with the additional allure of the absent – which made Prue want to weep for her unfairness.

'How are we doing with the plan to encourage Jane's friends?' Max asked as they went to bed that evening.

Prue was cleaning her face at the dressing table. 'Lydia is coming over this weekend.'

'We must make more of an effort.'

'You mean *I* don't?' said Prue sharply.

'I didn't say that.'

Prue reached for the tissue box. 'I'm busy at the moment.'

Max flung open a drawer and searched for a clean pair of pyjamas. 'However busy, there are some things on which neither of us should compromise,' he suggested.

'No.'

Prue patted her skin with a tissue while her heart somersaulted and dived. He knows. *He knows.* She folded up the tissue and threw it away. 'No, Max, I suppose not.'

In bed, Max reached for Prue. She submitted, taking a perverse pleasure from her submission, sickeningly aware, so tortuous and labyrinthine is the female psyche, that the frisson she derived from her suspicions added an essential ingredient to the punishment. And Max, suspecting his wife and suspecting that Prue might know that he knew, exacted his dues as he wished, silently and a little desperately, and Prue paid up.

Thus, out of the other's complicity, a strange but mutual dependence was created.

Max rolled away from her. 'Sorry,' he said. 'I'm tired.'

Prue pulled herself upright on the pillows and gazed down at her husband. He seemed more brittle and less substantial than she had realized, and the shadow of her treachery beat its wings over the bed they had shared for so long. There was a tiny scar at the base of Max's neck, a mole on his shoulder and a line had trammelled its way down his cheek. Anguish and the pity she dreaded stirred in her.

'So am I,' she said.

'You've always been good at the soft-soap.' Max swung his legs over the side of the bed and went into the bathroom. She heard the click of the medicine cabinet, the sounds of pills being shaken from a bottle and teeth being cleaned.

Prue threw back the sheets and, clutching her bunched-up nightdress against her, joined Max in the bathroom. He was inspecting his reflection in the mirror and their eyes met. With a sigh, Prue leaned against his back and slid her arms around him, hoping to gather up his tiredness and hurt. Their image merged in the mirror.

'My dearest Prue,' he said and, busy with her own thoughts, she missed the bitter, mocking note.

Perhaps, she thought as she lay rolling the edge of the sheet under her nails, it was her love for Max that provided the source of her love for Jamie. Perhaps love is like an amoeba; if it existed, it divided and continued to do so. Once you had learnt to love, it multiplied, leaving the original intact.

Darling Prue,
    [Jamie's letter had arrived at the bookshop a
couple of weeks after the Becketts had come home]
I'm sitting in this café and I might as well be on the
88 bus for the place is full of English. We are all in
one piece. Just. It's hot. The baby has been ill. Violet
is worried about her work. You will sympathize.

Well, no, I don't sympathize, Prue thought, not entirely immune from a little malice.

    It is beautiful here and I would love to share it
with you. I love the olive trees but I'm not up to
describing on paper what I see. I'll tell you about it
instead. It's also painfully apparent that I've forgotten
all my Italian . . .

Prue was conscious of a tinge of impatience at the peripheral detail.

I miss you, Prue. More than I can write. Each
night before I fall asleep, I picture you and I imagine
kissing your face. This morning in Siena cathedral
(which looks like a black and white ice-cream) I
found myself lighting a candle and saying your name.
It is not the sort of thing that I normally do but I was
reminded of Winchester. Luckily, Violet was seeing to
Edward. She is doing her best to cope and, I must
say, being very patient, for her . . .

Prue looked up from her letter. The sensation of nails
scraping down the inside of the chest cavity was not an
everyday experience and she was taken aback at how physical
jealousy can be. Violet, the wronged wife, was bad enough. But
Violet, the good and the patient, was unbearable. Violet, who
had told Prue repeatedly that she hated her, that she was only
a convenience and boring, boring, boring . . .

I want to tell you something, Prue, something I find
awkward to say and is easier to show, or to write, but
what I feel for you, Prue, influences everything. It
gives me enormous joy to tell you that, but also
anguish because our lives are arranged as they are
and the situation is as it is.
    PS I bought you this card of the Botticelli
Madonna. She reminded me of you.

It is as it is.
The card was one of those small rectangles of thick paper
on which was reproduced a suitably religious painting to be
sold in Catholic churches and shops. On the back he had
written, but not signed, 'I needed you to see Italy properly. I
love you.' In the paler English sun, the colours in the figures

and landscape beyond glowed with an enigmatic radiance: pink with a green tinge, blue, a hint of gold. Rich, joyous and assured.

Prue destroyed the letter, even though she desperately wanted to keep it, but decided she could risk keeping the card. There were several caches untouched by the male hand in Hallet's Gate. The plastic box where Prue stored bathroom cleaning equipment, the Hoover and the linen cupboard. But guaranteed absolutely inviolate was the mending bag. Prue hid the card under a torn summer skirt unlikely to be resuscitated and Jane's green poloneck sweater with a hole in the elbow.

It is as it is.

Prue ran a bath as hot as she could bear it and soaked herself until her skin turned the colour of salmon mousse. She washed her hair in two different shampoos and applied conditioner that had been so expensive she would not dare to confess its purchase even to Kate. The hairwashing was followed by applications of body and face creams and scent.

So had women prepared for men since time immemorial, but when Joan, repeatedly harried over this knotty problem, had been asked about her male clothing, she stated that the matter of dress was a small thing.

Scented and arrayed, Prue dialled Kate's number where Jane was staying for the night.

'Kate? Just checking that Jane's all right.'

'Fine. She and Judy are dressing up at the moment and arguing as to who should be the tragic Queen of Scots and who the executioner.'

'What are they using for the axe?'

'Good point, sweetie. I'll check.'

Prue listed the possibilities in her head, all of them menacing.

'Prue. That reminds me, let's set a date for the Christmas

concert now.' Kate was showing signs of settling down to one of their extended conversations. Prue cut her off.

'Kate,' she said, 'I don't want to do it this year. I think someone else should have a go. I want . . .' she gestured into the air, 'I want time off.'

'Prue! You always do it.'

'Precisely.'

Kate's voice had gone a little cool. 'It's not like you to back off. You were so keen earlier in the year.'

'Sorry. I think fresh blood is called for.'

The silence at the other end indicated that Kate was waiting for the confidences which both women would normally expect from the other after such a revelation. None was forthcoming.

'All right, Prue. You don't *have* to say anything. I suppose Molly did warn me—'

'Molly warned you of what?' Prue gritted her teeth.

'Nothing really. She just mentioned that you had been very preoccupied, which wasn't like you. Apparently, you've signed off the flower rota.' The rising inflection in Kate's voice indicated the friend with proprietorial rights of two decades or so of friendship who suspected something was up and wanted to know. 'Have you and Molly had words?'

Terror that sharp, nosy Molly had worked it out, made Prue reckless. 'Sometimes I wish Molly would jump in the ford.'

'Prue!' Kate was genuinely shocked, but also rather titillated at the spectacle of Prue letting rip.

'I think we'd better finish this conversation,' said Prue and put the phone down. She sat and looked at it, very sand-coloured, very plastic, and came to the conclusion that it was one of the ugliest she had ever seen. Then she dropped her head into her hands and pictured her vengeance on Molly. After a minute or two, she dialled Kate's number.

'Kate? I'm sorry I lost my temper and you're wonderful to look after Jane. I'll reciprocate. Promise.'

'OK.' On occasion, Kate could brood on a slight like a Greek fury but she was reluctant to relinquish capital advantage in the shape of an uncalled-in favour. 'Since you're my friend, I won't tell you what I really think of you.'

Just as well, thought Prue as she sat, tense and excited, in the London-bound train. I'm like an animal, streaking back to its lair. A she-wolf. A jackal, caught on camera lens as it lopes across the horizon. Clever. Feral. On heat.

The train slid into Basingstoke station. Basingstoke apparently had the highest figures for divorce in the south of England. Or was it suicide? Set out in bland, box-like estates – the Home Closes, Hill Rises and Manor Gates – the houses in Prue's line of vision looked too neat and new for divorce and death. Yet behind the net curtains and pots of begonias, messy things were taking place and people were behaving badly.

She considered good behaviour and was forced to conclude that hers – dutiful wife, loving mother and village stalwart – had been easy because it required no special effort, a depressing conclusion for someone who had spent twenty years imagining the opposite.

Unfolding the *Independent*, she tried to concentrate on an article on whether child benefit should be stopped or not. We should not be selfish, wrote the journalist. Shouldn't we? Selfishness is a sucker which shoots without warning from the main stem and threatens to destroy the whole. Rose manuals counsel that suckers should be snapped off – not cut – at the root base. Prue looked up as the train drew out of Basingstoke. The truth was, she wanted to be selfish. She no longer *wanted* to behave well, but to let go, to step out of her skin and, exposed, pulsating, blood racing, sun-warmed and supple, fly through thin, singing air.

Fleet, Farnborough, Woking, Surbiton . . . a litany of southern England rushed past, bathed in a hot yellow light – the kind of places immortalized in black-and-white films starring Kenneth More and Richard Todd when there was forever tea at the Pantiles and everyone played cricket according to the rules.

Discarding the newspaper, Prue picked up the glossy magazine she had bought at the station, which was filled with articles on women's positions in African tribes, and the latest in face-lifts and ferocious diets. Inserted among them was one on unfaithful wives, purportedly in-depth. The women recorded their need for fulfilment. Yes, yes, thought Prue. She recognized the power of an affair – the power of a secret – to consume an ordinary life. To make that life seem more significant, precisely because it was secret.

Yes.

The aphrodisiac of terror at being discovered. How to deal with it: run, fight, defend? The need to occupy territory that had nothing to do with your family. A place where you were not viewed as a wife or a mother.

Yes.

None of them spoke of the ravening need, the greed, the hot pulsing rage for another's body. Of lust and tenderness, of darkness and desire, of the sweetness of gorging on another's mind.

Neither did these women speak of the loss of innocence that Prue had found more shattering than relinquishing virginity or giving birth. She *knew* now, for certain, that all of us harbour secret areas of darkness. And those who know this are truly exiles from the Garden of Eden.

Thus, gentle, hitherto contained Prue, hurried along the platform at Waterloo and Jamie, waiting by the barrier, watched her search for him and hoarded anticipation for a few extra seconds before he raised his hand and waved.

They stood looking at each other with famished and desperate eyes. Then, unaccountably, Prue took fright. A summer holiday was a long time and it was possible that things had changed.

'Prue.' Jamie's eyes had settled deep into his tanned face. 'I can't touch you because if I did . . .'

Relieved, she moved towards him. 'You're brown.'

'Boiled to be precise.'

For a second, he was back in the Tuscan hills retasting the vividness of longing, reluctant to yield up the intenseness of the feeling.

'How long have you got?' Prue asked.

'An hour-ish.'

'No time for the hotel.'

'No.'

They walked across Hungerford Bridge to the Embankment Gardens. A hot wind whipped at their clothes and below, slapping at the bridge's moorings, the Thames flowed, dull, poisonous-looking green water in which drifted an assortment of flotsam.

It was less windy in the gardens, and the ground was scabby with dried earth and litter and, because it was mid-morning, they were empty of people, except for a couple of tramps who sat on a bench sharing the contents of a cider bottle. Jamie and Prue sat down on an adjacent one, and only then did Jamie's brown fingers slide up over her hands and catch her by the wrist. 'You've hardly said a word.'

She moved closer and smelt warm body and familiar aftershave. 'Words are not useful at the moment.'

He smiled. 'I wish.'

I wish. She wished. She wished what? That, like a moll in Boswell's London, he would grab her, drag her into the shadows of the bridge and take her against the wall. A knee-trembler, in the hot, airless city, hard and fast enough to assuage the tormenting wen of desire.

She listened to his account of outings, meals, Edward, paintings, the primitive kitchen . . . grateful that he kept his account shorn of Violet.

'And you?' he finished.

Prue supplied an account of house painting, Jane, the disappointing school report, the garden. In her ears, she sounded dull and uninspired but Jamie, observing the movement of her generous mouth and the soft, creamy skin on her cheeks and neck, felt his feelings renew and expand.

'That's all,' Prue finished a little helplessly.

With a sudden movement, Jamie put his arm round her and turned her face up to his.

'Enough,' he said, and kissed her.

Suborned by the mouth on hers, Prue drank of it with the greed of the dehydrated. She murmured his name, her husband, her home, her child pushed into a dark area where she could not see them. Jamie ran his hand across her shoulder, caressing the soft part of her upper arm and gave it a little pinch.

'Fat,' she said.

'Don't you start.' Jamie kissed the area of softness behind Prue's ear which especially fascinated him. 'I love you, Prue, and I missed you.'

Prue stretched and closed her eyes. The sun shone down on the lids and orange and red exploded into her eyeballs. She had never, ever felt so easy in her skin, so absorbed into life. One of the tramps shot them a look and laughed.

'That's right,' he said in a surprisingly cultured voice. 'Go on.'

Jamie released Prue and got to his feet. 'I'll ring you. Soon.'

He's had enough, flashed through Prue and her happiness

vanished just like that. She got up from the bench, suddenly weary of her vulnerability and of a situation that absorbed so much of her energy. Jamie took her by the hand, tucking his thumb into the hollow of her palm and they walked up the stone steps in Buckingham Street.

Prue heard herself cry out, 'I don't think this will do, Jamie. It's no good, I can't bear it anymore.' She meant the switchback of emotion and despair that she was on, but Jamie misunderstood her.

'I don't think I can either.' Jamie's thumb pressed hard into her cupped hand. 'Let's go to the hotel.'

'That's not what I meant.'

'Let's go to the hotel. I'll make an excuse at work,' he repeated. 'Will you wait? Then we can discuss what we're going to do.'

Prue was expected back by Jane, the supper required attention, Kate might be busy. Her absence would look odd.

'Yes,' she replied, shuddering in anticipation, at the mercy of the rolling waves of joy that, after all, he loved her. 'I'll wait.'

She paid no attention to Jane sounding tearful when she rang, to Kate's obvious annoyance, to Max coming home to an empty house – to the sort of considerations that she had poured her energies into over the years and imagined were enough.

No. As she and Jamie tore off their clothes in the hotel, Prue realized that her vision had changed, as once she had made the change from black-and-white television to colour, and could not now remember the former.

'Say you love me.' Jamie was peeling off his socks.

Head inside her T-shirt, Prue told him and pulled it over her head. Then, conscious that Jamie had come from Violet's beauty to her mature body, she folded her arms across her chest. Jamie pulled her to him and she felt the deliciousness of rediscovery, and the burn of his skin against hers.

'I'm so surprised at myself,' he said. 'And I think you are too. This was not part of the life plan.'

She reached up to touch his face. 'Don't say anything. Not now.' She raised her arms towards the ceiling in the ancient gesture – a sun god blessing the earth, or Moloch claiming his victims. 'I'm here, Jamie.'

He ran his hands down her arms and encircled her wrists with his finger and thumb. Then he led her towards the bed.

She thought later, I can't give this up. I can't.

The winged mirror on the cheap dressing table reflected the image on the bed in triplicate and later their separate images as they dressed and said goodbye.

CHAPTER TWENTY

JANE CLICKED THE MOUSE WITH HER MIDDLE FINGER, once, twice, three times, and the icons on the computer screen arrived and departed at her command.

Click. She conjured up a line that elongated across the screen and which another snap of the mouse turned into a circle. This she wrapped with a ribbon (summoned from the icon treasure box), 'painted' it in with light green and the ribbon a darker green. Underneath she used the mouse to call up HAPPY BIRTHDAY DADDY in green type and centred it under the circle.

Gravely she considered the design, checked it for imperfections and printed it out. The result was just what she had striven for. She folded the paper to make it into a card, and inserted it into an envelope ready to give her father the following morning. Well satisfied, she switched off the computer and tidied the desk.

The swing mirror on her dressing table had tipped over and gave Jane a fine view of her ankles and an empty area of carpet. She got up to adjust it, and her image came into view.

A child's face was caught in it, on to which she busily superimposed the features she wanted to see. Underneath the fair-skinned face and thick dark eyebrows, there was a body on the cusp of change which she examined with the same absorbed attention, and played the what-will-I-look-like-when-I-grow-up? game.

Tall, blonde, thin? Alice said she looked like a horse without a chin. Implying that it almost was, Lydia had said that wasn't *quite* right, which if it was meant to be loyalty ranked with the rottener variety.

Would Alice and the others like her next term? Apprehension at what might be in store settled on Jane with the weight of a hundred preps undone and a hundred hundred loathed steamed puddings. She hated herself for being weedy and fragile, for minding, but the memory of the previous term's misery made her feel sick.

'You can't run away,' her mum had told Jane (with a catch in her voice) when Jane had cast herself into Prue's lap and begged to be allowed to leave.

'Why not?' asked Jane with the straightforward logic of the child. 'Why can't you run away if it saves you?'

Why not? Prue asked herself, but said, 'We have to stay and stick things out otherwise we would always be running away, because quite a lot of things we find ourselves doing have their bad moments.'

Prue gathered Jane into her arms and they talked over the problem for a long time.

Jane raised her eyebrows and stuck out her tongue; the image in the mirror responded. She had failed to make her mother understand that *understanding* was not enough: it did not *change* anything. It did not make Alice and the others like her.

'But you will change,' her father pointed out when they took the problem to him for a second opinion. 'Do you remember,' he said, 'when you wouldn't go downstairs because they seemed so large and frightening?'

'Wasn't that Violet?' Jane accused him. 'She was the scaredy one.'

'No, darling,' said Prue, 'Daddy's right. You wouldn't go down those stairs for ages.'

Some comfort was available, for only half the holidays had gone. Seven weeks was a long time, as adults kept informing her infuriatingly. But it depended how you looked at it, and how it seemed to *you*, and Jane was inclined to pessimism. Three and a half weeks would vanish. Just like that. She knew – she just knew. However hard she tried to make the holidays different and special, they would slip from her grasp.

Diverted by the pinkness of her tongue, she waggled it, practised a smile and pulled back her hair to check on the effect. Then she stood sideways to examine the outline of her body and sucked in her stomach which she reckoned stuck out too much. Jane frowned. She was too fat. *Much* too fat. Yet again, she wished that she had a sister with whom to ruminate over these problems. Half-sisters, or rather Violet, were no use.

The inspection over, Jane launched on a hunt for the green corduroy skirt and polo-neck jumper that she planned to wear for her father's birthday supper. The skirt was unearthed from underneath the bed and she smoothed the creases out as best she could. Her next task was to bully her mother into ironing it for her.

Finding the jumper proved a problem, until she hit on where it would be.

Jane winged down the stairs that had once given her so much trouble and launched herself into the drawing room. The chest of drawers in which her mother kept her sewing materials and wools was pushed against the wall under the window and, most weeks, Prue liked to put a vase of fresh flowers on the top. This week, she must have forgotten for the flowers had died. A smell of decay pricked at Jane's nose and she wrinkled it in disgust. Some water had been spilt accidentally on to the wood beside the vase, bleaching a stained whorl of grain into the dark wood. Knowing her mother would be upset, Jane scrubbed at it with the cuff of her cardigan but it was too late.

She opened the drawer.

A couple of hours later, Molly spotted Jane trudging up the main street and hailed her.

'Enjoying the holidays?' Her briskness faltered as Jane turned a blotched and stained face towards her.

It was as if, Molly informed Keith over a supper of mince and cabbage, the child had grown up, almost aged, overnight. 'There was such a funny, bleak look in her eyes,' she said. 'It made me shiver.'

After she had cleared the dishes, Molly got on the phone to Kate.

At the same moment, Max was in a partners' meeting being invited, in addition to his usual duties, to take over administration of the Brussels and Madrid offices. Would he have any objections?

Various thoughts chased through Max's mind, among them pleasure at the recognition. Aware they might be offering it to him because no one else would take it, he concentrated on savouring the sensation before replying that, yes, he would be delighted.

His subsequent thought was that he would be spending less time at home.

Was it worth waiting for? Prue enquired over their after-dinner coffee. Oh, yes, he replied. I'm no saint and, believe it or not, ambition is not necessarily diluted by age. Of course not, said Prue, eyes fixed on his face. Of course not.

At that moment the telephone rang and Max got up to answer it. Prue went out to make more coffee.

'How nice to hear you, Molly,' said Max, at his most impassive.

'It was you I wanted to talk to, Max.' Molly was uncharacteristically hesitant. 'I've just had a word with Kate.'

'Have you?' Max knew at once that the conversation had a subtext, and he marshalled defences to protect his wife. 'But why ring me up to tell me this fascinating fact?'

'We're both worried about Prue. She's sort of gone off.'

'You make her sound like a dairy product. What do you *mean* precisely?'

Although not intimates, Molly and Max knew each other well. At least, Molly reckoned she knew Max well enough to take the bull by the horns. 'Stop being the lawyer, Max. You know what I mean. Do please persuade Prue to do the Christmas concert as normal. Kate is quite upset at having to do it on her own.'

'Why doesn't Kate talk to Prue?'

'She will, she will.' Molly sounded impatient that Max should fasten on peripherals. 'But I thought I would drop a word in your ear first. It's better if you talk to her.'

Is it, my God? Max extracted his tartan handkerchief from his lapel pocket and folded and refolded it. These two women had discussed and weighed and analysed his beautiful, private Prue, and his mood darkened.

'Look, Molly. It was kind of you to ring. But Prue must do as she wishes—'

'There is the *village* to think of and we're not so large that we can afford slackers.'

'Perhaps she's done enough? There are others.'

'Goodness me!' Molly's exclamation contained genuine outrage at the idea that anyone should sign off Dainton – and Max, folding and refolding the tartan material into patterns, had to concede that Molly's brand of – irritating – integrity was the stuff of heroines. Boudicca and Florence Nightingale probably said much the same things. And, of course, the wretched Joan.

'You know as well as I do, Max, it's only a certain type that does things and Prue's one of them.'

'Perhaps she's changed type.'

'Well, she can't.'

'Prue's owed a break, but I'll see what I can do,' he said. 'You'll have to leave it at that, Molly.'

Max terminated the conversation and gave a little smile as he returned the handkerchief to his pocket. Whatever pain she caused him, at least Prue was his, not theirs.

What happened to Joan? asked Jamie on the phone. Many things, said Prue. Abandonment, martyrdom, rediscovery, deification. By the time of her capture, she had become an embarrassment to the Dauphin, whom she had helped to crown, and he made no effort to ransom her. That, she added, in an age when ransoming was as commonplace as presenting a credit card is today.

Poor, wonderful, blazing, sincere Joan who wanted to kick the English out of France, what must she have thought in her miserable cell?

Never trust anyone, said Jamie. She should have known that. Politics always rate higher than religion and morality.

Not always, Prue threw back. They paused at this point to savour the erotic frisson engendered by this tiny disagreement, and became sidetracked.

Whatever happened, said Prue later, this time to Max (these days all her conversations seemed to be conducted three ways, but at different times), it was clear the English were not going to be cheated of their bonfire. 'We like bonfires, don't we?' said Max. 'Guy Fawkes and all that.'

Prue looked at him. 'You don't understand about Joan, do you?' she said. 'Not really.'

'Perhaps not.' Max sighed as he conceded the point.

The Church fell over itself to condemn Joan as a heretic, that most tricky of states to prove and requiring intimate knowledge of the accused.

'How did they do that?' Max asked.

Prue found herself breathing very quickly. The Church's insurance policy was the presumption that the accused is always guilty until proved innocent, this *a priori* conviction being useful in a case like Joan's.

'Ah,' said Max. 'Yes, I see.'

'But,' he queried after a long pause, 'did this not mean that the King of France had been crowned by a heretic?'

'Let us say,' replied Prue, 'that, having ennobled her brothers, the King ordered a certain Guillaume Bouillé in 1450 to prove that the English had rigged Joan's trial. It was the first of many procedures to rehabilitate her – for complicated political reasons, not because she was a saint and a heroine.'

'What else happened to her?' Jamie took up the subject again when he next telephoned.

Her image got used, and by her immediate family too, Prue told him. And the irony is: it was their greed and smallness, admittedly harmless, that ensured, rather like advertising a product, the spread of the story about Joan's extraordinary career. Five years after her death, her brothers pitched up in Orléans leading a woman in armour on horseback. She was, they maintained, Joan risen from the fire. People loved it.

They were exposed but, unabashed, the brothers were present in Notre Dame in 1455 to aid the touching tableau of their mother begging a papal commission with cries and groans to rehabilitate her daughter.

In later centuries, when Joan's life and death had faded into a footnote, and she had been almost forgotten, descendants of her brothers used her unimpeachably chaste and chivalrous image to prove that the family was, in essence, noble, and published books to that effect. As a result, Joan was again talked about and the interest in her led, eventually, to her canonization.

'No service to France,' wrote one of these impeccably noble authors, 'can be compared to the Maid's.'

He would, wouldn't he?

'But he was right, wasn't he, Jamie, even if it was for the wrong reasons?'

Ergo. You do not have to ride out to battle with your precious standard streaming behind you and your courage screwed to its limit . . . You do not have to be burnt at the stake in front of a howling crowd to be immortal. You do not have to be in almost daily conversation with God and bring off feats of the near miraculous and boot the English out of France. To save you from a second death you merely require a bandy-legged, pendulous-nosed king who could sign and stamp a piece of paper which ennobles your no-good brothers.

The peripherals to the story.

AUTUMN

CHAPTER TWENTY-ONE

'LEGS APART,' ORDERED THE BEAUTY THERAPIST.

Violet obeyed. She was shivering slightly, having been ordered into the shower to wash off the exfoliant which the therapist had rubbed – a little too enthusiastically – all over her with a loofah. Now, in the tricky part of the operation, Violet was being wrapped in wet bandages, wide flannel ones used in hospitals to conceal gaping wounds but now moulding the contours of Violet's (imaginary) cellulite to her hip.

'You're a lovely colour, Mrs Beckett.'

'Yes,' she said with a degree of satisfaction. 'We were in Italy in June and the tan seems to have stayed.'

'Wider,' said the therapist, whose own face and body glowed electrified and slender, and extracted a roll of plastic wire from the clutter on the shelf. Beginning with the right leg, she coiled it round Violet's bandaged body and a prolonged tussle ensued to anchor it properly. Keeping her legs obediently apart, Violet closed her eyes while hands invaded parts of her body not normally in the public domain and summoned a composite image of Cindy Crawford/Jane Fonda/the Princess of Wales as a compensation for the indignity.

'Hop up on to the table, Mrs Beckett, dear.'

Hop! It was doubtful if Violet was in the running for

breathing. Nevertheless, she wriggled herself as best she could into a horizontal position.

'Fine,' she said faintly.

The therapist attached electrodes to what, Violet devoutly hoped, were the correct areas of her body, and wrapped her in a length of plastic sheeting which she anchored with clothes pegs. Thus, like a chicken on a supermarket shelf, Violet lay and gave up her soul – and a lot of her money – in yet another pursuit of the body beautiful.

'Coming up now, dear.' The therapist busied herself with the machine, punching in numbers and flicking switches.

A sensation remarkably like the first stages of labour invaded Violet's torso, which shuddered under the impact. Neither the sensation nor the memory it engendered did she wish to dwell on. Reinforcing her unease, an extra strong charge of electricity shafted through her pelvic region and she winced.

'Bear up, Mrs Beckett.' The therapist patted her face. 'Are we all right?'

At least, the injunction was not 'Bear down.' Anything but that . . .

Violet closed her eyes and visualized electric worms – no, centipedes digging with busy legs through her dimpled cellulite and tossing it aside into her drainage system. Gathered up like Nile silt, it surged past pink muscles and vitreous green and red organs the colour of thirties china . . . to where? Not quite sure of the process of excretion, Violet and her Pilgrim's Progress of fat came to a halt. It would be disgorged somehow, in a glistening, creamy flood into the pipes bisecting London.

Bliss.

'We are very quiet at this point, Mrs Beckett, in order to work on our serenity.'

Eyes tight shut, Violet worked on her serenity and counted

numbers with a miser's loving, lingering relish: one centimetre, two, three even, off the hips.

The telephone shrilled in the tiny room. The therapist clicked her tongue with annoyance and squeezed past the table on which Violet lay to answer it. Violet tossed one more centimetre into the equation.

'Yes, she is here,' said the therapist with some surprise. 'But my client is undergoing a treatment and cannot be disturbed.'

There was a long pause, interposed by several 'buts' from the therapist. Violet's eyes snapped open. Her first thought was that the auction she was conducting had gone wrong. Her second that Gardener's, the American publishing house who was bidding in the auction, had backed down. If nobody was going to come to the ball she would look pretty damn foolish. Her priorities established, only then was a further thought at liberty to form: Perhaps there's something wrong with Edward?

'Well, if you *must*,' said the therapist in icy tones. 'Just a minute.'

There was a great deal of jerking and pulling of telephone flex and the receiver was inserted under Violet's chin.

'Hallo,' she said in a manner designed to disguise the fact that she resembled a mummy in the British Museum. An evening breeze of electric current played up and down her stomach.

'Violet, it's Lavinia. Gardener's have faxed in with what they say is their best offer of a hundred thousand. I thought you ought to know. They want our answer this afternoon otherwise they're withdrawing it.'

There was no apology from Lavinia for the interruption, neither did Violet expect one. 'They seem dead keen,' continued the voice, which was all breathy and excited. Bound to her sides, Violet's fingers twitched. She nudged the receiver with her head.

'Any more come in?'

'Nope.'

'Right. Tell them I'll get back to them in a couple of hours and could you tell Hayden where it's at, and say I'll be in the office to deal with it in an hour.'

'Yup.'

Almost too late, Violet realized she had made a strategic error. It was not a good idea to let it be known to the managing director that she was out enjoying a long lunch – at least, not these days. She changed tack.

'Scrub that, Lavinia. Just ring Gardener's and say we'll be back to them before close of play, our time.'

The evening breeze switched location and shifted to her bottom where it rippled in and out of the creases.

'OK, Violet.' Lavinia sounded suitably impressed by Violet's decision-making qualities. The phone went dead.

'Sorry,' said Violet, who was anything but at having her status so satisfyingly confirmed, if only to a beauty therapist.

'Well, dear, it seems you can't have much peace.' The therapist returned to dial-twiddling and did not look particularly impressed. She had witnessed this sort of thing many times. 'Not very good for the stress levels.'

'How much longer have I got on?'

'To get the real benefit, I should keep you here for another three-quarters of an hour.'

A brief but violent battle was waged in Violet's head. Three-quarters of an hour on the machine, half an hour to get back – leaving only the minimum to ring round and whip up from other bidders in the ring. If she was going to perform prodigious feats and pull in maximum dollars – and therefore the maximum kudos – she needed to be at the end of the telephone.

On the other hand, there had been an outrageous wait to

get on this machine and she wanted to extract every ounce. Correction: she wanted every ounce extracted from her.

'Everything all right, Mrs Beckett?'

Lianas of fat roped Violet to the table. Pound and dollar signs glinted on the ceiling where a fan whirled. What if a decision was taken in her absence? The memory of the disastrous meeting when she had annoyed the managing director had left its scars, and others – notably that prat Sebastian Westland – were keen to gobble up Violet's territory. In addition, the MD was hot on observing good corporate behaviour and had made it clear he thought it would be proper to sell the book to their mother house in the United States. Their mother house was not offering as much as Gardener's but it was just possible that the corporate view would throw a spanner in the works she had so carefully orchestrated.

'Turn the machine off, please,' she said. 'I'm afraid I've got to go.'

'Well . . .' The therapist's expertly tinted skin turned pink with annoyance.

'Don't worry. I'll pay. Do you have another appointment?'

'Except for Monday at seven thirty nothing for two weeks.'

'Fine,' said Violet, and waited to be un-shrinkwrapped. 'Book me in. I'll come on from the office.'

What about Edward? said a voice in her ear as she flagged down a taxi. You're already going out two evenings next week.

Emmy will cope said a second, louder, one. And Edward is far too young to notice whether I'm there or not.

Violet emerged much later that evening from the office, elated. Clever negotiation – a combination of insinuation, nerve and tricksiness – had ensured a deal thirty thousand dollars up on the Gardener's offer, and Violet had been congratulated all round.

'I'll get Julia to run out to the offy and buy a bottle of wine,' said Sebastian, flicking his expensive patterned tie in Violet's direction. 'Or has the little woman to run home?' Sebastian was given to comments like that. He thought they were funny. Violet, who had perfected the art of pretending to scratch her left arm so that she could check her watch without seeming to do so, rubbed at her wrist. Six o'clock. Just OK.

Julia, his secretary, told Sebastian to run his own errands, thank you, which resulted in a sharp little exchange. Eventually, a couple of bottles of chardonnay were opened and the office got stuck in.

Violet did not drink much: alcohol had never appealed to her, and she distrusted its power to make one lose control. She did not mind others losing control, providing they were not too disgusting – it was all grist to her mill. Rather, Violet did not care to let her guard slip but she was happy enough to watch her colleagues make inroads, and concentrated on sparkling. Tonight, however, she felt that her store of energy – which she had come to realize was finite – was being depleted. After a while, she slid off the desk on which she had arranged herself for the others to take advantage of her short skirt.

'Must go, folks.'

Sebastian also disengaged himself from a group. Violet's nostrils flared slightly, a wildebeest having been given a warning signal. 'I'll share a taxi with you, Vi.' He inflected the 'Vi'. 'We go in the same direction,' he said and gazed blandly into her face. It was the look he always assumed before he contradicted someone in a meeting.

Violet opened her mouth to say no, for she wanted some peace, but remembered the advice she had read in an American magazine – never neglect opportunities to bring enemies round – and thought better of it.

The London streets wore the distinctive air of a wet summer. Moisture oozed from the roads and pavements. Still oily from her session, Violet longed for a bath.

Sebastian indicated the nearest café. 'Like a proper drink?' Thump went the hoof on the savannah floor.

'No, thank you.' Violet was at her most gracious.

He did not press her but hailed a taxi and gave directions. Violet sat with her briefcase across her knees, hoping it suggested the ultimate in female power-broking and debated with herself as to whether it was sensible to bring up the changes she had suggested to the marketing meetings and which were still being discussed. Caution won, and she remained silent. Sebastian moved closer.

'What does your old man do?'

'Merchant banker. Why?'

'Just wondered.' Sebastian's fingers wandered over her thigh and then retracted. 'Sorry.'

Violet opened her mouth to suggest he kept his hands to himself but was forestalled by Sebastian leaning towards her, a mocking little smile stretching his lips. 'You're very beautiful, Vi.'

'Thank you.' Violet suddenly remembered that she had not planned anything for supper and it was seven o'clock.

'Very.' This time Sebastian's hand found its way to the opening of her blouse.

Violet was forced to abandon thoughts of tinned soup and (wholemeal) frozen pizza. She looked at Sebastian. 'Sebastian,' she said. 'Do you mind?'

He squeezed, rather painfully. 'Come on, darling.'

'Sebastian. This sort of thing is very old fashioned, you know, and politically incorrect.'

He paid no attention and Violet knew she had to make a decision. Bear this ridiculous performance for the sake of her ambitions at work – Sebastian being senior and rising – or not. (Actually, he did smell nice and expensive and obviously had a bit of money.)

Not. She moved her briefcase sharply to the right which blockaded Sebastian's access, wriggled free, tapped on the driver's partition and ordered him to stop. Safely on the pavement, she thanked the driver and said, 'Good night, Sebastian. Thank you for the ride. See you tomorrow.'

Not in the least embarrassed, the smile still in place, he sent a little wave through the window as if to say that this was a scene he had played many times and it was neither here nor there as to how it ended. The suggestion that she was only a piece of skirt stung just a little. Nevertheless, Violet skimmed rapidly over the implications of the episode in relation to office politics and made the mistake of watching the taxi out of sight. Then, a pleasing thought occurred: she was smarter and tougher than Sebastian Westland and who was to say who would survive if it came to war.

Taxis being plentiful in Waterloo, she decided to walk to the rank at the station, but became confused with the new layout for the Channel Tunnel terminus and found herself in the station concourse.

It was busy with commuters and holiday traffic, including an army of backpackers heading for the night trains. A few businessmen were swallowing beers in the bars, the more prudent, coffee in the coffee bar. Other passengers were bunched by the magazine racks in W. H. Smith and picking over bargain books. Violet sniffed. She liked the smell of a station.

As Violet made for the taxi rank, she saw Jamie.

He was talking to a woman wearing a short-sleeved,

stone-coloured linen suit with her back to Violet. She was familiar . . . but not, and was looking up at Jamie as she talked. It took a few seconds for the vignette to register properly with Violet and she searched for a comparison. Long ago, before she became ambitious, she had read a novel by Elizabeth Bowen about a meeting in a station. A residual memory fought its way up through the depths of her memory. She then recollected the clever, indulgent, detached French films she had seen many times in New York because it was the thing to do in her circle. In those films people were always meeting in stations. The rendezvous usually constituted or presaged disaster.

The man who looked like Jamie was wearing a grey suit and paisley tie – she had seen them this morning. Black shoes, yes. She was sure about those. Pink-striped shirt. Yes, yes. Grey socks. You see, she acknowledged to herself during the seconds that had stretched and billowed over her head, I know my husband down to the last thread on his back.

He would not be here at seven thirty at night because he comes home on the tube.

In the taxi, Violet stared out of the window into the dusk and noticed, for the first time, Vauxhall Bridge's disintegrating brickwork and the queue outside the doss-house. One of the tramps, frail and bearded, was parked in a wheelchair like an abandoned species. A nuisance who had no use.

Jamie at Waterloo? Why?

Emmy, who was waiting in the kitchen with her fringed suede bag slung over her shoulder, was uncharacteristically short with Violet when she arrived home. Violet got the point.

Emmy hitched the bag over her shoulder and got to her feet. 'Edward's fine. He ate second helpings of all his food.'

'Thanks, Emmy.' Violet spoke with unusual gratitude and added, 'I'm sorry to have kept you.'

Emmy looked at Violet and Violet found her eyes sliding away from Emmy's direct ones which looked angry. 'Is anything wrong, Emmy?'

Emmy wanted to reply that a few things would benefit from brushing up (wages, hours, consideration) but confined it to one. 'I know you don't want Edward to sleep during the day, but I let him nap this afternoon because he was so tired.'

Violet had issued the instruction on the happy assumption that it would make Edward sleep better during the night.

'You mean *you* wanted a rest.'

The words escaped before Violet could reconsider her management technique. At the end of her tether after a long, fractious day, Emmy found herself shrugging. 'If that's the way you want to look at it, Mrs Beckett.'

Violet did see it that way. Her eyebrows snapped together. 'It means I'll be getting up in the night.'

Emmy's mouth opened to say, 'Tough titty' but she thought better of it. Violet opened *her* mouth to say something cutting but was forestalled by the mixture of rebellion and genuine anger on Emmy's face. Violet's annoyance shrivelled and, all at once, she felt exhausted, depressed and uncharacteristically apprehensive.

'Well, Emmy.'

'Well, Mrs Beckett.' Emmy resisted the urge to stick her hands on her hips and glare Violet down; she plaited the suede fringe instead. 'I did what I thought best.'

'Yes,' said Violet, 'I suppose you did.'

Emmy was thoroughly taken aback by Violet's capitulation and told Marie-Laure in the wine bar later that her employer was in danger of going soft. Marie-Laure, who came from Brussels, and held dogmatic notions on routine and discipline and who had the misfortune to be working in a liberal family, remarked that Emmy was lucky to know where she was.

'Am I?' said Emmy, struck by the notion, and ordered another beer.

Normally, Violet fell like a stone into sleep from which she was only dragged by Edward's whimpers. Tonight, she read *The Wakeful Toddler: The Problem of Sleep Deprivation and Its Successful Management* until her eyes felt sore. Why she had been vouchsafed a child who considered sleep a form of torture she would never know. Only that she came near murder when other mothers opened their eyes wide and made remarks such as, 'Oh, heavens, mine slept through the night at three weeks.'

Then she lay awake, brain jogged into frantic activity as she analysed the bits of her life: motherhood, marriage, job, melded together into a rock that she was being forced to carry. Worse, at the heart of the rock was the mass – as easily chopped as the tofu she favoured – of her worry and fatigue which she worked so hard to conceal. Of her dislike of her son.

There, she had admitted it. Terrible words. Terrible meaning. But the confession brought no relief, no cooling hand over her hot, burning guilt. No sudden release of the poison draining from a boil.

Violet shifted tack.

No one could accuse her and Jamie of having a *bad* marriage. On the contrary, it was good. Violet thought back over the early days in New York when Jamie could not have enough of her and power came as naturally as breathing.

Jamie would *not* have been at Waterloo, talking to a woman who was so familiar, and yet not.

Under the sheets, Violet slid a hand towards her sleeping husband and touched his hip, as once he had felt for hers. Jamie lay inert and Violet sighed.

She was still awake when Edward gave his first cry, as usual in the wave band between one thirty and three o'clock, and Violet stumbled out of bed. The plan, à la *The Wakeful Toddler*, which had seemed so sensible and constructive during the day, was to give Edward a bottle of water instead of juice or milk, the idea being to bore him into sleeping through the night.

Edward had other, better ideas and fought for them with vigour. The house seemed to ring with the cries of the helpless, dependent – and unreasonable. At one point, Violet raised her face to the dark ceiling and her own face crumpled. She was tired, oh, so deeply tired, of the business of being in a female body, of babies and female curves, and feeding, and monthly rhythms that caged her as surely as the rat in the laboratory.

'Oh, God,' she whispered. 'Is there no rest anymore?' Sweating with fatigue and a depth of anger she had never experienced before, Violet held her son's wriggling body and pressed into it with her scarlet-tipped fingers. Edward roared in response, as much from surprise as hurt.

'Just shut up, you little beast,' she hissed at him. '*Just shut up.*'

Edward wailed harder. Beatrix Potter frieze, teddy bears, flickering fires, alphabet wall-paper, and empty space which her mother should have occupied, memory and need whirled like the snowstorm in the paperweight inside Violet's thudding head. Rage, betrayal, bitter grief had been trapped there and almost unfathomable fatigue and Violet, goaded to madness by the whole damn bloody business of what she was, of what had been taken away by motherhood, slammed Edward – her unloved son – back into his cot.

The crying stopped. Just like that. Silence enfolded the room.

'Violet! *What* are you doing?' Jamie stood in the doorway. Gasping noises came from the cot. Violet pressed her hands to her mouth, 'Oh, Jamie,' and felt the strength trickle away from her knees. 'Oh, Jamie.'

During those seconds, falling like hot coals between husband and wife, anything could have happened – murder, hysteria, welcome unconsciousness.

Jamie pushed Violet out of his way and picked up his son who, red-faced with the effort, was endeavouring to suck in air. Jamie held him up and, for several desperate seconds, Edward struggled. Then he let out a howl, filled with surprise and terror. With an anguished sound, Jamie cradled the little body to his chest and swivelled towards his wife.

'Get out.'

Violet fled to the sanctuary of her bed. Peace. Darkness. Escape?

She was cradled in her conditioner-scented sheets and duck-down duvet from Peter Jones. It was not her fault that she was so tired that she could not think anymore. Perhaps not even be responsible for what she did?

An image of her son flailing for the breath she had stolen from him superimposed itself. She turned and buried her face in the pillow where her pulsebeats thudded in both ears.

She thought of death.

When she surfaced, Jamie was standing by the bed. 'I've calmed him down,' he said, 'and given him a bottle of milk.'

'Thanks,' said Violet, looking up at him with an expression that Jamie interpreted as defiance.

'I'm going to sleep in the spare room. I think you need some rest.'

'I'm fine.'

'I also think you should go and see a doctor tomorrow.'

He spoke as if she was some distant, and tiresome, relation.

'There's no need to sound like that.' Violet was aware she should apologize. 'I'm sorry I did what I did.'

'You should be.'

At that point, Violet realized that he was seriously angry – and the enormity of what she had done finally sank in. As she so often did, Violet responded with attack. 'It might help if you were around a bit more. You leave it all to me.'

'I do my bit.'

On safer ground now, Violet reared up from the pillows and her eyes narrowed. 'Oh, do you? Who thinks about the shopping, about what to eat, whether the loo needs cleaning? If we have enough nappies, writing paper, shampoo? Tell me who does all that. And tell me if it's just a question of doing it once or week in, week out?' She wrapped her arms around her slenderized shoulders and hugged herself tight. 'It never ends, Jamie, and it makes me tired. Lunch, tea, supper, ironing, beds, cleaning. Chuck in a difficult baby—'

'Shut up, will you?' Jamie had to make a huge effort to stop himself shaking. Violet watched his fists bunch and his conscious effort to relax them. 'Other women manage, and you have Emmy and Mrs Stone to come and clean.' Only just in time, he prevented himself saying, 'Prue does.'

'Other women don't have full-time jobs.'

Oh, God, she had fallen into that one again. Violet saw her mistake too late. Jamie leaned over her, a hand either side of her body. 'You don't *have* to have one. I earn enough.' His breath jetted on to her cheek.

In a curious way, Violet was beginning to enjoy herself. 'That's right, fall back on the caveman and the bank balance. What if I *want* to work and I'm good at it?' She subsided back into the pillows. 'Anyway, you've missed the point.'

'Being?'

'The buck stops with me. You leave this house every morning confident that when you return you will be given an evening meal, your shirt will be ironed, your bed made. Yes?

Who plans all that? Who thinks about it before going to their own work so you can enjoy your meat and two veg?'

There was silence and Violet, sword whirling, drove it home. 'You don't, do you?'

She prepared to continue the fight, to exercise magnanimity in the face of his defeat, to say again she was sorry but, suddenly, Jamie withdrew. Literally. She felt him retreat to a place that did not include her.

And that frightened her most of all – more than the battle, more than her nightmares, more than the selfish, unmaternal side of herself that she did not care to think about too much. More than what she had done to Edward.

'Goodnight.' Jamie sighed, tightened his dressing-gown belt and made for the door, taking this new, puzzling picture of her husband with him.

'Jamie. Wait. Were you . . .' Violet found herself grasping the duvet tight, 'were you at Waterloo station this evening?'

There was an infinitesimal pause. 'No, I wasn't,' he lied. (Prue had met him for a drink before she joined Max at a business dinner, which she was occasionally obliged to do.)

Violet absorbed the information. 'I don't think the bed is made up in the spare room,' she said, with a satisfaction that bordered on the savage. After he had gone she sank down into the bed.

Food, lashings of it, swam across her vision. Muffins dripping with butter. Strawberry shortcake. Beef swimming in thick glossy gravy. Rosy pink shrimps curled into clarified butter, like babies tucked into their cots.

A few hours' sleep were sufficient for Violet to grout the cracks in the carapace – and to convince herself of several things. One: she needed to take a few days off and book into a health farm to recharge her batteries. Two: she had not done anything so very dreadful. Scratch any mother and find a hidden incident, a shaming accident – or four. Three: she had not seen Jamie at Waterloo station with a strange woman. It had been a mistake. A trick of the eye. Thus Violet had no need to worry about her marriage because there was simply no question of failure. Her marriage would survive, come what may.

In the mirror that morning, she drew a line of scarlet around her lips and filled it in.

CHAPTER TWENTY-TWO

THE SUMMER HOLIDAY CAME AND WENT, AND AS PRUE wished, the Valours did not go away. Max finished the decorating, gardened and watched Prue. Prue grew thinner and watched Max.

Jane spent a lot of time with Kate's daughter, Judy, hours with her computer, and frequently disappeared on her bicycle. She also avoided her mother, skipping meals and being unusually difficult. Prue, dividing her time between the bookshop and running the house, unable to meet Jamie (apart from that snatched meeting at Waterloo) because of the school holidays, was driven to exasperation and, finally, a burst of temper.

Jane informed her that she was unfair, unloving and furthermore that she, Jane, was too old to be bossed around by someone like *her*, adding that Prue did not care one bit about her.

Not true, not true, Prue wanted to cry out.

But the cry might not have sounded entirely genuine. In her heart, Prue knew she was missing something important about Jane. But that same heart was too full, too greedy exploring new sensations, too preoccupied to look outside itself.

Prue was discovering the fascination of being entirely self-absorbed. She justified it by telling herself that she was allowed to be selfish, that she was permitted a life other than the one devoted to her family, just once.

Eventually Jane was dispatched back to school for the autumn term, with panic, on behalf of Prue, over nametapes, games equipment and rebellion, on behalf of Jane, over a pair of skin-tight leggings that she had wished to take back and Prue considered inappropriate. Jane went, hugging her software disks, quiet, secretive and distracted, as if, her mother concluded, she was listening in to conversations from another world.

The school always gated the girls for the first two weekends of term and, for the third weekend, Jane was invited to stay with Lydia, a hopeful sign that the friend situation was ameliorating.

Early in the morning on Friday 25 September, the day a twelve-year-old boy in Florida won a 'divorce' from his natural parents, Mrs Harriman, Jane's housemistress, rang Prue. She was brisk but concerned and asked outright if something had occurred during the summer holidays to put Jane off her stroke.

'No,' said Prue. 'I don't think so.'

'She isn't putting any effort into her work, Mrs Valour. In fact, her work is sub-standard for Jane.' Mrs Harriman allowed that information to sink in and then said carefully, 'A little more worrying perhaps is her eating.'

'*Eating!*'

The pause at the end of the phone managed to convey accusation *and* condemnation. 'Yes. I'm afraid Jane is not coping with her food very well.'

'Have you spoken to her?'

'I felt we should speak to you first.'

'I shall come right over after I've finished work.'

There is a world of difference between the detached 'we' of

the school and the anxious 'I' of the mother. Prue rang Gerald to warn him she would have to leave early. She also rang Kate and cancelled tea, and Molly to excuse herself from the parish council meeting.

'I see,' said Molly.

No, you don't, Prue wanted to say. You don't see anything. 'I'm so sorry, Molly, but I think I must go.'

'Yes, well . . .' Molly implied that Prue's dereliction of duty ranked on a par with selling her grandmother to pay a gambling debt.

Autumn was beginning to run tongues of brown and gold over the trees and into the folds of landscape and shorn fields, and the light held the season's milky, tender quality. Ready to move off south, birds were gathering on the telephone wires or wheeled in untidy circles.

Hunched at the steering wheel, Prue, for once, took no notice.

Full realization of culpability does not, she realized, come suddenly. Rather, it seeps into the consciousness, drip by drip, gathering in depth and volume until it is flooded.

Prue's neglect of Jane came home to roost. She had not strained to listen to the voices in her daughter's head, only to her own. She had not perceived that Jane's quietness was, perhaps, a mask placed over turbulence.

She clenched her fingers around the wheel. The luxury of being able to do something without the rest of your life being dragged in was, it appeared, given only to a few: the very lonely and very determined.

'I've gone wrong.' Prue pulled off the band that confined her hair the way Jamie liked it and felt a corresponding surge of anger and frustration at the limitations of her existence.

Two minutes later, Prue had convinced herself that she was being ridiculous, that Mrs Harriman had made a mistake, and that Jane was only taking her time to settle down after a long holiday.

Well, no, Mrs Harriman contradicted Prue as they sat in her austerely appointed room. What they – 'they' again – had noticed in Jane was not naughtiness. Anyone with experience of children could recognize the difference between disobedience and a child who was angry and withdrawn. *She* knew that and – so went the implication – Prue should have known. Further, Jane had been caught at least twice stuffing her food into a paper bag on her lap.

'What do you think it could be?' she asked, directing a please-don't-trouble-to-pull-the-wool-over-my-eyes look at Prue. 'Is there a problem at home?'

Her tone suggested that Prue would probably lie.

Unsettled, furious at being judged, guilty, Prue felt a little sick but forced herself to remember that Jane's welfare came first and to acknowledge that Mrs Harriman had experience in this area. Furthermore, losing one's temper brought only fleeting benefits.

'No, there are no problems, Mrs Harriman,' she said, and imagined a blush spreading in a great, surging red stain over her body. She imagined, too, what that blush would convey to Mrs Harriman. Prue's anger stirred, one of the new emotions thrown up from the whirlpool that now swirled inside her.

Why should taking off her clothes in front of a man other than her husband, an act which had been kept apart from anyone who mattered, not remain private?

Because humans are not rabbits. Pick on any great love story, and an injured party always ends up crying into their pillow. King Mark, Octavia, Mr Karenin, poor simple Charles Bovary. Peter Abelard got it both ways – mental and physical castration (but at least he did not have to hunger and burn for years in a convent like his poor Heloïse).

Because, said the voice, you don't live in a vacuum.

Oh, Joan, she thought, how clever you were not to have anything to do with the flesh.

Peremptorily, she asked to see Jane.

When she saw her mother, Jane gave a visible start and her bottom lip quivered. Prue held out her arms, but Jane held back and avoided the contact.

'Everything all right with Dad?' she asked anxiously. 'He's not ill?' Her fingers left smudged prints on the highly polished brass door handle.

'Yes. Absolutely fine.' Prue swallowed. 'Can you come here, darling? Mrs Harriman is a little worried about you and I thought we could talk about it.'

Jane ducked her head with a gesture that told Prue nothing – and too much.

'I'm fine, Mum,' she said angrily. 'I wish everyone would stop fussing. I'm just not hungry.'

Prue had not mentioned food.

'Darling—'

'Please don't, Mum.' It was no longer a little girl who spoke, but an uneasy hybrid see-sawing between the baby-skinned, silk-haired image embedded in Prue's mind, and the pale, cross, hungry adolescent into which it had metamorphosed.

Prue knew that, sooner or later, innocence is taken away, usually by an adult – that is unavoidable. But if she had been responsible for taking away Jane's innocence too early, she would never forgive herself.

'Darling—'

'Really, Mum,' repeated Jane.

'But—'

'*Don't* fuss,' said the new Jane, tight and unforgiving, and, for the first time in their lives, a door was shut in Prue's face. The blow it dealt, and the grief that flowered like blood after the bullet, shocked Prue into making an audible gasp. Jane's gaze drilled into her mother and Prue imagined that she detected a gleam which was both manipulative – and desperate.

'Darling . . .' She dropped on to one knee. 'Don't be like that.' She captured Jane's hand, the penitent in the painting, and kissed it: the hand off which she had scrubbed dirt and paint, had cradled in her lap after a bath to cut its nails and folded kisses into the damp shell of its palm.

My child.

Jane tugged it away. 'I'll go and get my bag.'

Shorn of her maternal power or, rather, feeling she had forgone it, Prue was left looking stupid on the floor. Children sensed things, did they not? Every act had a consequence, she knew that. Added to which Jane was growing up and quitting the foothills guarded so carefully by her parents.

It was as if, she explained later to her lover and husband (in those separate, three-way conversations), Jane had cut a ribbon and retied it behind her against those who remained. Jamie did not have much to say about it except to tell Prue that she must not put coincidences together – Jane's growing up, their affair – and consider it a case for hanging.

Max said even less.

After saying goodbye to Mrs Harriman, Prue waited for Jane in the car. A trickle, then a flood of girls emerged through various doorways, the smaller ones still drowned and innocent in their uniforms, the older ones looking more knowing but not quite.

Or so it seemed to Prue.

She waited a long time for Jane. Lydia and Fee, another refugee from the bully Alicia's camp, said, 'Hallo, Mrs Valour,' and disappeared. Still no Jane. Prue fiddled with the knobs of the radio, stuffed rogue sweet papers into the ashtray then changed her mind and put them into her pocket. A draught played on her cheek from the open window and she shut it with unnecessary vigour.

Eventually, Jane emerged from the side door and walked, a little unsteadily, towards the car, her knees smooth bone hub-caps under which ran spoke-like legs, a changeling whose thinness had turned from the acceptable into the frightening. She put out a hand to steady herself before she opened the passenger door. Prue gripped the wheel,

'Thought you were never coming, darling.' Scrambled eggs, she decided, mixed with a little cream. Spinach puréed with cream? No Jane might guess. Pasta? Wholemeal bread?

She started the engine. Jane settled herself.

There was silence. No questions. No 'Thanks for waiting.' No 'What are we doing this weekend?' Just silence. Prue concentrated on driving.

'I've got a nice supper for you,' she said, wrongfooting it by mentioning food. 'And maybe we could go for a walk.'

'I don't want any supper.'

'Don't be silly,' said Prue in a mumsy voice and then wished she had kept quiet. 'Of course you want supper.'

At home Prue made hot buttered toast and tea. Jane took a mouthful and sawed at the contents in her mouth, which irritated Prue. For heaven's sake, she wanted to say, refugees are starving. It's good food. Jane piled the toast under her knife. Smudges of exhaustion underlined her eyes.

'How about that walk?' suggested her mother.

The leaves had lost their full-bellied summer note and made a drier, thinner noise, which anticipated their autumn death. Prue listened to the message, and she walked beside Jane down the main street towards the bridlepath that led to the fields. Each day the sun was lodging further down in the sky, sometimes startling red-orange, sometimes diluted by cloud into milky pinks and mauves. A chill threatened.

They passed the village shop and Molly emerged, wearing a navy blue beret and her tweed skirt.

'Any second thoughts about letting us down over the Christmas concert?' she asked abruptly and without preliminaries. She bent over Jane. 'It's not like your mother to back off.'

Prue shoved her hands into her pockets and grimaced as she encountered layers of fluff as deep as time.

'I didn't feel up to it this year, Molly. Besides, others should be allowed to have a go.'

'Not if they're no good at it. That's doing no favours to anyone. It won't do, Prue.'

It won't do. Some women knew what was what and bullied those who did not. Molly was one and, thus, the world behaved itself. Thank God for them, thought Prue.

Jane loitered behind on the bridlepath and Prue waited for her to catch up.

'All right, my sweetie?'

For a moment, it was like old times for Jane slid her fingers into the crook of Prue's arm, with a touch so bony and insubstantial that no impression was made.

'Fine.'

Prue placed her own hand over Jane's and some of her worst imaginings fragmented. The drag, so slight, at her elbow reminded her that this was where she should be, and had been only a few months back. Connected to her village, to her home, to her family. *There* for her daughter.

But instead of satisfaction and rightness, impatience and frustration beat at the bars confining Prue's existence. Their intense, ruthless quality shocked her.

That evening they lit the fire, the first of the season. Prue had forgotten to have the chimney swept and fretted at the army of birds' nests she was convinced lurked up there waiting to conflagrate. 'It's unlike you to forget,' remarked Max, who was on his knees in front of the fireplace trying to work up the flames.

He hunkered back on his heels with an expression that made her flesh prickle, for Prue recognized it. It was a calculating one. She had seen it sometimes when Max talked of Helen.

'I'll see about the sweep,' he said.

She busied herself clearing up the débris from the grate. The dust brushed obediently into a pile and Prue wished it was as easy to tidy up the untidy rag-and-bone shop of her heart. Max brushed ash from his corduroys.

'Nice to have a fire.'

'Ridiculous, really, so early in the year,' said Prue.

The fire struggled at first and then settled down into a respectable heat. Jane and Max plonked themselves on to the sofa and began to read. Uncertain, Prue hovered, trying to interpret any message conveyed by the back view of her husband and daughter and then told herself she was developing paranoia.

She was making the pasta sauce for the Friday supper-on-the-knees, which had become a tradition, when Max came into the kitchen. He uncorked a bottle of wine and poured some into a glass.

'She *is* too thin,' he said. 'We've got to do something. She must have been losing weight all through the summer and I hadn't noticed.'

'She's growing fast.'

Max swung round and stared out of the window. 'Well, what's the best thing?' His back remained turned.

Prue addressed it. 'I think we should watch her for a little longer before we do anything.'

At this, Max turned and stared at his wife with eyes that had turned hostile. 'Aren't you concerned that it might be something serious?'

'Of course I am,' she snapped.

Max took another mouthful of wine. 'Whatever the situation here,' he said, so softly that Prue was not sure that he said it at all, 'it is not permissible to take risks with Jane.'

'Of course not.'

'Eating disorders are usually a sign of anger,' said Max, 'often reflecting unhappiness in the family.'

Impatiently, Prue cut him off. 'Jane is growing fast. She's had trouble at school and she's never liked the food there. That's all.'

Prue reached for a glass – Max had not offered her one – poured out a generous quantity and drank some in silence. It was almost as if Max was waiting for something, but the trouble with playing games was that you required rules. She offered the olive branch.

'You're right, of course.'

'We'll discuss it later.'

Max quitted the kitchen and left a chill behind. Prue picked up the timer and set it for the pasta. At one of Kate's dinner parties, some years back, she had talked to a doctor. He had told her that epidemics followed a pattern, a pathology. The irony was intriguing – a disaster that was so far-reaching, possibly final for those at its centre, could be reduced to a predictable curve.

First there was the upward progression on the graph, the passage of a microbe digging into its chosen territory. Then, at the point when the line hesitated, curved and began its downward journey, was a check inserted – the guilt runnelling in dark veins into the love, madness and greed. Then, perhaps, the retreat.

QED: an epidemic shared much in common with adultery. From its discovery – the seeding in the mind and the body's answering counterpoint – to the greedy chaos it engendered. The tug of desire. Senses stretched until they were transparent and aching. Exhaustion that drove the body and did not permit rest. The selfishness.

Then what?

Prue did not know, for she had not climbed far enough up the graph.

'I don't want it,' said Jane, balancing the tin tray painted with pink roses on her knee. 'I'm not hungry.'

'Have a little.'

'Oh, Mum. Stop going on at me.'

Max's large hand descended on to Jane's skinny arm. 'Your mother is right. You should eat.'

Jane flashed a look at her mother, sighed and poked at the pasta with her fork. 'You can't *make* me eat.'

Again, she flashed a look at Prue. Help me, it said. Help me express my helplessness.

'Come on,' said Max. 'Not-so-plain Jane.' Using the baby nickname obviously touched Jane for she lifted her face, now infinitely weary and bewildered, towards her father. He slid his arm along the sofa and pulled her gently towards him. With the other hand, he picked up the fork with a mouthful of pasta.

'Open up,' he said. 'Storm troopers.'

Jane grinned at the reference to her latest computer game. 'Stupid, Dad.'

All the same, she opened her mouth.

'Chew,' he ordered gently. 'Go on. Bandits nine o'clock.'

Above her full mouth, Jane's eyes locked on to Max's and filled with tears. Prue found herself holding her breath in an agonizing lungful. Jane's jaw began to move. Prue's breath released in a sigh. She watched as Max, murmuring to his daughter, gently smudged away the moisture on her cheeks with his thumb, held her to his large body and fed her, forkful by forkful, until the plate was empty.

Then, cradled by her father, Jane went to sleep in front of the fire.

Max spent most Saturdays in the garden. In fact, he spent more and more time there, and the garden was beginning to acquire an obsessively manicured look.

Currently, he was relocating the compost heap.

That morning, he stood under the plum tree at the end of the garden, which was delineated by a stone wall between it and the road. It was going to be a warm day, but the warmth had not got going yet and the early mist was still in the process of being shredded by the sun. Plums in various stages of decay lay in the grass, jewels exuding a sweet slime above which hummed cones of flies. Amid the richness and plenty of autumn, he seemed a curiously lonely figure.

Or that was how he struck Emmy as she walked up the road.

'Hallo, Mr Valour.'

Down from London for the weekend, she had been walking up by the airfield and could not resist returning via Hallet's Gate, for the family's doings were, she informed Anna, beginning to really intrigue her. (Anna demanded a full-scale report and she wasn't to spare the dirt, and wasn't Emmy getting a bit toffee-nosed herself as she hadn't been in contact for ages?)

Sharp Anna. It was true, Emmy was changing, which was akin to being dragged into a room she had not planned on entering or being given glasses that widened the vision. Still, it was unlikely she would wake up as Cindy Crawford.

Max looked up. 'Hallo, Emmy. I was deciding where to put my compost heap. The old one isn't doing so well.'

This was a red rag to Emmy. She leant over the wall and squinted in the direction of his pointed finger. 'Are you planning to build one or two?'

'Build?' Max's shadow looked huge on the grass. 'I was just going to reposition the heap.'

Emmy got into her stride. 'It would be much better if you built a wooden one. That way the air won't get in and you can keep two on the go.'

'Why don't you come and advise me?'

Emmy didn't require asking twice. At once Max pinpointed the change in Emmy, who was looking much, much better – the jeans and Guernsey sweater moving her from one category to another, as did the short hair, liberated finally from its perm by Mr Twist of Clapham.

'Look . . .' Emmy hauled a piece of paper and a Biro out of her pocket, 'you can build one like this. You need four three-by-one corner posts. Four one-by-one, thirty-inch and twenty-seven inch floorboards. They're cheaper from a demolition contractor.'

'How do you know all this?' Max squinted at the paper.

Emmy shrugged and swiped at the flies. 'I like this sort of thing.'

She appraised the garden and Max suspected that she did not approve of the precise herbaceous border and circular bed in the lawn. It also amused him that he minded.

'I've been trying to get my mum to buy a wormery.' Emmy's face shone with inner conviction. 'But she won't have it.'

'Have you? Tell me.'

Max was fascinated. Emmy obliged and they settled to a conversation in which figured liquid manure, worm casts, air circulation, bacteria and slime.

Max borrowed Emmy's paper and was noting various things on it. 'You dig it twice?' He stooped over the paper and the sun struck his face, opening it to Emmy's inspection. He's upset, she thought in a rush of compassion and decided that she liked him far better than the more obviously attractive Jamie. Particularly if what she suspected – only suspected, mind – was true.

'How long will this take me to do?'

Before she could stop herself, Emmy offered to help. He smiled his sweet, tired smile. 'That would be very nice. Are you by any chance free now to help me buy the materials?'

A motorbike roared down the road and applied its brakes. Like a puppet jerked by its master, Emmy whipped round.

'*There* you are.'

A leather-encased giant leant over the wall and Max was fascinated to see a ponytail straggling from under the helmet.

'Angus.' Emmy looked from Max to the Adonis, every line of her thin face alight with longing, and Max shuddered for her. 'Sorry, Mr Valour. I can help you another time.'

Naturally, Max could not compete with the testosterone-charged Angus – never would have been able to.

'Tomorrow?' Emmy was being pulled out of the garden by an invisible force.

'Of course.'

Extraordinarily, they were back the next day. Both Emmy and Angus.

Building compost bins is a cohesive activity. Nails, planks, posts and fingers – more often than not wrapped in Elastoplast – are the constituents. Those, and the smell of wood: dry, resiny, strong enough to tickle the hairs in the nostrils. That, too, and the smell of earth, which blends the sourness of impacted soil and freshly turned sods, dampened by September rain. Fixing together four simple wooden sides and a lid to ensure that weed seeds and pathogens are destroyed establishes a bond, between material and maker, between bacteria and rubbish, between the cold outer layer which shields and conserves the heat at the core.

'Thank you,' he said to Emmy and Angus. 'Thank you.'

CHAPTER TWENTY-THREE

JAMIE SUGGESTED TO VIOLET THAT IT WOULD BE A gesture if they took the Valours to the theatre. 'Since when have you been a theatre goer?' Violet replied. 'But yes, fine. Get your secretary to organize it and it better be Shakespeare.' Perceiving he was puzzled, she added, 'Don't be witless, Jamie. Shakespeare is educational for Jane.'

They met in the foyer of the National Theatre. Neither Max nor Prue had been to the theatre for some time and Jane was excited. The theatre was brightly lit and humming with noise. As she pushed through the glass doors, Prue felt a stir of anticipation, a pleasing sense that she was out in the world, and it was an interesting place to be.

Violet, who looked in especially thin and confident mode, but felt acid and strangely rudderless, gave Prue a peck on the cheek.

'You look pale, Prue. Stewing too much over Joan of Arc?' She made it sound as if it ranked with unmentionable practices.

'Not over much.' Prue's fingers made their customary excavation of the fluff in her coat pocket.

'Perhaps it's the grey then. I never thought it was your colour.' Violet ran her eyes over Prue's crêpe suit.

Prue had not looked at Jamie, but now she did. 'This is very good of you both. I used to go to the theatre a lot before I married your father.'

'Ah, yes, the fifties,' said Violet, quick as a flash.

'I'm not *quite* that old,' said Prue.

'I know,' said Violet. 'Some days you really don't look your age.'

'Hi,' said Jane to Jamie.

Jamie bent and kissed her, and said, 'I've been looking forward to seeing you. I need some advice on a computer I want to buy.'

Jane lit up like an evening star.

Violet kissed her father. 'Get us some drinks, will you, darling Father. Mineral water for me. With ice and lemon.'

Max obeyed.

The foyer filled up and Prue felt the noise and colour stir her senses into action.

'By the way,' said Violet, placing herself adroitly in Prue's line of vision. 'I've booked in at a health farm.' There was a pause and Prue adjusted her expression into polite interest. 'I've been a bit exhausted lately and I thought it would do me good.'

Jamie appeared surprised. '*Have* you?'

Violet shot her husband a look. Jamie was back in her bed, but, these days, that was about all. 'I told you the other day.'

Jamie slipped a hand into his trouser pocket. 'I must have forgotten.'

A signal tactic of spouses existing in an uneasy silence at home is their rudeness to one another in public. It was a tactic that Violet was indulging in. 'Jamie, you're so stupid these days. Don't you ever listen?' She underlined the role of the-one-who-kept-things-on-course (which she played to the hilt) by casting her eyes to the ceiling.

'You're going somewhere nice, I hope,' said Max, the only

one of the party who appeared to approve the idea.

'Yes, very.' Violet's attention was temporarily diverted by the sight of a woman eating a large smoked-salmon roll.

'I'm thirsty,' said Jane.

'Why didn't you say so earlier?' said her father.

Violet ignored them. 'It's near Newbury,' she said. 'I chose the one closest to Dainton . . .' Prue knew then what was coming. '. . . and I wondered if you could look after Edward for me. Just for the Saturday and Sunday. Jamie or Emmy could bring him down.'

'No,' said Prue, her sense of well-being vanishing. 'I can't.'

'*Can't* I have something to drink?' asked Jane crossly.

'I haven't told you the dates, Prue. How can you say no?'

'Very easily.'

'Mum, you are impossible to get through to these days.'

Prue glanced at Jane, and perceived, instead of her loved daughter, a lanky, avenging angel with a sulky mouth. Outside, the river shone with light, illuminating a thousand, thousand other lives.

Jane tossed back her hair in remarkable imitation of Emma Hughes, a sixth-former with whom, judging from the number of casual references slipped into the conversation, Jane had fallen in love. 'Mum pays no attention to anyone but herself and she's slipping. We had *packet* custard the other day.'

'Jane . . .' Max spoke softly but with a warning. Going in to play against a cross-grained adolescent probably resulted in the same queasy mixture of rage and laughter as embarking on a tennis match against John McEnroe. Prue flashed a smile at Max, the referee.

Violet ploughed on. 'About Edward, Prue. He wouldn't be any trouble. And Jamie can help out. And Emmy's only down the road.'

The bell sounded for the performance and Jamie ushered

the party through the doors to their seats. Prue's determination not to give in hardened. She thought of heavy, immovable objects: the Stone of Scone, the pyramids, the Giant's Causeway.

'Violet,' she said as they made their way down the aisle, 'I don't think you understand. I don't want to look after Edward. I have other things to do.'

'Do change your mind, Prue.' Settled in the middle of a row in the stalls, Violet leant across her father and prodded Prue on the thigh. She had no intention of giving up, and dropped her voice a note or two to add urgency, skilfully conveying surprise that such a reasonable request was being refused. 'Don't worry about the packet custard.'

Acid welled to the surface. The acid distilled from years of distrust, dislike and of knowing that whatever she did, wherever she turned, Prue had failed with her stepdaughter, both failure and guilt sharpening dislike. Prue struggled not to be small, with the obligation, as she saw it, to treat the world with care, struggled to forgive if she could not forget.

She turned in her seat and said, loud and clear enough for the audience in the seats around to take an interest, 'Will you shut up, Violet?'

'Violet,' said Jamie, obviously uncomfortable – almost, Prue observed, aghast at Prue's response, as if he had been betrayed – 'why don't we leave the subject?'

Violet gave her husband one of her wide-eyed looks. 'I was trying to tell Prue not to worry too much about everything.'

She looked so earnest, believable and beautiful. Clever, clever Violet, hiding her secrets so well. Jamie touched his wife on the shoulder. 'Careful, darling,' he said, and Prue's determination melted into a hot tide and she wanted to cry out, 'Don't, don't touch her. Touch me.'

Jamie registered Violet's sharp shoulder blade under his

hand. He had never seen Prue in a temper (neither, of course, she him) and the experience would alter, subtly, the image he carried.

Violet leant forward. 'Prue,' she hissed, 'are you by any chance menopausal?'

'My God, Violet. You're the limit.'

Rage streamed through Prue, plus the urge to behave badly and she gave in to it. She leapt to her feet and squeezed her way along the row, provoking disgruntled murmurs and a great deal of rearranging.

'Mum.' Jane's uncertain, muted whisper followed Prue's progress. 'Mum?'

Prue ignored her daughter. Another black mark. Another cold stone for Jane to lay on the wall building between them.

At the door to the foyer she turned and looked back. Jamie seemed stunned, Max impassive, Jane frightened and Violet, well, Violet looked like Violet when she had won an encounter. Otherwise, they were a perfectly ordinary group on an outing to the theatre.

Outside the theatre on the river embankment she drew in London air, feeling the weight of her emotion choking the oxygen out of her lungs: pain, jealousy – and a passion that was in danger of going sour from too much weight upon it.

She was missing the first act of a play that she had wanted to see.

A wind blew off the Thames, a dank, sour wind, smelling of people and lives lived too close together. She wanted Jamie. How she wanted him. She also wanted her daughter, as perfect and unblotted by the world as the day she entered it. She wanted the second baby she had never managed. She wanted Max not to mind. She wanted to be in charge of herself again.

'Before you get caught in a great passion,' ran the letter of a seventeenth-century Portuguese nun, which Prue had come across during her research, 'think well of the excesses of grief, of the uncertainties, of the diversities of impulse, of despairs, doubts and jealousies . . .'

Prue had not considered well at all. So unlike her. She had let herself slip into a rushing stream and had not cared about the rocks. The nun, she should have remembered, had been abandoned by her aristocratic French lover.

Prue breathed in the alien river smell, traffic fumes, and a sense that she had lost her way.

In the interval, she sought them out to apologize, the old Prue on whom they relied. Of course she would look after Edward, it would be no trouble. Jamie was welcome to stay, too, and she was sure Emmy would not be needed. After all, Violet was a busy working mother and needed all the back-up she could muster. (Prue trusted she sounded convincing.)

Max and Jamie heard out this orgy of repentance in silence. Violet was repairing her make-up in the ladies.

'That's very good of you, Prue,' said Jamie at last. 'We appreciate it and realize it's a big favour.'

'Fine, I'll tell Violet.'

'Don't worry,' said Jamie, 'she said you'd come round.'

Prue stared at him. That was possibly the most tactless thing her lover had ever said to her and her faith in him was shaken. To stop herself from saying something irretrievable, she drank a slug of gin and tonic. Max slipped his arm round her shoulders.

'Well done, darling,' he said softly into her ear.

His tone conveyed complicity and understanding of her bad behaviour, and Prue was filled with gratitude for Max's goodness. She turned in the circle of his arm and kissed first Max's cheek and, then, his mouth.

Violet could be seen making her way towards them through the crowd in the foyer. She stopped to speak to an acquaintance.

Jamie gathered up their glasses and, as he passed Prue, touched her haunch in a secret gesture. Prue's flesh burned and the blood drummed in her ears.

She was helpless.

As they parted after the play, it was agreed that the Becketts would come down to Dainton for the following Sunday.

Since the Sunday morning looked promising, Prue revised the catering schedule and suggested a walk to Danebury Rings and a late lunch.

'Fine,' said Jamie.

'Not fine,' said Violet who, to do her justice, looked tired. 'I don't want to lug the baby up there. Besides, I've been there hundreds of times. I'll drive the car and meet you.'

Prue retrieved a stew from the larder and asked if Violet could put it in the oven.

'Oh, don't bother with lunch,' said Violet, repressing a vision of roast chicken, rubbed with tarragon, and roast potatoes. 'Cottage cheese and apple will do.'

Prue looked Violet straight in the eye. 'The rest of us would like lunch. You can eat apple and cottage cheese if you wish but I would be grateful if you did not make too much of a song and dance about it in front of Jane.'

Violet's expression darkened – and Prue turned away.

You betrayed me, Prue. No, worse. You did not supply what I needed.

What nonsense. Helen had betrayed her daughter long before Prue replaced her, or failed to.

But what of Prue's betrayal of a stepdaughter – for, surely, she stood, and must be judged as such, in *loco parentis*? But perhaps all families are busy practising the point-counterpoint of deceit and revenge on each other. She was at it; the next-door neighbour was it. The nation was at it.

Reluctantly, Prue faced the question. Was revenge the fuel of her love affair?

The weather threw up one of those warm golden days in which autumn specializes, and the morning heated up. The party filed along the lane, crumbling dry, crusted mud underfoot and watching air shimmer above the hedges. Naturally, the fields had been harvested and, patchworked with brown and gold, they rolled up the contours of the land, framed by a scattering of late poppies, hogweed and cascades of blackberries. In the verges, pimpernels made their tiny orange statements and periwinkle crawled up the stems in the hedgerows. A smell of hot fruit and vaporizing dew, of cool earth and ripeness was in the air. Notwithstanding the assaults made on it by chemicals and humans, the earth appeared in good working order.

Jamie stopped to shift the rucksack containing water and rations.

'Apple, anyone?' said Prue.

Jamie moved closer and his hand made contact. For a second, she closed her eyes. Jamie's thumb rubbed briefly on her flesh and then was gone. That's your lot, she thought.

They moved onwards down the path, lumpy with outcrops of chalk and summer drought. For some reason, an avenue of pine trees which led nowhere had been planted to their left. Rabbits played in the grassy ride between the pines where the shadows were cast, uneven and dark.

That grass: green and thick. To brush through it with bare feet, moisture squeezing up between the toes . . . She imagined sinking to her knees, waiting for Jamie. Lying back, allowing the damp to lap her body in a blanket, the nettle

317

to lash her skin and the outcrop of dry earth to lacerate the tender places on her body as she drew up her legs, and the sun striking them.

Jamie would blot it out and then, boneless and shaking with desire, she would give herself up to hot, juddering strokes of sex and love. She imagined, too, what she would look like afterwards: nettle-lashed, reddening, imprinted by grass, invaded and sated.

Prue chewed an apple. Jane needed new jeans. The freezer needed defrosting and Molly, apparently anxious to restore their *entente* back to the *cordiale*, had donated a quantity of tomatoes from the Greer greenhouse. They begged to be turned into sauce. The harvest supper committee required ten apple pies.

The vision of her naked, sated body fled down the pine trees, turned transparent, floating. And vanished.

The party halted by the edge of the biggest field lapping the perimeter of Danebury.

'Let's cut across.' Jamie squinted up at the slope beyond.

Max tested the soil with his boot. 'Too soft going. You'd end up with a sackload in your shoes.'

'Nonsense,' said Jamie, and struck out over the field confidently, stuck it out for approximately fifty yards and beat a retreat. The sun picked out his fair hair and the sheen of sweat on his forehead. He looked young and untroubled, and Prue drank him in greedily.

'You were right,' he said to Max and sat down to empty his shoes.

Once again, he brushed against Prue and her naked, desire-tormented body ran over the stubble and too-soft earth and sank to the ground.

They squeezed over a professional-looking fence at the foot of the ring and found themselves facing a clump of dense woodland which circled the lower slopes.

'Up, then.' Max beat a path through the undergrowth.

Jane disappeared through an interlaced hazel and beech after her father. Prue tied her sweater around her waist and drew in her breath.

'Damn and blast.' Max could be heard swearing. He slithered back down towards them. 'Someone's put a sodding great barbed-wire fence up. We'll have to walk round the ring and come up the other side.'

Jamie peered through the trees. 'We can get over that.'

Max sent him a look. 'I don't think Prue can manage.'

'Yes, she will.'

Max shrugged. 'She won't.'

'Yes, I will.' Prue surged forward. 'You lot can have the privilege of helping me over.'

In the event, Max held the wire down and Jamie draped his sweater over the barbed wire and Prue stepped across. The wire bit her hands, gave under her weight and every movement had an edge of danger.

Then they were up and over and into the open, treading ground impacted with history and myth.

Hundreds of years ago – 1000 BC? – an Iron Age people had singled out this outcrop in a valley basin. Actually, Prue explained in her best local-historian manner, it may be as old as 2000 BC, the height of the outcrop allowing the settlers to dominate the valley – unlike the village situated in the dip – and giving security from enemies.

The fort itself revealed considerable administrative, engineering and military sophistication. For instance – by now Prue had warmed thoroughly to her theme – the east entrance is cleverly placed at the intersection of several trackways.

'Rather like Sainsbury's,' said Jamie. 'Bagging the intersections outside towns.'

'It was well organized.' Max indicated the central area

where sheep were grazing. 'That bit contains hundreds of storage pits, one for each family, which were jealously guarded. You could probably steal your neighbour's wife but woe betide you if you pinched their grain.'

There was an awkward silence.

Max slid down the slope and landed, neatly for such a large man, in the ditch below.

'Catch me, Dad,' Jane yelled, and windmilled down the bank, which was knotted with treacherous roots.

'Catch her, Max.' Prue's heart was in her mouth.

Jane teetered and wobbled, failed to grasp at a branch, gathered speed and shot down like a bullet.

'My God!' Without a moment's hesitation, Prue launched herself after Jane.

But it was all right. Max assessed the angle of Jane's descent, moved into position and when his daughter tumbled towards him, caught her. He did not wait for Prue who was having difficulty making the descent but assisted Jane to climb up the inner earthworks. Thus, Prue finished in a heap at the bottom and, as she went over, she felt her ankle wrench, not badly, but it made her gasp all the same.

'Are you OK?' Jamie shouted from the outer earthwork.

She got to her feet and tested her ankle. 'Fine.'

Jane and Max had reached the top and were walking in a clockwise direction. Prue took a few experimental paces. Apart from a twinge, the ankle was fine. She looked up at Jamie, silhouetted against the sky.

'I'm going to find an easier way up,' she told him.

None of the party looked back at Prue, and she was left alone. She began to fight her way along the ditch, slashing through the undergrowth and densely packed grass. Once she glanced up, and there were Max and Jane walking in single file to her left, Max with his characteristic lope, Jane pattering behind him. Jamie had vanished.

Prue was alone with the muttering trees and a chorus of sheep cries. Above her was a sky with whipped-cream clouds and hot sun, around her, the slippery, treacherous sides of the fortified camp.

Wait for me, she wanted to call out to her husband and daughter, but felt, where once she had unquestionably possessed it, she no longer had the right. A bramble whipped at Prue's ankle, which sprouted a spray of needle pricks, and she cursed herself for not wearing trousers. She stooped to rub at the scratches.

'Still there?' Jamie stood above her.

She gazed up at her lover, so close and yet so removed, and never loved him so well.

'The others are coming.'

She turned to watch Max and Jane as they approached.

'This is cool fun,' Jane called out.

Across the divide separating Prue from the others, Max and Jane regarded each other and Prue, who could not bear to watch, bent her head and turned away. Max muttered something under his breath, slipped his arm around Jane and held her tight.

'Aren't you coming up?'

Prue swivelled towards her husband. He was looking down at her, eyes wrinkled in the sun, mouth compressed with his knowing, complicitous look.

What *do* I want? she cried silently.

'It's much easier to walk up here,' said Jamie.

Irresolute, confused, she looked from one to the other. She knew that this moment was significant, that the old Prue was gone, replaced by a woman who acknowledged both duality and the seeds of decay in herself, and accepted that these things were true of others.

It had been a difficult process, but there it was. Darkness creeps into most souls, leaving them lost, suffering and frightened. It had crept into Prue's life.

Gradually, her fists uncurled in her jacket pockets. Superimposed over the sun, the chain on a gate flapped in the autumn wind, and a flurry of sharp air blew over the stubble which made it rustle. Black on gold, crows rose in an aimless cloud. Prue stood motionless. For the first time, she understood what she had done by annexing her stepdaughter's husband, the measure of the transgression she had dealt Max in violating his family.

'I'll stay down here,' she said.

But a hundred or so yards further on, Jamie called down, 'I'm coming to get you,' which he did, pulling Prue up by the hand to the outer path where they walked in silence, in the opposite direction to her husband and daughter.

CHAPTER TWENTY-FOUR

From the first-floor landing window in Austen Road, Emmy watched a couple of redwings and a fieldfare feast on the red traffic-light berries of the *Viburnum opulus* in the next-door garden. Not natural democrats, the birds made a great deal of fuss although there were plenty to go round.

Emmy moved one of Violet's statements-in-bronze out of her way and propped her chin on her hands.

'Did you know that birds are attracted to red?'

'Nope,' said Angus, slipping his hand under Emmy's red jumper.

'Yes.' Emmy's flesh crawled with pleasure. 'If there's a choice between red and white berries, they always choose red.'

'Yes,' said Angus, and continued.

Emmy bit her lip. 'They prefer that end of the colour spectrum.'

'So do I.'

She turned her head over her shoulder. 'What about Sal, then? She wears black.'

'So she does.' Angus edged closer. 'Can we go upstairs and explore other spectrums?'

Emmy's mouth twitched. 'No, you devil. I've got the baby to look after.'

323

Angus cocked his head to one side and listened. 'Sounds as if he's asleep. I can tell.'

Downstairs in the kitchen, the washing machine and the dishwasher were banging out a cacophony. The drawing room had been cleaned, Edward's things ironed and Emmy had been on the point of tackling her own room. She had not been expecting the doorbell to ring, or Angus to step into the hall, kick off his boots as he always did and say: 'I was passing.'

Somehow, despite the faithful teachings of *Cosmopolitan*, sex at ten o'clock on Monday morning did not seem right. Emmy swivelled her body towards Angus so that her meagre breasts were pressed against his chest.

'Why were you passing?' she asked, curious to know.

'Just was.' He grinned. 'I hadn't seen you since last week.'

Four days, actually.

'Been with Sal, then?' Emmy kept her gaze fixed on the birds. 'Over the weekend, I mean?'

'Always knew you could read my lips. How did you know?' Angus shifted so that he could trace interesting pathways over her breasts.

'I can smell her.'

Indeed, traces of that ghastly musky perfume Sal poured over herself lingered on him. Emmy turned her head. Angus made a dive for her trousers and she squeezed her legs shut.

'Go away.'

'No.'

'Go away, Angus. Go back to Sal.'

His fingers arrested at the junction of her thighs. 'Do you really want me to? Shall I?' He was tracing small circles of desire which fanned out through Emmy's concupiscent body. 'I don't know why I bother with you, Em, but I do.'

'Don't bother, then. I can get along fine.'

'Do you believe that?' Angus went further. 'Aha.'

'Will you stop it?'

Angus feinted, grabbed for and captured Emmy's arm, and pulled her into the nearest doorway, which happened to be the main bedroom – Jamie and Violet's bedroom. She struggled and protested but by this time his hand had found the target it sought.

Sex at ten o'clock on a Monday morning was fine, she thought afterwards. Absolutely fine. But after such abandon, how did you face the rest of the day? The rest of the week?

Angus rolled over on Violet's lace-edged (and staggeringly expensive) pillowcases from Macy's in New York and kissed Emmy's naked shoulder. She closed her eyes, the better to savour the gesture. Then she stiffened, and shot upright.

'What if they find out?'

Angus pulled her down and made himself more comfortable. 'Stop fussing.'

She tugged at the hair trailing over his shoulder. 'Stop being a nag.'

'Nag, nag.'

An hour later, Emmy's eyes flapped open like a submarine hatch. Oh, my God, she thought, sleep vanishing. The baby. She raised her head and listened, but the house was quiet – even the machines were silent. Breathing quietly, Angus lay beside her, muscles and skin slackened by sleep.

For a few precious seconds, Emmy bent over him and allowed herself the luxury of a private view.

There was the slope of his haunch, and the line between the tanned chest and the loins which were paper white. The sinew running down his forearm, the angle made by ankle meeting foot . . . He was a map on to which she routed her desire but not her hope.

'Nice, aren't I?' Angus sounded slow and sleepy. 'An oil painting.'

'Yes, oh yes,' she found herself murmuring in that unguarded, private moment.

Slowly, he reached up and touched the slight mound of her breast. 'So are you.'

Emmy jumped out of bed and pulled on her underclothes. 'I must check on the baby.'

'Sure.'

In the doorway, she turned to look at him sprawled shamelessly over the bed. He returned her look and said something that took him as much by surprise as it drove the breath from Emmy's body.

'I want us to get hitched,' he said. 'How about it?'

Over a mug of Violet's decaffeinated coffee and with Edward on her lap, Emmy explained the reasons why she had no intention of getting married at the moment.

She was too young.

'Twenty,' said Angus. 'Hardly a chicken.'

She wanted a career and to travel.

'You could have fooled me,' said Angus. 'Have a career looking after me.'

She was not sure if she agreed with marriage.

'Shack up with me, then,' said Angus.

He leant forward over the table and sent his ponytail up and over his shoulder, and asked her why she was making excuses. Did she not love him? He asked so sweetly and with such tenderness that Emmy felt faint, and promptly succumbed to a tidal wash of fear that Angus was playing the worst of tricks, and could not, for the life of her, understand why.

Neither did it escape Emmy that he had not mentioned loving her, a prerequisite she rather thought was necessary in a marriage proposal.

Did she not love him?

'I'm not sure I do. Love you, I mean,' she lied, and had the doubtful satisfaction of watching his expression darken. She shifted Edward, who was playing dangerous games with the empty mug at the edge of the table.

'Yes, you do. I know you do.'

He leant back in the chair and folded his hands behind his head. It took a lot to crack Angus's confidence.

'Not enough to marry you.' Emmy's lips shook as she forced out the words. 'I want someone I can trust.'

Angus listened in silence and then got to his feet. 'You're out of date, Em.' He picked up his jacket. 'I'll be off, then.'

'Angus . . .'

He padded out of the kitchen into the hall and reappeared, boots in hand. 'What?'

'Sorry.'

He stuffed his feet into the boots and bent down to lace them. 'Don't bother to see me out.'

Too late, she realized she had hurt him, and badly.

The front door clicked shut and Emmy was left holding a wriggling baby and contemplating the empty coffee cups on the table. Edward made noises that indicated he wanted a drink and Emmy put him into his chair while she fetched one. He drank thirstily and Emmy interpreted the squall that followed as a demand for a refill. After he had finished, she carried him upstairs and peeled off his sopping nappy. Delighted with the attention, Edward kicked his bare legs into the air and made cooing sounds. Emmy cleaned him up and smothered his bottom with cream. At that, he laughed.

A clean bottom, a dry nappy, a drink . . . if only life was that simple.

Downstairs the kitchen seemed so quiet and empty that Emmy switched on the radio and cradled in her hands the mug that Angus had drunk from which still retained a residual warmth. The vision she had once nurtured of the house, with cork matting and potted plants, seemed dim and inappropriate.

The mug was empty, Angus was gone, and Edward was due his morning walk.

Jamie first noticed the change in Emmy.

'She's gone very quiet,' he said to Violet.

Nowadays his and Violet's conversations tended to domestic topics – a tacit acknowledgement, perhaps, that for the moment it was best to keep to safe ground. Violet searched in her briefcase for the minutes of a meeting she meant to go over.

'She looks fine to me.'

'She seems different.'

'Rubbish. There's no difference at all. There's still a layer of dust in the spare room which I've told her to clean several times.'

'Her heart doesn't seem to be in the job.' On several occasions, Jamie had caught Emmy staring out of the window in what struck him as a despairing fashion. Her misery sounded an echo with him, an empathy rooted in his own confusion – and who was to say if that empathy was less acceptable because it had been born out of deceit rather than honesty?

Whatever. Jamie now perceived how little he had understood, how life had flowed around him and how he had not taken the trouble to take note. This shamed him. (Don't be ashamed, said Prue, when he confided this. How can we understand everything all at once?)

'Her heart not in the job?' Struck by the implications of Jamie's statement, Violet slumped back on to the sofa. 'Jamie, are you serious? Do you think Emmy wants to leave? Had I better talk to her?'

'It might be an idea.'

Violet ran through her schedule. 'I've got Frankfurt in a couple of days, then the States in November. She *can't* leave.' She seized on a solution, the easy one. 'Maybe we should give her a pay rise.'

Jamie shrugged. 'We can't make her stay if she isn't happy.'

'Yes, we can. I'll make her stay.' Violet stuffed the minutes back into her briefcase. 'She owes it to me.'

Jamie's expression was not kind. 'You have funny ideas sometimes, Violet. Emmy doesn't owe you a thing.'

Violet began totting up figures on a smart black leather notepad. 'I'm sure it's the money. They always want more.'

Jamie sighed. Alerted at last, Violet's head jerked around. 'Don't go all snooty because I mention money. You work with it all day, so don't pretend you're above such vulgar pre-occupations.'

Until this moment, Emmy had not registered the exact honey colour of the kitchen floor: yellow, dashed with transparent wax, its mirror brightness now washed with the slight cloudiness of cream cleanser. As Violet talked, she stared at it. These days, most things had an unpredictable quality. Her feelings. The workings of her body. The patches of wakefulness during the night when she woke and stared into black and nothingness. The sudden pitchfork into exhausted sleep. Surprise at what she herself said and did.

Above all, Emmy was conscious of astonishment as to how hidden her feelings were, had been, from herself, the person who obligingly provided the receptacle in which they sloshed. Question: what were the chances of comprehending others if the chances of understanding yourself were pretty low?

'I mean, is there anything that's worrying you, Emmy?'

Violet was saying. 'You seem so quiet. So unhappy. Do you need anything?' Far too shrewd to mention money in the opening moves of a negotiation, Violet was banking on the I'm-terribly-concerned-about-your-welfare-approach, which worked a treat on the staff at work.

Emmy swallowed. 'I'm fine, thank you.'

The kettle boiled and Violet poured water over mint teabags and fished them out with a spoon. Then she placed a mug in front of Emmy and sat down opposite with hers.

'You would tell me,' she said, opening her eyes wide – yet another tactic that conveyed the appearance of absolute sincerity – 'if you needed help.'

Oh, yes, I do, I do, thought Emmy desperately.

'I mean, Jamie . . .' Violet still hesitated a little over the Christian names, 'Jamie and I would hate to lose you. We feel you're almost family.'

This gave Emmy the opportunity to reflect on the number of times she had been requested to take her supper upstairs on a tray, to fetch and carry shopping, forbidden to socialize during her work hours and had her movements scrutinized. The funny-peculiar aspect of it was: compared to the silence and isolation of her own home, it *had* been more like belonging to a family.

Across the table, Violet's lips moved and her glossy hair undulated and flicked obediently into its expensive cut. From a distance, Emmy watched her. Then Violet turned, glanced out of the kitchen window, and Emmy was hit by a clap of recognition. For Violet's expression revealed a fleeting uncertainty and, even more unexpected, loss.

She, too, thought Emmy. How extraordinary that, after all, she and Violet shared the same skin.

The moment passed as quickly as it arrived. Violet sipped the mint tea, argued the toss with herself and plunged in.

'You're not thinking of leaving us, Emmy, I hope? We would be very sad.'

Emmy grimaced and stared into her mug.

'Would you prefer camomile?' Violet asked.

'I'm fine,' said Emmy and, to her horror, tears welled in her eyes. 'Absolutely fine.' She struggled with herself. 'Would you like me to take Edward to the clinic today? He's due his twelve-month injection.'

It was Monday morning and Violet was not up to dealing with tears before work. She followed on the lead thoughtfully provided by Emmy. Waiting with a hot, restless baby in a hot, noisy clinic had not been written into her blueprint of motherhood when she devised it in those pre-conception days of sunlight and balm. Neither was it now. She looked at her watch.

'Yes, do.'

She dickered with the idea of trying once again to get to the bottom of whatever was worrying Emmy, then decided that ignorance on the behalf of the employer was the better part of valour.

Alone, Emmy resisted the impulse to ring Anna. What's up, then, you old cow? Anna would say, heavy with the weekend's excess. Keeping your legs tight together? Tell us the gen on Madam. How many pairs of knickers has she got through this week? Have I got news for you . . .

No, Emmy would say. Have *I* got news for *you*.

Instead, she plodded up the stairs to the first floor. The door to the main bedroom (Emmy could not bring herself to look through it) was open, revealing abandoned clothes and an unmade bed. The cistern in the bathroom gurgled quietly.

She held on to the newel post and hauled herself up the next flight to her flatlet. Here the doors were kept tight shut, for Emmy's standards had dropped lately and she was pretty sure that Violet checked up regularly on the rooms. Well, Madam could get her eyeful of piled clothes and overflowing wastepaper baskets.

Her sitting room smelt . . . of what? Despair? It should. Disuse? Certainly, the room *looked* despairing and out of sorts. Emmy stabbed her finger down on the table (a cast-off from the garage and Hallet's Gate with a split top) and wrote 'Fool' in the dust.

It was no use ignoring any longer what she had to do.

The bathroom door made its familiar popping noise and the displaced air raised the edge of the carpet, which had not been fixed. Emmy registered the wet flannel lying in the bath, the shell-shaped soap dish floating its burden of jelly and soap, five bottles of shampoo, each with a different set of promises, and one of Edward's rubber ducks.

A moth to the flame, her gaze was riveted on the test-tube she had left on the shelf above the basin.

Hundreds, no millions of women had crossed this bridge. No, no, nothing so comforting as a bridge, more a thin, rotting plank balanced over a big question mark, with the scatter from spoilt lives clotted into heaps underneath – like the discarded cars, bits of pushchair, kitchen waste and old clothes of the council tip.

It was Emmy's luck that she had had no practice at plank walking and was the sort of person who developed vertigo on a deep-pile carpet.

Imagine inching forward and hearing the rotten fibres give under her weight with the sodden, sullen sound! Imagine the shake of her body and the freezing blood forcing its way through her arteries and, down below, the gap into which she was falling.

Twenty, thirty years ago – Emmy did not know enough to estimate precisely – she would have had no choice. Stuffed, finished, probably banged up in some home and saddled with the stigma for the rest of her life. Now Emmy had three options, which made it worse because she did not know what to do – either what she wanted, or what was right.

Emmy surprised herself, for she was not in the habit of considering ethics and it did not come easily.

Jamie stepped neatly out of the way as Emmy jumped down the last six stairs into the hall. It was odd activity for an adult, and Jamie was transported back to the time when he did just that for a dare with his friends, the era of long shorts and scratched knees. He did not associate Emmy with those moments of shivering abandonment and free fall.

'Are you practising for the next Olympics?'

Emmy flushed and muttered something unintelligible, but there was something in the manner in which her eyes glittered that told Jamie that she had been crying.

'I thought it was only Eddie the Eagle who did that sort of thing.'

Emmy regained her balance. 'I don't know what came over me,' she said, with perfect truth.

Jamie looked at her thoughtfully. Guilt had unpredictable and physical results, and Jamie had been suffering from a diminished appetite and fretful sleep. But it also led him to another door. Jamie wanted to find out about other people, was ravenous to do so, because it gave him a sense of being earthed. By contemplating the mistakes and suffering of others, Jamie gave himself licence not to think too badly of himself.

Quite forgetting that it was loose, Jamie leant back on the

radiator and sprang forward again when it cracked and shifted in its moorings. He collided with Emmy.

'Oh, Lord, sorry, Emmy.'

He flashed her a wry grin. 'If there's anything we can do, Emmy, you only have to ask.'

Peaky, thin, shivering in the recently intensified autumn chill, Emmy was the incarnation of misery. A spot of red crept into her cheeks and Jamie mistook it for anger. Later, he realized it was a badge of courage, for Emmy shook as she said: 'I'm going to have a baby.'

Then Jamie made the reply that was to haunt him for many months: 'Is that all?'

Violet's reaction was not much better.

'I hope she doesn't want it,' she said, but had the grace to stop there. A flush suffused her cheeks and her red mouth twisted. 'I mean, I don't want to make it sound as if a baby is a disposable asset.' She paused, thinking of the offer she had made Jamie and which had never been spoken of since. 'They're not.'

'Well, we agree on one thing.' This time, Jamie's smile was a formality.

Well . . . in a way, a baby was. Helen, darling mother Helen, had thought so. Bye, bye, little daughter. I'm off and I don't want you hanging on my arm like a weekend bag (the sort that Violet had bought from exclusive shops: elegant but hell to carry). It doesn't suit me to have you along with Jack.

Violet often wondered if it would have been better if Helen had popped into the local pregnancy advice bureau and, hey presto, Violet would have been disposed of down the municipal drain. (Presumably, she would have been in good company down there. Consider all those film stars, politicians, aristocrats who found themselves lumbered with the prospect of an awkward weekend bag, let alone the career girls, potential unmarried mothers, mistresses and one-night stands.)

The strange thing was: Violet did not think the worse of them for it. Life had to be got through. Far worse to be born and then not loved. Correction: not to be loved enough.

Violet's analysis terminated at this point. She did not make the connection between Helen's treatment of her and her attitude to Edward.

'Do you want it?' she asked Emmy, who was retching over Edward's meal of puréed soya beans and tomato. 'Here let me.' She wrested the spoon away. 'Go and sit down. I'll feed him.'

Endeavouring to be practical was no defence against bone-deep confusion and anxiety. 'I don't know.' Emmy's hand fluttered in the region of her stomach.

'Well, you must decide quickly, otherwise it becomes worse.'

Violet remembered her surprise when she woke up one morning, twenty-four weeks' pregnant, to encounter the definite, writhing bulge under her ribs and thought: Legally, I could still get rid of it. And also, Not now. It is *alive*.

Emmy sat down in the kitchen chair. Even now, Violet was no expert in the business of shovelling food down her son and, the bout of nausea having subsided, Emmy was able to watch with scientific interest the false moves and baffled impatience on Violet's beautiful face.

'If you wait between mouthfuls,' she said at last. 'He likes to eat slowly.'

Clearly, this was news to Violet but she took the advice and harmony was achieved between mother and son for the remaining mouthfuls. At the finish, Edward threw himself back in his chair and flashed his mother one of the smiles that came from nowhere. Violet found herself smiling back.

'Cheeky monster,' she said, softer than Emmy had ever seen her, and dabbed Edward's face with a wet flannel.

Emmy breathed out slowly, and tried to imagine that her stomach did not belong to her. Violet captured one of Edward's flying hands and held it at an exaggerated distance while she tackled the grunge clinging to the fingers.

'Is it tactless to ask who the father is?'

Emmy swallowed and waited for the word Angus to form on her lips. It did not. If she expected something sharp and stinging from Violet she was mistaken, for Violet returned Edward's hand to him – rather as if it was a bag full of rubbish – and said: 'Don't worry. It's none of my business.'

Emmy revised her ideas on Violet.

Two days later, the postman delivered a parcel for Emmy elaborately tied up in string.

'You don't see that often,' Jamie commented as he passed it over to Emmy, who knew at once who had sent it. She held it between her cold hands, knowing that it contained the books she had lent him and her CD of Shakespear's Sister. The string, so carefully and determinedly knotted, undid Emmy – it was so like Angus to wrap things up well. To her surprise, she dropped her head in her hands and wailed from sorrow and nausea.

Within seconds, Jamie was on his feet. 'Violet, I'll leave you to sort this one out.'

Violet shot him a look which said, 'Typical', but the next thing Emmy knew was an arm circling her shoulder.

'Look,' said Violet in her ear, 'you've got to wise up, Emmy. You can't go on like this. I suggest you get along to the clinic this morning and get some advice.'

She glanced at her watch – Piaget and new – saw that she was running late, but made an effort. 'I'll ring up and make an appointment for you if you like.'

336

Emmy promised to do something, blew her nose and un-picked the string surrounding the parcel. Inside was the novel by Virginia Andrews that Angus had kidnapped before she had finished it. It was a novel about children in danger. Inside it, he had inserted a note: 'It was nice knowing you, Em. Don't worry about anything. Me and Sal have gone off to live in the country for the winter.'

It was so like him, too, to return everything.

Autumn had settled heavily over the city. Ringed by the cease-less traffic, Wandsworth Common was damp underfoot and mud-clogged. Here and there a light shone out of a building, or the bright red of a bus cut through air layered by damp and pollution. Trees, roofs, gates dripped. Emmy's feet left dark footprints on the grass and the buggy bucked and snagged.

What do I do? She watched a couple of mothy Canada geese by the edge of the pond, panic routing her resolution to be sensible. A jumble – abortion, welfare payments, coping alone, labour, a council flat – clogged her mind, which had lost its ability to concentrate.

She strove to pin down a rational thought, to settle on a concrete plan that would help, and failed. Her thoughts slid, despairing, muddled and without much hope, to the only thing she wanted to think about: Angus.

She had sent him away, and she did not know if she had the language to call him back.

CHAPTER TWENTY-FIVE

P RUE NOTICED THAT THE PHOTOGRAPH OF HELEN IN Max's study had been returned to its prominent position on the table.

'I hate you,' she told it, then admitted, 'but I think I understand you a bit better now.' Helen's face glistened mistily with non-comprehension.

She attacked the pile of papers on Max's desk and emptied an ashtray, releasing a whiff of stale tobacco and dust. It was then she noticed the box of gun cartridges on the right-hand side of the desk. Frowning a little, she checked the contents and refastened the lid. It was almost full, and should not have been left lying around. It was a strict house rule that the guns and the cartridges remained in their safe.

Upstairs, Prue retrieved the key from its hiding place under the bathroom basin and unlocked the safe. There was plenty of room so she pushed the cartridges inside and relocked it.

Later, when she was ironing Max's tartan handkerchiefs into the precise rectangles he preferred, Prue remembered something. The iron, which was on its last legs, hissed and an overabundance of rusty-looking water spilt on to the linen. Prue cursed and propped it on its side. Why, she asked herself, had there been so much space in the gun-safe?

In her mind she ran over the contents. Max possessed two guns: the one he had inherited from his father, and the other from an uncle. Max preferred the latter and it was his father's that was missing.

She tackled a shirt. Perhaps it was being overhauled.

The shirt-sleeve panned out under the iron, crisp and smooth. The smell of clean, hot clothes filled her nose. Strange that the cartridge box had been practically full. But not absolutely. Was Max becoming careless? The iron hissed in protest as she jerked it upright. Where was that gun? Prue snatched up the iron and ironed until there was a pile as high as her shoulder.

She was in the kitchen when the phone rang.

The phone call had been Jamie.

'Will you come, Prue?'

She had glanced at the kitchen clock and the clutter of cooking ingredients and utensils. This was as good a moment as any to say, No. It's over. Enough. Finish.

'Please, Prue. We haven't been together since the summer, and I can't wait any longer. It's been difficult.' Jamie meant Violet, work, a creeping restlessness, some money worries for, healthy as Jamie's salary was, its chief characteristic was a tendency to melt.

No, Jamie, she could choose to say. I no longer wish to be overwhelmed. By guilt. By deceit. By love. It has to stop. Sometime. It will stop. Why not now?

But her body said something different, and Prue was already opening the drawer and putting away the kitchen knives and frowning as she tried to remember what time Max was coming home and whether or not there was a stew in the freezer.

There was, and she left it to defrost on the sideboard and moved quickly around the kitchen wiping surfaces and stowing saucepans in cupboards. Since her affair, Prue's kitchen had changed. The more she entangled with Jamie, the more snowy and starched her tea-towels, the more polished the furniture. All of these achievements (snowy tea-towels, for goodness sake!) would offer clues to the observant, for Prue had never been a fussy housewife. Now, providing the sink was rid of its coffee stains and supper was on the table, Prue felt a balance had been struck, and part of the bargain held.

From her position on the boiler, Bella stared at her mistress and folded her paw carefully underneath her plump body. 'Not quite as simple as that, Bella, is it?' she informed the large, unblinking eyes.

Prue drove a third of the way to Winchester and, at the last minute, turned the car back. She had been using her country handbag, a terrible old plastic number, which accommodated her notebooks, and had neglected to transfer her cheque book and credit cards into the smarter London leather version. Ergo, no train fare.

She swore and headed back at top speed.

'How do you manage to get away from the office?' Prue asked Jamie when they eventually caught up with each other in room number 35. Prue was late and Jamie a little irritable as a result. 'Surely someone must be putting two and two together?'

It was, perhaps, significant that they did not fall on each other but sat down to talk.

'Office life is a monastery requiring poverty and obedience, until you have learnt the rules . . .' Jamie sat down on the bed, '. . . which are to do precisely as you wish and explain later.'

'How is the office, and is anything happening?' Prue tossed the leather handbag on to the chair as if it had not cost her extra petrol, panic and most of the things she required in a handbag for it was much too small.

'Work? Busy. And Dyson is still very difficult in meetings.'

'Tell.'

Jamie's eyebrows twitched together. 'There's nothing *to* tell, really. His views and mine are poles apart and we clash. Meanwhile, the world is in its usual turmoil and the infuriating thing is, the problems with Dyson take up far more of my energies and attention than anything else.'

Prue touched Jamie's knee. 'We're not so far apart, then. I've realized that I spend my life tiptoeing between alliances and hostilities. But it's not such a terrible thing.' She was silent for a minute while she considered what she wished to say. Her hand fell back into her lap. 'I have a feeling Max knows something,' she admitted at last.

Jamie went quite still. 'You're sure?'

'No, I'm not sure. It's a feeling. A feeling that he's watching me all the time.'

When you have wronged someone, it is helpful if they behave badly, too, however slight the transgression. The idea that Max was watching Prue provided Jamie, who tried not to think of his father-in-law, with a small opportunity to think less well of him.

Prue read her lover's thoughts and her protective instincts towards her husband were roused. 'Don't,' she said almost sharply. 'Don't think badly of him. Didn't you do the same with Lara?'

Lara? Golden, lying Lara. Be honest, Jamie Beckett. As lying as he himself had turned out.

Jamie caught Prue's hand and pulled her roughly down beside him. She gave a little laugh, and pretended to protest.

He brushed his mouth along the line of her jaw until it rested on the soft point pulsing beneath her ear. 'Yes,' he said. 'I watched her long before she knew I knew.'

She drew in his subtle smell, and turned her head so that their lips were almost touching. 'How did you find out?'

Jamie's mouth lingered on Prue's and she nipped his bottom lip luxuriously. 'Jenny was the one to tell me about Lara. She didn't realize she was doing it, of course. She just said that Mummy was spending the afternoon with Uncle Robert.'

'Poor Jenny.'

'Poor Max.'

Prue was still amazed by herself. How was she capable of talking about Max while she slid her hand under Jamie's shirt? Perhaps, perhaps, the things she had chosen to dictate the shape of her life had merely been props.

'Max may well suspect something,' she said. 'I'm distracted and forget things. I keep dashing up to London and I lose my temper. Relations between me and Violet took an all-time plunge at the theatre. Then there is Jane – and her problems.' She paused. 'And there I do blame myself.'

Jamie covered her hand and pressed it against his well-honed stomach. 'Shut up, Prue.'

She pictured what lay beneath the still faintly tanned skin – a pulsing, coiled and looped landscape that existed to service Jamie's taut, fresh-skinned body.

'Max once said, Jamie, that there are worse things than being a pander. I couldn't think what he meant at the time.'

With the sharpened hunger of the condemned man, for Jamie sensed that he and Prue had moved to another stage, he again plundered the closed eyelids with his mouth and the line between the clean silk of her hair and her temples. 'I do need you, Prue.'

She put her arms around his chest and held him. Their intimacy, a compound of sex, gratification, danger, shared guilt and indecision, intensified.

'What do you want to do, Prue? For I think you do want to do something.'

She hesitated. 'I don't wish to be responsible for a ship-wreck.'

'I see.' Jamie disengaged himself and got up from the bed. 'So we don't go on till we're old and past it?' From his height, he bent over Prue and twined his fingers into the hair at the nape of her neck and pulled her head back. 'Plenty of people live double lives, you know.'

'I understand that now,' she replied, feeling the tug at her neck like the tug of sexual desire. 'I just hadn't been looking before.'

Jamie tried to imagine what it would be like to be normal again, to conduct a Monday-to-Sunday life minus Prue. 'Have your feelings changed?'

'No.' Prue stretched out her hand, fingers quivering. 'Look, Jamie, it shakes for you. My mouth aches. My legs are weak . . . and all the rest of it. Can I prove it any other way?'

Jamie had a sudden, disconcerting vision of the future – Violet (where had all his feelings gone?), Edward, the office, bills, office cars, a little gardening, negotiations, last-minute holidays in Italy – and yearning and loss flooded him.

'Leave Max.'

He had spoken on the spur of the moment, but the sensation of an oiled, purposeful spring uncoiling inside him suggested that he had been thinking about it for some time.

'What did you say?' Prue's face twisted with a mixture of joy, fear, but not surprise.

'Leave Max.'

Against all advice, Joan had been desperate to take the

impossible, the city of Paris. The largest city in Christendom, with its hundred thousand citizens, moats, guns on the ramparts. Ranged against it, Joan's army and a wavering king who was conducting secret negotiations with the enemy and pursuing his own agenda. Joan had also broken her sword – the one she claimed had been given to her by God – by striking a camp prostitute with the flat of its blade. It was a bad omen and was seen as such. The offensive against Paris was a doomed enterprise, too, and Joan lost badly. Paris refused to be taken and she was borne away on the tide of a retreating, surly army.

Thereafter, Joan's luck, her vision, her whatever-you-choose-to-call-it ran out.

Leave Max? It seemed as impossible and as wrong as taking Paris.

'I could get a job abroad. It would be exciting, Prue. You'd like it. You need a change.'

Do I? Leave Dainton? Leave jam-making, gardening and flower-arranging and the balancing of the WI's accounts with which she did battle each year. Abandon a home, a husband and a child. Abandon the idea that a marriage should be made to work. Shut the door behind her, shake the dust from her feet – it had been done before, often. Helen had done it. Statistically speaking, women do it more frequently than men. The ideal soured by years of wielding Brillo pads and baby lotion, they leave their husbands, not the other way round.

'What about the children?' she asked him.

'Yes, what about them?' He sounded bleak.

Silence fell between them. Jamie looked down at his hands. 'Let's go out,' he said abruptly.

She glanced around the room which, over the months, had been scaled of its glamour, rather as the scales were flaking away, in little pearly scabs, from Prue's eyes. Once, its shoddiness had been exciting, now it appeared unjoyful and makeshift.

They left the bed as smooth and unoccupied as they had found it.

The November afternoon exuded a lost quality of threatening fog, congealing cold and orange neon. Oxford Street was dense with shoppers and fractured by coloured slabs of Christmas decorations. There was a hum of noise, the grind of traffic and the restless beat of shoppers pressing in and out of the stores. The pavement was too crowded to walk two abreast, which made their progress uneven. Jamie's irritation returned.

'Where to?' Prue slipped her hand through his elbow.

'I don't know,' he said, wishing it was late enough for a drink. 'Coffee?'

They made for the coffee shop in Selfridges and commandeered a table. Cappuccino arrived, foamed and flecked with chocolate. To give herself time before she tackled the issues, Prue stuck her spoon into the foam and scooped it up, struck by the childishness of the gesture.

As powerful as the released genie, a picture of Max in his city suit forced its way into her mind, followed by a thin white Jane. She watched them walk into the distance, knowing that for a long time she had ignored her connection to them. Or theirs to her. She looked up at Jamie and her mind cleared. What was left? A drained coffee cup, shame and regret mixed with intense happiness, the knowledge that she had grown, and a half memory of the old Prue.

She tinkered with cup and spoon, aware that Jamie's scrutiny was accompanied by a certain acerbity, which she was also aware indicated he was determined on something.

'I had no idea that kicking over the traces . . . sinning . . . would be so exhausting.'

'What do you mean?'

'It intrudes into your mind and acts like the magnetic pole. Everything is pulled towards it. And you can't stop thinking about it.' Prue pushed her empty cup into the centre of the table. 'Instead of being automatic, everything becomes self-conscious. I didn't think it would be so difficult. I imagined it was just a question of taking off your clothes and that was that.'

Jamie was conscious of a tinge of impatience. He gave one of his half-smiles which clients had learnt meant he was thinking strategy. 'Whoever sent you to a convent, Prue, did you a disservice. Sin does not come into it.' Jamie had the benefit of a more or less secular education, which allowed him to be more direct. He leant towards her. 'You haven't answered my question, Prue. Will you leave Max?'

'I don't want to answer it because I can't.' Prue took a deep breath, terrified suddenly at the thought of losing Jamie. 'I don't know what to think, or what to do.'

Jamie looked at his watch. 'I've got to go.'

For the first time ever, their meeting had proved unsatisfactory. Prue watched him pay the bill and leave. She knew she would never fully understand how or what she had got herself into, only that she was overflowing with a feeling to which she had become addicted, so strong, so consuming was it and she wondered what on earth she had done with her life before Jamie.

Prue emerged into the street and, skilled now in managing London's crowds, threaded her way through the crush along Oxford Street towards Marble Arch. She had no fixed idea as to where she was going, neither did she care very much. At the junction, she paused and then descended the stairs to the subway.

Underneath stretched the tunnels of no-man's land, spiked with sudden turns, blind alleys and hidden entrances, urine-impregnated, splashed with dirt and pulverized food, lit by a dirty light from yellow lamps.

Half-way along, Prue became aware of footsteps. They

were gaining on her – fast. Various thoughts jostled for precedence, but she herself to walk purposefully: there was no reason to panic. She debated turning round to look, decided against it and hoisted her bag further up her shoulder. Despite these precautions, her heart tattooed against her chest with stabs of panic.

The subway lights blinked, and time elongated into seconds of intolerable tension, long enough for Prue queasily to construct a case that she deserved this: a squalid mugging, the stinging corrective of assault. Should she turn to receive the lash and the bruise, much as she had her lover's caress?

'Prue!'

She came to a dead halt, swivelled and, relief and ruefulness making her furious, cried, 'Jamie. *Why* did you do that?'

He gripped the lapels of her coat and dragged her towards him. 'I wanted to frighten you. And I did.'

'Not very nice,' she whispered, as her head fell back and her knees trembled with both fear and desire.

'No.'

When he kissed her, she tasted grime and exhaust fumes and supposed that he tasted it on her. Breathing rapidly, she buried her head in his shoulder.

A woman passed them, glancing at their locked figures with an expression of distaste. Prue recollected the times when she had been confronted by couples eating each other, and did not care.

'Jamie, we can't stay here.'

They moved off down the subway, up the stairs, and into the park, which was still open. Welded into a mass by the dark, the trees were tipped by neon and hugging blackness at their centres. A solitary man walked towards Speaker's Corner, his shoes clicking on the path. Otherwise, it was deserted.

'Why did you want to frighten me, Jamie? Why? *Why?*'

His hand forced its way inside the fastenings of her coat. 'If I was able to explain the things I feel about you, and as a result of you, then I would be a rich man.'

Prue shook her hair loose from her coat collar and arched her head back so that Jamie could cover the exposed skin with his mouth. Then he pulled her, smiling, towards the blackness and concealment, their feet leaving matching depressions in the damp ground.

'Here,' said Jamie and pressed against the furthest tree. 'And don't say no, otherwise I'll make you.'

'Yes,' said Prue, as his hands travelled roughly up her skirt, experiencing the triumphant thrill of yielding, of being at her most female and feminine. She moved a little to accommodate him. Jamie pressed closer.

'Wait,' she said, and altered her clothing, shivering as tongues of cold air licked the inside of her thighs. Then she said triumphantly: 'Now.'

Afterwards, Jamie leant slack and heavy on her and pinioned her to the tree. He was panting and laughing.

'I never, ever imagined . . .'

Prue let her head rest against the bark and smiled at the lights of an aircraft moving in an arc through the sky. Where in the world had it come from? From plague, starvation, political uncertainty? She did not care. The episode had taken only a couple of minutes but she, Prue Valour, had travelled to the outer limits of lust.

She turned his face towards her. 'I love you,' she said, searching for his face in the dark.

He appropriated her hand in his and ran his thumb over her palm in the intimate and tender gesture that made Prue catch her breath.

'I love you,' she repeated, imprisoning his thumb by curling up her hand. 'And I must go home.'

Gently, he buttoned her blouse and straightened her skirt and she brushed at her hair with her fingers. The temperature had dropped and their combined breath streamed into the night.

'When do I see you again?'

She took a deep breath. 'I don't know, Jamie.'

On the train at Waterloo, Prue searched in her too-small handbag for a piece of paper, and began to make a list of Christmas presents. Then she divided the page into 'food' and 'things to organize'. Gradually, the wild, primitive feelings rocking her body dispelled along with the longing, and the urge to touch the stars. The train swayed from side to side, and the smell, peculiar to electric trains, seeped up from the floor. The dark outside the window was as thick as a blanket. Prue let the list drop into her lap and closed her eyes.

'Is that ZBD Software?'

'Yup,' replied a terminally bored voice.

Prue squinted at Jane's list of Christmas requirements, which made no concessions to legibility. 'Look, I don't know what I'm talking about but I want to order some things for my daughter.

'Name on credit card, please.'

'Before I order I want to check it will arrive before Christmas.

'Sorry, can't do anything without credit card details.

After a tussle over the spelling of Dainton, Prue asked for what Jane wanted.

'We don't have that one but could supply a similar model.

'Could I send it back if it's not right?'

'We charge an administration cost.'

The telephone emitted a dead silence. Prue took the plunge. 'OK, I'll order.'

'That will be five pounds postage and packing.'

'But that's nearly as much as it costs.'

'Do you want to order?' The voice had turned impatient.

'I'd better have something else to make it worth it.' Prue held up the ZBD advert and named a second item.

A keyboard tapped away. 'That will be an extra six pounds postage.'

'But you've just charged postage.'

'Each item has a postage charge I'm afraid.'

Prue slammed down the receiver and dropped her head into her hands. If I sit very quietly, she thought to herself, then perhaps everything will go away. If I am extra, extra still and quiet perhaps it will turn out to be a dream.

Christmas presents, school runs, hotel rooms, making wild, outrageous love in a public park, a hurting, bleeding husband, a lover who had hacked his way through the hedge of thorns to the modest house (and modest life) where she had lain sleeping. A stepdaughter. A daughter whose accusing face and bewildered eyes were locked on her mother's.

Life had to go on.

CHAPTER TWENTY-SIX

IT WAS LUNCHTIME, AND, AGAINST ALL EXPECTATION, AN early Christmas rush in Forsight's bookshop had gathered momentum. The shop was unusually full and stuffy. The more swingeing the recession, it seemed, the more the book as a present grew in political correctness. 'Indisputably cheaper than caviar,' said Gerald, propping up a sagging dumpbin. Either that or the free warmth and an undemanding dose of piped classical music kept the customers coming.

For the umpteenth time the telephone rang and Gerald held it out to Prue, who balanced the pile of paperbacks she was sorting against the counter and took the call pressed up against the wall to avoid the crush. It was Mrs Harriman.

'We would like either you or Mr Valour to come and collect Jane today,' she said. 'We think she needs a few days at home.'

Fear took Prue in its jaws and shook her. She could barely articulate. 'Why?'

'Jane has been very under par this week. So has her work.' Fatigue and real concern toned down Mrs Harriman's disapproval but she managed to suggest – yet again – that the situation was Prue's fault. Buried in the part of Prue that did not want to listen, a voice said: She may be right.

Feeling squarely in the wrong was something else with which Prue was coming to terms.

Time to admit that life was tougher and more draining than she had allowed? Prue observed her fingers curled round the receiver, and concluded that, for most of her adult life, she had been in retreat.

'Yes, Mrs Harriman,' she said.

'The headmistress had a word with her this morning and it seems to have upset Jane a great deal, in fact she grew quite hysterical, so we judge it best that she goes home to calm down,' said Mrs Harriman. 'We have been keeping an eye, as you asked us, on her eating.'

'So have we,' said Prue, ironing any suggestion of defensiveness out of her tone. 'Her weight is stable at the moment, yes?'

On this occasion, Gerald was not so accommodating when Prue asked if she could go early. He took off his glasses and slammed them into their case.

'If the job is becoming too much,' he said, 'you must tell me.'

'I'm sorry to let you down.' Prue looked Gerald squarely in the eyes but he merely extracted his glasses from the case and turned away.

Prue's gaze roved along the bookshelves and stopped at Fict.: W. Wasn't it in Evelyn Waugh's *A Handful of Dust* where Brenda Last, having been informed that John is dead, lets out a sigh of relief when she discovers that the dead John is not her lover, but her son?

Prue understood now – for she *knew* there had been times during her battle when she would not have given up Jamie. Never would, perhaps, but Prue reminded herself that, if she shared a complicity with Brenda, it did not mean that they were the same person. But yes, she and Kate had agreed during one of their no-holds-barred talks (that were not honest enough, it seemed) that they would never put their children in jeopardy. Both had spoken from innocence but, then, the so dedicated, so home-centred Prue had not understood a lot of things.

Feeling guilty about Gerald, Prue sorted the paperbacks into the shelves and went to fetch her coat. 'Letting down' people had become a regular debit on her account. Who else could she let down? She had already let down her employer, her husband, her daughter, her friends. The cat?

Jane was waiting in the front hall of the school and plainly in no state to be lectured. The junior mistress who was guarding her, handed her over with the jolliness that hides extreme embarrassment and Prue bundled her into the car.

'Home,' she said.

'Home?' Jane made the word sound as if it was recently acquired foreign vocabulary.

In Hallet's Gate, Prue stood her silent daughter in the kitchen and unwound her scarf, removed her woollen gloves and eased the school coat off bony, unresponsive shoulders. Then she rubbed Jane's hands between her own. They felt cold and unlived-in.

'Jane.' Where once Prue would have been confident, she was now uncertain. 'Can you tell me what's the matter?'

Jane shook her head. 'Leave me alone, Mum.'

'But something's wrong.'

Prue did not require verbal confirmation, and nor could Jane give it. She allowed her mother to fuss over her and, while Prue did so, she observed her with a grown-up pair of eyes. This was not the parent who had guarded Jane and taught her the shape of the world. This was no longer the mother who was on her side but, apparently, a stranger with a secret. Jane knew, she just *knew* that the secret was harmful. Above everything else, Jane hated Prue for changing.

Back at school, Victoria (she of the divorced parents) had said that people always stopped loving each other. Jane was disinclined to believe her, but Victoria insisted. 'It always happens. Wait and see. Then you get someone else.'

Of course, Victoria had no option but to say that. Imperfect as her knowledge was of what took place between men and women, however, Jane grasped enough to know that the card with its glowing painting and hasty inscription that had rested against her jumper had the power to hurt her father.

Her *mother* could hurt her father.

Jane thought of the loneliness of being teased, the bewilderment of realizing that the world was ranged against you, and not knowing why, of hearing girls snigger as you passed, of finding unwelcome objects in your desk, of lying awake at night, alone, cold and afraid. She could not bear the idea that her father might feel the same. Jane spent so much time thinking about the card, puzzling out what it meant and what to do, that she could not sleep and her appetite, which had picked up a little, dwindled.

'I want you to have a cup of tea, darling.'

'I don't want one.'

'*Please*. I'll have one, too, and then we'll talk.'

The regulation shoes looked frighteningly too large for Jane's feet and her tights were baggy around the ankle.

'How about hot buttered toast?' Prue reached for the bread board.

Wanting to throw herself on her mother and bury her head in her shoulder and, in the same breath, wishing to inflict hurt as she was hurting, Jane glared at her. 'I don't want to talk to you. I don't want anything to eat. I want to watch *Neighbours*.' She added under her breath because she liked the effect it would have on her mother, 'And I'm going to make you watch me starve.'

Prue went white, then red. Then she sat down and put her head in her hands. Trying to forget I'm here, I suppose, thought Jane angrily.

She left Prue to contemplate the corpse-like shape of Jane's outdoor things on the floor. Bending down, she picked up the coat and smoothed out the sleeves. Then she folded the scarf and restored the gloves to their proper shape. Such everyday, mundane things whose wool was soft and worn to the touch, and she held them as tenderly as if they contained a breathing imprint of her daughter. She looked up and her gaze locked on to the garden. In the winter dusk, the *Prunus autumnalis* looked stark and unyielding.

'Joan's life', wrote one of her biographers, 'had been led on the high planes of feeling and it was fitting that death should meet her in the same high key.' In other words, it would never have done if, after the Paris débâcle, Joan had meekly returned to Domrémy to tend her sheep or sat down and hemmed handkerchiefs for her bride chest. It was required by everyone that she died dramatically – the ones who loved her, or rather her image, the ones who hated her and wished for the tongues of fire to sear her bones. Courageous, heroic, the woman who, voices ringing in her head, had done much to change the idea of what a woman could be, Joan required it of herself.

Imagine. If you have stood beside your sovereign in Reims Cathedral as he was anointed by the holy oil and crowned at your instigation, the oriflamme grasped in your hand. (All other standards were excluded but Joan's. As she said: 'It has borne the burden and it was right that it should have the honour.') If you have ridden with the wind in your ears and the sun at your back, smelt the sweat and horse and blood, wept with anguish and pain at your own wounds, experienced the noise and exhilaration of the charge, fought with your comrades over the white dust and through black mud, listened to their oaths, the sound of the trumpet signalling victory, and the quiet commands of God, how could you give it up? How could you return to the spinning and dusting?

Imagine, too, standing on the ramparts of the city of Mélun and listening to the voices of St Catherine and St Margaret telling you that you would be captured shortly, that you must not be surprised, that you must take everything as it came, however difficult.

That God would look after you.

Then what?

'I want to talk to you, Prue,' said Max that evening, and rose from his armchair, his face set and drained of all humour. He walked to the window and looked out, one hand shoved into his pocket. 'We've got to do something.'

She did not dare to ask what he meant and sought refuge in evasion. 'Oh.'

'We have to face some things, Prue.' Max swivelled round to look at his wife. 'I . . . We . . . are failing to do so.'

She heaved up from the chair with the sagging seat which she had always meant to replace and went over to stand beside him. 'Are you talking about Jane?'

'Partly.'

She noticed that his hand was trembling and she put out her own to touch him. Quick as a dart, he moved back out of reach and she was left, hand suspended, with a sensation that he had kicked her.

'I see.'

'No, you don't.'

Prue said quietly, 'You're angry with me, Max, aren't you?'

He turned back to contemplating the dark garden that reminded him of the one through which in his childhood dark monsters had slid. The frog monster. The bad fox. The fanged weasel. Clever, hungry killers. 'I'm angry with myself.'

Impatient that, at the crucial moment, she should feel so weak, Prue wanted to say, So am I.

'Prue. Go and sit down. I can talk to you better from a distance.'

The past *was* a different country. How many times over the years had she and Max talked, sitting close to one another, often with his arm draped over her shoulders? How many times had he played with a strand of her hair, or wrapped his big fingers around her longer, finer ones while they debated this or that? Which car to buy. Which school for Jane. Which holiday to take. Countless.

And how many times had Prue cast herself on Max's shoulder and wept over Violet, then the baby who came, and then the baby who never did, with fatigue, with frustration? And how many times had he comforted her, and she him? Many, many.

Life was made up of a series of losses – loss of confidence, faith, love, money, health, taut muscles, eyesight . . . Max had imagined that he had that knowledge safely under his control, and understood how to use it. From the opposite side of the room, he regarded his wife and knew that he had lost the will to remain silent.

'Stay there, Prue,' he said to reinforce the point.

Back in the sagging seat, she flinched at what was to come. Courage, she muttered to herself. Courage, courage.

Max cleared his throat. 'We *must* sort Jane out, Prue. The situation can no longer be ignored.'

'I agree.'

'Do you know why she is like this?'

'No.'

The silence that followed her denial was broken by the clink of keys of the gun-safe which Max tossed from one hand to the other.

'I think I know, Prue.'

Stop, she wanted to cry cravenly. Turn the clock back. I don't want anything to be said. Let's leave it at that point when the balance goes neither one way nor the other.

Clink went the keys.

'Are you . . . are you unhappy, Prue?'

Perhaps Max had meant to ask other questions outright but at the last minute, pulled back by caution or an understandable shrinking from pain, failed to do so. His expression was quite calm and no one, not even Prue, could have gauged what it hid.

As the one who had built and consolidated for as long as she could remember, Prue now found herself cast as an agent of destruction: on a par with the vandal with the Stanley knife – or with Joan's men, who plundered the city of Orléans after her first great victory.

'To go back to Jane,' she said desperately. 'Puberty. And she's being teased.'

The keys disappeared inside Max's fist. 'I thought you would answer a direct question,' he said. 'You disappoint me.'

She sighed. 'Of course I'm happy.'

'You forget I have experience and I know the signs.'

'Yes,' said Prue bitterly. 'You do have experience and I'm sorry for it. I know I lag behind you in that. But, Max, I paid the dues. Helen and Violet were hung round my neck until I thought they would stifle me, and I could never get away from them. They've always been there in our marriage.'

As she spoke, a memory nagged at Prue of someone else saying the same thing.

'You never said.'

'I suppose there's a lot I've never said.' She moved slightly and the light played on her thinner face and accentuated the strain visible on it.

Of course. Jamie had told her once that Violet had accused him of hanging Lara round *her* neck.

'But you would not lie to me, Prue?' He knocked his fist gently against the wall. 'I wouldn't like to think that.'

'No, I wouldn't, Max. There's no reason.'

'So, there is no need for me to worry?' Max had got himself under control.

Her grey eyes met his blue ones. I understand perfectly that the price is silence, was the message in hers, provided I do nothing to rock the family boat. So why are you asking me now?

Darling girl, take what I offer in the spirit it is meant. I understand better, far better, than you can imagine. But have pity, for it's tougher than I had imagined.

On such collusions do marriage draw their nourishment, grow and even bear fruit, she asked herself.

'No need is there, Prue?'

Prue took a deep breath . . .

'I'll ask you again,' said Max. 'There's no need for me to worry?'

Prue stared at him and did what she thought best. 'No,' she said. 'There's no need to worry.'

Max stuffed trembling hands into his pockets.

The sight of those shaking hands brought a lump into Prue's throat. She was a lying and would carry the weight of her lie on her back, up hill and down dale, until her skin was bruised and torn and beaten – as a result of her daughter starving herself because she suspected something was wrong, and her husband's hands were shaking with grief at the effort of sustaining a marriage.

'We must concentrate on Jane.'

'I am thinking of Jane.' Prue felt her heartbeat return to normal. Relief made her terse. 'I think of her most of the time.' She continued, 'I think we should keep her at home for the rest of the week and then send her back. Otherwise she will fret at missing what her friends are up to. In the holidays, I will help her make up some of the work.'

'The eating?'

'Worrying. But I've checked out her weight with Matron and she tells me she has not lost any till this last week. So I think she was eating more or less OK. Plus, she's growing fast . . . Mrs Harriman did say that the girls had been talking about anorexia among themselves and one or two of them had been trying it on.'

'Dad?'

The door was pushed open to reveal the figure of their daughter in an old pink nightdress that she insisted on wearing even though Prue had bought her new ones. She was hugging her copy of *Goodnight Mr Tom*.

Max looked up with the softened expression he reserved for his women. 'Why aren't you in bed?'

Pale and huge-eyed, Jane advanced into the room. 'I was listening at the door,' she said, her mouth stretched in a smile that neither of them recognized on the face of their eleven-year-old daughter. It was a smile which belonged on an older face and with an older spirit.

'You naughty girl,' said Prue. 'Straight back to bed.'

She put her hand on Jane's shoulder. Jane fixed her with a look which combined hatred and yet love – betrayed love, Prue supposed – and shrugged herself out of Prue's grasp. The book fell open in her hands and a piece of thin cardboard fluttered to the floor. It fell with the painting face up.

Max picked it up. He looked at it, then turned it over.

Prue felt the rushing and beating of her pulses build to a crescendo and, for a second or two, was in danger of fainting. Max looked up. Jane hovered by her father's chair, one leg bent behind the other in the attitude of innocence. A smile remarkable for its bitterness pulled at Max's mouth, but his eyes were damp.

It is true, said those eyes as he handed it over to Prue.

'Is that yours?'

The pulses shrieked in Prue's ears and wrists. You knew, said her eyes in return. She took the card and examined the serene, sinless Madonna. 'Oh,' she said. 'That's Kate's. I liked the picture, so she gave it to me.'

'What does it mean, Mum? What does it all *mean*? Why was Dad so sad?'

Prue was putting Jane to bed, removing the pile of computer magazines from the bed, brushing the fair hair and proffering a toothbrush in front of her daughter's nose. 'Funnily enough, grown-ups do get sad. One day,' she said, 'I will explain but not now.'

'Why not?' Jane mumbled through a mouth full of toothpaste.

'Because you are too young and you must accept that.'

'But who was the card from?'

'From an old boyfriend of Kate's, I think.' Prue watched Jane in the mirror. Jane rinsed her mouth and spat out quantities of toothpaste.

'Oh,' she said, and Prue relaxed a little.

When Jane was in bed and tucked in, Prue bent to kiss her. Her lips made contact with the sweet, fresh skin and lingered.

'But you see, Mum, it's frightening when I don't know about things,' Jane said out of the blue.

Prue sat down on the bed. 'I agree. But in good time. Till then, you must trust Dad and me.' She ran the edge of the sheet under her fingernails. 'Why did you take the card? It wasn't yours.'

Jane's eyelids masked her expression. 'I don't know,' she said. 'I just did.' She was silent. 'Why was it there, Mum?'

Downstairs in the drawing room, Max was sitting quietly in his chair, his hands on either arm. A glass of whisky stood untouched on the floor by the armchair.

As she came back into the room, the twilight had been finally routed by the dark, and his figure was shrouded. She bent to turn on the table-lamp and went over to draw the curtains.

'Is she settled?'

Prue nodded.

'I love you, Prue.'

Unlike his wife, Max was used to solitude and suspected that, as in the past, it might be his portion in the future. He was well acquainted with it; it was his companion in life. Its prospect emptied the mind and cleansed the spirit and allowed the emotion and feeling to wash within the bone shell that housed his brain.

Life had to go on, and tranquillity was a luxury. Wars may lay waste, tornadoes lay waste, recession was laying waste, but, surely adultery lays waste far more lives than any of these.

'Have a glass of whisky,' he said, 'and we could watch the news.'

Prue thought her heart was in danger of breaking.

CHAPTER TWENTY-SEVEN

H ALF-WAY BACK FROM WINCHESTER ON SATURDAY morning, Max remembered the gun.

It was due for collection from the gunsmith's where he had taken it for repairs. The repair had not really been necessary and guns were best left in their safes. Nevertheless, Max had taken it to the gunsmith.

With an exclamation of impatience, he guided the car into the centre of the road, checked that it was empty and made a U-turn.

The detour would make him late for lunch. Not that that mattered too much, except to Max who was hungry, for the house was in chaos on account of the Valours' annual pre-Christmas drinks party due to take place the next day.

The Becketts were also staying for the weekend.

'Do you want to go ahead with it?' Prue had broached the curious – and ominous – calm that suggested everything, but also nothing, which had settled over their home life. 'Shall we drop it for this year?'

'Why?' he had replied.

Because, Prue had begun to say, feeling much as Joan must have done as she kicked her heels at the beginning of her journey, requiring the catharsis of some sort of battle, some point of engagement, some reference as to where one was. But Max cut her off.

'Then if you want the party,' she conceded, 'that's fine.'

If, thought Max, one reflected hard enough on events it was possible to predict what was going to happen. How the same things, betrayal, disappointment, lack of love, greed, foolishness, repeat themselves in each generation, in each family, in each relationship.

Max drove on. He needed time to rebuild the dignity he now perceived as more important at his stage of life than he had bargained on. *If* he was to survive, Max had to think of himself, and Prue must make allowances, as he had done for her.

With difficulty he located a parking place, for Winchester was crowded with shoppers (and garish with Christmas lights), and retrieved the gun.

'It's a beauty,' said the assistant, running his hand over the butt. 'Capable of doing big business. I see you take great care of it.'

'Yes, I do,' said Max. 'I do.'

It lay beside him in the car and, from time to time, he glanced down at the age-cracked leather case. He never used this gun on his shooting days. It had belonged to his father.

When people asked Max about the incident – and there were not many around to remember it now – he shrugged the question aside. At the time it had been newspaper fodder, and caused his family acute embarrassment.

What it was exactly that tipped his father over the edge Max had never been sure. Drink? The drip, drip of disappointment and frustration? A wish to make the day different from all the others stacked up on each other like old newspapers, and clumped into years.

Anyway, one morning in late spring, William had got up,

eaten a hearty breakfast and then turned a gun on Max's mother whom he threatened to kill.

Of course, he did not. Instead, he had blown a small hole in Antonia's foot and a large one in the kitchen floor.

So much for the grand Wagnerian finale crescendoing to a terrible howling end with wind and storm that William craved. Instead it had been a muddled, not terribly bloody, incident in a suburban kitchen, the Tristram with a whisky-mottled face and the Iseult in flowered print overall.

Extraordinarily, prison life contented William and, on visiting days, he enquired with more interest after Max's affairs – exams, games – than he had ever shown previously. When he emerged, considerably less ruddy and stout than when he went in, he went to live in a remote cottage on the Ardnamurchan peninsula where he chopped wood and planted trees (having become something of a tree expert in prison) until he dropped dead of a heart attack. Max stayed with him often and they spent companionable evenings in the pub drinking the local malt and walking the hills above the glen.

Once the initial shock (and discomfort) had diminished, Antonia also flourished and spent the remainder of her life happily in Croydon with a spinster cousin. Accommodations, however bizarre, having been made with the general messiness of life, everyone, it appeared, was a great deal more content.

But Max never liked the gun.

'It's the Christmas season, all right,' said Max, forty-five years later, edging through the kitchen door at Hallet's Gate. 'The men are all demanding whisky. Either that, or the party is awful.'

The kitchen at Hallet's Gate was unrecognizable under a sea of glasses, bottles and remains of the not-very-imaginative snacks, which Prue, in an uncharacteristic spirit of grudge and groan, had put together early that morning.

'Tough,' she said, wrestling with a tray of ice-cubes. 'I only bought one bottle. Make them drink the sherry. It's a good one and they should think themselves lucky.'

'Hallo,' said Kate brightly from the doorway. 'I haven't really talked to you yet.'

In honour of the occasion, Kate had progressed from Lycra leggings into a pleated wool skirt. She looked wholesome, straightforward and keen-eyed. The ice-cubes ejected out of the tray and shot over the sink. Prue made a grab for them.

'Take these, will you, Kate? I'm just coming.'

Kate was not in any hurry and lingered by the sink.

'Molly is having a go at Richard over the church cleaning rota,' she reported. 'Richard ain't too pleased.'

Prue had a distinct impression that Kate had levelled her radar at both her and Max with the aim of gathering as much information as possible.

'Will you see to the refills?' Prue turned to Max, and stopped herself adding her habitual 'darling'. She whipped open the oven and extracted prawn vol-au-vents. They looked overdone.

'Earn your keep,' she said to Kate. 'Open those packets of Kettle Chips, and dismantle the radar.'

Kate's eyebrows suggested outrage and innocence, and that she had no idea what Prue meant.

Prue flipped the oven gloves over her shoulder. 'If you must know, Max and I are going through a bit of a bad patch, in fact a bloody one, and I don't know how it's going to end. Somehow, the Valour party went ahead and I've got to get through it.' She smiled in a way that was new to Kate. 'Is that a good enough update for you?'

Kate looked like the woman who, having determined to learn the worst, decides to stick to the Noddy version of life from now on. 'Oh, Prue,' she said with distress and some distaste. 'I'm sorry.'

Too late, Prue realized that Kate would rather not have known about her marital problems, and felt some sympathy with this ostrich position. Oh, well, she thought. What did I expect?

The drawing room had been denuded the day before of most of its furniture, and echoed slightly. The party had reached the halfway point between the stiff beginning and the we-must-go-home-the-joint-is-overcooking stage and the atmosphere had worked up into a fug of cigarette smoke and bodies meeting central heating. Prue's arrangement of red ribbon and fir cones (not her best) sat below a water-colour of a Highland scene. As she came into the room, Violet was pointing out the painting to a guest, a woman dressed in an outfit that shrieked Emporio Armani.

Molly pounced on Prue. Molly was not dressed in Emporio Armani. As a concession to the Valour party, she had unearthed a shirtwaister dress of the type Doris Day favoured in the fifties, plus sensible lace-up shoes.

'Where's Jane?' Molly cast a beady eye around the room.

She made Prue feel uncomfortable. 'She's over with Judy. The two of them decided the party was boring news,' she said.

She was glad when Richard, the vicar, bore down on them both, cherishing his empty glass rather obviously. Prue grabbed a bottle and filled it for him. God knew, Richard had little enough luxury in his life.

'Now you two are together,' he said gratefully, 'we can discuss the cleaning rota.'

Every sense aware that Jamie was standing only a couple of feet away, Prue refilled Molly's glass. Molly launched into a tirade and Prue knew that if she had any shreds of grace left, if her love for Jamie was to mean anything, she must concentrate.

You could not drop in and drop out of your life, however tempting, however badly the frenzy of sexual desire itches and frets, however secret your inner life, however far you had travelled.

'. . . dusting,' said Richard.

If the pew-polishing rota was the vehicle by which the collective life in Dainton was conducted, so be it.

'. . . dusting,' she said, watching Jamie out of the corner of her eye.

Over by the window, Emmy held out a cross, crumpled-looking Edward to his mother.

'Why on earth didn't you change him? He's smelly.'

'Sorry, Violet.'

Edward was suffering from a slight stomach upset (he would, thought his mother grimly). Violet's glossy head ducked in annoyance. She had taken to wearing lipstick of an even brighter scarlet, which suited her and which acted as a beacon, although that was not necessarily her intention, for if Violet craved attention, she did not wish to take it further than that. (She was merely copying the look of a very OK author interviewed in depth in *Vanity Fair*.) A couple of the older men at the party had brightened at Violet's entrance, and hovered hopefully.

'It's better to journey than to arrive.' Prue nudged Kate and indicated the hopefuls.

'I particularly wanted to show Edward off,' Violet whispered to Emmy at a level calculated not to be heard while her red lips smiled and glistened with – false – invitation. Bet you did, thought Emmy. 'I can't if he smells.'

Unaware of the exchange, Edward gazed out of the window at a couple walking their retriever who, as non-invitees, were pointedly not looking towards the window of Hallet's Gate. At the sight of the dog, his face creased in a sudden, devastating smile and he bounced up and down on Emmy's shoulder.

'I'll change him,' said Jamie, materializing out of the group which contained Mrs Patterson, known as the Praying Mantis because she had presided over the deathbeds of three husbands, who had followed each other with staggering rapidity.

Edward was handed over and his father bore him off. Violet frowned in the direction of her hopeful cavaliers who backed off hastily, picked up a handful of dirty glasses and made for the kitchen. Emmy was left with a damp stain on her T-shirt, clutching a muslin nappy. Uneasy in the company, yet fascinated and just a tinge envious at the affluence in the room, she twisted the nappy between her fingers, knew she could never belong and wondered if she could make a bolt for home.

'Hallo,' said Max, waving the sherry bottle in her face. 'Would you like some?'

'No, thank you, Mr Valour.'

'Max,' he said.

He smiled his gentle smile which made Emmy, whose life for the last two months had been a compound of fear and a churning stomach, feel almost witty and beautiful and normal.

'Actually, I've been wanting to talk to you.' He placed the bottle carefully on the window sill and paused. 'I gather you're going to have a baby.'

Emmy felt a blush the colour of peonies mount her face, but there was no point in denying it.

'Have you decided what you will do?'

'Yes,' she said. 'No. I mean, yes.' She bit her lip and her peaky features were accentuated by her obvious agitation. 'I'm going to have the baby.' She paused. '*That*'s final.' Her fingers clutched the nappy. 'Mum can have me for a bit, I think. I can live off the social and then when the baby is older try and get a live-in nanny job with the baby. Some nannies get flats, you see.'

She made Max feel infinitely old. In his day, the social was somewhere you went for a good night out. He winced, too, for the trust that underlay Emmy's sad little plan.

'Don't fret,' he said suddenly, and his kindness made her want to cry. She looked up at him, and a strand of her hopeless hair lay against a cheek now so white that Max could swear no blood ever pulsed in it. As ever in situations like this (and Max had experience in dealing with pregnant women), his chivalry was stirred.

Acid was burning in Emmy's stomach and she longed for something starchy to mop it up. 'Mum's got to talk to Dad first. She's waiting for the right moment.'

'I've had an idea.' Max took Emmy completely by surprise. 'And I'd like to make a suggestion.'

It took a couple of seconds for Emmy to absorb what he said. Then her eyes widened and hardened with suspicion. You dirty old man, she thought, deeply disappointed. I thought *you* were straight.

Max understood. He took a step back until a space was between them. 'Don't worry, Emmy. This is perfectly above board. No question about that. I'll be in touch.'

Thoroughly bewildered, Emmy reckoned she could make a dash for it. Without a muted goodbye, she slid past Max and disappeared.

In the hall, she struggled into her inadequate jacket.

What will you do?

The answer was: I don't know, so stop asking me, everyone. Alongside the nag of *that* question was the ache and mystery of her love for Angus which she tried so hard to pretend did not exist – unlike his baby inside her.

Lady Truscott polished off her third glass and swayed, just a little, as she accepted a fourth. Smiling, Prue circulated and did her best to draw in a shy bachelor who appeared inextricably welded to the wall and debated introducing him to the Praying Mantis.

His nappy-changing duty completed, Jamie was back in the room and talking to Major Hutton. His attention remained fixed on the Major – except for once when he raised his eyes and met Prue's.

Prue moved in measured fashion around her guests offering vol-au-vents as if her heart was not beating to a wildly sexual rhythm, her conscience was as light as the flaky pastry and her home was not crumbling around her.

In the end, Joan was taken by the Burgundians and her former friends and allies abandoned her. The King, her King, in particular did nothing, he for whom Joan had risked so much.

Poor Joan. After capture, she grew so desperate and ex-hausted from constant questioning and prying that she threw herself from the tower at Beaurevoir, a leap of sixty to seventy feet. Astonishingly, she survived almost unscathed. She must have been very, very desperate, and she must have believed very hard.

Prue gazed out from the tower of Hallet's Gate on to the unyielding terrain below.

The last guest having been steered out of the door, the Becketts and the Valours sat down to eat bread, cheese and salami.

Max put down his knife with an expression, the careful, impassive, lawyer's expression that Prue knew well.

'I have some things I wish to discuss,' he said, 'and I might as well do it here.'

A hand grasped Prue's heart and closed, and she was not sure if it indicated fear, or a curious exultation that the worst could be about to happen. Oh, Mum, Jane had said, hadn't the

Woman Taken in Adultery *wanted* to get into trouble?

Once upon a time, Max would never have broached a subject publicly without first consulting Prue. If her life equalled the reading of a book, Prue sensed she had reached the crisis or drama in the story where events cried out to be tied up.

She had wanted and taken Jamie: she had wanted him badly and allowed the flames of that desire to lick and burn her body, as Joan's had been seared on the pyre. But, at the bottom of her only half-explored female soul, Prue expected to pay a price.

'This may surprise you . . .' Max did not seem agitated, 'but I will be living in London for the next six months or so in the company flat.'

Prue helped herself from a bowl of fruit salad. 'Max!'

'I'm going to be heading up the Brussels and Madrid offices, plus working to set up the additional European offices, and I feel the commuting is too tiring. Prue's staying here.'

Prue's spoon assumed a life of its own, and clattered back into the bowl. Apparently, she had misunderstood the bargain that had been struck.

'I'll come home for some weekends, of course, if it's possible.'

Imperceptibly Jamie relaxed but Violet's mouth opened.

'What on earth are you going on about, Dad? Leave Prue for six months?' She gave Prue one of her examining-an-animal-behind-zoo-bars looks. 'Do you mind, Prue?'

'If that's what your father wishes to do.'

Prue's tone, and the rigidity of her body, alerted Violet that there was more to this announcement than lay on the surface. Violet's eyelids closed over eyes that were suddenly suspicious, and hid the calculations she was making. Then she looked up and the obstinate look had settled into place. 'Jamie,' she ordered her husband, 'tell Daddy this is a bad idea. Not only bad but unnecessary.' Jamie hesitated, and she tutted impatiently. 'For goodness sake, Daddy, you've been commuting all your life. What's different?'

Max smiled at his daughter. 'There's no need to get upset, my darling.'

'You can't,' said Violet, and Prue could have sworn Violet was close to tears. 'It isn't good, and it isn't done. If we all went galloping off into the sunset every time we fancied a change, which is what I suspect this is, everything would collapse.'

Violet had no idea that she had hit the target.

Full marks, Violet. For common sense and for a certain courage. Reluctantly, then with a rush of admiration, Prue thus conceded to her old adversary.

'Darling,' said her father, 'you can't organize everything, much as you'd like to.'

'Think of Jane,' responded his daughter, who, over the years, had not made a practice of it herself.

Taken aback by Violet's late discovery of sisterly responsibilities, Prue picked up her spoon and chased a cherry-stone around her bowl. 'I don't think it's as dramatic as all that.' She assessed her husband. 'Is it, darling? You do have a lot of work with the commission.'

'The reason I'm discussing this with you,' Max continued, 'is that I will suggest to Emmy that after she leaves you she comes to me in the flat in London until she can sort herself out.'

With a noise that sounded suspiciously like a wail, Violet dropped her face into her hands. 'You've gone *mad*, Daddy. What will people think? You'll be accused of child molesting or something. Or they'll think the baby's yours.'

'She needs a helping hand and I will need a housekeeper.'

'For God's sake . . .' Violet raised her head and bunched up her napkin on which lipstick was imprinted in bloody rings. 'You have a wife.'

Lipstick, thought Prue, searching through the housewifery manual kept in her head. How do you get it out? Paraffin? Petrol?

'Pregnant women are no trouble,' said Max, as if he had not heard. 'They're easy to look after. It's what comes afterwards that's the problem.'

For a couple of seconds, Prue was bewildered and thrown off the scent, and then she understood. Helen. In many ways, what had happened to Max, and to her, was the result of Helen and that story.

She, too, wanted to drop her head into her hands and wail. Instead, with a curious disappointment, she looked at her watch and said, 'It's time to pick Jane up from Kate's otherwise we'll be late for the carol service.'

St Mary's held its carol service earlier than most parishes. Otherwise, said the admirable and wise Richard, Christmas was an indigestible lump.

Once again, St Mary's had been decorated – over-decorated in the opinion of some – by Dainton's army of flower-arrangers (which this year did not include Prue). Swags of ivy hung from the pillars, snaked over the pulpit and lectern and wreathed anything that possessed a circumference and did not move.

The much-argued-about candles had been lit in their dozens and the effect *was* magical, both familiar and yet mysterious. The church smelt of hot wax and was spiced with evergreens. Every last seat was taken, and parishioners who could not face the trials of Series B and tub-thumping, hugging and kissing matins, which Richard insisted on for younger members of the parish, were there in force to store up their annual tally of grace.

Once-in-Royal-David's-Citying, the choir progressed up

the aisle with Richard in tow, his expression serene. We must live and let live, it said. (Anyway, only a moment's reflection brought a forward-looking vicar to the conclusion that the majority of those who clung to the old ways would be dead quite soon.)

Violet had stayed behind at Hallet's Gate, declaring she needed a bit of peace or she would go mad, but Jamie had come. Standing in the pew beside Jane, Jamie on the other side of her husband, Prue felt sick and shaky and, perhaps for the first time in her life, completely alone.

'What about Jane?' she had whispered to Max in the hall as they collected their coats. 'What about her?'

'I think about her more than anyone,' he had replied.

'Why didn't you talk to me first? In fact, we *must* talk, Max . . .'

It was then that Prue saw Max was crying. She wanted to tear her heart out of her chest in expiation and give it to him to do with as he wished.

'Max . . .' She tried to touch him, but Max put up his hand to shield his face and turned away.

The Angel Gabriel saluted the Virgin Mary and, via St Luke, gave her the news of her impending pregnancy, which Molly read out at gunfire pace. Clearly, she did not feel easy with the subject.

'Il est né, le divin enfant' intervened in Prue's thoughts. It was sung in a jolly fashion by the choir, and then St Luke took up the story again, read beautifully this time by Mrs Paulton who owned the village stores.

In the pause, as choir and congregation gathered for the assault on 'Adam lay y-bounden', Prue felt the candlelight lap her like a second skin, and its tongues of flame run through her body. She turned her head and looked at Jamie.

A hunger has woken in me, she thought, and it will be

impossible to quiet it yet, for I am not yet old and dried up.

The high, clear voice of Jane beside her singing 'O Little Town of Bethlehem' made Prue screw up her eyes in pain. Where had her hunger led her?

'Do you believe you are in a state of grace?' was the trick question posed to Joan by Cauchon, her inquisitor at her trial. The question was so unfair that one of the other judges (who were there, after all, to condemn her) protested. But canny, passionate Joan knew that there are many answers to a question. Always.

'If I am not,' she said, 'may God put me in it, and if I am may God keep me in it.'

How did they take the reply, these men of God? Actually, not so much men of God as men of the Church, a distinction that should be noted. Further, they were men of the Church caught up in a civil war and those trying Joan in Rouen had chosen to work with the English and the Burgundians. To be fair, the Duke of Bedford and Philip the Good of Burgundy represented a decency and order that neither Joan's unstable Charles nor his cohorts could match.

Middle-aged, celibate, learned, these men were faced by a young, obstinate, extraordinary female who went to a great deal of trouble to hide her sex. They were men of peace. She was a woman of war. Her message was political – unheard-of for a woman. Boot the enemy out of France was Joan's cry. Further, she declared, she did not have to pay attention to those who sat in judgement on her unless God (through her voices) told her she must. In other words, Joan was not going to pay lip-service to the theological or ecclesiastical orthodoxy of the day.

You can imagine their horror, their bafflement, their fury that their authority and stature – the existing structures of Church and state – should be, thus, so undermined.

But when she was brought to face the court and the crowd

at the cemetery of Saint-Ouen at Rouen, Joan was placed at all times so that she could see a waiting cart and executioner. Unlike many martyrs, she did not seek out pain and had a healthy wariness of suffering. Perhaps the sight of that silent bringer of death was too much.

Joan recanted. She disavowed her voices, she renounced her male clothes, she submitted fully to the Church.

What agony she suffered as a result can only be conjectured, especially when she discovered she would not be set free. Her voices angrily informed Joan that she had committed a crime in confessing, and the rough English soldiers made her cell almost unbearable with their daily petty assaults. Joan was probably at the end of her tether when the more imaginative among them took away her woman's clothing so that she was forced to resume doublet and hose.

Once Joan had done this, the die was cast. Her determination returned and she was again ready for battle. Anyway, she would rather die, she told Cauchon, 'than endure longer my pain in prison'.

Then she informed him that it had been solely her fear of dying by fire which had made her sign the confession.

Nothing could have been more satisfactory to Cauchon, who desired only her death and, with those words, Joan had delivered up to him the disposition of her physical body.

She had also made a choice: to die. In the wrong done to her and the wrong she had done to herself by confessing, there had also been a rightness.

I was wrong, thought Prue of her own actions, but also right. In the bleakness there is also to be found healing, because there are many answers, because nothing is black and white and people need the grey as much as they need absolutes. I did not know that before.

At the end of the service – Prue swore she would never

willingly sing 'Hark the Herald Angels' again – the congregation filed past the collection tray by the door into the cold, dark world. Prue put in five pounds, Jamie twenty.

'Buying your way into good grace,' she muttered at him.

'Correct,' he said. 'It's traditional at Christmas.'

After exchanging greetings, the congregation dispersed and groups, breath streaming into the cold air, walked briskly back to their homes. Max had gone ahead with Jane and Molly, and Prue tugged at Jamie's arm. 'Wait.'

He half turned, and she sensed at once how tense he was. 'Max has won, hasn't he?'

Their faces were barely discernible in the dark. Prue permitted her hand to linger on the smooth cashmere nap of his overcoat. 'No,' she said. 'Not Max entirely. But the whole thing. It is too much to ask of us all.'

'Hasn't Max decided to make the break? That's what I assumed.'

She stopped by the recent grave of Molly's sister and stared down at it. 'I don't know because I haven't talked to him about it.'

Jamie did not reply.

They walked past the other graves with their uneven headstones, their carvings obliterated by lichen, and plodded up the slope from the church to the lane above. The grass was slippery and treacherous. Prue tripped, and landed on her knee. Jamie waited until she had brushed herself down. Then he said, 'You mean it is over?'

Further down the lane, a large, shambling figure beside Molly came to a halt.

CHAPTER TWENTY-EIGHT

WAS TELEVISION LIKE LIFE? OR LIFE LIKE TELEVISION? Compare and contrast.

Prue looked up at Jamie, felt the dust clogged under her fingernails, and compared and contrasted. No glossy television drama, no scriptwriter, no director could convey the impression that she was being cut into pieces, the rawness and anguish of her feelings, or the answering pain and desire on her lover's face. Neither would a director choose a backdrop of a sloping piece of grass slicked with dried mud.

The dialogue would not have passed muster. Neither Prue nor Jamie was capable of saying much, certainly not capable of articulating what this moment *felt* like or how they perceived the future without each other.

He licked his finger and scrubbed at her cheek. 'You've got a smudge.'

Prue submitted to his finger. 'Do you think Violet has any idea? It seems impossible that all this feeling is being expended and she hasn't sensed it.'

'No, I don't think she does.' Jamie considered Violet. 'That is her strength.'

'Don't ever tell her, will you, Jamie? Not even when you're old and grey.'

'That's my business,' he replied savagely.

'We don't all have to fall down.'

'*What?*'

'Ring-a-roses. Atishoo, and we all fall down.'

'I thought that was about the plague.'

'Exactly.'

Negotiating his way in the dark, Jamie sighed, full of regret, and aware that he was thoroughly netted. Not so much by his wife, but by being his age, a parent, and by who and what he was. Depression lowered a blanket over him.

'Won't you reconsider, Prue?' he asked abruptly.

She swallowed, and Jamie waited. Two or three seconds stretched out, and slipped into the past.

'No,' said Prue. She scrambled up the slope and into the lane, and contemplated a life once again simple and conducted on one level. 'I can't explain, but I know you know.'

At this point, Jamie probably understood less than Prue imagined.

'I didn't know how much it would hurt. That's all,' Jamie told Prue, frowning with the effort of talking sense.

Nothing he had said before had ever hurt Prue so much. Nevertheless, she managed a half-smile while she battled to put her life back on straight lines, to return it to the mundane where preoccupation with sausages, clean sheets, cat fleas and Hoover bags would help to blot out the radiant, shining, scented, achingly happy landscape that she had walked with Jamie.

'The others will be back by now and wanting supper,' she said.

Without warning, Jamie pulled Prue towards him. For a couple of seconds, she allowed herself to lean against his shoulder and closed her eyes.

*

Swaying circles of light in the lane indicated the torches shone by returning parishioners. They dipped and swayed, an *aurora borealis* sweeping back to base for gin and sherry, comfortable in the knowledge that church had been done, some even having found nourishment in the service.

'I say,' said Molly to Max, 'shouldn't you go back and see what Prue's up to?' It was too dark for Max to see Molly's expression.

It was at that instant that Max stopped walking. 'I'll see you on Sunday, Molly.'

'Right,' she said and, shrugging her dreadful tweed coat more tightly around her, set off home where Keith was waiting for her to serve him yet another supper with cabbage.

Max's large shadow moved back along the patched and rutted surface of the lane, dipping in and out of the light directed by the wind ripping over from the ridge, which was sending clouds scudding across the moon.

Max was about to say, Are you coming Prue? when the words were stillborn.

In the freeze-frame, looping and spooling in slow motion, he watched his wife, who was outlined in the light from the church porch, climb the bank and lean towards his son-in-law. He saw, too, Jamie's hand touch his wife's cheek, and pull her to him. Then he understood.

Prue looked up from Jamie's shoulder, the rough fibres of the material rubbing her cheek and saw a large figure back away, then turn and run.

'Oh, my God, Max has seen us,' she said.

And with that, Prue pushed Jamie away and also ran, streaking like an animal, its hunting finished, streaks home like a bullet from a gun.

At the entrance to the drive, she skidded to a halt, her feet sending a spume of gravel across the grass verge. Something moved and the security light flooded the area. Then she froze. 'No, Max,' she said, her hand across her mouth. 'No, not that.'

For Max had materialized out of the darker patch of shadow where the car was parked. The gloom made him appear even bigger, his face more set and white than she had ever seen it. In his hands gleamed the polished barrel of his father's gun.

'Where did you get it?' asked Prue in a stupefied fashion.

'It was in the car,' said Max.

'But you *always* put the guns away.'

'I didn't this time, did I?'

'Get back, Prue,' said Jamie urgently from behind her. 'Get out of the way.'

But Prue was not listening. She took a step forward but Jamie's arm swept out and pushed her aside. The shock made her gasp and she stumbled.

'What are you doing, Max?' Her voice rang thinly in the night. The gun shone into her face.

Max loomed over his wife. 'I want to kill you,' he said calmly. 'Painfully and slowly.'

She scrabbled at the fluff in her coat pockets. 'Max, where's Jane? Tell me where Jane is.'

'I don't know. Inside I imagine.'

Husband and wife stared at each other. The guns. Those guns had been there all their married life, waiting to be used.

'Max,' Prue inflected her voice into that of a supplicant, 'please don't do anything silly.'

A second later, she thought, How funny that I never realized the gun barrel was the colour of beech leaves in autumn. Another second elapsed, and she reflected: Max is going to kill someone. How will Jane cope with a murderer for a father?

382

'Put the gun away, Max.' Jamie sounded in control. 'It doesn't solve anything.'

'I know the truth now.' Max moved the barrel up to the level of Jamie's chest. The truth . . .'

'Yes,' said Jamie. 'And I'm sorry.'

'*That* makes it worse. At least, if you're going to fuck my wife you should be wholehearted about it. If you were going to betray my daughter—'

Max could not finish the sentence and took a gasping breath. Jamie was silent, and edged an inch or two across the gravel so that part of his body came between Max and Prue. 'I am. I was wholehearted. And this', he gestured at the gun, 'is not a resolution.'

'Shut up,' said Max.

Every movement the trio made appeared magnified, and so was the silence, broken by the shuffle of their feet, and their urgent whispered conversation.

And I had imagined we were so civilized. Prue was grasping at straws. Then she remembered the wild hot lust and tumbled bodies, the urgings, pantings and satiations, the greed for more, the ruthlessness that went out and took it, and knew that, ultimately, no one was civilized. Why should Max and a gun be any different?

Max felt a darkness fogging his brain, the rage he had been hiding from himself for so long. For a lifetime. Slowly and patiently, he lifted the gun and pointed it at his wife.

'What's the pattern, Jamie? A quick foray and then off? Do you hang around to estimate the damage? Is that the form?'

'Believe me,' said Jamie, breath streaming into the night, 'I do not make a habit of it.'

'Max.' Suddenly Prue was furiously angry. 'You know that's not what you think. You know what's been happening and you sat on the sidelines. You *cannot* take issue now.'

He looked steadily at his wife. 'I never thought you were stupid before. Adulterous . . . maybe. A liar . . . of necessity. There are worse things. But *stupid*.'

'Oh, my God!' Prue understood. 'It's because of Violet, isn't it? Not me.'

She stretched out her arm. 'Max, my darling. Listen, listen to me—'

With a gasp of rage and pain, Max tightened his grip on his father's gun. 'Was it not enough that you had your freedom, Prue? I could take that. I could manage it, and understand. And cope. Just. But I can't forgive that you have transgressed against my daughter.'

'Max!'

'Was it some sort of revenge for having to take on Violet when you married me?'

He only married you for convenience.

I hate you, Prue.

'Max. Shooting me or Jamie is only a gesture. It won't erase what's happened. What happened, whatever the suffering, is worth more than just a gesture.'

Prue's teeth chattered uncontrollably and inwardly she wept with pity and grief. She was frightened, my God, she was frightened. Demons take up residence in the wronged, even in gentle, wounded giants like Max.

'Max,' she said, knowing now that it was she that Max wished to kill, not Jamie and, strangely, accepting it, 'would you like me to get down on my knees?'

Down she went on to the gravel, the sharp stones biting her flesh like toothed animals. A St Joan of the shires. Penitent, but hungry. Awoken but grieving.

Sensing that this exchange between a husband and wife excluded him, Jamie remained motionless where he was. He found he could not bear the sight of the figure kneeling in the drive and he turned his head away.

'You threatened Violet's happiness, Prue. That is your greatest sin against me.'

'Is it? Are you sure?'

Prue would never understand fully the complicities of her marriage, and terror blunted her responses.

'To harm my daughters is to harm me,' said Max heavily. 'How could you think so little of it?'

The wind was rising. A dead, cold smell of winter blew in with it, and the silence of suspended life settled around the group in the drive. Prue's knees ached and stung and the shapes under them indented her flesh, but no less punishingly than Max's words stung and wounded.

Somehow, in the dark woods and ravines of blindness and folly, reason, humour and wisdom *had* to be found. Prue got to her feet.

'You must understand, Max, it did not seem like that,' she said, savouring (for the last time?) the beat of passion for Jamie deep in her body. She took a deep breath. 'If you kill me, Jane will suffer.'

Jamie's eyes suddenly narrowed as he saw that Max's aim had slackened.

Prue raised her arms in a gesture asking for forgiveness. 'The awful thing is, Max . . . that it doesn't have anything to do with you, or with Jane. It was to do with me, that's all.' She pointed towards the gun. 'Max, please let me have it.'

With a cry of pain, rage and release, Max raised the barrel, aimed and squeezed the trigger – and shot the sky.

The report ripped apart the silence and travelled through the village. Prue imagined she felt the air part above her fingertips and the passage of hot metal. Her hands dropped to her sides.

Edward began to cry inside the house and the curtains at

Jane's bedroom window were ripped apart. The back door was wrenched open and Violet peered out.

'What on earth . . . ?'

Then the telephone rang.

Behind Prue, Jamie tensed, leapt forward, and took the gun from Max. The muscles in both men's jawlines were rigid – the still-young versus the ageing. Sweat sprang out on Jamie's forehead.

'Don't worry, Violet,' he called out. 'The gun went off by mistake as Max was bringing it in from the car. Tell Jane not to worry.'

'How stupid of you, Dad.' Violet disappeared to answer the phone.

'I'm sorry, Max,' Jamie said. 'For all the reasons in the world.'

With a little cry, Prue snatched the gun from Jamie and cradled it awkwardly to her chest. 'Sorry, I'm so sorry,' she whispered to it.

A minute dragged by as the three remained, frozen and unmoving. Then, together, they entered the house.

'That was Molly,' Violet said as they entered the kitchen. 'For some reason, she wanted to know if you were all right. Since you could have blown us all to pieces, I said it was lucky that she was keeping an eye on us. Then the vicar rang to enquire what the shot was.'

'Hot chocolate, anyone?' asked Prue. 'I'm going to make some for Jane.'

'Yes, please,' said Jamie, and caught Prue's eye. Hot milk, passion and a threat of death, was the message it conveyed. How does that strike you?

It struck her as absurd, comic and profoundly truthful. 'I'll take Jane's up,' she said.

She shrugged off her coat and went into the study to put away the gun. The patina on the barrel gleamed at her, expensive and cared-for. She touched it with her fingertip and then locked it away.

When she returned, Violet and the two men were sitting at the table discussing the stock-market. She joined them, cradling her mug loosely between her hands.

Stock-markets and clean socks could not be denied their place and love, sex and passion had to be given theirs. But if that was true, which the tableau around the kitchen table appeared to confirm, neither was it deniable that in between the interstices of shopping, cooking, getting pensions flourished deep-rooted and tenacious emotions that sometimes erupted into violence and bloodshed.

Sometimes an irony lurked at the heart of these flaring eruptions. For Violet, who had done so much to cause trouble, was the reason – the reason, at any rate, to which they clung – that the three remained sitting round the table and kept silent, and would continue to do so.

Jamie drained his mug, a freebie from a petrol station that Jane had insisted on collecting, and got to his feet. He gestured towards the empty mug. 'Thank you . . .' he said, and for one farcical moment, Prue thought he was going to thank Max for not killing him. Violet stretched and pushed her mug towards Prue, which the latter took to mean she should wash it up.

'I'm going to have a bath,' she said.

How unprivate Prue's love affair had turned out. How impossible it was for it to exist as an island. Falling in love with a man other than your husband could never be private, and she had lacked the perception, or experience, to realize this.

'I won't be staying.' Jamie tapped the mug, which gave off an echo. 'I'll square it with Violet. Fabricate a work crisis.'

Max did not look at Jamie. 'I want you gone,' he said, and now he did not sound at all civilized.

Jamie appeared to approve Max's attitude. 'I'll go back by train in the morning. Violet can drive herself up later in the evening.'

'Right,' said Max.

And that was that.

Violet insisted that, even if her stupid husband was insisting on working through their well-earned, statutory weekend, she was not. She wished to be with her family.

In fact, Violet did not relish the idea of a Sunday on her own with Edward in London.

'Look, Daddy,' she said, bending over Max who was sitting by the drawing-room fire after breakfast. 'This is our pre-Christmas get-together. If Jamie wants to abandon his family, so be it. I'm staying put.'

Prue, who was writing yet more lists at the desk, fingered the silver paper knife and stared into the omnipresent photograph of Helen. Helen who had run away from her daughter. You launched more than a thousand ships, you witch, she informed the image, with a shiver of knowledge that left her cold, but at least you were honest. Yet if Helen had introduced the dogs of war into the family, it was Prue who had let them loose.

The patter of pine needles falling from the Christmas tree interrupted the silence. The movement caused one of the silver balls to rotate, catching the light.

Max reached up and grasped Violet's hand. 'Whatever you wish, my darling.'

'Right,' said Violet. 'We'll dispatch Jamie to his London vastness and we'll make ourselves comfortable. In some ways, it's easier without him.' She thought for a moment. 'You know what, Dad, I just might stay until Monday morning.'

She slipped her arm around Max's neck and rested her cheek on the top of his head.

Thus it was that Prue found herself delivering Jamie to Winchester because Violet wanted to watch the cookery programme *Gourmet Dieting.*

'You can drop Jamie off anywhere, actually, providing there's a station.' Violet made him sound like dry-cleaning. Max said nothing, but Prue suspected he was allowing her to say goodbye in private. Max had always been generous.

It was a cold, raw morning and the wind whistled up the line, bringing the sting of salt, smut and sewage from the coast. The tiny waiting room on the platform was stuffy and smelt of gas fire. A couple of women in sensible shoes were discussing their planned assault on Christmas shopping. They glanced at the intruders and their conversation broke off. By mutual consent, Prue and Jamie retreated outside. Here, the damp and rawness stung their exposed skin.

'*Annus horribilis.*' Jamie addressed the foot passenger bridge. 'Is that what it's been, Prue?'

Prue managed a joke. 'At least we haven't been photographed sucking toes.'

They were silent. She dug her hands into her pocket. 'Where next, Jamie?'

'I thought it was goodbye. In one sense, anyway.'

'For you, I mean.'

'Abroad,' he said with a little shrug of his shoulders. 'I think I can arrange the old job back in New York.'

'Violet?'

'She'll be pleased.'

The future stretched out, for the moment flat and dispirit-ing, a jigsaw puzzle into which the pieces still had to be fitted. Jamie paced away up the platform, then he stopped and re-turned to where she stood and put both hands on her shoulders.

'Prue. Darling Prue. I'll ask once more. Come with me.'

She stared into the face she loved so painfully, alarmed and unnerved by her desire to say yes. The price of her love for him had been her sense of wholeness, of belonging to the garden of Eden. But whatever the discord of the lost harmonies and innocence, it had been worth it. It had to be, otherwise all the mess and pain caused to others would have been for nothing.

The train came into sight, a steadily enlarging dot on its front plate registering like a borehole on Prue's vision. With a hiss of wheels on the rails, it drew into the station. Doors clicked open and shut with a hollow sound. A couple of voices rose above the noise, shouting instructions to one another. Passengers went in an untidy stream towards the ticket barrier.

Prue rubbed her fingers together, feeling the roughened texture from too much washing-up without rubber gloves.

'Prue?' Jamie questioned, his hands heavy on her shoulders.

'It's impossible.'

'It's perfectly possible.'

In the end, I would not have wanted not to have been buffeted, she thought – the sheet fluttering on the washing line, bouncing and whipping in the wind. Even though the end of this is going to half kill me.

Faith? Prue possessed only the form, not the substance. Belief in marriage? Yes . . . and no. A sceptic's view of passion? Never.

'The real reason,' Jamie prompted.

'Jane is the reason.' She smiled into the face of her lover. 'And Edward.'

'Are they the only reason?'

'They are quite good enough,' she replied, 'but no.'

She had been searching through sleepless nights and the fret of sexual frustration, and longing for the formulation which had, so far, eluded her.

Weeping copiously, Joan went out to her death wearing a black shirt, and a kerchief on her head. Nailed to the stake was a board which said:

> Joan, who had herself called the Maid, a liar, pernicious deceiver of the people, sorceress, superstitious, blasphemer of God, defamer of the faith of Jesus Christ, boastful, idolatrous, cruel, dissolute, invoker of demons, apostate, schismatic and heretic.

Such a small sign to carry so much invective – and wasted on nine out of ten of the waiting crowd who could not read. And as if this panoply was not enough, the sermon directed at a frightened, weeping girl waiting for the fire to strip the flesh from her bones took as its text a quotation from the First Epistle to the Corinthians: 'Whether one member suffer, all the members suffer with it.'

Joan was then formally cast out by the Church and handed over to the secular authorities to finish off. Then she was crowned with a mitre. 'Heretic, relapsed, apostate, idolater.'

They must have been very frightened of Joan, all those men, and of her power to change things.

Because the scaffold had been built so high, she had taken a long time to die, longer than necessary, and because the executioner had been unable to climb up and strangle her, as was the custom. She would not have been aware of that little detail when she threw back her recantation in Cauchon's face and, thus, gave her enemies everything they needed to structure the careful wall of faggots and wood.

Nevertheless, Joan had made her death her own decision.

Prue's decision was also her own. She spoke slowly, fighting to find the correct words. 'If I give up the marriage, it will have been for no good reason,' she said. 'There is no reason not to see it through. It's the same for you, Jamie. There is no reason to abandon Edward and Violet, and every reason to stay.'

To his credit, and this was one of the many things for which she loved him so passionately, Jamie saw the point.

'My darling Prue.' His hands dropped from her shoulders and he bent to pick up his bag. He stood upright. 'I did try.'

'Yes, you did,' she agreed.

When the train had become a dot on the horizon, Prue finally quitted the platform. She walked over the passenger bridge, through the ticket barrier and out into the station car park. She sat there, surrounded by cars belonging to day-trippers. A man also sat on one of the benches, holding his poodle as carefully and tenderly as if it was a child. Every so often, he bent and whispered into the dog's ear and the dog raised his face and butted his master's cheek. Prue tried squeezing her eyes to see if it hurt less. Then she dug her nails into her palms so hard that they left red crescents. The corresponding pain made absolutely no impression on what she felt inside. The homeopathic approach did not work.

She started up the engine of the car and drove home.

It came as something of a shock to Jamie staring at the newspaper in the train that he was probably suffering more than Prue.

The landscape was transmogrifying into suburbia, and the variety and colours of heaped and abandoned plastic toys in the back gardens stretching down to the line struck Jamie, and he wondered if his mind was similar – cluttered with soiled, greyish detritus that had once given the illusion of being inviting.

Had he really meant to leave Violet and his son? *What if this happens again?* also flashed across his mind.

Is this the pattern?

The train drew into Clapham Junction. Jamie looked without interest at the station sign, picked up his bag and stepped down on to the platform. The station had recently been tarted up with British Rail paraphernalia. Even so, it exuded a lost feeling and the litter rattled in the December wind.

He ducked down into the underpass.

As he made his way home, Jamie planned tactics and the strategy for the job in New York that he had already discussed with his boss. His bag grew heavy and he shifted it from one hand to the other and lengthened his stride.

The morning wore out over London.

In Hallet's Gate, Violet fastened Edward into his travelling high chair and surveyed the lunch laid out on the table.

'I'm glad Jamie's out of the way,' she said, 'because I want to talk to you about this London business.'

Max helped himself to ham, salad and a baked potato and sent a wintry smile in the direction of his daughter. Prue sat down beside him. Not now Violet, he thought wearily. It was one thing to make life-turning decisions and to choose what was right, or at least best; it was quite another to be lectured.

Violet returned to a favoured theme. 'Daddy, there is such a thing as the *male* menopause.'

Red stained Max's face and his fork stopped half-way to his mouth.

'It happens all the time. Middle-aged men get restless and do all sorts of funny things. But it's hormones, nothing more.

They'll soon settle down.' Violet turned in her chair to pinion Prue. 'Aren't I right? When you get older you mourn your lost youth.'

In all the battles and uneasy peaces that had attended their relationship, Prue had never once imagined that Violet would end up defending her position.

'So they say,' she managed to get out.

Violet pressed on. 'It's worse for women because they lose their looks, isn't it, Prue?'

Prue felt unable to comment.

'There,' said Violet with some satisfaction. 'She does understand.'

'Darling,' said Max. 'I do think you have to be careful with your advice. You can't always be sure what you're talking about.'

Violet dropped back against her chair. 'But I am, darling Pa. I've read about it in a lot of places. You really mustn't go shacking up with young girls, however innocently. It gives one a bad name. You can't have Emmy living with you.' Having grasped a line of attack, Violet was, as ever, reluctant to relinquish it. She added as the *coup de grâce*, 'Think of Jane.'

Max and Prue found themselves looking at each other, their shared thought passing silently between them, as the warp and the weft shares the thread in the cloth. Indeed, there was a price for ensuring the well-being of children.

CHAPTER TWENTY-NINE

EMMY HAD BEEN BROODING ALL WEEKEND OVER THE letter she had been sent the previous week.

> You might think it odd that I am writing to you,
> but I ask you to read this letter before making up
> your mind whether to ignore it or not.

A lawyer to the last, Max's formality was accentuated in his correspondence.

> As I mentioned last time I saw you, I have been
> thinking about your position. I am writing this on the
> assumption that you will be bringing the baby up on
> your own. (Please forgive me if I have got this
> wrong.)
> I will be living in London during the next few
> months, possibly longer. I know that Violet feels that
> it is difficult for you to continue with your job with
> them, especially when you have the baby. This, I
> imagine, leaves you with a problem and I would like
> to suggest a solution. I am offering you the post of
> housekeeper. Duties would be minimal – to cook and

clean and shop. *Nothing* else is required. I am
suggesting this because I think it might be of use to
you, and I would like to think that you and your baby
would have a roof over your heads.

Emmy reread the letter – written on Max's high white laid
paper – and looked out of the kitchen window of Number 5
Hallet's Lane. It was very much the same view that could be
seen out of the kitchen of Hallet's Gate, but the eyes and mind
processing the visual information thus received assessed things
differently. However, after a year of living with the Becketts,
Emmy had seen enough to know that the general messiness of
life applies at all levels.

Her father was in the pub, well on the way, no doubt, to
oblivion, and her mother had caught the Ride'n'Shop Christmas Saturday Special bus into Salisbury. A faint smell of disinfectant overlaid by the sicklier one of ceramic hob cleaner
assaulted her queasy stomach. Powered by a crystal battery, the
clock stared down at her from a wall that glistened with endless
applications of cream cleanser. It did nothing so old-fashioned
as to tick.

Tick, tock, Emmy.

Whatever she did, whatever happened, Emmy decided that
the first thing she would do was to buy a clock with a proper
tick.

In the midst of the muddle in which she found herself,
someone had bothered to stretch out a hand to help. To help
her, witless, ugly Emmy, who had fallen into the oldest trap of
them all. Max's gesture touched a healing finger to the abraded
areas of her spirit.

The view outside failed to provide any definitive answers,
and she dropped her head into her hands, pressing them
against her eyelids. Angus threaded his way through the

dancing circles and blobs of light. He did not look happy and Emmy, no saint, felt better.

Mrs Horton shrugged her shoulders. It was not a gesture designed to give reassurance and Emmy took none. 'Your dad's livid,' she said. 'And doesn't want you here.'

Emmy was not surprised. 'Don't worry. I won't bother you.' Inside, her guts heaved with dread and panic.

'Why on earth did you have to go and fall?' Mrs Horton attacked the microwave with a specially impregnated cloth and rubbed vigorously. Emmy pictured the war between loyalty to her daughter and loyalty to her husband being waged behind the frosted perm, and was rendered speechless when her mother announced that Emmy was a chip off the old block because she had married her dad for the same reason.

Emmy reached for a chair and sat down. 'You *never* said, Mum.'

It was only when, later that evening, she lay sleepless on nylon sheets so clean that they emitted sparks every time she moved that Emmy asked, Why don't you bloody help me, then?

Consequently, the idea of a roof over her head, a place for the baby, help and support, grew rosier. She pictured putting the baby to sleep in a freshly painted room in which hung a dancing mobile of grey and red elephants like the ones she had seen in Mothercare. She pictured, too, sitting at a kitchen table eating soup and fresh bread, with the radio playing.

These were stubborn, hard-to-ignore images, and they featured Emmy alone.

Emmy had no feminist axe to grind, or any views on the absolute necessity of looking after yourself which allowed her a degree of flexibility and willingness to contemplate surprising courses of action.

I could make myself live with Mr Valour, she informed the darkness. It's easy, really. Just for a little while. Until I'm on my feet. Then me and the baby will bugger off.

She regretted the element of self-serving in her plans, but it could not be helped for she understood intuitively that being on your own did not guarantee liberty – rather the opposite. It took away the freedom to be soft and generous.

The bedroom was chilly and Emmy's lips felt dry. She heard a scuffle outside in the garden. A fox? A rat up from the river? She pictured the latter trotting, head down, from its damp moss-licked mud-hole to the frost-scented, hollow pile of leaves under the beech, its feet leaving the imprints of curtain hooks on the lawn.

Did she have to be alone?

Towards dawn, Emmy got up and stood, shivering, by the window, still fogged with night vision. Soon, the mistle-thrushes would be waking, shaking out their white underwings and pale wingtips. Soon, they would signal the new day in harsh, rattling chatter and set about the business of finding a slug, a snail, a berry. After the breeding season, missel-thrushes often fed together in family groups.

Dix points the mistle-thrush. *Nul points* humans.

It would not be so bad living at close quarters with someone you did not care for. After all, Emmy claimed experience in non-affectionate co-habitation. Her parents had done it for years.

She washed, brushed her obstinate hair into some kind of shape and put on her black leggings. Black and white were magpie colours. Apt for someone who was about to occupy someone else's husband's nest.

She trod stealthily down the stairs to the kitchen – anything to avoid her father and his temper this morning. Two spoonfuls into the Frosties and her stomach rebelled. Her knees went odd, too. She bet she'd been right about what was up with that nice Mrs Valour and Mr Valour. She just knew something was wrong. Mind you, Madam and her husband were not exactly a pattern for the young and in-love. At least, she still had the energy and interest to be curious. That was something.

All day Emmy hovered by the telephone, notting. That is, not picking it up, and wasting considerable time and energy in not doing so. Yes, please, she *could* say to Max. I'll come and be housekeeper. I'll have the baby in Winchester, stay with me mum for a bit and then I'll come. That would be very nice, he would say, and puts my mind at rest.

Emmy recollected the thick carpet, the dry-cleaned curtains and pretty china of Hallet's Gate. She smelt the drift of pot-pourri and the expensive beeswax polish Mrs Valour favoured. Was she selling her baby for a brand of furniture polish? Her soul for a bowl of rose petals and a cushion with tassels?

For in her heart, Emmy did not *quite* believe that the housekeeping bit would remain so.

And what of Angus, wherever he was? Did he ever think of her as he stripped the knickers from the Sals and Cherrys and buried his body in theirs? Did he remember their secrets, the jokes, the whisper of breath over their passion, the drift of hair on a pillow and a shared thought?

Emmy did, but also hugged the knowledge that memory was a mist: it distorted the shapes of objects, and concealed hazards.

Just before he had left the house in Austen Road that last time, Angus had turned back, boots dangling from his scarred, tough-skinned hand.

'I never thought you'd be frightened, Em,' he said. 'I thought you were made of strong stuff.'

'I'm not,' she had told him. 'I don't want risks.'

What was she doing now if she wasn't taking a risk? And

how much more, silly cow that she was, would she prefer to be taking the risk with Angus?

Seventy pounds a week *in hand* from Mr Valour. Tax and insurance paid (unlike his daughter who had not got round to it). It meant she would not be able to go on the social once she had started, but the deal was a good one.

Emmy did what she always did when she felt trapped and went out. Christmas trees shone red and green pinpoints, mixed with dazzling white, from windows on to a day that was not going to bother over much about getting light. Emmy looked up. The huge beeches that dominated this end of the village were still, frozen into dormancy.

The village and its occupants appeared to Emmy's fevered, bothered mind to be waiting. For what? Christmas? For the recession to end? For more optimistic times?

She trudged on, her life wedged awkwardly in the lap of others. Someone else's house, someone else's husband to look after.

The light at the top of the rise was dull and flat, the land dripped brackish water and the puddles were frozen around their edges. Was she still capable of discerning the beating life in the woods and under the hedgerows from which she derived so much pleasure, which she needed to exist as she needed the glass of pure, cold water? Was that also suspended, and driven underground so that she could not find it? Suddenly, Emmy found herself clinging to the gatepost into Oven's field and sobbing.

Emmy dialled Cherry's phone number and a woman answered. Her voice was familiar.

'Is that Sal?' Emmy asked, surprised.

'Yeah.' She did not sound friendly.

'This is Emmy. Remember? Do you know where Angus is?' And why aren't you in the country? she wanted to add.

The voice hardened further. 'Since you ask, I haven't seen the bugger for weeks, which is typical.'

Emmy swallowed, paused and made the hardest request of her life. 'Do you know where I can get hold of him?'

'What's it to you?'

Emmy licked her lips. 'Plenty.'

Boredom, disenchantment or perhaps a spirit of mischief overcame Sal's reluctance. She gave Emmy the number and, in a rare moment of feminine solidarity, offered the following advice. 'He'll always have his hand up a skirt, you silly idiot. Do you want that?'

No, Emmy did not. Neither, judging from her tone, did Sal, after all. Well, well. On balance, there were worse things. Lack of understanding. An ultra-clean kitchen and a bare heart. The mess and pain of Angus and his women terrified her, but she had learnt that terror was portable and life was composed of a series of loads . . . the basket of shopping into which purchases were chucked, heavy breasts – not that she had any idea of those, not yet anyway – the overdraft weighed down by failure to deal with it.

Thirty seconds later, she dialled the number.

'Can I speak to Angus, please?'

'Who is it?' asked a bruising sort of voice.

'Tell him Emmy.'

She heard the echo as Angus's name was shouted through the house. It took some time before anyone came to the phone, and her mother's colourful china plate beamed down on a shaking Emmy.

'Who is it?'

'Emmy.'

'Hell. Are you all right?'

Emmy found that her throat was blocked and her eyes were streaming. 'Of course.'

There was a silence. Clearly Angus was not going to be cracked easily and Emmy realized she had been stupid. She could not ring Angus up, coolly inform him that she had changed her mind, and then reveal her little bundle of news. You cannot declare the war over and then drop nuclear tonnage when signing the peace treaty.

'Are you going to say anything, then?' Angus sounded frighteningly cold and distant.

'No. Yes. No.' Emmy's voice did not sound right either.

Angus softened. 'You *are* OK?'

'Yes. It's nothing. Forget this.'

'Where are you?'

'At Mum's. I'm staying till Monday morning. Look, Angus, it's all right. I'm fine. Bye.'

The receiver was back in its cradle and she was left to stare at it and the pad beside it which, for some reason, was disguised as a liquorice allsort. Emmy pressed a hand to her stomach. It's you and me, she thought. You and me. Us.

After their tea, Mrs Horton sallied out to an underwear-selling party. Her father was sleeping off the day in his bedroom. In desperation, Emmy turned on the television. The script-writer on *Casualty* had decided that a stomach haemorrhage was highly entertaining. Shackled to the sofa by repulsion, Emmy watched for a few minutes and then turned it off, just as the luckless doctor and the wall were being artistically splattered by an actor who, to his credit, looked as though he could wring the script-writer's neck. If that was entertainment, then Emmy was beautiful.

She went to bed and slept.

Up at seven o'clock, she went through the routine. Teeth. Hair. Leggings. T-shirt. Since she was feeling masochistic, Emmy stared at herself in the diamond-bright bathroom mirror. The sight was not reassuring. On impulse, she reached for a relegated bottle of Charlie and dabbed some behind her ears and on her wrists. Too late, she forgot that scent made her feel sick.

A noise like a wounded aircraft coming in to land advanced up the lane and, bottle in hand, she froze. It brought back the days when Angus flew down the lane on his gleaming machine and swept her away, a knight on a bike, smelling of sump oil.

Her sadness and loss made her throat swell and she watched in the mirror as tears dammed in her eyes and slid on to her cheeks.

Look at me, jeered the image. That's all you've got, Emmy.

So absorbed was Emmy by this touching vision of tragedy that she did not, at first, take on board that the noise had stopped. By the house, in fact. The gate banged shut, and someone squelched up the path.

Only one person did that.

Emmy screwed the top back on to the scent bottle and put it with extreme care in its place on the shelf. Pregnant women were known to have funny ideas – think of the stones of them eating coal, or longing for exotic foods.

Someone thumped on the door and her father bawled, 'Go to hell.'

Emmy went down the stairs and opened the front door. There, looking cross and tired, stood Angus. Emmy's hand flew to her mouth.

'What . . . ?'

Angus yanked her outside on to the concrete doorstep. 'I've come to find out what's going on.'

Emmy began to shiver from cold and excitement, the smell

from the scent making her nausea rise in retch-making waves.

'Well?'

Emmy's defences fell with a crash.

'Oh, Angus, help me.'

He watched her for a moment or two, long enough for Emmy to grow really frightened. Then he said, 'What do you think I'm here for, you silly cow? So. What is it?'

She lifted her pale, tear-stained face to him and her lips formed the words, but nothing emerged. Instead, she laid her hands on her stomach. Angus's eyes travelled down Emmy's body and came to rest on the bunched fists.

'Oh, Emmy,' he said, enlightenment percolating slowly into his brain. 'You would.'

'Shut the door,' Mr Horton roared from the top of the stairs.

Angus cocked his head. '*Are you coming with me this time?*'

This time, Emmy did not hesitate. She pulled the front door shut and said, 'I'm here.'

'*Good* girl.'

She followed him down the path and through the squeaking gate. Angus rummaged in his carrier and chucked her a pair of leathers and the spare helmet. Emmy caught them with both hands.

She imagined the comments – the sort she had learnt while living with the Valours – being uttered behind the doors of Dainton's houses and cottages as they passed with an ear-splitting noise emitting from the bike's engines. Yobs. Selfish. Should be shot.

Hallet's Gate and its damp, heating compost heap peeled away to their left.

It was a nice idea, Mr Valour. I'm sorry. I would have done my best. I *would* have done my best.

A few cars were straggling out of the drives, driven by men in shirtsleeves, the white bloom of their aftershave still overlaying their complexions. As usual, the traffic on to the main road had clogged to a standstill, apart from pin-striped cyclists in trouser-clips, who sailed past. A bus drew up at the stop by the junction and a couple of girls in short Lycra skirts, Doc Martens and permed hair shining with moisture got on.

Emmy was shivering uncontrollably. She tugged at Angus's back. 'I'm going to die of cold.'

'We'll stop at the services.'

Andover now lay behind them and Emmy sang a farewell to the town she knew best. In the market place, stalls – pink polythene mushrooms – would be springing up, and those in trouble and on the dole would begin their creeping progress in search of bargains.

Good oxtail there, and cheese, Emmy told them silently. Rabbits are cheap, too.

The doors to the precinct would be reset for their daily open/shut performance, and synthetic aromas would waft from the shops specializing in potions and knick-knackery. How do they make a living?

An assistant would paste up another 'Special Pre-Christmas Sale' sign on the china and electric store, and the butcher would assemble shrink-wrapped chicken thighs, ham, and mince the colour of terracotta. Barclays Bank would continue to shine its hideous turquoise signs into the arena, a reminder that shopping and money were as linked as peaches and cream, love and marriage.

She and Angus?

Goodbye, said Emmy, heart thumping, teeth chattering, baby fluttering.

Angus rode up to the Fleet services as if Hell's Angels were on his tail. He stopped the bike and helped Emmy, frozen into a state resembling *rigor mortis*, on to the ground. Her knees buckled and he grabbed her.

'Tea,' he said. 'Egg and chips.'

'Can't wait,' said Emmy.

The Muzak was hard at work in the restaurant, which was already fugged with steam and cigarette smoke. Angus steered Emmy past the smokers and settled her by the window.

'I'll get you the best breakfast of your life. Trust me, Em.'

That was it. Emmy must wait and trust. Trust, even though it was a risk. *Precisely* because it was a risk.

Half dreaming, she closed her eyes. Then she opened them to watch as Angus balanced a loaded tray in one hand and two bottles of milk in another. He slid the tray down on to the table. Both plates were lapped in fried eggs, baked beans, overdone bacon and grilled tomatoes. Once again, Emmy's eyes closed.

If you make me sick, she told her baby silently but fiercely, I'll never forgive you.

'OK?' Angus flicked at Emmy's chin with a finger that stung her skin.

The nausea that threatened at the sight and smell of grease and food rose alarmingly.

Don't you dare.

It subsided.

'OK,' said Emmy and picked up her knife and fork.

CHAPTER THIRTY

PRUE TOOK THE PHONE CALL LATER THAT MORNING.

'Yes, Emmy,' she said eventually, after a prolonged interval. 'If I told you how delighted I am at your news would you believe me?'

She went to find Max. He was in the study, polishing the butt of the gun that Prue had last seen illuminated by the moonlight. Weak at the knees, she stopped abruptly in the doorway, reliving the sensation of stones biting into them, and smelling the cold night air scented with smoke and leaf-mould.

'Shouldn't you put it away?' she asked after a while.

If twenty years had not qualified you for superior knowledge or wisdom when it came to dealing with yourself, they certainly did not qualify you when it came to dealing with a spouse. The only thing of which Prue was now sure was that she knew less than at the beginning, and that life was a state of flux, but cunningly hidden.

Max shrugged. 'Don't worry, I won't use it again.' He did not look up.

Prue bit back the temptation to reply: That's what they always say. Instead she slid her hands into the pockets of her cardigan and wrapped them over her middle, aware that the gesture revealed her nervousness.

'Emmy's just phoned to say she's sorry but she can't take the job, after all.'

Plainly disappointed, Max looked up at last.

'She's going to live with her boyfriend, the father. That's very good, though goodness knows how they will manage.'

Max contemplated the perfect gloss and smooth grain of the butt. 'I should think they'll manage perfectly well,' he said, and his tone suggested that Prue had been guilty of patronage.

So she had been. She advanced into the room, which felt cold and, because no one had cleaned it lately, sported a thin veneer of dust on the furniture.

'Can we talk, Max?'

Asking for forgiveness was akin to the executioner asking the victim to absolve him. (Joan's executioner never was absolved. He pitched up at the Frères Pécheurs shaking with terror. God would damn him, he wailed, for burning a saint. He is also said, traditionally, to have insisted that, despite the quantity of oil, sulphur and fuel he had thrown on to the pyre, he could not get Joan's heart or entrails to burn. They, and anything else left of her, had been thrown into the Seine.)

Still hugging her cardigan around her middle, the old, soft, sleepy-eyed Prue stood by her husband – except that she was not. 'Max, please put that thing down, the gun, I mean, and talk to me.'

Her closeness stirred his senses, honed after twenty years into the conditioned reflex. He knew now that the image he held of his wife was deceptive – and why should it not be? So was his own. Funnily enough, the one person who had not bothered to hide anything had been Helen, and how thin a person she had proved. Max sighed, and placed the gun in its case, shifting his bulk out of the daylight coming through the window into the shadowed area of the room.

'Do you want a divorce?'

The locks on the case snapped shut and Prue breathed a sigh of relief. Max inhaled her scent and the freshness of recently ironed clothes, lifted the case off the table and opened the gun cabinet.

'It's curious, isn't it . . . ?' Prue held her breath and Max continued. 'You imagine your life has a certain foundation . . .' Prue winced. 'In answer to your question, Prue. I'm not sure what I want, or what is going to happen.' He stowed his father's gun in its place and took out the Purdey.

Prue thought of the clichés in which she could take refuge. She and Jamie were separate from her and Max's marriage. The itch of her flesh made no difference. Max and Jane were too important to throw away. No words would do because Prue had loved Jamie and it had mattered, and had altered things at home.

'Do you have to do that?' She gestured towards the Purdey.

He squinted over the bifocals at his wife. 'Yes, I do. They need attention.'

A sigh escaped her. 'I am sorry I hurt you, Max. I wish I hadn't.'

'You showed admirable judgement in finding precisely the point where I would hurt most.' Max took off his glasses and rubbed his eyes. 'Why weren't you cleverer, Prue? You could have been, you know.'

'Forgive me, Max. Forgive me.'

Yes, Prue *could* have been a great deal more clever. More principled, tougher, she could have stayed at home. But she (as are others) was locked in an unconscious drama, propelled by ancient, primitive forces.

Prue looked at Max and raised her shoulders. Oddly enough, Max understood the gesture. It embodied the spirit in which he had married Helen, against reason and sense. You

409

did something because it was unavoidable. He decided to talk and laid the Purdey on the table.

'As I said before, I knew about it for some time,' he said, 'but I did not know whom.'

'I was so careful.'

'You forget that I know you very well. I may not know what you think, but I know your mental geography. It changed, Prue, and I couldn't find my way anymore.'

This was true.

'Anyway, you bought a new set of underwear and there was dust on your St Joan notes. But, you see, I had prepared for all that.'

'Was I that *obvious*?' Prue looked at the carpet, so in need of the Hoover. 'It's a cliché, I know, but it was nothing to do with you.'

'That's one of your sillier statements.' Max went over to the drinks tray.

'Isn't it a bit early?' Prue watched him pour a whisky.

'Shut up.' Max measured out some water.

She thought of Jamie bending over her in the bed at the hotel, tense with passion, kissing her naked shoulder and thought she would die from the pain.

'I imagined you together,' said Max. 'I thought of what you did when we made love and I wondered if he took that bit of you which was mine as well. Or were you different with him?'

She felt a tidal blush flood her face. 'I never compared notes.'

Max leant against the mantelpiece and toyed with the glass. 'I know I'm getting older, Prue. We all know what happens to potency and I realized that by marrying someone so much younger I had to make allowances. In a way, I felt you were owed an affair. My mistake was to think I knew it all. You see, I thought Helen had taught me that the flesh was everything,

410

but also nothing. I did not see what it would cost. I did not foresee it would involve my daughter. My daughters. And that cannot be.'

She turned away her head and fought her tears.

'Anyway,' Max continued, 'it taught me a thing or two about sex. The degrees of complicity. Imagining, you see, which is what one does a lot of at this stage of life, instead of doing.'

The tears slid down Prue's cheeks. 'So the gun and that stupid scene *was* for me as well as for Violet . . .'

Max's fingers tightened on the glass. 'I found it unforgivable,' he searched for the words, 'unbearable, wicked, that you had taken my daughter's husband, and I had to do something for her.'

Prue knew then that she would never be free of Violet. Ever. Ever. That was her punishment. 'The dustman or the mayor would have been fine, or any old Tom, Dick or Harry, but not Violet's husband,' she said.

'You must see that, Prue.'

She accepted it in silence. 'The tiger principle,' she said eventually and wiped her tears with the back of her wrist. 'You've made the point. Will you have me back?'

Max's whisky made a glugging sound and displaced dust pricked at Prue's nose. She waited.

'For Jane's sake, probably,' said Max.

'No. *You*'ve missed the point. Not for Jane's sake, for mine. Because I've asked you. Because I decided to ask you to help rebuild our marriage.'

'And Jane?'

'It has to be between the two of us.'

Max turned away from Prue and jiggled the contents of his glass from side to side.

Prue held out her hands, fingers stretched and quivering. 'Max, please.'

He did nothing. She gestured again. 'Give me your hand, Max.'

Still he waited.

'Give, Max.'

Slowly he put out his hand and laid it in hers, his cool, manicured lawyer's hand, so familiar against her hot, unsteady flesh. Their fingers held, moved and twined together.

'Oh, Max,' she said, her gaze fixed on the white slash of Helen's wound.

'There's a brick coming loose in the wall by the gate,' he remarked. Then he said, 'What's for lunch?'

After a while, he picked up the Purdey and replaced it in the gun cabinet, which he locked with a click of metal on metal.

The Reverend Richard Williams looked a happy man. Although Easter was, of course, hugely important, Midnight Mass was the colourful highspot of the year. Lit by candles, the church looked so beautiful, so swathed in mystery and light. Unlike the world.

Regardless of his parishioners' sleep quota, Richard had decided to give a sermon. He felt something was needed to mark a bad year, financially, politically and spiritually. Was there anyone left untouched by cynicism and who trusted a politician? He thought not, although the Church could be said to have benefited from the misery brought on by recession even if the unemployed *arriviste* churchgoer was only there because it marked out a day in the week.

Keith, her husband, relegated to the seat behind the pillar, Molly sang 'It Came Upon the Midnight Clear' loudly enough for two, and Richard suspected she had had a couple of nips. The Valours were in the pew behind. Mrs Valour looked strained and he wondered if she was sickening for something.

Mind you, the daughter was very pale and, now he looked properly, far too thin.

His sermon was one over which he had brooded long and hard, in the belief that, in the end, you must stand and be counted. Vicars were there as sacrificial lambs or, worse, Aunt Sallies, but also examples to their flocks. He knew he was going to cause offence and viewed it with trepidation, but with a sense of martyrdom searched for and found, he mounted the pulpit.

'The family,' he announced, 'is under assault and I want to talk to you about it.'

Prue stole a glance at Max out of the corner of her eye, but he was staring ahead.

'Easy options . . .' Richard was warming nicely to this theme, 'It's easy to conclude that your spouse is dull, or doesn't satisfy you, and to decide to seek out someone else. It is far harder to stand by the vow of marriage and to make a go of it. I accuse those who are listening of giving in to these temptations at one point or another.'

Several stifled yawns issued from the Paulton family and Keith Greer had taken advantage of his cover to slip quietly into a doze. Quite a few in the pews adjusted their expressions into blankness and wished that the vicar would shut up. Jeremy North thought of several little episodes with some pleasure, Fred Stokes with less. Old windbag, the latter thought, keeping his eyes fixed on the vicar and attempting to look stern.

Prue thought of the tides beating inside her body that would take years to subdue and subside. Of extremes of feeling, of the scars still unhealed, of the moments when she soared above ordinary levels, of her daughter's misery, and thought, savagely and stubbornly. Even so, I *can't* regret it.

'What do we want?' Richard Williams's question was rhetorical for he did not wish to run the risk of being given the wrong answer. 'Security, real security, for our children to grow up in. We want families, real families, to make our communities and to set an example to future generations. We want standards.'

Newly married, newly arrived in the parish, exuding a fresh-minted quality, Carole and Peter Danby shifted closer together and tried to disguise that they were holding hands. Max turned his head and indicated the Danbys with a nod.

What's in store for them? he asked Prue silently.

She returned his gaze, and took on board its new speculative quality and concluded that, in a strange way, the events of the last year had revitalized Max. In some indefinable manner, repossessing had turned out to be an aphrodisiac.

Against that, Prue had to remember that he would not forget what she had done, and that she must accept his anger. Prue could never again regard her husband in the same light, neither would Max her, but her vision was wider.

She turned her attention back to the vicar.

Yet that was not quite how Max viewed the situation. He was thinking: There is no fool like an old one. Nevertheless, when he looked at his wife his eyes suggested that he accepted the perversities of the spirit – the contradictions on which deep-seated, long-term relationships often thrived. Particularly his own.

There was an audible rustle as Joe Tatchett got up and walked out, throwing his prayer book on to the table by the door with a thump.

The candles burned lower and the yawns got louder.

Jane moved restlessly beside Prue and Prue bent over her.

'Not much longer,' she whispered.

'So boring,' Jane whispered back, and leant briefly against her mother.

'The promises we make to ourselves and to others,' Richard

wound up with a flourish, 'should be made on the absolute assumption that we try to keep them. Not on the I'll-give-it-a-go basis.'

I suppose, thought Prue, concentrating on her love for Max and Jane, the Church has to say that and it *is* useful. But it is not the whole story. Not at all.

Twelve days later, the tree needed to be dismantled and the decorations replaced in their box. Max would put them back in their place in the attic beside the fishing rods – at which point he usually retrieved the latter to look them over.

Prue and Jane were wrapping silver balls in tissue paper when, true to form, Max entered the room and dumped canvas-shrouded rods and a cobwebbed fishing bag on the sofa.

Prue got in quick before he became sidetracked. 'Can you help with the tree? I think we'll have to cut it up before we take it out.'

'Plain Janey,' Max used the old nickname, 'can you get the clippers from the shed and a black plastic rubbish bag?'

Prue held up a ball to the light. It was made of delicate, transparent glass and the light slid over it like coloured oil. 'Pretty,' she said.

Both Max and Jane were reflected in its curve, distorted, distant reflections. I've been away, Prue told herself, suppressing her grief. I went and looked at another land, and wandered beside a river flowing with honey. But I had to come back, and I had to find the way home.

The image blurred under the warmth of her fingers and, after wrapping the ball carefully in the tissue, Prue put it in its place in the box.

Many women turn back from strange lands to light the fire

and tend the hearth. It was not a bad decision – quite the contrary – but not every woman's. But to arrive at it, it was necessary to beat it out in blood and pain, otherwise the fire would not burn with heat and light.

Prue had an idea that the roar and buffets of the battles ahead would strengthen her power. Love, after all, was an act of will. Passion was not.

Jane returned with the clippers and handed them to her father.

'Hold the tree steady,' he said. 'And hold the bag open, Prue.'

Cursing gently when the needles punctured his skin, Max pruned the tree of its branches and stuffed them into the bag. It rained needles on to the carpet, which disappeared under a green sea, and the tree shrank and became bald.

After the last branch had been disposed of, Max straightened up. 'That's Christmas over,' he said. 'Let's get this thing outside and I'll chop it up.'

Prue bent over and fastened the plastic bag because she did not want Max or Jane to see that she was crying.

Jane watched her mother. Her expression suggested that she had learnt something about the precariousness of the adult world. It also contained a provocative element – how can I use this knowledge? – but mainly relief. 'Hurry up, Mum,' she said. 'I'm hungry. What's for supper?'

Acknowledgements

Many thanks are due to many people including my agent, Caroline Sheldon, and my editor, Suzanne Baboneau, for their back-up and expertise, to Peta Nightingale whose input was vital, and to Hazel Orme, on whom I rely absolutely. Last but certainly not least, to my family.

There is a huge body of work devoted to the life of Joan of Arc and I would like to mention two in particular: Edward Lucie Smith's *Joan of Arc* (Allen Lane, 1976) and Marina Warner's brilliant *Joan of Arc: The Image of Female Heroism* (Weidenfeld & Nicolson, 1981). I took factual information and drew on ideas from both of these works.

If you enjoyed this book, why not join

Elizabeth Buchan's Mailing List

Members are the first to hear all the latest **book news**, have the chance to win in regular **competitions**, and get **exclusive** writing from Elizabeth Buchan delivered straight to their inbox.

Plus you'll receive a FREE short story by Elizabeth Buchan as soon as you join.

To join, simply scan the QR code or visit
www.elizabethbuchan.com
for more information

Lose yourself in the atmospheric novels of bestselling author

Elizabeth Buchan

CORVUS